FORSAKEN COMMANDER

THE ATERNIEN WARS BOOK #1

G J OGDEN

Illustration © Tom Edwards
TomEdwardsDesign.com

Editing by S L Ogden
Published by Ogden Media Ltd
www.ogdenmedia.net

PROLOGUE
THE POST-HUMAN REVOLUTION

IN THE YEAR 2257, people from across the Planetary Union of Nine witnessed the creation of the first digitally immortal human - a being whose very existence would challenge the limits of life and revolutionize the fate of humanity forever.

The Aternus Corporation, the wealthiest and most powerful consortium in the Union, succeeded in creating a neuromorphic brain, into which the consciousness – the soul – of the Corporation's President and CEO, Markus Aternus, was uploaded. Together with a synthetic body many times stronger and more resilient than flesh and bone, Markus Aternus showed the nine planets that human beings could transcend mortal boundaries and become as eternal as the cosmos itself.

It was humanity's greatest achievement, and its most deadly mistake. Within the first decade alone, hundreds of thousands of human beings had been 'ascended', beginning with Markus Aternus' closest friends and advisors, quickly making the Aternus Corporation wealthier than the superpowers combined. To his people, collectively known as Aterniens, Markus Aternus became more than merely a visionary leader. He became a god.

Driven by prejudice, fear and jealousy, billions of organic

humans demanded an end to the practice of digital transference. Protests erupted across the Union, sparking riots and violence that engulfed the nine worlds. The Aterniens fought back, defending their god-king and their new, superior society. Lives were lost on both sides, but humanity suffered the first of what would become a series of bruising defeats. Tens of thousands of organic humans were killed, while the resolve of the Aterniens merely grew stronger. Soon the conflict had spiraled far beyond a clash of ideals – it became a fight for the very survival of humanity itself.

The Union's response was decisive and punishing. In partnership with other planetary leaders, the President acted swiftly to implement the Aternien Act. Post-human practices were immediately outlawed across the Union of Nine, and all research and development pertaining to artificial intelligence and human-machine interfaces was banned. A segregation order was ratified, forcing the Aterniens into permanent exile on a distant world deemed too hostile to support organic human life.

The Aterniens resisted, led by their god-king, Markus Aternus. Isolated pockets of rebellion quickly evolved into organized terrorist attacks on a city-wide scale, killing tens of thousands. But the Aterniens numbered too few, and before long the Union had beaten them back. Markus Aternus called for a cessation of hostilities and the Aterniens were allowed to voluntarily go into exile.

A border outpost was built on the demarcation line between Aternien and Union space, to allow for the possibility of future diplomatic relations. But while the Union always sent a representative, year after year, the Aterniens never came.

After a decade without any contact, the Union took a risk and decided to send a probe across the demarcation line, to the planet the Aterniens had been exiled to. The probe arrived but found only abandoned cities, inspired by Egyptian culture and mythology, and the remnants of a civilization that was long gone. Further searches were conducted, but no sign of the Aterniens was ever discovered. Soon, they faded into history, becoming a distant memory. For a time, there was peace in the Union of Nine.

But the Aterniens were merely biding their time. Lured by the prospect of eternal life, flocks of human beings risked their lives in a continual migration across the demarcation line, in a desperate effort to find the Aternien home world and attain immortality. The convoys were never seen again, but unbeknownst to the Union, the Aterniens had received the refugees with open arms, and before long they had transferred enough minds to build a vast army.

The war began in 2297 and lasted for thirty-five years. Outgunned and out-matched by superior Aternien forces, led by twelve Solar Barques – warships of incalculable destructive power – humanity turned to the technology and practices it had outlawed to survive. An elite force of bio-engineered and technologically-augmented humans were created, along with a fleet of twelve Longswords; the most powerful and advanced warships ever devised by human minds.

The Longswords and their bio-engineered, post-human Master Commanders were instrumental in turning the tide of the war, but eventually the losses, both human and Aternien, became too grueling to bear. An armistice was declared, the cost of peace being a mass and permanent demilitarization on both sides. The five surviving Union Longswords were decommissioned, and their post-human crews callously cast aside and sent back to a society that feared them almost as much as they did the Aterniens. Strict restrictions on technological development were reinstated to ensure that a post-human incident like the one that had given birth to the Aterniens could never happen again.

The Aterniens also abided by the terms of the armistice and cast their five surviving Solar Barques into the distant Piazzi asteroid field, which had also become the graveyard of the decommissioned Longswords. Their remaining forces withdrew to their new home; a world known only as New Aternus, its location unknown.

For a long time, there was peace, and humanity lived without fear of conflict. But a century after the armistice, the gears of war began churning once again. It began with isolated raids, at first attributed to pirates and criminals, but soon the skirmishes became more frequent and coordinated. There was only one conclusion that could be drawn; after a hundred years of silence, humanity's old enemy was stirring once more.

The Aterniens had returned, but in their complacency, the Planetary Union of Nine no longer possessed a fighting force that was able to match them.

THE INCIDENT

BRIDGE COMMS LOG: UNION FRIGATE
YAMATO

//**Location: Union Outpost 6**//
//**Role: Defensive Patrol**//
//**Timestamp: 2434-01-17.16:40**//

Tactical: "Captain, I'm detecting a soliton warp signature at bearing three-two-nine, mark seven, range five thousand meters."

Captain: "Are we expecting any new arrivals, Lieutenant?"

Tactical: "Negative, sir, there's nothing scheduled to arrive until 19:00 hours, Zulu. Sensors are reading a single vessel, configuration unknown."

Captain: "Identify that ship, Lieutenant. And put it on the screen."

XO: "What the hell is that? Lieutenant Hoyle, hurry up on that ID."

Tactical: "Report coming back now, sir, but it doesn't make sense…"

Captain: "Out with it, Lieutenant."

Tactical: "Sir, the ship is reading as Aternien."

XO: "That can't be right. Recheck and verify."

Tactical: "Checked and verified, sir. It's Aternien."

Captain: [standing]. "Tactical alert! Hail it."

Operations: "No response, Captain."

Tactical: "Sir, I'm detecting an energy build-up from the Aternien ship… It's firing!"

//Recording interrupted. Resuming at 2434-01-17.16:43//

Captain: "Return fire all weapons!"

Tactical: "Weapons are offline! We have hull breaches on decks four through seven. Critical damage to main reactor. Helm offline…"

Captain: "All hands, abandon ship. Repeat, all hands…"

//Recording ends//

//Union Frigate Yamato confirmed destroyed, 2434-01-17.16:44//

ONE

THE HUNT

CARTER ROSE PUSHED through a dense thicket of thornbushes and lowered himself onto his chest in a shallow ravine that cut through the centre of the alien timberland on Terra Nine's forest moon. A razor-sharp thorn scraped across the side of his face, and he could feel blood slowly trickling across his cheek. Yet by the time the first droplet reached the corner of his mouth, so that he could taste its salty, metallic flavor, the cut had already healed over.

"Optics, give me a status report," Carter said, speaking to his scouting drone, which was hovering above the tree line.

"Target directly ahead, range twenty-nine meters," the sterile, computerized voice of the drone answered.

Carter shifted onto his side and lifted his head above the ravine. It was late evening, and the sun had already dropped below the horizon, but his bio-engineered vision meant he could see the path ahead as clear as day. Suddenly, the trees rustled, and the thickets shook, and Carter's target crept into view.

"Target should be visible," Optics continued. "Species, Morsapri. Native. Mass, four-zero-two pounds. Height, four-point-seven feet to the shoulder."

Carter blew out a restless sigh. He'd been tracking the alien Morsapri – or 'death hog' as it was more commonly known to the small population of Terra Nine's moon – for three hours, and now he was finally ready to make the kill. Even so, the sheer, intimidating size of the beast, which was like an oversized, flesh-eating wild boar on steroids, was still enough to make his bio-engineered heart thump harder and faster.

Carter slowly lifted his hunting rifle, pressed the butt of the weapon into his shoulder, and took aim at the beast's enormous side. His custom-engineered weapon had been specifically designed to puncture the animal's thick hide and dense muscles. And, thanks to his superior vision and unwavering stability, he only needed iron sights in order to shoot the animal through the heart.

Inching his finger onto the trigger, he let out another slow breath, and was about to fire, when an alert squawked through his earpiece. The beast turned in his direction and snorted, pushing a plume of vapor into the cool night air, before darting through the undergrowth and out of sight. Cursing under his breath, Carter lowered the weapon and waited for the drone's report.

"Warning, new contact detected," the drone intoned, lifelessly. "Single human female approaching, ninety-two meters west of the target, and closing."

"What the hell?" Carter grunted, sliding his finger along the frame of the rifle. "Why didn't you pick her up earlier?"

"I am sorry, I cannot answer that," the drone replied, unhelpfully.

"Can you at least tell me if she's another hunter?" Carter grunted.

"I am sorry, I cannot answer that," the drone repeated. "However, she is unarmed."

Carter let out an exasperated sigh. "If she's unarmed then she's not a hunter, is she?"

The drone remained silent, and Carter shook his head at the patch of sky where the machine was lurking. The Union's long-standing ban on the development of advanced computer intelligence wasn't normally something that caused Carter Rose any problems, but on this occasion, he wished his drone wasn't so damned stupid.

"Where's the hog now?" Carter added, pushing through the thorns and hurrying in the direction of his quarry, and the woman who had foolishly walked into his hunting grounds.

"The target is forty-two meters, directly ahead," the drone replied. "The human female appears to have spotted the Morsapri and is fleeing from the beast, heading due south."

Carter huffed a laugh. "At least she's got the good sense to run."

The trees and thornbushes rustled, and Carter stopped dead, brow scrunched tightly. It was then he realized that due South meant that the woman was running straight at him. Suddenly, a figure burst through the bushes, clothes ripped, and face scratched from the inch-long barbs that covered the alien catkins from root to tip. Seconds later, the Morsapri charged through after her. Carter lifted his rifle to his shoulder, but the woman was directly in his line of fire.

"Get down!"

The woman's eyes grew wide, and she threw herself into the ravine. Carter squeezed the trigger, but the alien hog was already on top of him. The weapon discharged, carving a chunk of flesh out of the beast's massive shoulder, before the Morsapri barreled through him like a wrecking ball.

Carter was sent spiraling across the forest floor, each loose stone and broken branch biting into his flesh like a hundred bare-knuckle punches. Digging his fingers into the dense, mineral soil, he arrested his fall and ground to a stop. The Morsapri was directly ahead, plumes of vapor snorting from its wide nostrils. The beast's red eyes were locked onto him, and

Carter knew that their roles had been reversed. Hunter was now prey, and with his rifle lying broken beneath the beast's hooves, it would come down to a contest of strength and will.

His augments kicked into action, flooding his body with chemicals that enhanced his already exceptional speed, strength, and stamina. The beast charged, but Carter held his ground, drawing his hunting knife from its scabbard and facing down the Morsapri without fear. The animal drove its broad head into Carter's gut, but at the same time he grabbed the beast around the neck and tightened his hold on it like a wrench. The beast kicked and shook its body, trying to throw Carter off it, but he clung on, and thrust the seven-inch blade into the Morsapri's neck. The beast spasmed and its legs faltered, but he continued to add pressure, making use of his superhuman might to subdue the animal.

The Morsapri's knees buckled, and Carter bore down on it with his own considerable mass, while drawing the blade cleanly out through the front of the animal's throat, severing the carotid arteries and jugular vein. The Morsapri collapsed beneath him, steam still billowing from the animal's mouth and nose, but within seconds it was unconscious, and soon after that it was dead.

Carter released his grip on the animal and rested on its muscular flanks. His heart rate, which had climbed above two hundred, was already returning to a calm, resting rate of forty beats per minute. A normal human would have been exhausted, but the only sensation Carter Rose was experiencing at that moment was an expanding bubble of anger.

"Hey, thanks…"

Carter looked up from the animal and saw the woman who had been running from the alien hog standing in front of him. She was wearing a Union military uniform with the golden oak leaves of a major on its shoulder boards. The uniform was torn badly across the right thigh, mid-section, and arms. He could see blood seeping from the many cuts and scratches, but the woman paid them no mind.

"How did you stop that thing?" the major continued, nodding toward the dead Morsapri. "By rights, that beast should have torn you limb-from-limb, but you manhandled it like it was nothing."

"This animal could have killed you," Carter said, deliberately ignoring her question. He pushed himself up, using the dead animal as leverage. "Just what the hell were you thinking, coming out here at night, and unarmed too?"

"I was looking for you, of course," the woman answered, speaking her response as if the answer should have been obvious.

"You've got the wrong guy." Carter climbed to his feet, cleaning his knife using the lining of his jacket as he did so. "If it's military you're looking for, try the base in Ridge Town, about twenty miles west. I'm just a smallholder."

The woman narrowed her eyes at him and pressed her hands to her hips. It seemed obvious that his attempt to fob her off had failed spectacularly.

"You're Master Commander Carter Rose, veteran of the Aternien war, and former commander of the Longsword Galatine," the major replied, without taking a breath between words. "Why don't we cut the crap, okay? I wasn't born yesterday."

Carter thought that his lie had sounded pretty convincing, but the officer clearly had him at a disadvantage. Even so, he wasn't interested in speaking to the military; given the way they'd treated him at the end of the war.

"What you were was almost this thing's supper," he replied, still avoiding the major's probing questions and statements.

The major snorted with derision. "Come on, wild hogs eat nuts and fruits and that sort of thing, not people."

"Actually, hogs are omnivores, Miss Know-It-All, though these beasts are more closely related to wild boars," Carter said, wiping his bloodied hands onto his pants. "The difference is that this beast is predatory. And it's an effective predator too."

His answer seemed to intrigue the officer, and she took a moment to study the animal's muscular shoulders and horn-tipped nose.

"What do they usually hunt?"

"Whatever the hell they want," Carter said with a shrug. He then smiled, and added, "But they especially enjoy nosy busybodies who wander into the forest wearing military uniforms."

"I'm not a busybody," the woman snapped, bizarrely more concerned about Carter's insult than the fact she had almost become dinner for an alien beast. She then returned his smile. "And if I were easily frightened by bad-tempered, angry beasts, then I wouldn't still be here, talking to you, would I?"

Carter snorted a laugh, appreciating that the officer gave as good as she got. However, since it had been his intention to scare the woman away, her sarcastic quick wit didn't help him get rid of her. Before he could think of another ploy to convince the woman to give up, she stepped around the dead beast at her feet, and offered him her hand.

"My name is Major Carina Larsen, by the way," she said, hand outstretched. "I'm from Union Intelligence."

Carter laughed and sheathed his blade. "Military intelligence, you say?" He shook his head at the woman. "I guess standards must have slipped quite a bit since I left the service."

Major Larsen's eyes narrowed and her back straightened. If her hair hadn't been tied back into a tight ponytail, Carter wondered if it would have bristled like the hairs on the hog's back.

"So, you *are* Master Commander Rose," she said, and Carter winced, realizing his slip. "And considering I managed to track you down, I'd say my intel was on the money."

Carter had to admit she'd got him dead to rights, and because of that, he allowed her some extra leeway.

"Look, Major Larsen, I haven't been an active member of the Union Military for a very long time." He returned her interrogating stare. "But you already knew that."

"To be honest, I wasn't even sure you'd still be alive," Carina said, avoiding directly answering his question. "No-one has seen or heard anything from you since before I was even born. They all told me it was a wild goose chase, coming out here."

"The fact you found me doesn't change that it's still a wild goose chase," Carter answered, while removing his pack and setting it down. "Whatever you're here for, I'm not interested."

"I'm here on an urgent matter of Union security," Carina said, ignoring his protests. "You must have seen the news reports?"

"I don't watch the news, and I don't care why you're here," Carter countered. "I don't wear the uniform anymore. Your predecessors saw to that."

Carina watched with morbid curiosity as Carter removed a transport bag from his pack and spread it out on the ground. Grabbing the carcass of the Morsapri by its front legs, he hauled the beast inside the bag then closed it over the body. Moments later, the bag wrapped itself tightly around the carcass and filled with an inert coolant.

"I know you're an old timer, but isn't hunting living creatures for sport a little barbaric, in this day and age?" Carina said, as grav-repellers hummed into life and lifted the refrigerated transport bag off the forest floor.

"This isn't sport, it's dinner," Carter grunted, running his hand through his silver hair. He then grabbed the handle on the top of the bag and began hauling it away.

Carina laughed. "Dinner? You can't be serious? Don't they have food markets on this moon?"

"Of course, they do, but in case you haven't figured it out by now, I prefer to keep to myself," Carter snapped. "I don't like people and they like me even less. And right now, you're top of the list of folks I don't like."

"You don't have to like me; you just have to hear me out." Despite his blatant hostility toward her, Carina remained undeterred. "Unless, you have a few more innocent creatures to slaughter first, that is?"

Carter threw down the handle and turned to Carina, hands pressed to his hips. His actions were so sudden that she almost walked straight into him. However, the shock was enough to put her on the back foot.

"I don't enjoy this; I hunt because I need to," Carter said, pointing to the bag. "And if it hadn't been for you bungling into the forest like a damned fool, this creature wouldn't have felt a thing. Instead, I had to kill it the hard way."

"I said thank you, didn't I?" Carina replied, her response as prickly as the thornbushes surrounding them.

"You're welcome, now will you finally get lost? I told you; whatever you're here to say, I'm not interested."

He quickened his pace, in the hope that the officer would finally take the hint and leave, but Carina continued to follow him doggedly. Before long, she had drawn level and was side-eyeing him with interest. Carter grumbled and tried to outpace her, but even with his augmented strength and stamina, the fact he was hauling a four-hundred-pound load meant that he couldn't get away. Even so, he was impressed that she was managing to stay with him, considering her regulation-issue footwear was wholly unsuited to the wild terrain.

"You're still here…" he said, after neither of them had spoken a word for several minutes.

"I'm not going anywhere until you agree to sit down with me," Carina replied, showing no signs of relenting.

Carter stopped again and dropped the bag, this time less suddenly, so as to ensure the major didn't collide with him. He was about to ramp up his level of unfriendliness from rude to downright hostile, until he noticed the cuts on Carina's arm.

They had stopped bleeding, but looked angry, and he could see that they were starting to aggravate her too.

"You'll need to get those cleaned, and take an anti-toxin as soon as possible," he advised, pointing to one of the longer scratches on the woman's arm. "The thorns on the shrubs in this forest can cause a nasty reaction. I wouldn't want you to die, especially after I just saved your life."

Carina looked at one of the cuts and scrunched up her nose. Carter could see sweat beading on her brow, and his bio-engineered senses could detect that her body temperature was climbing sharply. However, the major simply folded her arms and stood her ground.

"It's at least three clicks from here back to my shuttle, and I'm guessing you have a house or cabin that's much closer?"

Carter was only half-listening; the cuts were getting angrier by the second, and the major's heart rate was also beginning to slow.

"Show me your arm," Carter said, his tone urgent enough that Carina complied without protest.

He squeezed the cut and Carina hissed with pain, and almost passed out, as a blob of phlegm-like green pus oozed from the wound. He relaxed his grip, but kept a firm hold on the woman's arm, knowing that if he let go, she would fall.

"A little warning next time, maybe?" Carina said, her nose turned up at the gooey, green splodge oozing over her skin.

"I needed to see how bad it was," Carter replied, in an uncaring fashion.

"And?"

"And if you don't get these treated within the next thirty minutes, you'll be sent home in a sack just like this."

Carter grabbed the handle of the transport bag and set off again, though this time at double the pace. Carina, however, remained where she was, frozen in place by fear.

"Are you coming, or not?" Carter called out, waving her on. "I'll make sure you don't die, but that's as far as this goes."

Carina nodded and hurried to his side, though her footing, along with her vision, already seemed unsteady.

"Thanks again," she replied, grabbing Carter's arm for support. "Though while you're fixing me up, you may as well hear me out too…"

TWO
UNWANTED GUESTS

CARTER HOOKED a chain to the handle of the transport bag then hauled the four-hundred-pound beast above the floor of his shed, which was next to the log cabin he occupied in the woods. He then pulled his personal comp-slate out of his jacket pocket, and set a trio of drones to work, cleaning and preparing the animal, ready for storage in his food freezer.

"I half expected you to drop the animal on an oak slab and butcher it yourself," said Major Larsen, who was watching the gory spectacle unfold without any effort to hide her distaste for it.

"You sound disappointed," Carter said.

"Not in the slightest," the major replied, vigorously shaking her head. "The last thing I want to do is watch you slice and dice this thing in front of me."

Carter smiled and slid his hunting knife out of its scabbard. "In that case, maybe I will. It could be the only way I get rid of you."

Carina shot him a dirty look, but there was a hint of a smile hidden beneath it. The major clearly enjoyed sparring with him, and despite the fact she was continuing to pester him, he found the distraction of her company to be surprisingly welcome.

Suddenly, her knees buckled, and she grabbed hold of the door frame, which was all that was stopping her falling flat on her face. Carter was by her side in an instant, and managed to take her weight before her legs gave way completely.

"Come on, let's get you sorted before I end up having to hang another carcass in this shed," Carter said, guiding Carina outside and up the hardwood stairs to his cabin.

"Doesn't the toxin affect you too?" Carina asked, as Carter practically kicked in his front door. "You must have gotten scratched by those alien catkins."

"I did, but my metabolism is able to fight off toxins, as well as hostile viruses and bacteria." Carter dropped Carina into a kitchen chair and placed her hands onto the arms. "Can you grip these? I don't want you face-planting onto my nice, clean floor."

Carina gripped the arms of the wooden chair, and Carter released his hold on her, though he didn't go far, in case the woman still fell forward. Carina wobbled for a moment but steadied herself and smiled weakly at him.

"I'm good, for a minute or two, anyway."

Carter nodded then hurried to the far side of the kitchen and pulled open a wall cabinet. Rifling through the contents, which were as dusty and cobwebbed as his shed, he finally found a medical kit and removed it. He always kept one for emergencies, despite not needing traditional medicines himself, but had never had cause to use it before then.

"Is it a natural resilience?" Carina continued, still on to the topic of Carter's miraculous immune system.

Carter laughed politely and opened the med kit, setting it down on the kitchen table next to Carina.

"There's not a whole lot about me that's entirely natural," Carter said, while searching through the contents of the kit for what he needed. "My cell biology and DNA were re-engineered to give me the characteristics the Union thought were needed to fight the Aterniens."

"I guess that explains your crazy strength too?" Carina commented.

"Partly, yes, but it's more than just edited genes and tweaked cells." Carter found the device he was looking for, which resembled a pocket-pistol, and loaded the appropriate med tab into the base. "My enhanced blood contains billions of nano-machines, and my skeletal structure is a bio-hybrid, incorporating synthetic materials that dramatically increase bone density, strength and resiliency. There are dozens more augments too; so many, I've forgotten half of them."

"So, you're a bona-fide superhuman then?" Carina said, again offering Carter a weak smile.

"Superhuman is the nice way of putting it. Post-human is how people see me, which is why I'm not exactly Mr. Popular."

Carina's weak smile suddenly took on a roguish twist. "I don't know, maybe your lack of popularity has more to do with your disagreeable personality…"

He scowled at the major, then her eyelids suddenly fluttered, and she toppled forward, but thanks to his augmented speed, Carter caught her in time.

"I know this might be hard for you, but can you try shutting up for a second?" Carter said, propping her up against the chair back. He then went to press the pistol-shaped injector to her neck, but the major jolted away as if he were about to slit her throat.

"What the hell is that?" Carina snapped, eyeballing the device. "I know you're old-school, but isn't sticking me with a needle a bit archaic?"

Carter grunted a sigh. "I'll stick you with my damned knife in a second…" However, Carina's dagger eyes and unyielding stare suggested he wasn't going to get away without an explanation. "Look, it's a Lorentz-force injector. It's old-school, like you say, but there's no damned needle. I'm not that ancient."

Carina's narrowed eyes widened by the smallest fraction,

then she slowly leant toward the device, presenting her neck to Carter like a Vampire familiar offering herself to be turned. Wary of the possibility that she would back out again, he wasted no time in pressing the device against her skin and actuating the injection.

"There, give it a few minutes and you'll be right as rain," Carter said, replacing the Lorentz injector into the med kit. He then reconsidered his statement and pointed to his kitchen door, which was still wide open. "In fact, there's the exit, so you can get lost now."

"I haven't told you why I'm here yet," Carina said, rubbing the spot on her neck where Carter had injected her. "Besides, I still feel woozy, so how about you put the kettle on and make some tea, while I give you the facts."

Carter growled and slammed the med kit shut. "You're one stubborn asshole, has anyone ever told you that?"

Carina smiled again, though this time it was broader and accompanied by a flash of her bright hazel eyes.

"All the time; it runs in the family," she replied, sounding exceedingly proud of this fact. "It's also one of the reasons I got this assignment."

"I don't doubt it," Carter said, though it wasn't meant as a compliment.

He filled his old iron kettle from the kitchen faucet, which tapped an underground spring, before dropping it onto the wood-fired range.

"What's the other reason you got this sorry duty?" Carter asked, checking on the major out of the corner of his eye, to make sure the anti-toxin was taking effect.

"The other reason is because I'm the Union's foremost expert on the Aterniens," Carina answered, straightening up in her chair, and adjusting her torn and bloodied uniform as best she could to make it presentable.

The mention of Aterniens made Carter tense up and take notice. His hands were pressed flat to the top of the stove, which was hot enough to burn normal flesh, but his augmented skin resisted the heat.

"In fact, I'm probably the Union's *only* expert on the Aterniens," Carina corrected herself, unaware of Carter's fretful reaction. "But that's going to change, because if our intel is correct, they're back."

Carter turned and rested the small of his broad back against the stove. He folded his arms and studied the young officer's now stern expression. The jocular, forthright major had been replaced by a serious officer on serious business. Likewise, the mention of his old enemy had stirred the fire in his blood and sobered his thoughts. As much as he wanted that part of his life to be ancient history, there was always a corner of his mind that was occupied by the Aterniens, and what happened to them after the armistice that ended the war a century ago.

"Nobody has seen or heard from the Aterniens for more than a hundred years," Carter answered, gruffly. "The news reports are a lot of hot air; tabloid nonsense trying to stir up fear in order to boost ratings."

"I thought you didn't watch the news?" Carina responded. Tellingly, this time there was no hint of a smile. The accusation was plain – that Carter had been holding out on her.

"You have two minutes, Major Larsen," Carter grunted. The kettle began to whistle behind him, and he pulled it off the hot plate, without using a glove or towel to protect his hand against the scorching heat. "Make it good."

Carina reached into her pocket and removed a comp-slate, which was folded into a compact packet a quarter of the thickness of a deck of cards. She opened the device into a thin screen with a ten-inch diagonal and set it down on the kitchen table. Moments later, the image of a ship appeared on the screen. It was fuzzy and indistinct – the type of image taken from a long-range relay – but he knew at once what it was, and the sight of the vessel made his heart thump harder.

"This was taken near outpost five, about three months ago,"

Carina said. The image updated to show another similar ship, this time in greater fidelity, followed by a series of others, all of which improved slightly in resolution. "This last one was a couple of weeks ago, out by outpost six, close to the Aternien demarcation line. The probe was destroyed, so this is the best image we could retrieve, but I assume it makes my point."

Carter stared at the sharper image of the Aternien warship and compared it to the mental image of vessels he'd fought a century earlier. It was broadly similar in size and shape, but even the fuzziness of the image couldn't hide the fact it was more highly developed.

"We obviously have much more intel besides a few shaky images, and it will all be made available to you after the admiral's briefing at Terra Prime."

"I'm not going to any damned briefing," Carter said, pouring water from the kettle into a teapot before adding two spoons of Darjeeling tea leaves from a cracked jar to its side. "I've allowed you to say your piece, and you've said it. Now you can go."

Major Larsen shot out of her chair with such force that it toppled over and clattered against the dark hardwood floor.

"What are you talking about? Didn't you understand what I just told you?"

"I understand that it's no longer any of my business," Carter hit back. "You wear the uniform. I don't. So, go tell your admiral to find someone else."

The anti-toxin had already rid the woman of the physical symptoms of the thorn toxin, and she was back to her fiery best.

"You're still a member of this Union," Carina said, stepping in front of Carter, so that he couldn't avoid looking at her. "Our enemy is back, and you have a duty to fight."

Carter hammered his fist into the hot plate, causing the kettle to jump an inch off the surface.

"Don't talk to me about duty," he barked. Carina looked startled, but to the woman's credit, she stood her ground. "I was fighting Aterniens before your parents were even born. I sacrificed my body and my future for the Union, and what did it get me?" He gestured to the stark wall of his cabin, which he'd built on the barely inhabited moon of the Union's most distant world. "Decommissioned is what it got me," he added, bitterly. "It's just another way of saying thrown on the scrapheap. The Union was happy to toss out their post-human ideals when it meant they could make the perfect soldier, but once I was no longer needed, I was shut out, shunned, and left to fend for myself."

Carter cursed under his breath and poured the tea from the pot into one of the two waiting mugs. In truth, he was embarrassed by his sudden explosion of anger. Nothing of what had happened to him was Carina's fault, and she was the last person in the galaxy that merited bearing the brunt of his decades of resentment and anger.

"I'm sorry," he said, pouring tea into the second mug then setting down the kettle. "You didn't deserve that."

Carina shrugged. "Maybe not, but I understand why you feel that way." She picked up the mug and cradled it in both hands. "Actually, that's horse shit because there's really no way I can empathize with your experiences. But I do know that if my reward for decades of service and dedication was a boot up the ass then I'd be pissed off too."

Carter snorted a laugh then moved over to the kitchen table and dropped into one of the chairs. Despite his furniture being made from chunky pieces of the forest moon's equivalent of oak, the chair almost broke under his augmented mass.

"Even if I did come back, there's nothing I could do, anyway." He took a sip of the tea, which was still too hot for Carina's regular human mouth to drink. "What made me and those like me special wasn't just our augmented abilities, but our ships too. And the few surviving Union Longsword-class Battleships were all decommissioned, like me."

"We still need you," Carina said, remaining as dogged as

ever. "You're one of the only people alive who's even *seen* an Aternien, never mind fought one. The Union military are peacekeepers now. We haven't fought a major engagement in seventy years, and that was a tiny skirmish compared to the Aternien war. In short, we've forgotten how to fight, which is why your experience is invaluable."

Carter took a longer gulp of the tea, which was doing an effective job of soothing his frayed nerves.

"Experience is one thing, but surely, after a hundred years, the Union must have a fleet of ships even more advanced than the Longswords?" Carter asked, mulling through a hundred questions that had surfaced in his mind. "Superior firepower is far more valuable than any wisdom you'll get from an old fart like me."

Carina winced and her cheeks flushed with color. "Actually, our ships are all pretty old too. And because of the armistice restrictions on developing new computers and technology, they're not a patch on the Longswords. Not even close."

"Then build some more Longswords!" Carter could feel anger swelling inside him again. The solution seemed obvious, and he didn't understand why the Union had sent a major all this way to speak to him, instead of knuckling down and preparing for war. "If the Aterniens really are mobilizing, the armistice is null and void, as is the agreement not to develop advanced weapons, including more battleships."

His answer seemed to cause further embarrassment. Carina vacillated for a few seconds, before finally revealing why she appeared shamefaced.

"We don't know how to build more."

Carter almost fell out of his chair. "Why the hell not?"

"The blueprints were all erased seventy-four years ago," Carina answered, while staring into her tea, like it was black hole swallowing all sense and reason. "Besides, it wouldn't matter if we still had all the schematics. We don't have the engineers, equipment, or know-how to build anything that advanced."

Carter shook his head. "That still doesn't explain why the blueprints were binned. What the hell were they thinking?"

Carina continued to stare into her tea. "The Union President at the time apparently thought history might repeat itself if the capability to build such immense weapons of war remained in their keeping."

Carter laughed openly, almost spilling his tea in the process. "We *won* the Aternien war. That's a history worth repeating, wouldn't you think?"

"Look, you're clearly interested, despite your protests, so why not just come with me?" Carina said. She set down the tea, which was still undrunk. "All you have to do is meet the admiral and learn the full facts. There's no commitment. Like you said, you're no longer an active member of the Union military, so they can't force you to sign up. But I promise that I wouldn't have spent weeks tracking you down, then hauling my ass out here, if I didn't think we needed you desperately."

Carter grunted a sigh then finished his tea. Carina continued to peer at him with her piercing hazel eyes. He could hear her heart thumping in her chest, fast and powerful, like she was running for her life from a rabid Morsapri. Whatever truth there was in the reports of an Aternien return, he was sure about one thing; Major Carina Larsen was scared to death, and that she believed everything she'd said.

"I'll give it some thought," Carter replied, grudgingly.

Carina smiled. "Great, then if you can just drop me off at a motel or guest house in the nearest town, I'll await your reply."

Carter laughed again. "Did I mention that you're a stubborn asshole?"

"It may have come up," she replied, smiling with her intense eyes.

"Fine, I'll drop you in town, then at least you can finally stop riding my ass."

Carina punched the air symbolically then frowned. "Hey, is there a bar in town?"

"Of course there is; it's a hick town in the ass end of nowhere."

"Great, then I'll buy you a drink, as a thank you for saving my life." Carina headed toward the door. "You can at least manage that, right?"

Despite everything, Carter was surprised to find he actually liked the pushy, straight-talking officer. And he also couldn't deny that a drink sounded good right at that moment.

"I think that's actually the most sensible thing you've said since dropping in on me, uninvited," Carter said, returning the woman's smile.

Major Larsen winked at him then headed outside, but paused when she realized that Carter hadn't yet stood up.

"Are you coming then?"

"I'll see you out by the truck." Carter pushed himself up, causing the chair to creak and groan like old bones. "I just need to grab a couple of things first."

Carina's brow furrowed, but for once she didn't answer back, and instead merely nodded and headed out of sight. Carter used his augmented hearing to listen to the woman's footsteps grow quieter. When he was certain she was waiting by his truck, he walked over to a locked drawer, and pressed his thumb to the panel to open it. With another quick look over his shoulder to check he wasn't being observed, he slid open the drawer and removed a black block about the size of a bar of gold bullion.

The inscription read, "Primary Core Block | Longsword Class | Galatine."

Carter sighed and considered dropping the object back into the drawer. Instead, he slid the core block into the inside pocket of his jacket, before heading through the door and closing it firmly behind him.

THREE

PAST MEETS FUTURE

CARTER PULLED into a parking space in the center of Ridge Town and turned off the truck's engine. The burble of the ancient V8, which he'd restored by hand himself, had barely dissipated before the anxious and curious eyes of onlookers began peering at him through the windshield. He sighed, preparing himself for the unwanted scrutiny he was about to receive, and opened the door.

"You have to let me drive this thing before we head out!" Major Larsen said, jumping out of the passenger side. "I've only ever seen vehicles powered by internal combustion engines in museums. How did you even get fuel for this thing?"

"I built something called a Fischer-Tropsch converter, which creates synthetic gasoline out of trash and a few other things," Carter replied. He glanced at a woman who was eyeballing him from the sidewalk. She looked away, and sharply quickened her pace.

"Sounds dangerous."

"It is." Carter locked the truck and began heading toward the Red Hog, which was the only bar in town that didn't lock its doors when it saw him coming. "The first device I built blew up, and almost took my cabin with it. I ended up with second degree burns on my hands and face, which made the folk in this town fear me even more than they do now."

Carter laughed to himself as he remembered people fleeing from him, like he was some kind of demon, risen from the fiery pits of hell. Then, to his surprise, Carina placed a hand on the side of his face and turned his head toward her.

"I call bullshit," the major said, studying his features, while turning his head one way and then the other. "Wiry silver beard aside, there's not a mark on your face. Not even age-lines."

Carter drew back – the physical contact was uninvited, and unwanted. Carina appeared to notice this and tried to backtrack.

"Hey, sorry, I didn't mean to spook you."

"I wasn't spooked," Carter answered, though in truth it had been a shock. "It's just that the only kind of touch I ever get these days is from a fist or a boot. Sometimes a baseball bat."

Carina frowned then looked around the town center, apparently noticing for the first time that all eyes were watching them, and that none of the attention was of the friendly kind.

"What the hell is their problem, anyway?" she wondered.

Carter noticed that, perhaps intentionally, she had spoken loudly enough that anyone close by could hear her. However, if her purpose had been to embarrass the onlookers into turning away, it hadn't worked. Folk on the streets were still staring at them like lepers.

"The Union demonized post-humans like me a long time ago," Carter said, quickening his pace toward the bar. "It's an entrenched belief across all Union worlds, as powerful as any religion."

"Well, it's no religion that I believe in," Carina replied, while also giving the evil-eye to a man and woman who had stopped to glower at them as they passed.

"You're in the minority then." Carter stopped at the door to the Red Hog and grabbed the handle. "And, in case you're wondering, my advanced healing factor meant that any trace of the burns from the failed engineering experiment were long gone inside of twenty-four hours."

Carina huffed a laugh. "Maybe these folk are right about you being a freak after all."

"That's not funny," Carter grunted.

He pulled open the door and was about to step through when an older gentleman, who was on his way out, walked into him. It was like walking into a block of solid lead.

"Beggin' your pardon," the man said, staggering back while doffing his flat cap. "My fault entirely. I've probably had one too many." He paused and nudged Carter in the ribs. "Though I didn't fall on my ass, so maybe I've not had enough yet, eh?"

The man laughed freely and heartily, finding his own joke unreasonably amusing.

"Hey Joe, I thought I might find you in here," Carter said, grabbing the man's shoulders and guiding him out onto the sidewalk, so that he was no longer blocking the entrance.

"You know me; I like a tipple or ten," Joe replied, before laughing again. "What the hell else can I do with my retirement?"

"You could spend more time with your wife," Carter replied, raising an eyebrow.

Both froze then for a moment neither said a word, before Joe burst out laughing again, and Carter joined in. The man wiped a tear from his eye then suddenly noticed Major Larsen standing behind him. The man pivoted toward her like an old roly-poly toy and scowled, while swaying from side to side, like the upper branches of a tall tree.

"Oh, beg pardon, I didn't see you there, Miss," Joe said to the major, at the same time as straightening his shirt and trying to stand tall, without wavering. "It's a rare treat to see Carter these days, and even rarer to see him with company." The man's frown deepened. "In fact, I think you're the only person I've ever seen him with, besides me."

"This is Major Carina Larsen," Carter said, deciding that a

formal introduction was only proper. "She's here to make my life a misery."

"Major, huh?" Joe said. He scowled at Carina's torn uniform and raised an eyebrow. "The dress code must have changed somewhat since I was in the Navy."

"Let's just say I had an unwanted encounter with a thornbush, and a giant killer hog," Carina said, smiling at the drunken man. "It's nice to meet you, Joe. I'm glad at least one person in this town doesn't treat Commander Rose like trash."

"Most folk on this rock wouldn't understand service and sacrifice if it slapped them around the face," Joe said, suddenly fired up. "The military runs in my family. Pop was a Union Peacekeeper, and Grandpa fought in the Aternien war."

Carina nodded, respectfully. "I thank you for your service."

"I remember that my grandpa used to tell this amazing story about the Battle of Terra Five," Joe continued, suddenly swept away in his own reminiscences. "He was defending a position against a superior Aternien force. All hope was lost, he used to tell me. The enemy was closing in on all sides, and half his section were already dead…"

Carter smiled. He'd heard the story many times before, but Joe always told it well, especially with a few whiskeys in his belly. The man's measured, theatrical delivery and sweeping hand gestures were more worthy of a stage than a sidewalk. He glanced at Carina and was pleased to see that she appeared to be enjoying the recital too.

"Grandpa thought he was a goner, he used to tell me, but he fought on to the last, like Custer at the Little Bighorn. Then… boom!" Joe made a wide gesture with his hands, as if throwing confetti into the air. "The sky split open, and a great sword-like ship thrust through the clouds and cut down those Aternien bastards like King Arthur wielding Excalibur."

"King who?" Carina cut in.

"It doesn't matter; just myths and legends," the man continued, waving her off. "What matters is that my grandpa's life was saved that day, and if it wasn't for that ship and its crew, I wouldn't be here to tell you about it."

"Well, I'm glad that you are," Major Larson said. "It's a great story; one worth remembering."

Joe smiled broadly. The appreciation of a Union officer clearly meant a lot to him, Carter realized. The man then fumbled through his pockets for a few seconds before finally removing his comp-slate.

"Here, I actually have a picture of my grandpa, taken on that day," Joe said, clumsily scrolling through a gallery of photos, most of which appeared to be of his dog; a Shih tzu called Josie. "I've been trying to get hold of this from the Union central archive for years, and they finally sent it on, just this morning, as it happens."

Joe continued to scroll for a few seconds, until finally arriving at the correct image. He expanded the screen size of the device and held it up, like a photo frame.

"There you go; the battle of Terra Five," Joe said, proudly. "You can even see the ship that saved my grandpa, heading back into space."

Carter frowned at the image and pouted his lips. It had been one hundred and eight years ago, but he could still recall the day like it was yesterday.

"I remember it well," Carter said, as the sights and sounds of the battle a century ago flooded back to him. "It was early autumn on Terra Five, but it was unusually cold that day, despite the sun shining. The ground was softer than I expected, which hindered the Aterniens and made their advance clumsier than it ought to have been. That gave us the advantage."

He paused for a moment, recalling the final moments of the engagement, where he and his crew had cut down the remaining Aterniens hand-to-hand, while his Longsword-class battleship hovered above them, destroying the enemy armor, and providing cover. He sighed then smiled at Joe, who looked like he'd seen a ghost.

"And it wasn't Excalibur that cut down the Aterniens that day, but the Galatine," Carter continued, to a stunned silence. "That was my ship. It was named after another Arthurian legend; the sword given to Sir Gawain, by the lady of the lake. It was the shadow to Excalibur's light, and a fearsome weapon, in reality as well as in legend."

"But that couldn't have been you," Joe said. The man had sobered up like he'd been dunked in a barrel of freezing cold water. "The Battle of Terra Five happened over a hundred years ago."

Carter shrugged. "It sounds like you know a little something about myths and legends. Well, you're looking at one." He slapped Joe on the shoulder, which almost knocked the man on his ass. "Take care, Joe. Go home and spend some time with your wife. You're lucky to have someone who loves you."

Carter left the bemused man on the sidewalk and entered the bar. He held the door for Major Larsen then closed it behind her, leaving Joe outside, still in a state of shock.

"What a dump," Carina said.

"You were expecting the Ritz?" Carter looked around the bar, which was a typical spit-and-sawdust outer territories watering hole. "This is the sort of place people come to drink and forget. If you want champagne cocktails, I suggest you head back to Terra Prime."

"I'm more of a beer kinda gal," Carina said, brushing past Carter and pulling up a stool at the bar. "Now, what'll it be? Your reward for saving my life, I mean."

Carter walked up to the bar, ever conscious of the fact that the dozen or so others in the Red Hog were watching him attentively.

"I'm not much of a drinker, but scotch is tolerable," Carter said, sliding onto a stool beside the major. "You may as well ask them to leave the bottle."

"Thanks, but I don't drink whiskey or any kind of spirits, unless it's a toast."

"It's not for you, it's for me," Carter added. The major's reaction suggested she considered an entire bottle of whiskey to be somewhat excessive, so he chose to explain himself. "I have a bio-engineered metabolism, remember. Scotch is like water to me, just with a little more burn."

Carina huffed with interest then waved over the barman and placed the order. Carter didn't recognize the server, and though the barman attended to the drinks swiftly, he did so without making eye contact with him.

"We shouldn't stay long," Carter said, feeling suddenly hemmed in by the bar's four walls. "I haven't been into town for some time, and it looks like this place has changed hands since then. In my experience, it's never long before someone with too much alcohol in their blood takes issue with a post-human drinking in their bar."

Carina blew a raspberry that was so loud it made the barman look over. "Screw them. I was almost skewered by a demonic boar, then poisoned to death, so we're having a drink and that's final."

Carter found himself laughing. While he'd agreed to the drink as an excuse to drive Carina into town and get rid of her, he was surprised to discover she was his kind of people. Like himself, she put everything out there, completely unvarnished. After decades of being treated with prejudice and fear, it was welcome and refreshing.

"So, why the fascination with the Aterniens, anyway?" Carter said, necking the double scotch in one before topping up the tumbler. "You said you were one of the Union's experts on them."

Carina took a deep breath then paused to think. "I guess I'm fascinated by their culture, and how it developed so quickly. But you don't need me to tell you about the Aterniens. You must know more than I do."

Carter shook his head. "Truth be told, I only learned what I needed to know to fight them. Anything more was a waste of time."

Carina seemed surprised by his admission. "You obviously don't subscribe to the notion of, 'know thy self, know thy enemy' then?"

"I knew how to kill them, and that's all I needed to know," Carter answered, coolly.

"I disagree; I think knowing our enemy will be a crucial factor in the war to come." Carina suddenly sounded more formal and professional.

Carter emptied his second glass of whiskey and topped it up. "Fine, then educate me, professor Carina. What do I need to know about our enemy?"

Carina adjusted her position on the stool then wet her lips with a swig of beer before clearing her throat.

"For starters, their society and rank structure borrow heavily from ancient Egyptian culture, amongst others," Carina began. Her enthusiasm for the subject was already shining through. "They have a highly stratified civilization, based on when they ascended, and how long they've served the Empire. The first humans that ascended before the uprising and the war, many of whom were friends and acquaintances of Markus Aternus, are classed as nobility, while Markus Aternus himself is like a Pharaoh or a god."

"He's an asshole, that's what he is," Carter grunted.

"Some of the nobles are members of the Royal Court, which is an elite inner circle," Carina continued, undeterred by his gruff interjection. "The top amongst those is the Grand Vizier, who is Markus Aternus' right-hand man. Below the Vizier are the High Overseers, who are like generals, and below them, though outside of the Royal Court, are the regular Overseers. These include military captains, and top engineers and scientists."

Carter listened attentively, enjoying the major's enthusiastic delivery. In truth, he already knew everything she was telling him, but he didn't want to spoil her fun.

"Below the Overseers are a collection of lower ranks, which comprise the general workforce, who secure energy production and resources, and build their tools of exploration and war, but it's the soldier class I find most interesting." She paused and flashed her eyes. "They're known as Immortals."

"Cannon fodder," Carter grunted. "Every army has them, and the Aterniens are no different."

"I disagree," Carina countered. "The difference is that Aternien soldiers are much harder to kill. So long as their memory cores, or soul blocks as they are known, are retrieved from the battlefield, they can be reborn, with all their experiences and learnings intact. That's why they call them Immortals."

Carter sank another whiskey and slammed down the glass. "At least they respect their soldiers enough not to toss them onto the scrapheap, like the Union did to me."

Carina eyed him warily. "I thought you said that alcohol didn't affect you?"

"I said I metabolize it quickly. But, for a fleeting, glorious couple of minutes, I do still benefit from its intoxicating effects."

"All it's doing is turning you into a grumpy old fart…"

Carter made sure to shoot the major his most disgruntled and dirtiest look, before adding another slug of whiskey to the tumbler and sloshing it around the sides of the glass.

"Just how old are you, anyway?" Carina added. She was resting her chin on the back of her hand and studying him like a museum piece. "Joe, the drunk guy in the street, must have been at least seventy, but you said you fought alongside his grandfather?"

Carter sighed and took another sip of whiskey. Its effects were already waning, but he was no longer thirsty. He was also in a sulk, largely because Carina had – somewhat accurately – called him a grumpy old fart.

"You know when the war started and ended, so do the math."

"Really?" Carina said. "I have to say that's impressive. You don't look a day over fifty."

Carter pulled the glass away from his lips and shot Carina another dirty look.

"What do you mean I look fifty?" he snapped, trying to catch his reflection in the mirrored glass behind the bar. "The hell I look fifty!"

"What I mean is that you're a very good fifty," Carina added, quick to pull herself out of the hole she'd dug. "With those chiseled features and that dashing silver hair, you have a movie star quality to you."

Carter snorted a laugh. "You can stop hitting on me. As you bluntly pointed out, I'm far too old for you."

"You should be so lucky, old man!" Carina smiled then her expression took on a mischievousness that made Carter feel wary and uncomfortable. "Anyway, can you still, you know, get it up?"

"What?!"

"Hey, I'm not judging," Carina said, fighting hard to stifle laughter. "Most guys over a hundred would probably struggle."

"Don't worry about me, Major, my physical strength and metabolism aren't the only things that are augmented." Carina threw her head back, laughing. "Not that it's any of your damned business," he added, also laughing.

"I guess you must have dozens of kids, grandkids, and even great grandkids by now then?" Carina said, once she'd caught her breath.

The comment brought Carter down to earth harder and faster than a meteorite.

"Actually, all the augmented crew of the Longswords were sterilized. The Union didn't want any post-human babies running around after the war…"

Carina's shoulders sank. Of all the things she'd heard about him, this seemed to have surprised her the most.

"I'm sorry, I didn't know that."

Carter let out a long slow breath and pushed the whiskey away from him.

"I used to tell myself that it didn't matter, but it does," he said, running his finger around the rim of the glass. "The Union scientists tried to engineer emotions out of us, but we're still human. The five members of my crew were my family, and they tore us apart, like our feelings didn't matter. They didn't even let me keep my gopher."

"I take it you don't mean the rodent type of gopher?" Carina said, before finishing her beer.

Carter felt his cheeks flush hot. "It's actually kind of embarrassing. Gophers were little volleyball-sized robots that were designed to complement each of our skillsets. They were smart as hell, and funny, but to me and my crew, we loved them like pets."

"I already want one," Carina said, smiling warmly.

"Mine was a J-Class Advanced Commander's Assistant Bot, but I just called him JACAB for short."

Carina snorted a laugh. "Jacab?"

Carter scowled at her, but Carina held up her hands in submission, and allowed him to continue.

"Because they contained tech that was banned after the Aternien Act, I had to leave my gopher onboard the Galatine, before it was smashed into the Piazzi asteroid field." He sighed heavily. "Hell, I don't even know how many of us Longsword crew are left. For all I know, I'm the only one."

"You're not…"

Carter shot bolt upright. "Wait, do you know of someone else who's still alive?"

"I do…" Carina said, flashing her eyes again. She removed her folded-up comp-slate and set it out on the bar. "But if you want to know, then you'll need to buy me another beer…"

FOUR

CARTER ROSE TRIED to flag down the barman, but the man was avoiding his gaze and pretending not to see him, despite it being obvious that he had. Carter rapped his knuckles on the counter-top before coughing loudly, but politely.

"Yeah, what?" the barman eventually answered, when it became too awkward for the man to continue his pretense of ignorance.

"Can you get the major another round, please?" Carter said, maintaining a polite tone, despite the barman's rudeness. "If it's not too much trouble, of course."

The barman sighed before grabbing a bottle of pilsner from the fridge and placing it onto a fresh paper coaster in front of Carina. Carter couldn't help but notice that the man had stayed as far away from him as humanly possible, while still being able to serve the drink.

"Thanks…" Carter said, though the barman had already turned his back on him and walked away.

"I'm beginning to see why you spend so much time in the forest, hunting killer pigs," Carina said.

"Freak!"

The call had rung out from somewhere in the darker corners

of the bar. Carina twisted around on her stool in an effort to see who'd shouted the insult, though Carter just faced forward and continued to toy with his whiskey glass.

"Pay it no mind. I don't," Carter said. Carina was still scouring the bar, an angry look on her face.

"I don't know how you tolerate it," she said, turning back and picking up her beer. "All I can say is that you have a thicker skin than me."

"That's actually true; I am literally thick-skinned." Carter placed his hand on the countertop, palm facing upward. "The Union science guys engineered a type of cell they called a 'super keratinocyte', which makes the epidermal layer of my skin thicker and much tougher than yours."

Carina seemed unconvinced. "If that's the case then why doesn't your face look like lizard skin?"

Carter shrugged. "I moisturize…"

Carina continued to regard him skeptically, so he decided to perform a little demonstration. Sliding a pocketknife out of his jacket, he flipped open the blade and placed it on the countertop.

"Go on, try to cut me," Carter said, smiling.

Carina recoiled from him. "Are you out of your mind? I'm not going to cut you."

"It's fine, give it a try," Carter said, grabbing the knife and holding it out to Carina. "Just draw the blade across my palm and see what happens."

Carina continued to stare at him like he was a lunatic, but he could tell that he'd piqued her interest. He continued to hold out the knife, and eventually curiosity got the better of her, and she took it from him.

"How hard can I cut?" she said, placing the blade onto Carter's palm.

"Imagine it was your hand and start there," Carter replied. "Just don't carve me up like a steak, okay? I'm post-human, not made of stone."

Carina blew out an anxious sigh then slowly drew the blade across his hand. To her obvious surprise, the knife didn't cut him.

"No way, this thing must be blunt!" Carina flipped the blade and casually ran her finger along the edge, slicing her skin like a fine paper cut. "Damn it to hell!" she cried, shaking her finger vigorously before thrusting it into her mouth and sucking the blood.

"I told you," Carter said, reveling in his victory.

Carina scowled then jabbed the tip of the pocketknife into his palm, this time with enough force to cut through.

"Are you insane?!" Carter said, snapping his hand away from her. It hadn't hurt, courtesy of his sensation blockers, but it was still a shock. "You could have punctured the hide of a Morsapri with a stab like that!"

"I just wanted to see how tough you really are," Carina said, mumbling the words since her fingertip was still stuck in the corner of her mouth. "Go on, show me your hand."

Carter returned her scowl than placed the back of his hand onto the counter. "Just don't stab me again, okay?"

Carina leant in to examine his skin, like an anatomy student studying a dissected corpse.

"See, you bleed too," she said, sounding oddly heartened by this fact.

Carter smiled. "Keep looking…"

Carina watched as the cut from the knife slowly closed before her eyes, healing to the point of invisibility within seconds. It had the desired effect of stunning her into silence.

"Now, if you're suitably convinced, how about we move on to the rest of my crew?" Carter said, drawing his hand away. "You said you had information about who was still alive?"

"I do, but be warned that not many have lived as long as you have."

Carter nodded; he'd already accepted that, and it didn't deter him from wanting to know. At the same time, Carina took a long gulp of her beer then turned on the comp-slate that she'd set out on the bar earlier.

"Five Union Longswords were still active at the time the armistice was called, and with a crew of six each, that makes thirty officers who survived the war," Carina began. She tapped the screen and a list of names appeared, most of which were highlighted in red. "Unfortunately, twenty-one of those thirty are known to be deceased. You're one of the surviving nine."

The news hit Carter harder than he expected. "Are there really that many of us gone?"

"I'm afraid so," Carina nodded.

"How the hell did they die? As you've seen, we're pretty hard to kill."

Carina took a deep breath then began searching through the Union records on her comp-slate.

"From what I can see, some of the deaths were a result of simple accidents. Vehicle crashes and other random misfortunes like that." Her manner then became suddenly more somber. "It also says that several committed suicide. It seems that a few had a tough time reintegrating after the war."

Carter shook his head. "Yes, well, when everyone sees you as a freak of nature to be feared, it's hard to get along in polite society. That's why I've made a point of avoiding it."

"The majority appear to have passed from unintentional opioid overdoses," Carina continued, though even she appeared to be surprised by that fact. "That seems off, though. You mentioned being highly resistant to drugs?"

"We are, but the bio-engineering and cybernetic procedures we underwent during our transformation were agonizing, to say the least," Carter explained. "It was worse for some than others. I got lucky, for example, especially considering I was the first to undergo the procedure. The Union gave us Trifentanil tablets to manage the effects, until we healed."

"You're kidding?" Not for the first time, Carina had been knocked for six by a revelation he'd made. "Trifentanil is an insanely powerful synthetic opioid. A single tab of that stuff could put one of those 'death hogs' on its ass, permanently."

"You're not wrong, which is why they gave it to us," Carter answered. "Trifentanil takes the edge off, and then some, but it's easy to go too far, so I guess it doesn't surprise me that a lot of Longsword crew went out that way."

The news that more than two-thirds of the post-human officers who'd survived the war were dead had been difficult enough to swallow, but that many suffered mental trauma that had driven them to suicide or accidental overdoses was an added kick in the gut.

"The Union techs went to a lot of trouble to make our bodies strong, but they didn't give a second thought to our mental health," Carter said, speaking as much to himself as to Major Larsen. "Bullets aren't the only things that kill soldiers. War takes its toll in other ways too."

Carter was lost in his own thoughts for a moment, before he noticed that Carina was pouting, as if she were sucking a boiled sweet. And while that wasn't entirely beyond the realms of possibility, he guessed that she was instead working up the courage to ask him a difficult question.

"Do you still take Trifentanil?"

"No, not for a long time," Carter replied, keen to knock that concern on the head. "I need my edge, especially here. As you've already discovered, I'm not exactly welcomed with open arms wherever I go." He shifted in his seat so that he could better see the major's comp-slate. "Enough about the dead, anyway. Why don't you tell me who's still alive?"

Carina cycled through a few different screens then stopped on a set of personnel records.

"Three of your crew from the Galatine are listed as still being alive, besides you," Carina began. She pointed to the first record. "Master Operator, Cai Cooper, is believed to be alive and on Terra Six."

Carter nodded. "He was my ops and intelligence officer. A cold fish, to be sure, but his mind is sharper than a razor blade."

"The next is Master Navigator, Amaya Reid," Carina continued. "She showed up at a random Union checkpoint scan about six months ago, but we're still trying to fix her location."

"You'd like Amaya; she thinks she's a comedian, just like you..." Carina rolled her eyes at him, but, tellingly, didn't refute his accusation. "Amaya can fly anything faster and harder than you'd believe, but without a ship, a pilot and navigator isn't much use to anyone."

Carina nodded her agreement then scrolled down the list to the next name.

"Officially, Master-at-arms, Brodie Kaur, was recorded dead on Terra Three in the year 2335, when he would have been fifty-three."

Carter cursed. "That was only three years after the war ended. I should have reached out to him, damn it."

"Don't write him off just yet," Carina was quick to add. "Recent intel suggests he's very much alive and kicking on Terra Seven or possibly Venture Terminal, working a private security gig."

"That certainly sounds like the sort of thing he'd do," Carter replied, choosing to believe Carina's recent information over the much older official record.

Carina scrolled further down the screen, and the final two entries were considerably briefer.

"Master Medic Rosalie Moss died from a Trifentanil overdose in 2356 when she was ninety-one," Carina added. "And Master Engineer Kendra Castle died twenty-one years ago, in 2413." Her eyes narrowed. "It says here she would have been a hundred and forty-seven years old at the time of her death. Surely, that can't be right?"

Carter shrugged. "Sounds about right." Then his eyes narrowed too. "And don't ask again about my age. It's impolite."

Carina snorted a laugh and continued reading the screen. "There's no cause listed for Master Engineer Castle, either. The death was recorded by a close friend in a local news page on Terra Three."

Carter was immediately suspicious. "Who was the friend?"

Carina searched through the records for a few moments, during which time Carter noticed that a group of drinkers had gathered by the pool table, and were watching him closely. They were dressed casually in a mixture of dark denim and leather, and all of them wore caps or bandanas, with the Ridge Town emblem emblazoned on them.

"It says here that the entry in the news page was made by Orla Raeb," Carina finally answered.

Carter snorted and shook his head.

"Do you know this person?"

"In a manner of speaking," Carter replied.

He was about to explain his cryptic response when the group of six men began to strut in his direction. Three were brandishing pool cues, and all of them had a hateful look in their eyes that betrayed their violent intentions.

"Hey, freak," one of the men said, jabbing a finger into Carter's back. "Go drink somewhere else. This bar is for true-born humans."

Carter judged that the man was roughly two-eighty pounds, and while not in good shape, he could tell the drinker could handle himself. He sighed and was about to deflate the situation by agreeing to leave when Major Larsen spun around in her seat and stared down the ringleader.

"He was born human and still is human," Carina said, channeling the calm but authoritative tenor of a military officer. "And as citizens of the Union, we have just as much right to drink here as you do."

"It's okay Major, we're done, anyway," Carter said, still trying to avoid a confrontation.

In his experience, they only ended one way, with people

fearing and hating him even more. He slid off his stool, ready to leave, but the gang wasn't done. The six men loomed over Carina and Carter, trying to railroad them out of the bar. One of the men, a burly thug with a shaved head, glared at Carter and spat on his boot.

"That's right, freak, fuck off, and take this little bitch with you," the man hissed, while jabbing a finger at Carina.

Carter stopped and closed his eyes, trying to contain the rage that was boiling inside him. He was used to the attacks and insults, but the gang's bigoted resentment of him had spilled over to Major Larsen, and Carter wouldn't stand for it. Quite apart from anything else, he hated the f-word. Lesser swears he could tolerate, and in many ways were part and parcel of life, especially in the military, but the f-bomb had to be justified, and having it casually thrown in his face only served to rile him up even more.

"You need to take that back," Carter said, turning to face the gang leader, "and you also need to mind your language."

The leader laughed in his face, and his cohort joined in, cajoling, and jostling each other, as if Carter had said something hilarious.

"Fuck you, you post-human fuck," the man growled, squaring off against Carter. "The way I see it, hanging out with deviants like you makes her just as much of a freak." The man sneered and cracked his knuckles. "But if you have a problem with me calling your little major a bitch, I suggest we take it outside."

The group closed in, and Major Larsen also slid off her stool. They were backed up against the bar and in a bad spot, but he could see that Carina had managed to slip her empty beer bottle off the counter and was hiding it behind her back.

"I'll leave when you apologize to the major," Carter said. He knew it would have been more sensible to just back down, but as Carina had repeatedly pointed out, he was old school. "Hate me all you like, but you don't get to cast slurs on my friends."

The ringleader grabbed Carter's shirt collar and leaned in so close that he could smell the beer and cigarettes on the man's breath. "I'll do whatever the hell I like, freak. Starting with beating your ass."

The man head-butted Carter and there was a dull, organic crunch as the thug's forehead collided with his diamond-hard cranium. The ringleader rocked back on unsteady legs and toppled over the back of a chair, landing hard on the cold stone floor.

"Bastard!" cried one of the others, and a second later a pool cue was swung across his chest, but the shaft cracked and splintered like old driftwood.

Carter kicked the drinker who'd struck him, carefully measuring the power of the blow so as not to cave in the man's chest cavity. Even so, the kick bent the man double and propelled him half-way across the bar, and over the top of the pool table, scattering the balls, and even pocketing a couple of them.

The remaining four drinkers all piled in and Carter raised a guard, protecting his head against the barrage of frenzied strikes, combining fists, pool cues and bottles. Glass smashed and beer splattered his face, then a moment later one of the drinkers was flat on his back, blood pouring from a cut to his head. Carter looked up and saw Major Larsen with the broken stub of a bottle in her hand. One of the thugs took a swing at her, but she ducked under it and chopped a knife-hand strike into the man's throat, causing him to squawk like a strangled chicken. A spinning elbow strike then broke the man's nose and knocked him out cold on the floor, alongside his ringleader buddy.

With only two left standing, Carter dug in his heels then shoved the men off him, sending both flying through the air as if they'd been shot from a catapult. One crashed through a table, while the other smashed into the juke box, causing the old-fashioned player to skip to the next song. To Carter's amusement, it was one he liked – a new country-rock ballad from a band on Union Three, called The Deaf Wolves.

Suddenly a blast of gunfire rang out and splinters of wood from the ceiling beams fell onto Carter's head. He turned to see the barman staring at him, hands wrapped around a semi-automatic 12-gauge.

"That's enough!" the man yelled. "You two get out of here, right now, and don't ever come back!"

The order had been issued at volume, but Carter could detect stress in the man's voice, and he could see that his hands were trembling. The thump of the man's heartbeat was louder than the jukebox to his augmented ears.

"Fine, like we said, we're done here anyway," Carina answered, picking up her comp-slate and casually folding it back into a neat rectangle. "You could do with cleaning up the place, though," she added, hooking a thumb toward the pile of bodies behind them. "It's full of trash."

Carina headed for the door, as cool as ice, and Carter watched her leave with a smile on his face. Despite what the Union had done to him, the service was ingrained in his bones, like the letters inside a stick of rock candy, and watching how Major Larsen had handled herself gave him a sense of pride.

Picking up his whiskey glass, he finished the drink then headed out onto the street, where Carina was waiting for him.

"So, we're friends now?" she said, with an eyebrow raise and a smirk. "That's what you said in there, and there are no take-backsies."

Carter laughed and fixed his shirt, which had become untucked after the thug had grabbed him. "I guess I did say that," he admitted.

"Great, so since we're friends, how about you do your old pal a favor, and meet with the Admiral?" Carina added, getting straight back to business. "If you still don't want to help us after that then you can walk. You don't owe us anything."

"Your admiral probably doesn't agree with that sentiment," Carter sighed.

"Don't worry about the Admiral, I can handle her." Carina then nudged Carter with her shoulder. "Come on, what do you say?"

Carter sighed again then cast a glance back into the bar they'd just left in tatters. He'd arrived dead set on having a drink, then sending the Union major packing, but hearing about how so many of his old brothers- and sisters-in-arms were dead had changed his perspective. He had been augmented and trained for one purpose alone, which was to defeat the Union's enemies. And if Carina was correct, his old enemy had returned. He couldn't allow the sacrifice and service of the Longsword crews to have been for nothing, so while blood still flowed through his veins, he knew he had to fight.

"Okay, I'll meet your admiral," Carter said, causing Carina's smile to broaden and become beaming. "But I promise you, she won't like me."

FIVE

IT'S WORSE WHEN YOU'RE OLDER

CARTER STUDIED the Union military ship with interest, while Major Carina Larsen piloted their compact two-man shuttle toward the vessel, which was slowly orbiting the forest moon of Union Nine. He'd moved from planet to planet a few times since being decommissioned, before finally settling on the distant, sparsely populated moon. He wracked his brain, trying to remember when his last interstellar jaunt was, and realized he hadn't been into space for at least forty years. However, looking at the Union ship, cast into sharp relief against the blackness of the cosmos, it was hard to believe any time had passed since the end of the Aternien war.

"That old junker looks like it's been around longer than I have," Carter said, as Carina began docking maneuvers.

"It probably has," Carina admitted, without embarrassment. "The Dexterous is an old Hunt-class countermeasures ship from the Aternien war. She's fifty-two meters long and has a crew compliment of thirty-six. Thirty-seven with you on-board."

Carter blew out a long, low whistle. "My god, I never thought I'd see a Hunt class again." He shook his head and studied the vessel more closely. "It looks like the hull armor has been replaced and reconfigured since my day, but now that you mention it, it's a

Hunt through-and-through." He laughed and shook his head. It was like seeing an old friend for the first time in years. "Those things used to get deployed in the vanguard and were used to launch decoys to misdirect Aternien torpedoes. Some of the bravest men and women in the fleet crewed those ships." He shook his head again, though this time in bemused curiosity. "What the hell is the Union doing still using Hunt-class ships? You should be generations beyond these old hunks of junk by now."

"Hey, that's my ship you're dissing, so watch your mouth," Carina chided him. She was scowling, though by the lightness of her voice he could tell it wasn't meant in a hostile way. "The Dexterous has obviously been retrofitted significantly since the end of the war, so she's more advanced than you remember, but you're right that the bones are the same."

"I hope you have a spare cabin, because I guess you don't want me bunking with you?" Carter added.

Carina laughed. "Easy tiger, I have a cabin for you, so don't worry. The soliton warp jump back to Terra Prime won't take long, though. That is one aspect of ship technology that has moved on."

"That's good, because as I recall, a sardine tin is spacious compared to the living quarters on the Hunts."

Carina rolled her eyes at him and was then distracted by comms messages from the Dexterous, confirming their final approach and docking pad. The major locked in the landing pattern then set the ship to automatic and relaxed back in her seat.

"I take it the Union has built some newer ships in the last hundred years?" Carter said. "Because if the Aterniens do come back, these old buckets won't cut it."

Now that the nostalgia of seeing an old Hunt class had worn off, he found himself consumed with concern that the Union had been sleeping on defense research and development. The way that Carina squinted her eyes, pursed her lips and cocked her head to one side suggested his fears were founded in reality.

"We have built some new vessels, but new doesn't necessarily mean better." Carina glanced at him out of the corner of her eye. "Like I said back on the moon, the armistice and restrictions imposed by the Aternien Act heavily curtailed any R&D. And defense spending isn't exactly what it once was."

Carina's answer had given him a sinking feeling of dread. She'd skirted around the edges of the issue to make her point, but he understood the meaning well enough. The Union wasn't prepared for a fight, and if the Aterniens did return, they'd be caught with their pants down.

"The ban on developing new tech went way too far and left us vulnerable." Carter rubbed the wiry bristles on his chin, which could have used a trim. "I said so at the time, but no-one listened. I was already *persona non grata* by then."

"The Union was afraid of creating another post-human movement or, worse, the birth of a true AI that might turn around and stab us in the back one day."

Carter laughed. "Humanity's worst enemy has always been itself."

Carina sat more upright and folded her arms across her chest. "Don't forget it was the Aterniens that were the aggressors, not us."

"That's just the Union's warped view of history that they teach to young, impressionable officers like you." Carina's eyes widened. He could tell she was ready to defend the uniform, but she had the grace to allow Carter to finish his point. "The truth is it was human fear and prejudice that started the war, not the Aterniens."

"Whose side are you on, anyway?" Carina snapped, with more bite.

Carter could have backed down, but he was already slipping

into his old ways, and he figured that this could be a teachable moment for the major.

"I like to believe that the truth is always the side to bet on," Carter said, unsmiling. "But the truth isn't always virtuous, or kind. The Union is far from blameless, in more ways than one, and if we let ourselves believe otherwise, we're doomed to repeat the same mistakes."

Major Larsen quietly reflected on his words while the shuttle touched down and mag-locked to the landing pad and was conveyed in the shuttle bay. Carter noticed that a slightly frosty atmosphere had developed between them, and they both waited in silence for the bay doors to close and the hangar to pressurize. Carina then shut down the shuttle's system and opened the side hatch, allowing a breeze of recycled air to rush inside. Compared to the fresh Autumn air of the forest moon, it felt suffocating and artificial.

"Welcome to the Dexterous," Carina said, inviting Carter to exit first.

He unclipped his harness and stepped down the sloping ramp. The gravity, like the air, had an artificial feel about it, and Carter had to remind himself that Union standard was 1g, like on Terra Prime. The forest moon was a touch above that, and while most people wouldn't have noticed, Carter's augmented senses didn't miss a thing.

"We should get straight to the bridge, and start the warp jump," Carina said, jogging down the ramp to Carter's side. "The Admiral is not a patient woman."

Carter looked the major up and down. Under the harsh lights of the hangar bay, the frayed edges of her ripped uniform were more obvious, as was the dirt and the smell of stale beer from the bar fight.

"You might want to change first," Carter said, while plucking a loose strand of fabric from a tear in the collar of her uniform.

"Good point..." she replied, tugging at a few more loose

strands. "We can detour past my cabin. After all, it's not a big ship."

Carter followed the major through the narrow corridors of the vessel, though in truth he already knew the way. While the décor had changed, and the materials had been given a makeover, it was still a Hunt-class, and walking through its passageways felt like stepping back in time.

"Just hang around outside for a second; this won't take me long," Carina said, stopping by a door and pressing her hand to the pad to unlock it.

"I'll be right here," Carter said, as the door slid open, and Carina disappeared inside.

With the major gone, he suddenly felt exposed, and out of place, like a trespasser. A couple of crewmembers turned the corner and began heading toward him. He cursed under his breath and stood tall, straightening his jacket and shirt, but no amount of pruning could disguise the fact he looked like a vagrant, wandering the ship.

"Hey there, how's it going?" Carter said, as the man and woman shuffled past, eyebrows raised.

Neither answered his polite question, and both scurried away as soon as they could, casting anxious glances over their shoulders and muttering to one another as they did so. However, rather than feel put out at the fact he'd been given the cold shoulder, he was angry that neither crew member had confronted him. He wasn't wearing a uniform and had no form of ID. For all they knew, he could have been enroute to sabotage the ship.

Standards really have gone to shit… he thought to himself.

The cabin door slid open, and Carina reappeared, wearing a fresh uniform. She smiled at him and did a 'ta-da' style twirl to show off her new regalia.

"Better," Carter grunted.

"Okay, let's do this," she said, leading the way. "The bridge is just along here."

"I know where it is," he muttered, still brooding from their earlier, frosty encounter.

Carina frowned but didn't question his surly response, and before long they had stepped on to the command deck of the Hunt-class countermeasures ship. The lieutenant occupying the commander's chair immediately jumped to attention.

"Captain on the bridge…"

"This is your command?" Carter said.

"It's a temporary assignment, so that I could venture out and find you." Carina stood in front of the commander's chair and gestured to an auxiliary console to the side of the bridge. "You can park yourself there for the jump. Unless you want to remain standing?"

"Hell no," Carter said, hurrying to his assigned position. "I hate soliton warp travel. It feels like getting fed through a meat grinder then being glued back together on the other side."

"How long has it been?"

"Not long enough…" Carter planted himself in the chair and gripped the armrests.

Carina chuckled to herself, somewhat unkindly in his view, then turned to the navigator and pilot. "Take us back to Terra Prime, Ensign. A single jump if you can manage it."

The fresh-faced young officer acknowledged the command and the crew set to work. However, despite the sudden bustle of activity, the officers on the bridge still found time to gawp at him. Carter scowled, checked that his flies weren't undone, then sniffed his armpits, but he could see no reason why he merited their attention.

"Soliton warp drive is spinning up," the pilot announced, though the rising beat of the engine as it reverberated the deck plates was declaration enough. Carter blew out a long, slow breath and tightened his grip on the arms further, warping the metal due to his strength. "Jumping in five, four, three…"

The final two seconds of the count were always silent, in part because the warping of space around the ship distorted time. This was a tradition that annoyed Carter because it left an annoying element of uncertainty as to exactly when the jump would occur. And despite having experienced interstellar travel literally hundreds of times, it always caught him off guard. It did again.

By the time his head had stopped spinning, the arms of the auxiliary seat had been twisted inward like the handlebars of a chopper, and he was hunched over, on the verge of being sick.

"You okay back there?" queried Carina. Though the question indicated her concern, her sarcastic tone had displayed none.

"I'm fine, don't worry about me," Carter groaned.

He sucked in a deep breath and sat upright, still feeling nauseous. The rest of the crew were looking at him, though every head on the bridge snapped sharply back to their panels once Carter met their gaze. However, he saw enough to know that the jump had left them green around the gills too.

"Was it like you remembered?" Carina wondered, this time with more curiosity than mockery.

"No, like most things, it gets worse with age," he replied, gruffly. "But it won't take me long to adjust. You should be thankful you never got to experience gravitational maneuvering on the Longswords; that really twists your guts."

Carina frowned, suggesting that she wasn't aware of gravitational maneuvering, which further indicated that the technology, like so many others, had been a casualty of the armistice imposed at the end of the war.

"Captain, message from Station Alpha. We are ordered to dock immediately at pylon seven," the pilot said. "Fleet Admiral Krantz is waiting for you."

"Very well, take us in, best possible speed," Carina replied.

The crew responded and the ship began moving toward the towering space station orbiting Terra Prime – the planet formerly known as Earth. Carina pushed herself out of her seat, wandered over to Carter and reclined against the bulkhead next to him.

"Long warps are a kicker, ain't they," she said, smiling.

"All warps are a kicker when you have augmented sensory receptors," Carter answered, before blowing out a shaky breath of air. "So, tell me about this Admiral Krantz. Anything to help distract me right now would be good."

Carina shrugged. "I'm sure you know admirals, so there's not much to tell you that you don't already understand."

"Humor me…"

Carina chewed on her bottom lip for a moment while she gathered her thoughts.

"She's confident, driven, and strong-willed, like all senior officers of her ilk. And she's unblinkered. She sees the threat for what it is, while others in similarly lofty positions continue to downplay it."

"That's the good, what about the bad?" Carter asked.

Carina huffed a laugh. "I wouldn't wish to speak ill of my commanding officer, but to say she's blunt and impatient would be an understatement. There are great white sharks that are less cold and ruthless."

"Sounds familiar. What does she think of post-humans?"

This was the key question that Carter wanted answered. The rest was as he'd expected.

"To be honest, I've never asked her," Carina admitted. "But I will say this; she's fair minded, and she judges people by their actions, not who or what they are."

Carter grunted, thoughtfully. In his experience, the senior commanders were simply better at hiding their prejudice, but he chose to give Admiral Krantz the benefit of the doubt.

"I suppose we'll find out soon enough," he commented.

A heavy thump reverberated through the ship as the Dexterous thudded into the docking port on pylon seven. The pilot confirmed they had a hard seal.

"Come on, you can decide for yourself what you think of

her," Carina said, heading off the bridge. "She's no doubt already impatiently waiting to meet you."

Carter pushed himself up, grateful that the dizziness and nausea had subsided. Ironically, while it was his highly-attuned senses that caused the adverse reaction to soliton warp, it was also his augmented biology that swiftly rid him of the aftereffects. And, thanks to the nano-machines in his blood, his body had already re-learned how to counteract the effects, meaning that future warp jumps would be mercifully free from discomfort.

An officer was already waiting at the inner hatch door when he and Carina arrived. The pressurization light turned green a moment later, and the door was swung open, allowing processed air of a slightly different artificial flavor to flood in. As Carina had predicted, the Union's highest-ranking officer was already waiting for them.

He studied the woman, able to make out every detail of her uniform as if she were standing directly in front of him. Among the twenty decorations and badges, he spotted a Silver Star and Legion of Merit with clusters, along with a Presidential Service badge, which told Carter she was versed in politics, as well as combat. Her square, serious face was framed by light brown hair, fashioned into a chin-length bob that was as neat as her uniform and posture.

"She looks too young to be an admiral," Carter commented under his breath, as they approached.

"I think they call it being ambitious," Carina muttered, glancing across to him. "Besides, everyone is young compared to you."

Carter snorted then Carina came to an abrupt stop and saluted the admiral, who returned it stiffly. He almost found himself saluting too but managed to rein in the urge. He hadn't been reactivated, at least not yet.

"I take it that you are Master Commander Carter Rose?" the admiral said. Each word was like a pinprick in his eyeballs.

"It's just Carter these days," he replied. Already he felt on edge and under attack.

"That changes today," Admiral Krantz replied. "You were decommissioned, and now you are not. Report to briefing room five in thirty minutes, that's an order." Krantz then turned to Carina. "See to it, Major."

Carina acknowledged the command then Admiral Krantz turned on her heels and marched away without another word spoken between them. Carter was lost for words, but it turned out that the admiral hadn't quite finished. Stopping suddenly, she looked back.

"Oh, and Master Commander, you are out of uniform."

Seconds later, she was gone, and all Carter could do was grumble and shake his head.

"I knew this was a bad idea..."

SIX

OUT OF UNIFORM

CARTER ROSE STOOD outside briefing room five on Station Alpha, waiting to be called in by the fire breathing dragon, otherwise known as Admiral Clara Krantz. Major Carina Larsen was by his side, fidgeting with her uniform and obsessively picking imaginary bobbles of fluff off her jacket sleeves.

"Will you stop squirming around like a damned river trout?" Carter demanded, after her fidgeting became too unbearable to witness. "I thought you said you could handle Admiral Krantz? It looks like you're about to pee your pants, like a week-one cadet."

"I do not!" Carina hit back, scowling at him. "It's just that this is important, and I don't want to screw it up."

"If you don't want to screw it up, then take a breath," Carter said, staying calm, in the hope that his Zen would rub off on her. "I've been dealing with admirals for longer than you've been alive, and Clara Krantz is no different to any of them."

Carina continued to scowl at him, then looked at his dirty clothes. "You should have changed into uniform. Defying her will only start things off on the wrong foot."

"I'll wear the uniform again if, and only if, I decide that I want to," Carter answered. "And trust me, if I choose not to, there's not a damned thing Admiral Krantz or anyone else can do about it."

There was a stern shout of, "Enter!" and Carina immediately straightened to attention. Carter snorted a laugh, which drew another look of ire from the major, before she hit the button to open the door. Carina marched in first, and he followed her, back straight and senses on alert, as if he were expecting a fight.

"You are still out of uniform, Master Commander," Krantz said, her blue eyes drilling into him like cobalt-colored lasers.

"I agreed to this meeting to hear you out, and that's all I've agreed to," Carter answered. "If I don't like what you have to say, I walk."

Admiral Krantz pressed her hands to small of her back and puffed out her chest. At nearly six feet tall, Carter admitted that she cut an imposing figure, at least for someone who wasn't augmented like he was.

"Union law is clear on this matter, Master Commander Rose. In a time of war, I have the authority to recall you to active duty at any moment. You do not get a choice."

"We're not at war, Admiral, unless you can show me different," Carter countered. "And make no mistake. If I rejoin, it will be my decision, and no-one else's."

He pressed his hands to the small of his back, mirroring the standoffish posture of the admiral. He could see his reflection in the glass walls of the briefing room, and despite his ramshackle clothing and unkempt silver beard, his post-human physiology meant he still cut a far more imposing figure than the admiral did.

"I could have you arrested," Krantz replied, coolly. "Perhaps twenty-four hours in a cold cell will make you more amenable?"

Carter smiled. *This dragon has claws...* he realized.

Carter respected strength, if applied correctly, and if Major Larsen was correct about the Aterniens, the Union Military would need strong officers in spades. However, Krantz had to realize that he wasn't her 'asset' to do with as she pleased. He'd been there and done that. If he was going to fight another war, it would be on his terms.

"Admiral, let's speak plainly; your officers and crew are as soft and green as grass, and don't know the first thing about fighting. If I wanted to, I could walk out of here, take a ship and leave, and there's not a damn thing you could do to stop me. So, if you want my help, you'd better cut the crap."

Carter glanced at Major Larsen, intending to reassure her that everything was going fine, but she was pink-faced, stiff as a board, and looked about to ready to pass out. Admiral Krantz, on the other hand, remained remarkably unflustered. She continued to regard him for a few moments longer, before she walked around the meeting table, and perched on the edge nearest to where Carter was standing. Her penetrating stare was beginning to become uncomfortable when she finally folded her arms and spoke again.

"Okay, Commander, let's air out all our dirty laundry, then see where we stand?" Krantz began. Her tone had shifted, and she was speaking to him as a peer and equal, rather than as admiral to subordinate. "The Union treated you terribly at the end of Aternien war, and I'm truly sorry for that, but you have to understand it was a time of deep unrest. The civilian population remained terrified of post-humans. Decommissioning the Longswords and their crew, and ratifying the Aternien Act, was the only way to restore public confidence."

"You can spare me the history lesson, Admiral, I lived through it, remember?" Carter was angry that Krantz was lecturing him about something she'd only read about in books.

Krantz drew in a deep breath and let it out slowly, before turning her attention to Major Larsen.

"So, this is the man you're so sure is our best hope of winning the coming war?"

"Yes, ma'am," Carina replied, confidently.

"I disagree," Krantz said, fiercely. "This man is insubordinate, rude, and mired in the past." She pushed away from the table and turned her back on him. "We're done here, Major Larsen. You can escort Mr. Rose back to your ship and return him to whatever rock you found him under."

Carina stepped forward. "Admiral, I appreciate Commander Rose might be a little short on charm, but I've already seen what he can do. And he's right when he said he had a choice whether to come with me. Respectfully, ma'am, he's here."

Krantz stopped but kept her back to Carter. "You vouch for this man?"

"I do, Admiral," Carina replied, finally getting into her flow. "We need him, it's as simple as that."

Krantz let out an aggravated sigh then turned around and again locked her eyes onto Carter's.

"Very well, Commander, let's cut the crap," Krantz said, returning her hands to the small of her back. "You're right that our forces are ill-prepared and inexperienced. The terms of the armistice and the ban on weapons development has left us critically vulnerable. By now, the Aterniens may even be able to match our numbers, and their troops, ships and weapons are superior. The bastards don't sleep or bleed, and once destroyed, they rise again. In short, if the enemy comes in force, we will not be able to resist. So, the only question that matters is, are you still a soldier or not?"

Carter felt a swell of anger building inside him, but it was matched in force by a sick feeling of guilt. The admiral had called him out and he didn't like it.

"You are certain the Aterniens are back?"

"They are," Krantz replied. She nodded to Major Larsen, who began working on a comp-slate built into the briefing table. "See for yourself."

A holo projection appeared in front of him, comprising a dozen separate information displays. Some showed ship-to-ship engagements at the Union outposts near the demarcation line, in which Aternien vessels outclassed the older Union ships in both tactics and firepower. Others showed intelligence reports, and statistics on their losses to date.

Then there were the screens displaying body camera footage from Union soldiers fighting Aternien Immortals on the ground, and on outposts four and six. The Aternien warriors were like literal machines, advancing without fear, and cutting down the Peacekeepers with pulsed particle weapons that were light years ahead of the gauss firearms the Union still employed.

His eyes narrowed as he watched an Aternien Immortal get shot a dozen times in the chest; his synthetic body damaged beyond any ability to function. It should have meant death, but another Immortal simply removed the soldier's soul block – a receptacle that contained the digital essence of every Aternien – and continued onward. Later, the dead solider would be reborn, wiser, and more experienced, and with a thirst for revenge.

To an ordinary human, the jumble of displays was an onslaught of information that would have been impossible to digest, but Carter could assimilate it all. And the story it told was one of impending war, and certain defeat.

"If I'm to wear the uniform again, I want broad authority," Carter said, while still watching the screens. "That means I pick my crew, and I plan the ops. If you want me, you have to accept all of me."

Krantz pressed a single button on the comp-slate and the images fizzled to nothing.

"We plan the ops, together," she said. "And you can select your team, with one exception." She gestured to Major Larsen. "The major will serve as your executive officer."

Carter looked at Carina, but her expression did not betray any surprise. If anything, she was fizzing with excitement and anticipation. He realized that she not only knew that this would be a condition of his return, but that she had personally requested it.

"I've seen Major Larsen fight, so I know she can handle herself, but she's still just a human," Carter replied. He looked Carina in the eyes, feeling honor-bound to express his feelings to her directly. "I mean no offense, but I'd likely just get you killed."

"I've met you part way, Commander, so the least you can do is afford me the same courtesy," Krantz cut in. "Major Larsen is your XO. It is non-negotiable."

Carter stroked his unkempt silver beard and continued to look into the major's eyes. To her credit, she had not immediately begun protesting her case, stating X and Y reasons why she would make him a great second-in-command. Ordinarily, the idea of a regular human serving in his unit would have been dangerous and ridiculous, but Carina had already proved her mettle. And more than that, he actually liked her and trusted her.

"All of this is academic without a way to fight the Aterniens," Carter said. He chose not to explicitly confirm his acceptance of Carina as his XO, but the smile on her face told him that she knew she was in. "I need a ship, but not just any ship, and the major told me that the Union scrapped the blueprints for the Longswords."

Admiral Krantz pouted and appeared to be chewing the inside of her cheek. She glanced at Major Larsen and gave her a subtle nod, as if giving her permission to reveal a secret. Carter felt a flutter in his gut, and his mouth went dry.

"We believe that one of the Longswords from the Aternien war is salvageable, and can be returned to the line," Carina said.

The flutters in his belly grew stronger, but he wasn't about to accept Carina's statement at face value.

"We hurled those ships in the super-dense Piazzi asteroid field close to TESS-961S," Carter answered, his voice betraying none of his internal jitters. "I don't see how any of them could have survived that."

"Once it was clear the Aterniens were ramping up their

attacks, we sent probes to the Piazzi asteroid field, in the hope of recovering some of the Longsword's lost technology," Carina continued. "We discovered that one of the vessels had been captured by the gravity well of a planetoid. The ship appears to be intact."

"Which ship?" Carter replied, electricity racing through his body.

"The Galatine…" Admiral Krantz cut in.

Carter looked into the admiral's eyes, but her heart rate was steady, and he detected no other indicators of deception. So far as his augmented senses could tell, she was telling the truth.

"The Galatine was my ship."

"I know," Krantz replied, coolly.

"You could have started out by telling me that," Carter said, feeling a little betrayed. "It would have made things a whole lot simpler."

"Perhaps, but I wanted to be sure you were all-in first," the admiral replied. "This isn't a nostalgia trip, Commander. This is war."

"I know war," Carter grunted. "But if the Galatine is intact, I'll need an engineer who knows the Longswords inside and out. And that isn't any of your men or women."

Krantz nodded. "Who do you suggest, Master Commander?"

Carter thought back to Carina's briefing in the bar on the forest moon, and to the unusual entry regarding the supposed death of Kendra Castle.

"There's only one person I'd trust with the Galatine, but she won't be happy to see me."

"Who?" asked Carina.

"Master Engineer Kendra Castle…"

Carina stroked her top lip, her brow scrunched up. "But Master Engineer Castle was one of the crewmembers confirmed dead? You saw the record yourself."

"Kendra's middle name is Orla, and her gopher, her

engineering helper, was an R-class Autonomous Engineering Bot."

Carina still looked painfully confused, but then the penny dropped, and her eyes grew wide. "R-class Autonomous Engineering Bot. RAEB. Orla Raeb! So, Kendra Castle faked her own death?"

Carter nodded and smiled. "Kendra isn't dead. She just wants us to think she is."

"Then I suggest you find her, Master Commander Rose," Admiral Krantz said.

She walked back around the far side of the briefing table, sat down, and began working at the comp-slate. Carter looked at Carina, but she simply shrugged.

"In order words, Commander, you are dismissed," Krantz said, after he and Carina had remained in the room, looking awkward.

"Yes, ma'am," Carter replied, before about-turning and heading toward the door.

"Oh, and one more thing Commander…"

Carter stopped and met the admiral's eyes.

"You are still out of uniform…"

SEVEN
HEIGHTENED PERCEPTION

CARTER HUNG around outside the bridge of the Dexterous, fussing with the jacket of his new working uniform, which he'd picked up from the stores before embarking. It felt stuffy and claustrophobic, and was a far cry from his old 'battle uniform'. Like himself, the Longsword battle uniform was imbued with nano-machines that allowed it to self-repair, in addition to a host of other benefits, including exceptional protection against incoming fire. In contrast, Carter figured that the regular Union uniform would struggle to stop a sharp pencil from penetrating its soft fiber layers.

Giving up his attempts to make the clothing fit better, Carter approached the door, which scanned his face and allowed him to enter. Blowing out an anxious sigh, he stepped through and was immediately greeted with the beaming smile of Major Carina Larsen. This was followed soon after by a thankfully somewhat restrained wolf whistle.

"Not bad, Master Commander Rose," Carina said, teasing him, as he fully expected she would. "You wear it well. And I'm glad to see that you've also trimmed that mass of silver hair."

"I think you mean, 'not bad, *sir*'," Carter replied, feeling his cheeks flush hot from the comments. "As Master Commander, I outrank you."

Carina raised an eyebrow. "I didn't know that. It's a rank that hasn't existed since the Aternien War, so pardon my ignorance."

"You are duly pardoned," Carter grunted, stepping further onto the bridge. "The Master ranks were only given to Longsword officers, so it makes sense that you wouldn't be aware of them. In today's structure, it would fit in somewhere between a Naval Captain and a Commodore."

Carina nodded then stepped aside. "In that case, the bridge is yours, Master Commander," she said, gesturing to the captain's chair.

At first, Carter assumed this was merely a continuation of Major Larsen's good-humored ribbing, but it quickly became apparent that she was being serious, and gracious.

"That won't be necessary, Major, but thank you," Carter replied, waving her off. "I only command one ship, and until we find her, you're still the captain of this one."

Carina nodded then took her seat, while Carter sat in the vacant XO's chair to her right. He waited as she gave the order to detach from the station and get underway.

"All we need now is a heading," Carina said, turning to him. "Master Engineer Castle was reported dead on Terra Three, so I assume we start there?"

"She'll still be there, though we might regret seeking her out," Carter said. "Or, at least I will."

Carina was intrigued. "Why is that? I thought you Longsword crew were like family?"

"Yes, we *were*," Carter said, emphasizing the past tense. "But when the decommission order came through, she was the angriest out of us all. The Galatine was her baby. She invested years of her life into that ship, and nothing was more important to her, not even the mission. And I ordered Kendra to scuttle her."

Carina puffed out her cheeks then sat back in her chair. "I can see how that might make her a little resentful."

"A little?"

"Hey, it's been a hundred years," Carina shrugged. "Time is a great healer, or so I'm told. I'm sure she'll have forgiven you by now."

Carter merely snorted a laugh, which did nothing to allay Carina's obvious concerns. However, she didn't press him further, and gave the order to her crew to jump the ship to Terra Three.

"Hold on tight, this is going to be another long one," Carina said, glancing at Carter from the corner of her eye, while wrapping her hands tightly around the arms of her chair.

"Don't worry, the cells in my body have a type of memory," Carter replied. "That first soliton warp back to Terra Prime kicked my ass, but this one will be as easy as taking a stroll."

Carina huffed. "Not for the first time, I envy you."

The pilot began the countdown to the jump, and Carter observed how everyone on the bridge of the Dexterous bore down, as if they were about to embark on the rollercoaster ride from hell. He smiled and relaxed in his seat. It was at times like these that he was grateful for his post-human augments, despite the trouble they had caused him in other facets of his life.

The ship jumped, transporting the Dexterous and its crew from one side of Union territory to the other in a near instant. Aside from a sudden white-out and brief stab of pain in his temples, as if someone shot a camera flash gun in his face, he felt fine. Glancing at the seasick faces of the crew, however, it was clear they'd fared less well.

"We have arrived at Terra Three," the pilot announced. The ensign, at least, had weathered the ordeal better than the others.

"Standard orbit, Ensign, and prepare the shuttle for launch," Carina said, while massaging her temples. "Master Commander Rose and I will be heading to the planet. Lieutenant Kallis has the bridge while we're gone."

The operations officer acknowledged the command and waited respectfully for Carina to vacate the chair before assuming command.

"You're up, Commander, tell us where we should look first," Carina said.

"Our best bet is the shipyard at Eastsea," Carter replied, walking beside the major as they headed off the bridge. "It's a major freight terminal and shipbuilding hub for the Union, as well as for private consortia. Kendra will always be where the ships are."

"Sounds like a plan," Carina said, hustling down the stairs, clearly eager to begin their mission.

"She won't be using her real name, of course, since Kendra Castle is supposed to be dead," Carter added, speaking his mind merely to fill time.

"That will complicate matters. Maybe we should start by looking for Orla Raeb, the woman who supposedly registered her death?"

"That'll be a wild goose chase," Carter replied, returning the anxious salutes of a couple of crewmen. "Kendra was a genius even before they boosted her abilities with tech implants and gene editing. She'll likely have just hacked the register of death and fabricated the records. And any mention of Orla Raeb will lead us nowhere."

Carina was undeterred and continued at a rapid pace into the shuttle bay. The craft was already prepared and waiting for them, and Carter's new XO dropped into the pilot's seat without delay and raced through the pre-flight sequence.

"She sounds more like a spy than an engineer," Carina commented as she worked.

"Kendra is too ballsy to be a spy." Carter smiled, thinking about what mischief his engineer had likely gotten up to in the last century. "If she's at Eastsea, I suspect it won't be that hard to find her."

The gull-wing doors of the shuttle swung shut, and the

lights in the shuttle bay turned red to signify that it was depressurizing. Seconds later, the bay doors opened, and Carina powered the shuttle into space. Carter ducked as the slabs of metal raced past; his pilot hadn't even waited for them to fully open before launching.

"I'm the one with augmented spatial awareness, remember?" Carter said, side-eyeing the major.

"Relax, I graduated top of my class in the pilot training program," Carina said, while increasing thrust and powering toward the atmosphere at a rate of knots.

"Then how come you ended up in Military Intelligence, and not flying combat craft?"

"Who is there to fly against?" Carina replied, shrugging. "If I'd have gone that route, it would just be endless training and patrols, and occasionally getting scrambled to scare off raiders and chase down freebooters. I preferred to chase down mysteries, and the biggest mystery of all is where the hell did the Aterniens go."

Carter grunted a sigh. "I suspect we're going to find out. And when we do, you'll wish you hadn't asked."

Major Larsen dove the shuttle through the planet's atmosphere and raced across the terminator into night, heading for the planet's most populous continent in the southern hemisphere. Before long, the industrial port city of Eastsea came into view. In truth, it was hard to miss. It was a manufactured island more than thirty kilometers square, built in the sea off the eastern edge of the original port town. Part of it was devoted to freight traffic, moving well north of a billion tons of cargo every Terran year, while the remainder consisted of enormous shipyards and repair and refit docks. The bright arcs of the industrial welders look like concentrated columns of lightning, captured in place, while enormous showers of weld spatter sparkled all across the city from the dozens of ships being built or repaired.

"Maybe there's time to get the Dexterous refitted down

there." A smirk curled his lips. "Lord knows she could do with it."

Carina scowled at him, but thankfully kept the bulk of her attention focused on the landing pad that they'd been directed to. As a Union military shuttle, their clearances came through swiftly, and it wasn't long before they touched down on the hard standing. Carina shut down the shuttle's systems and the gull wing doors swung open. Carter closed his eyes and sucked in a lungful of real air for the first time since leaving the forest moon of Terra Nine. It was the difference between drinking an alcohol-free lager and an ice-cold German-style pilsner; both were technically beers, but the real thing was unmistakable and a million times better.

"It's already past midnight here," Carina said, grabbing her pack and sliding out of the pilot's seat. "I suggest we find a hotel in the city and begin our search tomorrow."

Carter slung his bag over his shoulder and surveyed their surroundings. The sky was pitch black, but the ship building area of the city was still humming with activity. Every structure and building was illuminated brightly, while the constant bursts of weld spatter made it appear as bright as day. He wanted to suggest they get straight to work, but while he needed relatively little rest, he reminded himself that Carina was still condemned to the human need for regular sleep. Checking his watch, which was still set to the local time on his forest moon, he realized that he'd been awake for almost three days straight. A normal human being would have been a hallucinating, gibbering wreck by this point, assuming they were even able to remain conscious. But while his augmented biology meant that he could operate effectively for days without sleep, doing so wasn't without consequences.

"Sure, see if you can flag down a taxi into town," Carter said, jogging to catch up with Carina, who was standing by the road outside the landing area.

"Way ahead of you, old man."

A taxi was already pulling up, as if Carina had materialized the vehicle out of thin air. She opened the rear door and disappeared inside. Carter quickened his pace further, for fear of the taxi taking off without him, and tossed his bag onto the rear seat beside the major, before getting into the front passenger seat. A tired-looking man wearing a black turtleneck and weather-beaten baseball cap with a logo that had long since faded, stared back at him, bleary-eyed.

"Where to, bub?"

"Take us to the nearest hotel in town, please," Carter said, pulling on the door, which creaked shut with a rusty clank. "Scratch that... take us to the best hotel in town. After all, the Union is paying."

"That's easy, since there's only one hotel in town," the cabbie replied, setting off without looking where he was going. "Unless you want to try one of the flea-ridden guest houses that is?"

"The hotel will do fine," Carina cut in.

"You got it," the cabbie replied, finally returning his eyes to the road ahead.

The buildings flashed past at speed, and Carter was reminded of Carina's daredevil piloting. Before long, they had turned onto the city's main thoroughfare, which looked like a low-rent version of the Las Vegas strip. Dozens of gaudy bars, cheap eateries and seedy gambling venues slipped by before the taxi finally screeched to a halt outside a hotel that looked like it hadn't seen a lick of paint or a window cleaner in decades.

"That's the *best* hotel in town?" Carter asked.

"The best and only." The cabbie shrugged. "We're not exactly a tourist destination."

"It'll do," said Carina, thumbing the pad to pay the fare, then stepping out. "All I want right now is a shower and a soft bed."

Carter jumped out onto the sidewalk, grabbed his bag, then slammed the door. The cab sped away, wheels screeching like a wailing banshee disappearing into the night. The din from the bars was even louder outside the cocoon of the taxi, and he watched as a group of five revellers stumbled across the road and almost got run over in the process.

"It's certainly a lively place, I'll give it that," Carter said, listening to the sound of music playing, intermingled with the boisterous chatter of drunken voices.

"Places like this operate day and night, because of shift work on the ships," Carina said, staring at the hotel, which was literally humming with activity. "I guess the workers cash their pay checks then sink the profits into the bars and casinos along here."

Carter was only partially listening. His heightened sense of danger had just switched on like a lightbulb. The white noise of the bars and clubs had been filtered out, and his eyes and ears were instinctively drawn to the threat. It was as automatic to him as breathing, but it was a status he hadn't experienced for long time; not since he was last at war and being tracked by the enemy.

"Hey, are you still with me?" Carina said, slipping in front of Carter and snapping her fingers to get his attention.

"Come on, let's get a drink…"

Carter headed for the closest bar, which so happened to be over the street from the hotel.

"You're kidding?" Carina said, though Carter was already half-way across the road. She hurried to catch up. "I'm not normally one to pass up on a beer, but I really think we should save the celebrations until after we've found Master Engineer Castle."

"Trust me, Carina, and follow my lead…"

Carter pushed through the door of the bar and Major Larsen followed. She now looked more anxious than confused but stayed by his side without further protest. He checked the venue, which was less busy on the inside than the blaring music and gaudy, flashing lights suggested it would be, and headed for the bar.

"Watch the entrance, and be ready," Carter said, waving the barman over. He ordered a beer and a double scotch, then twisted on his stool so that his back was to the door.

"Who am I looking for?" Carina replied. She picked up her beer and casually swigged from it.

"I'm not sure yet," Carter said.

His senses were still on overdrive. The only voices he was attuned to were the major's and his own, but there was something else too. Hurried footsteps heading their way, and the flap of heavy fabric in the breeze, like the sails of a yacht.

The door opened; Carina's eyes twitched and her grip around the beer bottled tightened.

"Three guys just walked in," she whispered. "One looked our way."

"Describe them…"

"Nothing out of the ordinary," Carina said, doing an admirable job of observing the new arrivals without making it obvious she was doing so. "They're wearing waxed raincoats and heavy boots. They're probably just off-shift workers."

Carter's heart rate increased, another automatic response.

"They're not dock workers," he replied, muscles coiled and ready to spring. "Get ready…"

Carter looked into the mirrored glass behind the bar and saw the trio of men approach. The leader pulled back his coat and a knife reflected the neon glow of the strip lights outside. The blade was thrust at him, but Carter had already spun off the stool and caught the man's wrist.

"Who are you?"

His attacker cried out in pain as Carter added pressure and forced the man to drop the knife. It thudded into the wood floor of the bar like an arrow.

"Answer me!"

The man cried out again, then his two companions also

reached inside their coats, but Carina was alert to the danger. She darted forward and kicked the first man hard between the legs, sending him down in a tortured heap. The other reached for a pocket pistol, but Carter snatched Carina's bottle of beer and launched it at the man like a missile. It thudded into the side of his head, knocking him flat and sending the pistol spiraling from his hand.

"Last chance. Who are you?!" Carter growled, now grabbing the first attacker with both hands, and lifting him off the floor, like he'd been hung from a meat hook.

The man hissed and spluttered through teeth that were gritted and bared, but to his surprise there was no fear behind the attacker's eyes. Suddenly, his senses jumped again, and he picked out the distinctive metallic clack of magazine being slid into gauss gun. His eyes scanned every corner of the bar in front of him in a millisecond, and he saw a shadow flicker past the window.

"Get down!"

Carter dropped the man and dove at Carina, catching her around the midriff and pulling her into cover at the same time the door was kicked open. Two men in long raincoats burst in and opened fire, spraying slugs into the bar with chaotic abandon. He felt a projectile bite into his shoulder, but the pain was automatically nullified by targeted nerve blockers that were released by his battlefield augments.

Flipping a table onto its side, he pulled Carina behind it then grabbed a chair and launched it like a catapult firing rocks at a castle wall. The chair collided with one of the gunmen, knocking him out onto the street, before it ricocheted through the window, smashing the pane with an ear-splitting crash. The second gunman was undeterred and charged forward. Carter couldn't see him from behind the table, but the sound of his footsteps indicated he was heading straight for them.

He jumped up and snatched the attacker's sub gun, catching

the man completely by surprise. The gunman squeezed the trigger, but Carter deflected the weapon's aim and the slugs thumped harmlessly into the ceiling. Gritting his teeth, he then squeezed his hand into a fist and collapsed the barrel like crushing a soda can. The weapon exploded in the gunman's hands and the man howled with pain as shrapnel bit into his body, face and neck. Carter grabbed the collar of the man's raincoat and pulled back his fist, ready to strike, when two more figures appeared at the door.

"Police! Everybody, freeze!"

Straight away, the attackers who had not already fled the bar shot and up and ran. The police called out again, but to no avail, and the men had slipped into a back area of the bar in a heartbeat. Suddenly, the gunman Carter had held off slipped out of his coat and ran. He set off after him, but gunfire thudded into the ceiling, and the cry of the police officer cut through the air for a second time.

"Last warning! Stay where you are, or I will shoot you!"

"I'm Union military, damn it!" Carter snarled, glaring at the officer barring him from pursuing his quarry. "I have to go after them."

He took another step then felt the razor-sharp barbs of an electroshock gun pierce his skin. Electricity coursed through his body but the pain was numbed in an instant, and Carter grabbed the electrodes and yanked them free, as easily as pulling out a thorn. The police officer's mouth fell open, evidently at a loss to explain how Carter was not writhing on the floor, suffering incapacitating pain. The officer fumbled for his live sidearm, and Carter knew when his luck had run out. He raised his hands and surrendered.

"Are you okay?" asked Carina.

She'd climbed up from behind the table and was brushing splintered wood and plaster from her hair. The police officer immediately barked orders at her too, and she lazily held up her hands.

"I'm a little cooked, and a lot pissed-off, but otherwise fine," Carter said.

"I don't know how. I've never seen anyone eat a shot from a stun weapon and stay standing before." She then saw the gunman's raincoat on the floor and picked it up. "Who the hell were these guys anyway?"

Carter shook his head. "I don't know, but I doubt that's the last we'll see of them."

EIGHT

THE GROUCHY PATIENT

CARTER WALKED over to the bar and finished his whiskey, while Major Larsen smoothed things over with the local police. Her chameleonic charm, combined with her Union uniform and rank, seemed to be helping, and before long the officers had left to pursue the real culprits.

"All sorted, and they also told me to apologize for shooting you with a shock gun," Carina said. She placed the raincoat that one of the gunmen had shed onto the bar and reached for her beer, before realizing it wasn't there.

"Sorry, I threw your drink at one of those assholes," Carter said, shrugging. "Why didn't that cop apologize to me directly? It's not like he didn't have chance."

Carina laughed and shook her head at him. "Are you kidding? They were both terrified of you. You got hit with enough volts to light up half this street, and you shrugged it off like it was nothing."

"It wasn't nothing, trust me."

The barman arrived, slid a paper coaster onto the counter, and dropped a fresh bottle of pilsner onto it. The outside of the bottle was covered in ice-cold dew from the fridge, and the fizz as the cap was popped off made Carter feel immediately thirsty.

"I'm sorry about the trouble," the barman said, while adding another healthy slug of whiskey to his tumbler. "There have been some strange folk around these parts for a while now, all wearing coats like than one, come rain or shine." The man tapped the raincoat on the bar as he said this.

"What do they want?" Carina asked.

The man shrugged. "Same thing every damned time. 'Have you seen Kendra Castle? Is Kendra Castle here? Does anyone know Kendra Castle?'... They're like a damn stuck jukebox."

Carter and Carina exchanged anxious glances, but both were careful not to give too much away. Even so, the barman appeared to perceive they were hiding something, and eyed Carina with interest.

"It ain't you, is it? That would explain why those guys burst in here just after you two breezed in."

Carina shook her head. "My name is Major Carina Larsen." She tapped the name tape on her jacket. "Says so right here."

The barman looked at the tape, scowled, and grunted. "Shame. I thought if it were you then it might finally stop those weirdos from snooping around."

"Who is this Kendra person, anyway?" Carina said, still playing dumb.

"Beats me, I've never heard of her. I don't know anyone named Kendra for that matter."

Carter took a sip of the whiskey then looked around the bar. The slugs that the gunman had fired into the place with reckless abandon had made a holy mess.

"It looks like your bar took the brunt of it," Carter said, meeting the man's eyes. "I hope you have insurance?"

"Yeah, don't worry, I'll be fine," the barman said, removing a towel from his shoulder and idly mopping the countertop. "The shipyards bring in a lot of businessmen, and while they can get a bit loud, it's always good natured, so I'm paid up." He laughed. "Actually, I've been thinking about refreshing the look of the place for a while, so I guess now I don't have a choice."

Carter smiled and laughed politely, then finished his drink. "Well, it's way past our bedtime, so we'll be heading off."

Carina took a long drink from her beer then offered the rest to Carter, who gladly finished it off. He paid the tab and together they headed out onto the sidewalk, which was still as busy as it had been when they'd entered. Crossing the street to the hotel, they paused to allow a group of four inebriated men in suits to stagger through the door first, before entering and heading to the reception desk. It wasn't staffed and Carter dinged the bell, which chimed resonantly.

"Looks like there's some kind of conference going on," said Carina, leaning on the counter and pointing to a signboard that read, "Interworld Conference on Maritime and Shipbuilding (ICMS)".

"I guess that explains all the activity," Carter grunted, while dinging the bell for a second time.

The sudden movement of his arm caused pain to shoot through his shoulder and he grimaced. He pulled back the lapel of his jacket and touched inside, feeling blood wet his hands.

"Hold up, you're shot?" Carina suddenly sprang upright.

"It's nothing, I'll deal with it when I get to my room," Carter replied, calmly.

"You can't treat a bullet wound in a hotel room. You need a hospital."

The comment was made without her usual sarcasm. Carina had suddenly become stern and every bit as serious as her rank denoted, and Carter realized he'd need to give her a better answer if he was to stop her from dialing for an ambulance.

"I'll be fine, really," Carter said, matching Carina's sternness with an appropriate level of sincerity. "My dense muscle and bone structure is like a natural layer of armor. And my blood vessels and arteries are designed to close off and redirect in the event of trauma, to prevent major blood loss, and maintain circulation."

Carina raised her eyebrows, both impressed and shocked. "Doesn't it hurt though?"

"A little," Carter shrugged. "My engineered physiology automatically blocks pains in the heat of combat, as well as ramping up levels of cortisone, adrenaline, and norepinephrine. It's like a typical 'fight or flight' response, but amped up to a thousand. Once my heart rate and cortisol levels have dropped, my body slowly reintroduces the pain, so I don't forget to treat the injuries. Normally, the slugs just get pushed out as my body heals, but this sucker is wedged in."

His detailed response did the trick of setting Carina's mind at ease, and she relaxed against the counter again, blowing out a nervous sigh.

"You sure are one tough old bastard, I'll give you that."

Carter grimaced, though it was because of Carina's comment, not the pain in his shoulder.

"Less of the old, thank you very much."

A sleepy looking woman headed out from the back office, rubbing her eyes. She straightened up and smiled at Carter as he turned to greet her.

"Sorry to keep you waiting, it's been a little manic around here, what with the conference in its fourth day," the woman said, amiably. "Do you want your room key?"

"Actually, we're looking to book a room for the next few days, if possible," Carter answered. "We arrived a couple of hours ago. It's all a little last minute."

"Oh, no problem, let me see what we have…"

The receptionist spent a few moments accessing the hotel's booking system, then scrunched up her eyes. She looked apologetic, even before she'd apologized.

"We only have one room available, I'm afraid, and it's only a single," the woman said. "It's a Super Deluxe, though, so it's big and there's a good-sized couch."

"Is there a fully-stocked minibar?" Carter asked.

"Of course, sir," the woman smiled.

"Then we'll take it." He nodded toward Carina. "She's paying."

"Not a problem, let me get that booked in for you."

The woman smiled and moved across to another terminal. It was then that Carter noticed Major Larsen was gawping at him, mouth open.

"Relax, you're not my type," Carter said, guessing the source of the major's objection.

Carina closed her mouth and pressed her hands to her hips. "By 'not your type', I assume you mean than I'm under a hundred years old?"

Carter returned the woman's surly frown. "Very funny. You're quite the comedienne."

The receptionist returned, coughing politely to announce her arrival, before placing the keycard onto the counter.

"Here you go, sir and madam." She pointed to a scanner to the side of the comp-slate. "If you'll just look into the device, it will register your details."

Carina muttered something under her breath, then grabbed the camera and stared into it. Her details and photo were automatically populated into the system as she did so. Carter went next, but the computer simply bleeped angrily and a light on the device flashed red.

"I'm sorry, sir, the system hasn't been able to register your details, correctly," the receptionist said, sounding even more apologetic than before. She then laughed nervously. "It says here that you're a hundred and seventy-two years old!"

Carter turned the comp-slate toward him and quickly read all of the details it had registered.

"Looks correct to me, thanks for your help."

Without giving the woman an opportunity to respond, he grabbed the keycard and set off toward the bank of elevators, leaving the sleepy receptionist in a dazed and confused stupor. Pressing the button to call the car, he noticed Carina was giving him the side-eye.

"What?"

"A hundred and seventy-two years old?" Carina said, disbelieving.

Carter rolled his eyes then the doors pinged and slid open. He stepped inside and hit the button for the fortieth floor. Carina slid in quickly before the doors closed again, but she was still looking at him, now with a smirk on her face.

"Do you have something to say, Major?" Carter said, side-eyeing her right back.

"Nope, nothing at all," Carina replied. She paused a moment, before adding, "Grandpa..."

Carter shook his head, though he couldn't hide his smile either. The elevator door pinged open then he checked the keycard before heading to their assigned room. More suited men and women were milling around in the corridor, and it seemed apparent that a room party was in full swing, though he was glad to note it was happening at the other end of the passageway.

Carter opened the door and allowed Carina to step through first, though there was room enough for both of them in the entrance corridor.

"They weren't kidding about it being a big room for a single," Carina said, throwing her bag and the gunman's raincoat onto the bed. "They could have easily fit two super-queens in here. In fact, that couch is bigger than the bed in my quarters on the Dexterous."

"Sleep on it, if you like; I'll take the floor." Carter dropped his own bag onto the plush four-seater sofa then dropped himself into it. It felt like being absorbed by a marshmallow. "I find most beds to be far too soft. The Longswords weren't built for comfort, so I got used to sleeping on a mattress that was as hard as granite."

Carina opened her bag and removed a medical kit. Carter eyed her and it with suspicion, then watched her approach, kit in hand.

"Let me take a look at that wound, before you bleed out and die on me," she said, dropping onto the couch beside him. "I don't want to have to explain to Admiral Krantz how I found an unfindable man, only to have him die on me as the result of a bar fight."

"It wasn't much of a fight," Carter grumbled, while removing his jacket. Though he wouldn't admit it, the stuck bullet was beginning to sting quite a bit. "Whoever those men in raincoats were, they're not soldiers."

"So, the grey is natural after all," Carina said, fluffing a tuft of his chest hair that was poking out above his tank top. "I was wondering if you dyed it for the full-on 'silver fox' effect."

Carter slapped her hand away and scowled at her. "Do you mind? Don't they teach about personal boundaries at the academy these days?"

Carina flashed her eyes. "I must have slept through those classes…"

Carter grunted and reclined on the sofa, sinking deeper into the soft cushions. "Just grab the damned bullet already. There's a minibar over there with my name on it, and you're keeping me and it from being properly introduced."

"Such a grouchy patient," Carina hit back, smiling. She then removed the requisite items from the kit and inspected the wound. "The slug has barely penetrated but it looks to be wedged behind some costal cartilage," she added, continuing to be amazed by Carter's post-human body.

Carina sprayed the area with a sterilizing compound, which was unnecessary but he didn't interrupt her, then removed a pair of forceps and drove them at the wound. Carter could feel her poking around, but there was no pain. A few seconds later, she removed the metal slug and dropped it into her hand. It was squashed and bent, like a stubbed-out cigarette.

"What the hell are you made of?" Carina said, scowling at the mangled slug.

Curious, Carter plucked the slug out of her hand. It had

been a long while since he'd been shot, but the unpleasant sensation still perfectly matched his memory of it.

"I'm still flesh and bone, just a bit tougher than the average human."

Carina scoffed at the understatement then returned to the med kit. "Let me close up that wound with a cell regenerator… Assuming I can find the damned thing."

"Don't bother, it will take care of itself."

Carina turned back to see that the bullet wound was already closing and knitting itself back together, courtesy of the nano-machines in his cells.

"I don't think I'll ever get used to seeing that," Carina said, shaking her head.

"Hopefully, it doesn't become a common occurrence."

Carter got up from the sofa and walked over to the bed. "Let's see if this raincoat holds any clues as to who those jackasses were, and why they were looking for Kendra."

He emptied the pockets onto the bed then began searching through the items. There were some receipts, an unopened tube of gum, a packet of half-smoked cigarettes, and a well-used leather-style wallet. Turning to the wallet first, he flicked through it and found an identification card.

"Nico Wilder," Carter said, passing the card to Carina. "Maybe you can cross reference this with the Union database and see what you can turn up?"

The major nodded, sat down at the elegant executive desk and unfolded her comp-slate. She worked for a few moments, before swiveling the chair to face him.

"Nico Wilder is thirty-two years old and originally from Terra Three. A high-school grad, he held down a reasonable clerical job in an accountancy firm until four years ago, when he went off grid."

"That doesn't help us much, I'm afraid."

Carina turned back to the comp-slate, undeterred. "I'll run

his ident through the local police computer, as well as the interplanetary database."

Carter was surprised. "Can you do that? Legally, I mean?"

Carina shrugged. "Not exactly, but let's just say the admiral isn't one to let red tape stand in her way, and neither am I."

Carina worked for another couple of minutes, during which time she became increasingly frustrated.

"He's a nobody," she said, angrily pushing her chair away from the desk. "Just a petty misdemeanor on Terra Three when he was younger, but nothing that stands out. The Inter-web records are clean too."

Carter cursed. "Then why the hell is he attacking us? And how did he even know we were here, for that matter?"

Carina shook her head. It was a disappointing end to an unsatisfying day.

"I'm sending the data to the Dexterous to analyze further and pass on to command. Hopefully, they'll be able to turn up something I missed."

Suddenly, Carter's senses switched into high alert, and his hearing became attuned to the sound of scraping and erratic breathing outside the door. Then the sounds grew louder, so that Carina heard them too. He held a finger to his lips and pointed to the door. Carina nodded then carefully moved over to her bag and removed her sidearm, before taking cover behind the luxury super-queen bed. Carter crept up to the door and pressed his back to the wall. The handle rattled. He checked that Carina was ready then flipped open the lock.

The door flung open, and a man bundled inside. Carter was on him like a rash, hammering a punch across the man's face then grabbing his jacket and lifting him so high that his head burst through the plasterboard into the ceiling.

"Who sent you?!" Carter barked, slamming the man's back into the wall and almost putting him through it. "Answer me, or things are going to get ugly."

"Hey, Carter…"

It was Carina. She was standing in the corridor, no longer appearing alarmed, and had hidden her sidearm behind her back. If anything, he thought she looked embarrassed. Scowling first at her and then the man he still had pinned to the wall, the penny finally dropped. The intruder was wearing a classic grey business suit, with a nametag bearing the logo of the Interworld Conference on Maritime and Shipbuilding.

"Oh, shit, sorry," Carter said, sliding the man down the wall and back onto his feet.

"No, no, my fault entirely," the man replied, with surprising cordiality. Carter could smell the whiskey on his breath. "This is the wrong room…"

The drunk conference attendee then headed for the exit, reached for the handle, even though the door was already open, and walked outside. A second later, his legs wobbled, and the man fell flat on his face.

NINE
OLD CLASSICS

CARTER CLOSED the taxi door then walked over to Carina, who was already surveying the private repair yard, where they'd chosen to begin their search for Kendra Castle. He adjusted the cuff of his shirt and undid the top button, which went some way to alleviating the discomfort of wearing store-bought civilian clothes again. He missed the personally hand-tailored gear that was now sitting unused in his closet back home, and he also missed the cleaner air. The vast industrial complex surrounding them was suffocating in more ways than one.

"Have people forgotten how to make clothes in the last century?" Carter said, adjusting his other cuff. "First, you manage to change and mess up the Union uniforms, and now you have me wearing this rubbish."

"You look fine," Carina said, picking a piece of fluff off the navy-blue blazer she had picked out for him before they'd set off to the repair yards. "You need to look the part, and that 'wild huntsman' getup you brought from Terra Nine just made you look like a vagrant."

"I don't look like a vagrant in my old clothes, and saying I look just 'fine' in this new outfit is hardly inspiring," Carter answered, crabbily. "Besides, what part am I supposed to be playing, anyway?"

"We play whatever role is necessary to secure the information we need." Carina then set off toward the first industrial unit, and he followed. "For example, we might need to be investors looking to break into the ship building market. Or maybe we're fleet owners looking for a new repair dock contract. Basically, whatever works."

"I tend to find my hands wrapped around someone's neck is a good way to get the information I want," Carter grunted.

Carina smiled. "Let's hope it doesn't come to that."

They walked for a few minutes, but it quickly became apparent that their search was akin to looking for a needle in a haystack. The repair yard was a massive complex, with dozens of drydocks of varying sizes, in addition to hundreds of smaller workshops and units.

"I don't suppose you have any idea where to start?" Carina asked, pausing, and pressing her hands to her hips. "It could take us days or even weeks to fully scour this place."

"She'll gravitate to the most complex jobs, so that she gets to flex her engineering muscles." Carter replied. "That could be challenging refits or difficult engine builds, or maybe even custom commissions."

Carina checked her personal comp-slate and ran a search of the different businesses on the site, filtering by those catering to specialist clients.

"There's a cluster of industrial units about half a klik away that focus on engine rebuilds, refurbs and soliton warp engineering," she said, pointing the way. "That seems as good a place as any to start."

"Soliton warp drives are complex beasts, so that sounds like a good shout," Carter agreed.

They set off on their new heading, but it wasn't long before security intercepted them. A car with flashing blue lights screeched to a stop, blocking their path, and a security officer leapt out to challenge them.

"This is private property," the officer announced. He was stern, but not rude. "And I don't see any permits or IDs, so I'll have to ask you folks to leave."

"We're from the Union," Carina said, reaching for her military ID. "We just need to take a look around."

Carina held out her ID, and the officer took it then tapped the card to a sweatband-sized comp-slate wrapped around his left wrist. The screen turned on and displayed the major's credentials, the information steadily scrolling around the band in a circular motion.

"I'd have preferred it if you folks had called ahead," the man grumbled, while handing the card back to Carina. "We've had a spate of trespassing incidents over the last couple of weeks, you see."

"Angry men in long raincoats, by any chance?" Carter asked.

The officer's eyes narrowed. "Just how the hell did you know that?"

Carter stepped forward, sensing that the security officer might have information that could prove useful.

"We're looking for someone called Kendra Castle."

Carter removed an old photo of the engineer that he'd brought with him from home and was briefly distracted looking at it. Kendra was wearing her old Longsword battle uniform, and her layered chestnut hair was tousled up on top of her head. *She always had a way of looking like she'd just dragged herself out of a maintenance hatch...* Carter thought, smiling fondly at the image. However, despite her unkempt hair, no-one could mistake Kendra for a laughable figure. He'd once heard a Union officer describe her as "dangerously attractive", and Carter thought that summed up his engineer perfectly.

"Have you seen her anywhere around here?" Carter asked, finally showing the photo to the security officer.

The man studied the image for several seconds then pouted and shook his head. "That's the same person those other guys were looking for, but I haven't seen her, at least not that I can recall. There are thousands of folks working these docks, so the chances of me remembering all the faces I see are slight, to say the least."

Carter nodded then slid the photo back into his pocket. "Well, thanks anyway."

The officer grunted then rubbed his chin. "Anyways, since you seem to have God-level security clearance, I can't stop you from looking around, but do me a favor and call the office when you leave, just so I know you're safe. If you folks get crushed under a steel beam, or walk through a plasma welder, it'll mean paperwork for days."

With that, the officer turned on his heels and got back into his car. The flashing lights were turned off, and the vehicle drove away at a more unhurried pace than it had arrived.

"You heard the man; don't die, or it will cause him an administrative headache," Carter said, both disappointed and amused by the officer's selfish thinking.

Carina smiled, but the wind seemed to have been knocked out of her sails. "If the yard's security chief hasn't seen Kendra, it doesn't bode well for us finding anyone else that knows her."

"I wouldn't be so sure," Carter replied. "Kendra would want to stay off security's radar as much as possible, so it makes sense that our self-centered friend wouldn't recognize her."

Carina appeared to accept this, and her mood perked up. "Okay, so we head to the specialist industrial units first, and start asking questions, like a couple of private eyes."

However, after a solid three hours of going unit-to-unit, without success, even Carter was beginning to lose faith. A handful of people thought they might have seen Kendra Castle, or someone that looked like her, but none could give any concrete details. On one occasion, Carter thought they had a solid lead, but the trail of breadcrumbs merely took them to another dead end, and a Kendra lookalike that possessed none of his old engineer's dark wit or engineering flair.

"This is hopeless," Carina said, leaning against a park bench in a manufactured garden outside one of the office blocks. "There must be an easier way to locate her. Can't you just scan for her engineered DNA or something?"

Carter scowled at his irritable partner. "No, you can't scan for our DNA; it isn't possible to scan for DNA, period. But I know she's here somewhere, we just have to keep looking."

A man sauntered past, carrying a brown paper bag with the name of an on-site cafe on the side. He smiled at Carina, while also brazenly checking her out from head to toe and back again. The worker's blatant rudeness aggravated Carter, and since he was already in a funk, he decided to call the man out.

"You're obviously an observant young man," Carter growled, suddenly stepping into the stranger's path, and almost causing the man to walk into him. He removed the photo from his jacket and held it up. "Since you clearly enjoy checking people out, how about you tell me if you've seen this woman?"

"What? Who?" the man said, jerking back from Carter.

"This woman, have you seen her?" he repeated, thrusting the photo in front of the man's nose.

The worker's eyes darted back and forth between Carter and the picture, then he blinked rapidly a few times and shook his head.

"No, I ain't seen her."

Carter's senses jumped into overdrive, and suddenly he was aware that the man's heart rate had increased, and that his body was producing sweat from its apocrine glands. In time, interactions with bacteria on the man's skin would produce a tell-tale 'stress sweat' that indicated he was probably lying, but Carter's engineered senses were far quicker on the uptake.

"You're sure?" he pressed. "Her name is Kendra Castle."

"Look, I ain't seen her, okay?" the man snapped, while itching the side of his face. "Now piss off; I only get a half hour for lunch."

The worker tried to barge past Carter, but he grabbed the back of the man's jacket and threw him at the park bench. The man was barely a hundred and sixty pounds, and Carter's shove nearly sent the worker through the weather-beaten wooden slats.

"Fuck!" the worker swore, which only angered Carter further. "What the hell is your problem?!"

Carina moved behind the bench, while Carter boxed the man in, and gazed down at him, causing the worker to shrink deeper into the confines of the bench.

"You're lying about not knowing Kendra Castle," Carter said, holding up the photo again. "I'd strongly recommend that you rectify that mistake."

"I don't want any trouble, okay?" the man said, holding up his hands, and his paper bag. "I'm not even involved. All I do is get hold of a few things that Marco needs."

"Who is Marco?" Carter grunted.

"Look, I've said too much already."

The man tried to get up, but Carina clamped her hands onto the worker's shoulders and pushed him back into the seat. The worker grimaced, suggesting the major's grip had not been gentle.

"Just tell us what you know then you can go and enjoy your lunch," Carina said, playing good cop to Carter's bad. "Otherwise, he'll be forced to beat it out of you."

The man's eyes bulged. "You can't do that; it's broad daylight!"

Carter loomed closer and cloaked the man in his shadow, while clenching his hands into fists. He had a stern face at the best of times, but when Carter was truly pissed off – as he now was – even the hardest of men would find themselves intimidated.

"Okay, jeez!" the worker said, recoiling and shielding his face with his sandwich bag. "Check out the Deansway Industrial Park, about a hundred meters east. That's all I'm saying."

Carter was about to grab a hold of the man's overalls and shake a few more answers out of him, when Carina released her vice-like hold.

"Thank you for your cooperation," she said, amiably. "You can go now."

The man didn't need telling twice and ran like he was being chased by a Morsapri 'death hog'. Ironically, considering how attentively he'd protected the brown paper bag up until that point, he forgot his lunch on the bench.

"Why did you let him go, when he clearly knew more?" Carter asked.

"We're supposed to be the good guys, remember? He told us enough."

Carina picked up the paper bag, sifted through the contents, then removed a sandwich. Peeling open the bread, she gave it a sniff then started eating.

"Stealing a guy's lunch is playground villain level bad, you do realize that?" Carter said. He grabbed a bar of candy and tore it open. "Though I guess he won't be needing this anymore."

Carina finished the sandwich en route to Deansway Industrial Park, which turned out to be another cluster of small, specialist workshops. Compared to the rest of the shipyard, it was oddly quiet, Carter thought, and most of the units appeared to be closed. Then he saw an old road car parked outside a warehouse space and his senses stirred.

"Let's check over there," Carter said, nodding in the direction of the vehicle.

They approached the warehouse and the parked car, then Carina let out a long, low whistle.

"This is a Vinci XL100," Carina said, reverently tiptoeing around the vehicle while running her hand along its sleek lines and mirror-polished paintwork. "It's a bonafide classic, and one of the last commercial cars to feature an internal combustion engine."

"I didn't have you down as an engine head," Carter said.

He was teasing a little, but in truth he was impressed that Carina was impressed. Then he remembered how interested she'd been in his custom-built V8 truck engine.

"Well now you know. I love anything I can drive fast or fly hard."

Carter also had an appreciation for the classics, but he was studying the Vinci XL100 for different reasons. It had sparked a memory, and he was trying to extract it from the depths of his mind. Then it came to him, and he clicked his fingers.

"A Vinci XL100... Kendra always wanted one of these." He checked all around and underneath the vehicle, but for a car that should have been at least a hundred and twenty years old, it looked brand new. "I'd say this beauty was put together recently, and by hand too."

Suddenly, the warehouse shutter began to whir open, and Carter stepped away from the car, his senses on high alert. There was someone inside the unit, but the shutter kept the figure in shadow, until it had retracted enough to allow a man to step outside into the daylight. He was taller than Carter and were it not for his augments and increased muscle and bone density, the man would have been heavier too. Despite the business suit, he cut the look of a classic hired goon.

"Hands off the car; it's worth more than half the ships in drydock," the man grunted.

"We were just admiring it," Carter said, meeting the man's unsmiling eyes. "Hand-built right? Is that what you do here?"

"You've seen the car, now get lost," the man answered, keeping up his tough-guy act.

"We're actually here to see your boss," Carina cut in, moving around the back end of the vehicle. "Is she here?"

The man cast a wary eye toward Carina then back at Carter. The tell-tale indicators of stress lit up around him like an aura composed of pheromones and nervous energy.

"I suppose you'd better come inside," the man said, stepping underneath the shutters and gesturing for them to enter.

Carter took the lead, and Carina followed closely behind, though with enough separation between them to complicate any potential ambush. As soon as they were both standing on the concrete floor inside the unit, the man pressed a button on his wrist band to lower the shutter again. The trio remained silent as the mechanism whirred, then the instant the bottom bar hit the ground, the man reached inside his jacket. Carter was a blur as he dashed forward and tore the gauss pistol from the man's hand, before tossing it over his shoulder like a piece of trash. To his credit, the goon kept his cool and threw an overhand right that smashed across his jaw with enough force to break regular human bone. All it did to Carter was piss him off. A second punch came his way, but he blocked easily, before snapping a low-power kidney shot into the man's fleshy side. An anguished gasp escaped the thug's lips, and he was about to go down when Carter grabbed his shirt and pinned him to the shutter, causing it to clang like a trashcan being kicked over.

"Let's try this again," Carter said, adding pressure and squashing the air from the man's lungs. "I'm an old friend of Kendra's, so just take us to her, and I'll explain everything."

"Who the fuck is Kendra? I thought you were looking for the boss?" the thug answered, wheezing his response.

Suddenly, two men raced out from the back room, and skidded to a stop on the smooth concrete floor. For a second, nobody moved, then the two men pulled pistols out of their jacket pockets, and Carter heard the safeties click off. Dropping the bigger man, he dove for cover as slugs slammed into the shutter and chased him behind a stack of containers. Carina had dodged behind the controls for one of the crane lifts, and was soon under attack too.

"We're Union military, hold your fire!" Carina called out.

The shooters ignored her command and continued to pepper her position with gunfire. Carter could see that her protective barrier wasn't going to hold for much longer. He was about to warn her to move, when the bigger man charged and tackled him through the midsection, sending them both clattering through a tool chest. The cabinet fell on top of him, spilling wrenches, screwdrivers and more over his body.

He shoved the cabinet aside then was hit hard in the chest by the blunt end of a clawhammer. His sensation blockers had yet to fully engage, and it felt like he'd been kicked by a mule. The man roared then swung again, this time at his head, but he caught the hammer and tore it from the thug's grasp. A knee to the side forced the man to roll off him, but his opponent was back on his feet as quickly as he was.

"Give it up old, man, I don't want to hurt you!"

Carter was now beyond angry, but he had to rein in his strength, knowing that he could easily kill the goon with a single punch.

"You just hit me with a clawhammer," Carter grunted in reply, brushing grit off his shirt while casually meeting the man's eyes. "Do I look hurt to you?"

The goon had no answer, at least not one that involved words. Instead, the thug closed his hands into fists, and came at him again. Carter admired the man's courage, and for a big guy, his opponent was surprisingly agile, and clearly knew how to box, but none of it would help him. Attacking Carter was as futile and as stupid as trying to fight a silverback gorilla.

The thug landed a crisp right hand, which Carter allowed, merely because he was curious to learn how hard the man could hit. A second shot thumped into his ribs, but the crack of bone and grimace of pain told Carter that the punch had hurt his opponent far more than it had hurt him. Face warped in pain and confusion, the thug pulled his broken hand away, and Carter folded the man in half with a carefully-measured body shot that snapped him shut like an old book.

Leaving the man curled up in a fetal position, red faced and in a pool of his own snot and drool, Carter turned to where the other two men had been. The sound of gunfire had stopped, and he couldn't see either of them, nor could he see Major Larsen. Picking up a weighty monkey wrench, he stole toward the back of the workshop where he found Carina, gauss pistol in hand. The two other men were on their knees; one was bleeding from the mouth and had his hands behind his head, while the other had his chin to his chest and held his hands tightly in his lap.

"Good work, Major," Carter said, moving into plain sight, monkey wrench rested over his shoulder. The bloodied mouth and broken tooth were a dead giveaway for what happened to the first man, but he couldn't work out the cause of his companion's discomfort.

"What did you do to him?" he asked, pointing the wrench at the man cowering with his hands pressed into his lap. Carter noted that the man's eyes were also streaming, like he'd been cutting onions.

"Let's just say you don't need a wrench to crack nuts," Carina replied, with a mischievous grin.

Carter winced, feeling sympathy pains for the unhappy soul, but no actual sympathy.

"Okay you two fuckers, put your hands in the air!"

A woman had darted out of the shadows to Carina's left, so fast that even Carter hadn't seen her till it was too late. He wondered why his own early warning system hadn't alerted him to the woman's stealthy advance, then he saw her face and realized why.

"Carter?" the woman said, eyes scrunched like she was struggling to read a signboard. "What in the fuckity fuck are you doing here?"

"Hello, Kendra; we need to talk," Carter said, wincing at the repeated use of his least favorite swear. In an admonishing tone, he added, "And you also need to mind your language."

TEN

ARE YOU WITH ME?

CARTER DISCOVERED from his former Master Engineer that the heavyset man whom he'd incapacitated with a crippling gut-punch was the infamous Marco, and that he was actually Kendra's business manager, not hired muscle. He'd also turned out to be a thoroughly nice guy, which made Carter feel guilty for folding him up like a deck chair. Marco was currently serving them up a tea tray containing a pot of coffee, several mugs, and a plate of crisp-looking biscotti. His ambling advance suggested that the effects of Carter's punch were still lingering.

The other two men were Kendra's mechanics, and both were nursing their injuries in the workshop outside the office, where he, Carina and his Master Engineer had retreated to, after calling a ceasefire. Carter could see through the windows that one of the men had a bag of frozen peas pressed to his jaw, while the other was still hobbling around like John Wayne after a long saddle ride.

"Sorry about the punch," Carter said, as Marco brought him a coffee, which he politely refused, since he hated coffee. He half-expected the man to throw it in his face, but he instead handed it to Kendra, who accepted it with a wink. "If it makes you feel any better, you hit pretty hard, for a regular human," he added.

"It doesn't really make me feel any better," the man grunted, before pushing the plate of cookies under his nose. "Biscotti?"

"I don't mind if I do," replied Carter, cheerfully tossing a cookie into his mouth then picking up a second for a later date.

Marco then handed a coffee to Major Larsen, though she declined a biscotti, before turning to Kendra Castle, who was perched on the edge of her desk.

"You need anything else, Brenda?" Marco said, one arm wrapped around his gut.

"We're good, thanks, Marco," Kendra replied, shooting the large man a friendly smile.

Marco nodded then shuffled through the door, grimacing as he went. Carter felt sorry for the man, but on the other hand, it was good to know that his advancing years hadn't slowed his reflexes, or diminished his ability to take a punch, compared to the Carter Rose of a century ago.

"Why did he just call you Brenda?" Carina asked.

Curiously, she hadn't been looking at Kendra when she'd asked the question, and was instead distracted by objects in the office, and particularly in the storeroom, visible through an open door at the rear.

"Because that's who I am on Terra Three," Kendra replied, plainly. "Here, my name is Brenda Worthington. Kendra Castle died when I scuttled the Galatine, on *his* order..."

The word "his" was shot at Carter like a bullet, and he felt its impact with the full force of Kendra Castle's ire.

"I had my orders, Kendra," Carter answered, tersely. He had been expecting a prickly reception, but he wasn't willing to take even more flack for what had happened a hundred years ago. "Be mad at me all you want, but I hated scuttling the Galatine just as much as you did."

Kendra snorted and shook her head. "You're damned lucky I didn't pull the trigger when I saw you roll in here.

You've got a lot of nerve showing your face after all this time."

"Believe me, I'm as surprised as anyone to be back in uniform." He looked around the humble office space, and through the window to the equally humble workshop outside. "Though I am surprised to find you here. I thought you'd be managing major ship-building programs, or at least doing something more challenging than small-potatoes repair jobs in a place like this."

Kendra scowled at him; his comment had clearly insulted her, but that had been his intention. His old engineer was a secretive soul, who wouldn't easily disclose the true purpose of her operation. Accusing her of wasting her talents was an attempt to goad her into revealing the truth, but it didn't appear to be working.

"I was tossed onto the scrapheap at the end of the war, so dealing in scrap seemed to be a fitting occupation," Kendra replied, stubbornly.

"Don't forget that I was cast aside too, Kendra, so I know how you feel."

It irked Carter that his old friend seemed to think she was the only one who had suffered because of the Union's actions, but he continued tentatively, because he didn't want to start a fight.

"You have no idea how it made me feel, so don't insult me by pretending you do," Kendra snapped. "That ship was my life, and you took it away."

"It was my life too," Carter countered, finding himself becoming angry, despite his intentions to stay calm. "It was home for all of us."

"You're a safecracker?"

They both turned to Major Larsen, who had gotten out of her chair while he and Kendra had been bickering and was looking through a ring-binder filled with actual paper.

"She's a what-now?" Carter asked.

"The more old-fashioned way of saying it would be 'hacker'," Carina replied. "It's someone that takes black market tech, breaks the military security on it, and installs illegal, custom firmware. It turns restricted Union tech into equipment that can be bought and operated by anyone." She closed the ring binder and tapped her index finger onto it. "It's all in here."

"That's confidential!" Kendra said, snatching the ring-binder away.

Carter snorted and raised an eyebrow at his old engineer. "You kept hard copy records of all your criminal activity?"

"You know how I prefer physical materials to holo screens and photons," Kendra answered, more than a little embarrassed. "Besides, it's only a problem if the Union or the police find this place, and they never have and never will. And even if they did, I made sure that no-one could trace the hacked items back to me."

Carina coughed politely to get the engineer's attention. "You seem to be overlooking the fact that a Union officer has just read all of your incriminating evidence."

Kendra was unrepentant and unbothered by this fact. "What's the big deal anyway? All I do is recommission repair bots and service machines, plus the odd military comp-slate or core block. It's not like I'm selling weapons or secrets."

Carina had progressed from shock to incredulity. "What's the big deal? Everything you just said is banned under the Aternien Act. Only authorized and highly-regulated personnel are allowed to write and modify code, and the process is strictly monitored to ensure there's no risk of generating an AI, or other piece of code that might be applied to post-human experiments." She folded her arms across her chest and stood tall. "Union regulations give me the authority to arrest you."

Kendra Castle pushed away from her desk and squared-off against Major Larsen. Like Carter, her augments and genetic modifications had kept her in peak condition, despite being almost as old as he was. And while Kendra's specialty was engineering, her raw physicality and combat prowess were no less formidable than his own.

"You can try to arrest me, if you like, though I wouldn't recommend it," Kendra said, sounding as threatening as she looked. "But I'll wager you didn't come all this way just to bust a petty criminal."

Carina held her ground. "It's hardly petty criminality. They'd throw the book at you, and it's a damned heavy book. You could be looking at fifteen to twenty."

"None of this is important," Carter said. His comment cut through the tension like a laser. "We're here because we need you, Kendra. The Aterniens have returned."

Kendra narrowed her eyes at Carter then looked into Carina's eyes again, seeing in them the same sincerity, before she backed off and resumed her reclined pose against the edge of her desk.

"I've heard the rumors, but it sounds like paranoid horseshit to me," the engineer replied. Carter saw through her attempted skepticism and could sense she was concerned. "We haven't heard a peep out of the Aterniens in more than century, so why now?"

"That's what we need to find out." He nodded toward Carina, who was still on edge from her earlier confrontation with Kendra. "Major Larsen will make all of the intel available to you. Though, from the sounds of it, you could just hack the Union database and take it for yourself."

Kendra Castle stared at Carter for a few seconds, while chewing the inside of her mouth. The mention of the Aterniens had focused her mind, and for good reason. The Aterniens were more than simply their enemy; they were their nemesis.

"Why do you need me? I've been out of the game for a long time."

While Kendra's response suggested an unwillingness to cooperate, she was merely looking for a compelling reason to set aside her grievances and change her stance, and Carter had the perfect way to gain his engineer's full investment.

"We need you because the Union has found the Galatine."

He let that bombshell sink in for a moment then observed Kendra's reaction. Her engineered biology meant she was able to mask many of the physical and chemical 'tells' that reveal the truths human beings try to hide, but there was no disguising her excitement at the mention of their old ship.

"You'd better not be bullshitting me, Carter."

"I wouldn't do that, Kendra," Carter answered, sincerely, but also with an appropriate level of offense. "They want me to command her again, because the Union's forgotten how to fight, and how to build ships and weapons worth a damn. But she's been out there in the darkness for more than a century, on her own, and I'll need you to piece her back together."

There was another awkward silence, during which time Kendra Castle appeared to shift through a range of emotions. The excitement was still there, but it was being overshadowed by a growing sense of anger and resentment.

"She deserved better than to be discarded and left to rot," Kendra said, just about managing to keep a lid on her emotions. "And what's to say the Union won't do the same again once we've served our purpose for a second time? There's not a chance in hell I'm re-building the Galatine only to have her wrenched away from me again."

"I hear you, Kendra, and you're absolutely right," Carter said, maintaining a calm, measured tone. "This time it will be different, I promise. You have my word on that, assuming my word still means anything to you?"

Kendra still looked angry, but her response was cut off by a scuffling sound somewhere in the workshop space. Carina appeared not to hear it, but Carter's senses shot into high alert, and he sprang out of his chair, muscles primed and ready to fight.

"Marco, is that you?" Kendra said, inching toward the door to the office. "Marco?"

Suddenly, time seemed to slow down, and the crack of weapons fire split the air. Carter grabbed Major Larsen and pulled her down with him, as slugs ripped through the walls and crashed through the windows. Kendra had also thrown herself into cover, her augmented responses allowing her to perceive the attack moments before it happened. He was glad of the fact his Master Engineer hadn't lost a step, because now there were two of them in a position to fight their ambushers.

The gunfire stopped and Carter heard the metallic click of ammo magazines being released from semi-automatic weapons. He jumped up and spotted four gunmen through what remained of the windows, recognizing them instantly as being from the same group who'd attacked him and Carina in the bar. Marco and Kendra's two accomplices lay dead on the concrete floor, riddled with holes from the onslaught of solid slugs that had just ravaged the workshop.

His augments kicked into a higher gear, and he charged at his new enemies, smashing through the prefab wall like a battering ram, and poleaxing the closest attacker at full speed. In a flash, Kendra was beside him, her body amped up to the same level as his. She hammered one of the gunmen with a palm strike to the chest, cracking the man's sternum and propelling him into a stack of containers.

Another magazine was slapped into place, and Carter heard the sound of a slug being loaded into the chamber of a gauss sub gun. He spotted the assassin in cover behind a crane lift, and accelerated toward him, before shoving the heavy piece of machinery and crushing the man against the wall, like cracking an egg in his hand.

One gunman remained, but Kendra was already on him. She slapped the sub-gun out of the man's hands with the force of a sledgehammer strike, then took a punch flush on her jaw, but it did nothing other than cause Kendra's eye to twitch in anger.

Stunning the man with a fast jab, she then picked him up and threw him across the room like a sack of dirty laundry.

The sharp clatter of tools scattering across the floor persisted for a few more seconds, until the workshop fell silent once again.

"Holy shit, and I thought just *one* of you was badass," Carina said, staggering through what remained of the office wall. The entire fight had been over in a matter of seconds. "You two together are like a hurricane coupled with an earthquake."

"Just like old times, isn't that right?" Carter said to his Master Engineer, who smiled warmly in return. It was the first friendly gesture he'd received from her since their reunion, and he took it as a good sign.

Kendra then grabbed one of the unconscious gunmen by the collar and lifted him to his feet.

"These assholes have been asking around after me for a while," Kendra said, glowering at the man's bruised and bloodied face. She then side-eyed Carter. "I don't suppose you can tell me why?"

Carter shook his head. "They attacked us too, not long after we landed on Terra Three, though I have no idea why."

Major Larsen's comp-slate chimed an incoming message, and she pulled the device from her pocket and read the screen.

"It looks like I might have the answer," the major said, still skimming the content of the message. "Union Intelligence managed to ID one of the men who attacked us in the bar, and he isn't a random mugger. These people are part of a collective known as the 'Acolytes of Aternus'."

Carter scowled; it was a name he'd heard before, but not for a very long time.

"The Acolytes were an activist group that championed post-humanism and campaigned for the abolition of the Aternien Act, but their movement died out after the war. I haven't heard that name for maybe eighty years."

He looked at Kendra to see if she knew any different, but his

Master Engineer simply appeared intrigued and concerned in equal measure.

"According to my information, they became active again about ten years ago," Carina continued, still reading the screen. "These new Acolytes are different, though. They worship the Aterniens as gods and crave acceptance and ascension into Aternien society. It's more like a church than an activist group." Carina paused for a moment to assimilate and condense any other salient points, but she shook her head, finding nothing significant. "Intelligence claims they're merely a band of rabble rousers and nutjobs. The Union has been monitoring them for years, and it doesn't consider them a threat."

"That doesn't add up," Carter said, massaging his silver beard. "These men certainly aren't rabble rousers and malcontents. They were armed and had training, and they knew how to find us."

Kendra Castle nodded. "Still, the question is, why?"

Carina's comp-slate chirruped for a second time, though as she read the new message, her posture straightened, and Carter detected a sharp rise in her heart rate and stress indicators.

"It's the admiral; I need to take this…"

Carina answered the call then hurried inside the office; nerves jangling like a bag of spanners.

"Is she usually so fidgety?" Kendra asked, raising an eyebrow at him.

"Carina is okay," Carter replied, still half-watching the major. "She's tougher than you think, for a regular human, anyway."

"Carina?" Kendra repeated, recoiling from Carter. Her eyes then narrowed. "You two aren't bumping uglies, are you?"

Carter sighed then shot his old engineer a look that conveyed the full spectrum of his disappointment and displeasure in her comment. "No, we're not… Besides, I'm old enough to be her great, great grandfather."

Kendra snorted a laugh. "And then some…"

Carter scowled at her again. "She's a good officer. And you'd better get used to her if you're coming along with me."

"Why's that?"

Carter smiled. "Because she'll be your XO."

Kendra's mouth dropped open like a drawbridge, but the reappearance of Major Larsen put paid to the possibility of a response. Carter turned to his XO and awaited her report with eagerness.

"The Union President just received a communication from the Grand Vizier; our first official contact with the Aterniens in a century," Carina began, getting straight to the point. Carter and Kendra both straightened up, as if they'd been called to attention. "The Grand Vizier is Markus Aternus' right-hand man, so it's akin to getting a call from the Union Vice President."

"What did he want?" Carter grunted.

"The Union has been invited to a meeting at the Diplomatic Outpost on the demarcation line between Union and Aternien space."

"Then it's beginning," Carter replied. He found comfort in that certainty. "I take it the admiral has said yes to the meeting?"

Carina nodded. "There's a catch, though. They'll only meet with you."

"I wouldn't have it any other way," Carter grunted, before turning to Kendra. "I know we've still got some shit to work out, but this is real, so I'm asking you straight up... Are you with me or not?"

Kendra straightened to attention. "Our enemy has returned. So yes, boss, I'm with you all the way."

ELEVEN
DIPLOMATIC RELATIONS

THE DEXTEROUS CAME to a full stop and held position two hundred meters from the Diplomatic Outpost on the demarcation line. They had been joined at the rendezvous coordinates by Admiral Krantz's battleship, the Repulse, and a taskforce of Union frigates and destroyers. Both had hung back as the diminutive countermeasures ship advanced, like a pawn making the first move in a game of chess.

"How many Aternien ships are there?" Carina asked, directing the question to her tactical officer.

"We are reading three Aternien vessels, Captain," the officer replied. "Scanners identify them as destroyers, but it's a new class of vessel that was first detected during the raids on the border outposts."

"What do we know about those vessels, Lieutenant?" Carter stood in front of the view screen, studying the outpost and ships, while meditatively stroking his silver beard.

"I'm afraid we know practically nothing, sir," the officer replied, sounding a little embarrassed to admit this. "They are similar in size to the attack ships that fought in the Aternien war, but their hull configuration is new."

Carter grunted. "We should have brought more escorts."

Carina pushed out of her captain's chair and stood by Carter's side. He knew this was so she could keep her voice low and not be overhead.

"I suggested the same to the admiral, but she was adamant the Union not be seen as provocative. This first meeting is critical to any future diplomacy."

Carter scowled at his new XO. "They're not here to negotiate, Major. They're here to make their demands. The sooner Admiral Krantz realizes there's no negotiating with these people, the better."

"That's as may be, but for now, we play the diplomacy card, okay?"

"I wasn't made for diplomacy; I was made for war…"

Carina sighed then peered at him with beseeching eyes, as if she was afraid that he was going to storm up to the Grand Vizier and punch a hole through the man's synthetic chest. In truth, he'd thought about doing just that, but he was as curious as Carina was to hear what the Aterniens had to say.

"Okay, we'll play it your way," Carter said. His statement immediately caused Carina's muscles to relax and her heart rate to slow. "But I promise you, things will turn ugly before the day is out."

"Not all of us are jaded old bastards like you," Carina said, playfully.

"Not all of us are jaded old bastards like you, *sir*…" Carter corrected her, putting heavy emphasis on the word, sir."

"My deepest apologies, Master Commander," Carina replied, placing her hand onto her jacket, above where her heart would be.

Carter grunted again then waited as Major Larsen issued orders to her crew.

"Lieutenant Kallis, you have the bridge. Signal the Repulse that Master Commander Rose and I are taking a shuttle to the outpost."

The lieutenant acknowledged the order, and the crew set to

work. Following Carina off the bridge, Carter was acutely aware that the young men and women of the Dexterous were in a heightened state of anxiety. The stench of sweat hung heavy in the air, and their combined heartbeats sounded like a drum roll inside his head.

"Not a single one of these kids has seen combat, either on the ground or in space," Carter said, as he hustled down the metal staircase beside his XO. "They're going to have to grow up fast."

"Were you always such a pessimist?" Carina wondered, as they stepped off and turned toward the shuttle bay. "We're here on a diplomatic mission, so let's give diplomacy a chance."

"It's not pessimism, Major, it's experience." The door to the shuttle bay opened, and Carina took a step forward, but Carter slammed his hand against the frame to block her path. "You need to get your head into a different space, Carina. War is coming, sooner than you think, and you need to be ready."

"I am ready," Carina said, confidently. She then nodded to his arm. "Do you mind?"

Carter allowed her through, and his XO set a frenetic pace toward the shuttle that was waiting for them on the pad. Her heart was pacing even faster than her footsteps. Carter followed and slid into the passenger seat, while Carina readied the ship for takeoff. He watched her work in silence, unsure as to whether his words had reached her, and pondered whether to push harder.

Her unwillingness to relinquish the possibly that conflict could be averted was the optimism of youth, he realized. After all, Carina Larsen was also just a kid compared to him. They all were. Yet, whether they accepted it or not, Carter knew what was coming, and he knew that by the time Carina's head next hit the rock-hard pillow in her cabin on the Dexterous, she wouldn't be a kid any longer.

Carina piloted the shuttle out of the bay, and set a course for the Diplomatic Outpost, flying the small craft at her usual, breakneck speed. The three Aternien warships remained in position, but no similar shuttle had been launched from any of the vessels.

"The Grand Vizier must already be waiting for us," Carter mused, as Carina hurtled the craft toward the docking hatch on the Union side of the outpost. "Either that, or the bastards plan to keep us waiting first, before making their grand and illustrious arrival."

Carina accessed one of the consoles on her chair then shook her head. "The outpost's internal sensors are reading one synthetic lifeform on board." She smiled at him. "So, it looks like we're the tardy ones."

Carter accessed the same readings on the auxiliary console and scowled at the result. There was no indication of respiration, which was to be expected since the Aterniens didn't breathe, but a single heat signature was present in the central diplomatic chamber. He grunted under his breath; his early warning senses hadn't yet flared, but something still felt off.

His musings were brought to a sudden and abrupt stop when Carina thumped the shuttle against the docking ring of the outpost with more force than was necessary or prudent. This was followed by the whir of the docking ring closing around the hatch, and the hiss of air as the pressure between the shuttle and outpost equalized. Carina then unclipped her harness and made the short journey aft from the cabin to where the hatch door was waiting. She grabbed the lever and turned to Carter.

"Are you ready?"

Carter went aft, opened a weapons locker, and removed a gauss pistol.

"Now I'm ready," he said, fixing the holster to the belt of his uniform.

Carina looked at him like a disappointed mother. "No weapons can be brought onto the diplomatic outpost. You know that."

Carter removed another pistol from the locker and offered it to his XO. "I know the rules, Major, but they were written a century ago, and this is a different time." He pressed the pistol into her hand. "Trust me, take it."

Carina let out a frustrated growl, but she took the weapon and fastened it to her uniform. Grasping hold of the locking lever again, she yanked down hard then pushed open the hatch. A rush of cold air flooded into the shuttle. It was stale and lifeless, like the outpost itself.

"The diplomatic chamber is directly at the other end of this corridor," Carina said, taking the lead. Carter could feel her pulse quickening again. "If our scans were correct, the Grand Vizier should already be waiting for us."

"He's there," Carter said, coolly.

While the dimly-lit chamber would have been invisible to Carina's human eyes, he could already make out a single figure inside. Then as they both entered the Union half of the circular hall, the Aternien Grand Vizier stepped forward, and was illuminated sharply from above, as if being bathed in rays from a distant sun. He felt Carina's heartbeat quicken further, but to her credit, she remained outwardly calm and composed.

"Is that an Aternien?" Carina said, keeping her voice low. "I've never seen one before, not in the flesh."

"Not quite what you expected, right?" Carter replied, smiling at her. "Don't let their elven beauty fool you. Underneath that carefully-engineered exterior, the Aterniens are ugly, cold-blooded killers."

Carter approached the meeting table in the dead center of the room, and the Grand Vizier approached too, his gleaming blue eyes tracking Carter like laser sights. Despite their striking, almost supernatural appearance, there was something about the Aterniens that always struck Carter as off. Their skin was too unblemished; eyes too bright; symmetry too exact; movements too precise. In seeking perfection, they had made themselves bizarrely unreal.

The Grand Vizier stopped on the Aternien side of the table, behind the row of chairs that had sat unused for a century, despite the Union sending an envoy every year on the anniversary of the armistice. Carter stood opposite, studying the man's sinewy frame and golden armor that flowed with every movement of his body, like dragon scales. The chest section of the armor was engraved with intricate patterns that closely resembled Egyptian hieroglyphs. In the dead center was an ornate cross, known as the Ankh of Aternus. The language remained an enigma, but Carter knew that the Ankh identified the Grand Vizier as a member of the Aternien Royal Court inner circle. It was a small, but important detail, because it meant that the Vizier was at least as old as he was.

"I wondered if we would ever meet again, Master Commander Rose," the Vizier began, speaking with perfect pitch and diction in a voice worthy of stage and song.

"Do I know you?" grunted Carter.

"Yes, but I confess that it has been some time," the Vizier replied, smiling with pristine golden teeth. "Like you, I also fought in the war. I was commander of the Aternien Solar Barque, Senuset."

Carter thought for a moment, searching the depths of his memory. Then he remembered, and anger swelled in his gut.

"The Senuset razed entire cities to the ground, burned refugee camps and attacked medical and rescue ships without mercy." As his anger built, the augments in his body began to release chemicals to stimulate his responses, in anticipation of a fight. "You and your ship alone were responsible for the death of millions of innocents. You fought without honor, and with a brutality not seen since Earth's Middle Ages."

"So, you do remember," the Vizier replied, still smiling as if his own memory of those events were as pleasant as a summer's breeze. The man's eyes then sharpened, and the smile fell away. "But to us, a human is a human. It does not matter if it was a soldier or a babe in a mother's arms. All of humanity was our enemy. Your Union saw to that."

The more he heard the Vizier speak, the more he remembered about the former commander of the Senuset. It was like suddenly recalling a dream and being able to picture it in vivid clarity.

"I remember you now. You've done well for yourself, Grand Vizier."

"You, on the other hand, have fallen hard," the Vizier hit back. He shook his head, causing his perfectly straight hair to flow like strands of fine silk. "You talk about our lack of honor, but where was honor when the Union cast you aside?" He laughed, cruelly. "And you say that we are the monsters."

Carter heard Carina's footsteps approaching then he saw her draw level out of the corner of his eye. The Grand Vizier's upper lip curled slightly, and his nose creased. It was like he'd just witnessed a dog taking a crap on the floor in front of him.

"How dare you bring this sack of meat with you," The Vizier hissed. "Her presence is an insult."

"No, Vizier, what you just said was an insult. Insult her again and I'll rearrange that pretty Aternien face of yours."

The Vizier's self-righteous smile returned. "You are welcome to try."

Carter closed his hands into fists, but Carina was quick to step in and head him off.

"This is a diplomatic outpost. You requested this meeting, so presumably you want to open a dialogue, rather than start another war?"

"Warn this human not to speak to me again," the Vizier snarled. "If she does, they will be the last words to come out of her filthy mouth."

"The major's question stands." It was taking everything he had not to vault the table and rip the Grand Vizier's head from his slender neck "What is it that you want?"

The Vizier's posture stiffened, and the already towering and slender man appeared to grow taller by several inches.

"We want what was taken from us," the Vizier replied, his tone blunt and insistent. "The Union of Nine stole our lands and our homes. We demand that they are returned to us. This will begin with Terra Six. This planet will be vacated of all human occupiers and relinquished to the Aternien Empire."

Carter huffed a laugh. "That's all, huh?"

"Do not mock me, Commander Rose," the Grand Vizier hissed, his voice little more than a whisper. Despite transcending their original, biological form, Aternien emotions were as powerful and as raw as those of any human being. "We were victims of persecution. The Union acted out of prejudice and fear. The same prejudices and fears that led you and your kind to be outcast."

"If you're trying to create common ground between us then save your breath, or whatever putrid gas comes out of your mouth," Carter answered. "I was a Union soldier then and I'm a Union soldier now."

"Set aside your human pride!" The Vizier was almost pleading with him. "You have a simple choice to make. You can return the worlds to us or we will take them by force, and exterminate their human populations, along with anyone else who stands in our way."

Carter stood tall. "Then there really is no choice at all. War it must be."

The Vizier sighed elaborately. "Time means nothing to us, Commander Rose. For the Aterniens, the war never ended. The last one hundred years was merely a stay of execution for the human race. But if your fragile human mind requires a point of reference – a place and a time to say, 'this is where the new war began' – then you can say it began right here, right now."

The station shook and Carter was forced to grab hold of the back of a chair to steady himself. There was a brief moment of stillness, then the room shook repeatedly. Debris began to rain down around them and an automated alert blared into the room.

"Hull breach. Atmospheric integrity compromised. All personnel, evacuate immediately. Repeat, all personnel, evacuate immediately."

"You're attacking the diplomatic outpost?" Carter said, struggling to understand the Vizier's bizarre actions. "You mad bastard, if you destroy this station, you'll die here with us!"

The Vizier took two paces back, a sanctimonious smile still plastered across his perfect face.

"This body is but a vessel, Commander Rose. I was never truly here."

The Grand Vizier's gleaming eyes went dark, and the man collapsed to the floor, like an ancient robot succumbing to rust and age-worn joints. Then, in the pitch darkness at the far end of the Aternien side of the chamber, more sinister pairs of eyes lit up, and a squad of Aternien Immortals marched toward him.

TWELVE
FIRST CONTACT

CARTER GRABBED the edge of the conference table and pushed hard, ripping the bolts that fastened the legs to the deck plates out of their fixings in the process. The heavy table thudded onto its side and moments later, blasts of energy from Aternien particle rifles were hammering into the other side.

"Why the hell didn't our scanners pick up those soldiers?" Carina said, ducking behind their new shield and drawing her gauss pistol. She'd had to shout to be heard over the crash of particle blasts slamming into the table.

"They must have added some sensor shielding, which is why their heat signatures didn't register," Carter called back, also drawing his pistol. "This whole thing was a set up. The Aterniens planned this all along."

More energy blasts thudded into the two-inch thick table and sections of it began to glow hot. Carter popped up and fired four shots at the approaching Aternien Immortals, but the slugs simply rebounded off their metal armor, like a tennis ball thrown at a wall. He cursed, then ducked back into cover and checked their exit. The door leading to their shuttle was still open.

"We have to get back to the Dexterous and get out of here. If those new Aternien destroyers are anything like these Immortals then we're heavily outmatched."

The deck shook hard, and more debris fell around them. Carter looked at the high ceiling of the diplomatic chamber and saw that the room was steadily buckling under the stresses of the Aternien bombardment. Then the exit door on the Union side of the room slid shut, like a bulkhead sealing off a doomed section of a warship.

"Shit, we're trapped," Carina said, still huddled behind the upturned table. "Is there another way out of this room?"

Carter shook his head. "No, but I can get that door open, if we can reach it." He picked up the heavy table like it weighed nothing and held it out as a shield. "Get ready to move, and see if you can take out a few of those Immortals at the same time."

Still holding the table, Carter began pacing back toward the door, while Carina took pot shots at the Aternien soldiers. One of the Immortals went down, but the rest of her shots ricocheted off their golden bodies.

"These pistols aren't powerful enough to breach their armor," Carina said, pulling into cover behind the table, parts of which were now melting like candle wax. She was frustrated, but importantly, she'd held her nerve.

"Aim for their heads, or more specifically, their eyes," Carter replied, wincing as sparks from an Aternien particle blast showered his face and burned his skin. "You could blow their legs off and they'd just crawl toward us instead. You have to destroy their neuromorphic brain, or the soul blocks at the backs of their heads. It's the only way to put them down."

Carina reloaded her weapon then took a deep breath. Carter could hear the thumping beat of her heart and sense her internal struggle against the debilitating effects of primal fear. In all likelihood, this was her first contact with a real enemy. It would make or break her, but so far, her fighting spirit remained strong.

Darting out of cover, Carina fired three shots in close

succession, bouncing two slugs off an Aternien Immortal's skull before sinking the third through the soldier's glowing right eye. Blue sparks erupted and the warrior went down.

"Got one!" Carina called out.

"Good, now keep shooting!"

Carter dropped the table and positioned it in front of the exit door. Holes had been burned clean through the metal in several places, and the Aterniens were aiming shots through the cavities with the precision of sharpshooters. He took a glancing blow to the shoulder, which melted his uniform and cooked his augmented flesh, but his sensation blockers nullified any pain.

Peeking through one of the burn holes, he watched as an Immortal recovered the soul block from the cranium of a fallen warrior. He cursed, realizing that the memories and experiences of that soldier would be preserved, and integrated into another body. It was the reason they were called Immortals. Even death didn't stop them.

Readying his weapon, Carter danced out of cover and unleashed a torrent of gunfire, piercing the eyes and neuromorphic brains of three Immortals, then withdrawing before any of the soldiers could retaliate. He reloaded the gauss pistol and slapped the weapon into Major Larsen's empty left hand.

"Keep firing, while I make us a way out."

Carina continued to harass the Immortals, who were advancing more cautiously after Carter's last assault, but more had entered the chamber and were gaining fast. While the major defended their position, Carter tore open the control panel next to the door, and yanked out the wire bundle, like removing the intestines from a butchered animal. A blast hammered into the wall inches from his head, but he had no choice but to continue, and risk being shot. So long as the door remained closed, there was no hope of escape.

"I've almost got it!" Carter called out, while reaching through the emptied-out panel and trying to grasp his hand around the internal release lever. "Just hold them off for a few more seconds."

Suddenly, Carina's body was thrown against the wall, and she slumped onto the deck, barely conscious. Carter pulled his arm free and saw that an Aternien Immortal had rushed their position and knocked her down with a shoulder charge. A bayonet on the end of the warrior's rifle crackled with particle energy, and the soldier attacked, but he was faster. He grabbed the Aternien's forearms and fought the soldier to his knees, synthetic muscles screaming under the intense strain of Carter's overbearing strength. Teeth gritted, Carter let out a roar as an explosion of performance-boosting chemicals flooded his bloodstream, imbuing him with the might of a Titan.

Tearing the arms from the Immortal, Carter beat the once-human man with them, until his golden armor lay smashed and broken at his feet. Suddenly, two more warriors threw what remained of the meeting table aside and aimed their particle rifles at him. His superhuman reactions allowed Carter to dodge the first blast and tackle a warrior to the ground, before tearing the post-human woman's head from her elegant, slim neck.

The second Immortal was about to stab him with an energized bayonet, when the Aternien's body spasmed, and arcs of blue energy erupted from the synthetic man's mouth. Carter turned to see Major Larsen; gauss pistol held outstretched. Blood was running down her face and neck, and her eyes were glassy, but she was still fighting.

Carter got to his feet and recovered one of the Aternien weapons, using it to drive the advancing horde into cover. He continued firing until the weapon overheated, but it had done its job, and bought him more time.

"Hold on, we're almost clear…"

Ramming the energized bayonet between the edge of the door and the frame, he forced it open by just enough to get a solid handhold. Then with all of the strength his augmented body possessed, he tore the door open and powered through to the other side.

"Carina, let's go!" he called out, pressing his outstretched hand toward her.

Carina was still dazed, but she hauled herself up just in time to avoid another barrage of Aternien particle fire. Carter took a hit to his hip and grimaced as the pain of the burn briefly flooded his body, before being blocked by his augments. Carina had recovered enough to run unaided, and was firing blind along the corridor, but soon her weapon clicked empty, leaving them unarmed in the face of a renewed enemy force.

Reaching their shuttle, Carina dived through the hatch and flattened her body to the deck as blasts flashed above her head. Carter raced inside a second later, then slammed the hatch shut, and threw the latch to pressurize the cabin. Aternien weapons fire continued to hammer into the shuttle's exterior, but Carter knew they were safe inside the ship, at least for a time.

"Get the admiral on the line," Carter said, jumping into the pilot's seat and activating the systems. "If we're to make it back to the Dexterous in one piece, we're going to need some cover."

Carina scrambled across the deck and pulled herself into the second seat. Alarms were already ringing out, and Carter saw that the port-side armor was buckling. He released the clamps and punched the throttle to push them away from the Diplomatic Outpost, but it was a case of 'out of the frying pan and into the fire', because an Aternien destroyer was already bearing down on their location, like a shark hunting in shallow water.

"Shuttle Delta Four-One-Four to Union Battleship Repulse, do you read?" Carina said in to the comm system, but the channel returned only static.

Suddenly, a burst of particle energy erupted from one of the Aternien destroyers and swept across space toward them. Carter's augmented senses instinctively calculated the trajectory of the shots, and he rotated the shuttle and dove beneath them. The particle blasts missed by less than a meter, and instead lashed against the side of the outpost, causing an explosive decompression that battered the vulnerable shuttle with debris.

"Repulse, do you read?" Carina tried again. "We need cover, or we won't make it!"

Still, they heard only static.

Carter wrestled with the controls and managed to set the shuttle back on course to the Dexterous. The Union Destroyer Virtuous soared overhead and attacked the Aternien ship that had almost blasted them in half, but its barrage of cannon fire had barely any effect. The enemy ship returned fire, and the Aternien particle blasts tore through the Virtuous like a hot poker through flesh. The ship erupted into flames and listed heavily to port before exploding with the force of an atom bomb.

"I'm almost there," Carter said, pushing the battered and bruised little shuttle harder.

The Dexterous was directly ahead, shuttle bay doors open and waiting for them. Then a target-lock alarm sounded with strident urgency, and the Aternien destroyer swung back into view, ready for another attack run. Carter held his course. If they didn't make it back to their ship in the next few seconds, they never would.

"Carter, this isn't a Longsword," Carina said, staring at the Aternien vessel, wide-eyed. "One hit from that will finish us."

"It won't hit us," Carter said, hands firm on the controls. "It won't have a chance to."

"How the hell do you know that?"

A shadow crept over the shuttle, casting the cockpit into darkness, then moments later the massive hull of the Battleship Repulse cut across them. The enemy destroyer fired its particle cannons, reducing a section of the Repulse to molten slag, but it wasn't enough to stop it. The Repulse returned fire with a broadside at close range, but the Aternien vessel merely banked away, its armor dented and scorched, but still intact.

"Shuttle Delta Four-One-Four, this is the Admiral…" Clara Krantz's voice cut through them like the wail of a banshee. "Initiate emergency docking, then immediately fall back to Terra Six."

The comm channel closed and Carter made the final adjustments to line up the shuttle with the small docking bay of the countermeasures ship. Blasts of energy continued to crisscross space all around them, then suddenly they were hit. An emergency bulkhead closed off the rear of the shuttle and the control panel began to flash erratically.

"Our engines are gone," Carter said, making minute adjustments with the thrusters to keep them on course. "Buckle up; this is going to be rough."

Carina clicked her harness into place and tightened the straps; in the rush to escape, both of them had forgotten to secure them. Carter finished adjusting the controls then pulled on his own harness, and braced himself for what he knew would be an unpleasant landing.

The shuttle clipped the side of the bay door and was flipped onto its side. Carter gripped the arms of his seat as the craft was spun a full three-sixty degrees, before hammering into the back of the shuttle bay and coming to a painful, jarring stop.

Consoles exploded and a section of the cockpit burst into flames, filling the tiny cabin with acrid, poisonous smoke. He sucked in a breath and held it, then unclipped his harness and checked on Major Larsen, but she was out cold. With smoke stinging his eyes, he tore her harness away from the wall, then climbed onto the burning console and punched out what remained of the shuttle's cockpit-glass. The smoke billowed out and he filled his lungs with a breath of clean, recycled air. Ducking back inside, he grabbed hold of Carina and hauled her out onto the battered hull of the shuttle.

"Master Commander Rose to bridge, do you read?" he

called out, his voice unaffected by the smoke thanks to his bioengineered lungs.

"Lieutenant Kallis here, we read you Commander."

The young lieutenant's voice was shaking, but to his credit the officer had held position, despite the ease with which the Aterniens could have blown the Dexterous out of the ether.

"Signal the flagship that Major Larsen and I are on board, then get us the hell out of here."

"Sir, our soliton warp drive was knocked out," the officer replied. "It's reinitializing, but we can't jump till it's back online."

Carter punched the hull of the shuttle, leaving a fist-shaped dent in the metal. "How long, Lieutenant?"

There was an awkward silence before the officer on deck replied. "Maybe five more minutes, sir. It's hard to know."

"We'll be atoms in sixty seconds, Lieutenant," Carter hit back. "Where's Master Engineer Castle?"

Kendra Castle's voice cut through over the comm channel. "I'm here, boss, but these morons won't let me help. They say because I haven't been reinstated yet, I don't have clearance."

Carter cursed. "Lieutenant, listen to me and listen well. Until I say otherwise, Kendra Castle is God, and what she says is gospel. Is that clear?"

There was another pregnant pause before the officer responded. "Yes, sir, perfectly clear."

"I'm on it, boss," Kendra added, then the channel closed.

"Did we make it?" Carina was conscious again, though barely. Her normally fair hair was covered in so much blood it was as if she'd dyed it red.

"We're on the Dexterous, but we're not out of the woods yet," Carter answered. "Can you stand?"

Carina grabbed hold of his broad shoulders and tried to haul herself upright, but her legs gave way. "I think the answer to that is no…"

The flames inside the shuttle cockpit were growing taller

and licking his boots, and Carter knew he had to get them both away from the ship before the fire suppression systems kicked in. If they remained, they'd be suffocated by the gases and foams that would consume the dying vessel.

"Hold onto me, I've got an idea." Carter said, helping Carina to her feet.

She looked over the side of the shuttle. The drop to the hangar bay floor was almost five meters.

"Am I going to like this idea?" Carina queried, shooting him an anxious look.

"I don't like it, so my guess is no." Carter scooped up the major, and held her firmly in his arms.

"Oh, shit, you have to be kidding!"

Carter didn't answer. He stepped to the edge of the upturned shuttle, his augmented brain automatically processing the calculations required to make the jump safely, without either breaking his own legs, or turning Major Larsen into an unintentional airbag. She opened her mouth to protest, and at the same time he leapt.

Air rushed past his face and Carina screamed, then he hit the deck hard and rolled through the landing, protecting her head and using his own engineered body to soak up the impact. They crashed through a stack of storage containers, which unintentionally cushioned his fall, before coming to rest in a contorted heap, legs and arms intertwined with one another.

"Bridge to Commander Rose. Stand by for warp."

Suddenly, space folded in on them, and the Dexterous was punched through a hole in the cosmos and deposited hundreds of light years away in the blink of an eye. However, Carter remained on his back, every inch of his body throbbing from the cuts, bruises and burns that his augments were now screaming at him to get treated. Even so, he didn't know what was worse; the agony of his injuries, or the nauseating trauma of their defeat at the hands of a rejuvenated Aternien Empire.

THIRTEEN
WE ARE AT WAR

CARTER WATCHED the cut on his hand slowly heal itself, until all that remained was a patch of slightly redder skin. Then he blinked his eyes a couple of times, and the marks were gone completely. Sighing, he lowered his hand and walked to the window of the medical bay in Station Foxtrot, at Terra Six. Three more Union ships had warped in, making a total of thirty that had arrived since their retreat from the diplomatic outpost.

"It's a good job you still heal just as fast as in the old days," Kendra Castle said. She was also standing by the window, a couple of meters further along. "If you were a 'normie' then that energy blast would have burned all the way down to the bone."

'Normie' was the word that Kendra used to describe regular humans. It was a somewhat derogatory expression that Carter disliked, but trying to get his Master Engineer to drop the phrase was almost as difficult as stopping her from cursing.

"How's the patient?" Kendra asked.

"As you can see, I'm fine, or at least I will be in an hour or two," Carter replied, still gazing at the ships massing outside. Another seven had arrived since his last count.

"I don't mean you," Kendra said, rolling her eyes. "I meant the 'normie'."

Carter scowled at her, and she relented. "Sorry, Major Larsen."

As if on cue, the ward door swished opened, and his XO strolled out. She was cradling her ribs and had a few cuts to her face and neck that were held together with steri-strips, but otherwise looked strong and in good spirits.

"How the hell are you managing to look so sparky?" Carter said, feeling oddly annoyed that Carina wasn't suffering like he was. "I thought I was the post-human around here?"

"Thanks to you, I got lucky." Carina smiled then joined him at the window. "I suffered a couple of cracked ribs, and some cuts and bruises, but I avoided a concussion." She bowed her head slightly and parted her hair to reveal a long row of neat stitches. "These won't heal up as quickly as your cuts do, but all in all, I'd say I got away lightly."

Carina then noticed the burns visible through the patches of his uniform that had been destroyed by Aternien particle blasts. She scrunched up her nose and pressed her hand to the corresponding locations on her body, as if feeling sympathy pains.

"Why aren't you letting the medics treat you?" his XO asked.

"Union doctors don't understand how our bodies work," Carter answered. He checked the wounds and admitted that they looked a little gnarly, though they didn't hurt much. "It's why every Longsword had a Master Medic, an officer specifically trained in post-human physiology." A memory of Rosalie Moss, the Galatine's quirkily entertaining Master Medic, surfaced in his thoughts and he exhaled a slow breath. "Sadly, none of the Master Medics are still alive. I suppose there's a cruel irony in that."

Carina nodded, but didn't press him, correctly sensing that it was difficult for him to talk about crew that he'd lost, or who were still missing.

"I'm amazed you survived those blasts in the first place,"

Carina continued, returning to the subject of Carter's wounds. "A direct hit on the shoulder from an Aternien particle rifle would have probably taken my arm clean off."

"There's no probably about it," Carter said, wanting to make doubly sure that his XO understood the risks of getting caught by a blast. "But we're built differently, as it were."

He nodded to Kendra Castle, who picked up where he left off, since she was more knowledgeable and enthusiastic when it came to discussing the technological wizardry that had gone into creating them.

"The nano-machines in our cells react to heat and rapidly produce a silica-based nanocomposite layer on top of our skin," Kendra said, happy to accommodate Carina's curiosity. "It gives us significantly enhanced flame and heat-resistance, but our skin was also engineered to dissipate heat across our entire bodies. That's also why we can operate in extremes of temperature."

"Basically, the energy is partly reflected and partly dissipated, so instead of losing an arm, it's like being scalded by boiling water," Carter added, putting Kendra's explanation into simpler terms. "That's not to say it doesn't hurt, though, or that a few well-placed shots can't kill us."

Carina was suitably bamboozled, but before she could quiz him or his Master Engineer further, Admiral Clara Krantz marched in. She wore a thunderous expression that could have cracked concrete and was moving so fast that Carter worried she might set the soles of her boots on fire.

"What the hell happened back there?" Krantz roared. Carina looked like a rabbit in headlights, though it wasn't the first time that Carter had been confronted by an irate admiral or general, and so he took it in his stride. "You were sent in to conduct a sensitive diplomatic negotiation, and instead you started a war!"

Carter stood in front of the admiral and pressed his hands to the small of his back, pushing out his broad, and slightly scorched chest.

"There was no negotiation, Admiral," Carter answered, coolly. "This whole thing was a setup from the get-go."

Krantz's blue eyes drilled into him for a moment. While the admiral had burst in looking like she was spoiling for a fight, Carter could detect that she was calm beneath her fiery exterior.

"Explain, Master Commander Rose," Krantz eventually replied. "And make it good."

"The Grand Vizier demanded that we immediately surrender Terra Six to the Aternien Empire." Krantz's eyes narrowed, and he detected a quickening of her pulse. "And that's only the beginning. If we resisted or refused, the Aterniens would take the planet by force. It was an ultimatum, Admiral, not a dialogue."

"Go on…" Krantz encouraged.

"Once it became clear there was nothing to discuss, we were ambushed by Aternien Immortals inside the outpost. My guess is that they were planted there some time ago, in advance of our meeting."

"Then what was the purpose of the Grand Vizier requesting a meeting in the first place?" Krantz asked. She'd dropped her accusatory tone and was now simply angry.

"They wanted to see what we're made of," Carter replied. Since arriving at Station Foxtrot, he'd already given that topic considerable thought. "Border skirmishes and raids are one thing, but the Aterniens wanted to test themselves against the best we have, to learn how we might fare in a wider conflict. I'd say they got their answer."

Admiral Krantz bristled. Though he had not said so directly, Carter was making a comment on the poor performance of the Union taskforce.

"If you have something specific to say, Master Commander, then say it. I value honesty, and frankness, even if I do not like what I hear."

"Okay then…" Carter cleared his throat. "We pitted a force of twelve warships, including the Union's flagship, against only three Aternien destroyers, and had our assess handed to us." Krantz's eyes sharpened, but she did not interrupt. "By the end of the engagement, we'd lost five ships, and three more had taken heavy damage. In return, our attacks did little more than put of few dings and scratches onto one of their ships, which would probably polish out with a bit of elbow grease."

"I am well aware of the details, Commander," Krantz hit back, unamused by his glib description of the battle's outcome. "What I need from you is insight. How is it that these Aternien ships could so easily outclass ours?"

"Master Engineer Castle has already looked into that."

Carter nodded to Kendra, and she removed a comp-slate from her pocket and stepped closer to the admiral, so that she could see the screen. A tactical analysis of the new Aternien destroyer was shown on the display.

"This analysis is based on all the accumulated sensor data from the Repulse and the other ships that engaged the Aterniens at the diplomatic outpost," Kendra began.

Admiral Krantz looked so shocked that a strong gust of wind might have knocked her over. "How the hell did you get hold of this information? These logs are classified Top Secret."

Kendra shrugged. "It honestly wasn't hard to pull this data from Station Foxtrot's primary core, once you transferred it over from the Repulse," she said, admitting to breaching data security. "It's actually a good thing that Union ships maintained the policy of hardlined computer systems, carried over from the war, because if your systems were accessible remotely, the Aterniens wouldn't need to fight us; they could take us out with a few lines of code."

Admiral Krantz looked furious, though Carter wasn't sure if she was angry at Kendra Castle for hacking the station's core, or angry at how easy it had been for her to circumvent Union security. It was quite possibly both, he realized. Krantz then looked around the ward and noticed that their gathering had begun to attract quite a bit of attention.

"Everyone, could you please give us the room…" the admiral called out. The order was given firmly, but not snappishly. "Only Major Larsen, Master Commander Rose and Master Engineer Castle are to remain."

The medical and admin staff all stopped what they were doing and extracted themselves without delay or complaint. It seemed clear to Carter that everyone concerned knew not to trifle with Admiral Clara Krantz. Soon, the patter of shoes against the clinical white floor tiles grew to a miniature stampede, and within seconds, the space had cleared. It was like students rushing out of a classroom as the last bell of the day rang.

"I am prepared to grant you significant latitude, Commander, as was the case with the Longsword commanders during the first Aternien war. But if you go around me again, I'll snap you back so hard that even your augmented neck will get whiplash. Is that understood?"

Carter straightened to attention. "Yes, Admiral."

Carter took the reprimand without resentment, and Krantz appeared to recognize that her message had been received, loud and clear. The admiral then turned to Kendra Castle, who met her eyes without shame or embarrassment.

"Give me your assessment, Master Engineer."

Kendra tapped the comp-slate and the image of the new Aternien destroyer animated, while additional information cycled across the display.

"As you know, Union intelligence has designated this new warship as a Khopesh-class Destroyer," Kendra began. "The hull configuration is based on the Aternien D'Jah-class attack vessels of a century ago, but that's where the similarities end."

Kendra worked the screen and highlighted the armor covering the external hull of the Khopesh-class warship.

"This is the reason why our weapons had barely any effect," Kendra continued, while zooming in and highlighting the multi-layered armor. "The outer layer is constructed of a novel material that's highly-resistant to our kinetic mass weapons. There also appears to be a sophisticated reactive element that offers protection against explosive shells and warheads. Beneath that is a sandwich of ceramic and other layers to provide protection against heat, radiation and more. It's one hell of a tough shell that's been designed specifically to combat Union weaponry."

Krantz listened carefully then studied the schematics in detail, before her eyes flicked across to the engineer. "Continue…"

"Power generation has also been amped up, to say the least." Kendra highlighted the engines and reactor section of the Khopesh-class warship. "It uses a fusion-reactor power plant, but my analysis suggests that its output is at least double that of comparable ships its size. It's hard to tell, because my feeling is that they weren't operating at maximum power when we took them on at the diplomatic outpost."

Carter grunted and nodded. "That would make sense. The Grand Vizier wouldn't want to reveal his full hand just yet."

"My guess is that a high reactor output is necessary to power their new particle weapons." The image switched to highlight an energy cannon that occupied the entire lower two decks of the ship. "This weapon fires pulses of particle energy, like the weapons the Immortals were using on the outpost, except on a much larger scale. They're broadly similar to the plasma cannons that Longsword-class battleships employed, which is likely where they got the idea, but they're less powerful."

Kendra reset the image then spun it, so that the Aternien destroyer was slowly displayed from all angles. It was a typically sleek design, heavily influenced by the Aternien's love of Egyptian mythology, but it was also much more than a pretty face. It was a deadly warship, the likes of which the Union had never faced before.

"In short, Admiral, the Khopesh-class Destroyer has been specifically engineered to target the vulnerabilities of current Union warships," Kendra concluded. "In my estimation, a single Khopesh could match four Union heavy destroyers or cruisers. Perhaps more."

"I've seen enough, thank you, Master Engineer," Krantz said, wafting her hand at the comp-slate, like she was trying to get rid of an annoying wasp. "It would seem that we have our work cut out for us."

A subdued silence fell over the room, which was exacerbated by the fact Admiral Krantz had cleared all other personnel from the space, to allow Kendra to give her analysis away from anxious ears that were keen to learn of the new threat. It was Major Larsen who eventually broke the silence.

"The Aterniens had us beat at the outpost, so why didn't they pursue us to Terra Six to finish the job?"

It was a good question, Carter agreed, and one that he'd also put some thought into, without much success.

"My sense is that they have something bigger planned," Carter suggested. "Even with their new ships, a stand-up fight is messy and costly to both sides. They've had a century to plot our downfall, so whatever they have in mind, we may not see it coming till it's too late."

"What would you suggest we do, Master Commander?" Krantz replied.

There was a touch of desperation in her voice, as if she believed that the Aterniens had already delivered a killer blow, and all that was left was for the Union to fall and hit the ground, dead.

"We need to place all Union forces on a war footing, right now." Krantz had invited his opinion, and he was going to give it, in all its unvarnished glory. "Start running daily combat exercises, and I mean real ship-to-ship engagements, using training lasers. If you have reservists, call them up – all of them – and bring back your retired veterans too, especially those with any kind of combat or operational experience. And we need to build warships at a rate never before seen, because when the Aterniens come, the cost will be high."

"There has been no official declaration of war, Commander Rose," Krantz reminded him. "What you suggest could be seen as provocative."

"It doesn't matter how it's seen," Carter said, sticking to his guns. "I know this enemy, Admiral. They've just tested us, and we were found badly wanting. Whether it's official or not, as of this moment, we *are* at war. And if we don't prepare now, the Aterniens will tear through the Union of Nine, leaving death and destruction in their wake, until nothing of humanity remains."

Carter was suddenly aware that he could hear a pin drop. No-one said a word or even moved a muscle. It was like he'd just dropped the verbal equivalent of a nuclear bomb, and everyone had been caught in its blast. Finally, Krantz turned to Major Larsen.

"Is this your assessment also, Major?"

"I can't claim to know the Aterniens anything like as well as Commander Rose does, but I didn't see anything to suggest a diplomatic route was possible." She swallowed hard, as if her mouth had suddenly gone bone dry. "The Grand Vizier spoke to me like I was vermin. They have no interest in coexisting with us. Commander Rose is right; their endgame is our annihilation."

Admiral Krantz suddenly turned to face the tall glass window; her hands still pressed firmly to the small of her back. Carter understood the trick; it was to ensure that no-one could see the fear and doubt in her eyes, but he knew they were there. The chemical and physical signals had lit up around her like flashing sirens, but to the admiral's credit, she masked them well.

"I will return to Terra Prime and make my case to the President directly," Krantz said, still peering out of the window of the medical bay. "But we could build another thousand ships and they would be no use against their new destroyers."

"You're right, they won't be," Carter replied, bleakly. Admiral Krantz looked over her shoulder at him. "You have to build them better. The Aterniens never honored the armistice accords, and we were fools to do so, because now we're fighting a war with weapons that are decades out of date."

"I can't just magic a new generation of warships out of thin air," Krantz snapped.

"We don't have a choice." Carter wanted to ensure the admiral was left in no doubt as to the scale of the undertaking ahead of them. "But the first step is to task every shipyard and dock in the Union, whether private or military, with the mission of upgrading the current fleet. And the ban on technological development has to be scrapped now, no ifs or buts."

Admiral Krantz muttered a string of blue curses under her breath. "You do not ask for much, do you, Master Commander?" she said, looking away.

He knew he was asking nothing more than the reversal of a century-long way of life, but hard choices and sacrifices had to be made.

"Master Engineer Castle can give your crews a head start, but first we have to recover the Galatine, if she's still out there," Carter continued. "Only a Union Longsword can stand against these Khopesh destroyers. With the Galatine leading our forces, the Aterniens will think twice."

The admiral continued to stare out of the window, but while she continued to present a façade of calm, her heart was still beating like a hummingbird.

"What use is one Longsword against these Khopesh Destroyers?" she said. "Can the Galatine really make a difference?"

Carter managed a smile. "Admiral, I mean no offense when I

say that you have no idea. If we can find her, and get her back up to strength, the Galatine can be a difference-maker."

Krantz finally turned away from the window. Carter's sudden outburst of pride and confidence in his vessel had rubbed off on her.

"Very well, proceed with the mission to recover the Galatine," Admiral Krantz said. "In the meantime, I will gather every engineer in the fleet and beyond and get them working on new weapons and armor." Her expression then soured and became harder than granite. "And I will speak to the President directly about overturning the laws on technological development, so that we don't all end up in jail for what we are about to do."

FOURTEEN

TESS-961S

CARTER SIGHED AUDIBLY and side-eye Major Larsen with a look that he hoped displayed his frustration and displeasure at her constant foot-tapping. She had been fidgeting for the entire journey from the medical bay on Station Foxtrot to shuttle bay seven, where their new ride was waiting for them. Along the corridors, it was easier for him to walk ahead so that he didn't have to watch her twirl her hair, crack her knuckles or tap her fingers against her thighs, like she was playing an invisible instrument. Now, however, they were cooped-up together in an elevator and there was no escaping her squirming.

"Damn it, Carina, if you're going to be like this for the whole trip to the Piazzi asteroid field then I'm going to have to sedate you," Carter snapped, when he could finally stand it no longer. "Relax for heaven's sake. This is what you wanted, right? To uncover the mysteries of the lost Aterniens?"

"I was hoping to discover the ruins of their dead civilization, then get rich and famous by writing a book and milking the lecture circuit." She smiled at him, though she was continuing to rattle her fingers against her thigh. "I didn't expect to be called a 'primitive sack of meat' by the second most powerful figure in the Aternien Empire and end up starting a war."

Carter laughed. "Think about it this way; it'll make for a much more exciting book."

Carina smiled meekly then blew out a nervous sigh and began picking her fingernails. Carter scrunched up his nose as a piece of torn nail was tossed to the floor of the elevator.

"Seriously, I will sedate you, if you do that on the shuttle," he said, intentionally sterner. "Remember, you're under my command now, Major Larsen."

She stopped picking her nails and scowled at him. "I know you're a little behind the times in terms of Union regulations, but I'm pretty sure that sedating your XO for fidgeting is against the rules."

Carter remained stern. "Longsword officers were never really ones for following the rules."

The elevator finally thumped to a stop, and the door opened onto shuttle bay seven. Carter hustled out first, eager to avoid having a shred of his XO's fingernail flicked at him. Admiral Krantz had already cleared bay seven of all personnel, in order that the mission remain a secret. A single craft occupied the space, which was roughly the same size as a football field.

"That's what we're taking to the Piazzi asteroid field?" Carina said, scowling at the boxy Cyclone-class recon shuttle, which was just under twenty meters long. "Wouldn't we be better off taking the Dexterous?"

"Perhaps, but the Dexterous is known to the Aterniens now," Carter said, walking toward their new ship. "It's also too big. We need something small and innocuous enough to hide amongst the asteroids, in case the Aterniens have the same idea we do. This shuttle ticks the boxes and has enough hold space to carry the equipment we need to get the Galatine up and running again."

"I read the latest intelligence briefing on Piazzi, and there was nothing unusual out there," Carina replied, huffily.

"Maybe so, but according to our scans, there were also no Immortals hiding out on the diplomatic outpost." He stopped and looked his XO in the eyes. "I think we can assume that our scanners can't be trusted when it comes to the Aterniens."

Carina hummed and made a sort of smacking noise with her lips while she pondered what Carter had said. It was another one of her fidgets that drove him mad.

"You may have a point, Commander," she finally conceded. "The asteroid field orbits TESS-961S, on the demarcation line. It's a hell of a jump for a ship that size; are you sure it can make it?"

"I'm sure."

The reply came from somewhere inside the shuttle's cargo hold, rather than from his own lips. Master Engineer Kendra Castle then stepped down the lowered ramp and walked toward them, dusting down her hands.

"I've had to make a few special modifications to the soliton warp drive, but she'll get us there. It might be a bit of a rough jump, though."

"Rough is fine, so long as we make it intact," Carter replied.

His engineer was back in uniform, and he was astonished at how little she had changed, including the mass of tousled chestnut hair on her head. The engineer was even more "dangerously attractive" than he remembered.

"How the hell has a hundred years only made you look better?" Carter grumbled, while stroking his wiry silver beard. "Me, on the other hand…"

"Don't worry, boss, you've still got it," Kendra said, winking at him. She then turned to Carina and a wicked smile curled her lips. "Don't get any ideas, though. Longsword crew are like family, but not in the husband-and-wife sense, if you take my meaning."

"As if," Carina snorted. "You guys all need therapy, if you ask me."

"It's a bit late for that," Kendra countered. "Our psychoses were baked in a long time ago; at the same time they sliced and diced our DNA." She patted Carina on the back, which made her stumble forward a step. "You'll get used to it, and probably develop a few of your own." Kendra then spun on her heels and marched back into the recon shuttle. "I've already got her loaded up, so we're good to go when you are."

Carter followed his engineer and was surprised by the quantity of equipment she'd managed to pack into the compact hold of the shuttle.

"This is some heavy-duty gear. Won't it weigh us down?"

"Oh sure, she'll maneuver like a dinghy in a lake of soup, but we have no idea what state the Galatine is in, so I need to cover all bases." Kendra patted a stack of crates on the port side. "These are repair drones that I modified myself. I've also brought a fabrication station, in case we need to make some parts in-situ."

"What are these?" Carina wondered, looking at a rack of circular devices the size of manhole covers.

"Those are warp magnets," Kendra replied.

The engineer spoke with pride, as if the devices were her own invention. It then occurred to Carter that they probably were, because he'd never heard of a 'warp magnet' before in his life.

"What exactly is a warp magnet?" Carina asked. Evidently, the terminology was new to her as well.

"Well, if I had it my way, we'd be flying out there with an entire mobile repair dock, but that might look a little suspicious."

"A little…" Carter grunted.

"But, since I can't be sure that we'll be able to get the Galatine back online and warp capable just with these drones to work with, I came up with a plan B."

The engineer picked up one of the discus-shaped devices and activated it. The rim of the object began to glow yellow.

"If we can't jump the Galatine away from TESS-961S under

her own steam, we attach these all around the hull," Kendra continued, handing the activated warp magnet to Carina. "Then when we generate a soliton warp field from the shuttle, these magnets will pull the Galatine thought the space fold with us. It'll blow the shuttle's drive to hell in the process, but it will get us home."

Carter nodded. "Good work, Kendra. You're the best."

Kendra smiled, accepting the compliment. "I know, but it's nice of you to say so."

"So long as blowing the shuttle's soliton drive doesn't also blow us to hell, I'm in," Carina said, handing the warp magnet back to Kendra.

"No, we'll be okay." Kendra deactivated the object and slid it back into the rack. "Probably, anyway…"

Carina's eyes widened but Carter was quick to cut off any further debate. "Nothing we do here is without risk. But the one thing I have learned after years serving with Kendra Castle is that she doesn't set foot on a ship unless she's certain it won't blow us to hell."

"That's comforting to know," Carina replied, though it didn't take someone with augmented senses to see that she wasn't at all comforted by his comment.

"If there's nothing more, let's get going." Carter slipped past the other two officers and slid into the pilot's seat. "I'm flying."

"I call shotgun!" Kendra said, jumping into the seat next to him.

"You don't get to call shotgun; this isn't a road trip," Carina grumbled, folding her arms. "Besides, an XO's place is by her commander's side."

Kendra looked ready to argue back, but Carter shot her a stern, commanderly look, and she tutted and backtracked.

"Fine, I'll take the aux seat in the rear," Kendra said, climbing inelegantly over the back of the co-pilot's seat and dropping into the rear row. "I hope you still remember how to fly though, boss, because to avoid any potential Aternien sensor nets, we need to warp in as close to TESS-961S as possible. And you don't need me to tell you that is one nasty-ass planet with wild electrical storms and intense volcanic activity."

"Don't worry, I can still fly," Carter snorted, insulted at the insinuation that the years had dulled his pilot's instincts and skills. "Though, I don't know if my licenses are still valid after a century out of the service."

"You decide to mention that now?" Carina blew out a resigned sigh and dropped into the co-pilot's seat. "What the hell? It all makes for a better story for my future speaking gigs, right?"

"That's the spirit," Carter laughed.

Carina closed the hatches and doors, ready for departure, while Carter powered up the shuttle's engines and maneuvered the shuttle into the launch bay.

"Soliton warp coordinates are locked in. Our target is a low orbit of TESS-961S," Carter said, while working the controls of the shuttle.

"Control reports that we are clear to depart," Carina added. "The admiral wishes us good luck and Godspeed."

The launch bay depressurized, and the door opened onto what would normally have been the emptiness of space. However, on this occasion, three hundred Union ships hung in the void around Terra Six, the closest planet to the demarcation line.

"Let's hope the Aterniens hold off on their invasion plans until we get back," Carter said. The massing of ships had stirred up old memories of the war a century ago. "Otherwise, we'll be returning from one ship's graveyard to another."

"The soliton drive is spun up, boss," Kendra said, while reading a diagnostic panel on her left. "It's now or never."

"Then I guess it's now…"

Carter cleared the docking garage then initiated the warp jump, but rather than immediately triggering a rupture in spacetime and vanishing through it, the warp drive system in the shuttle began to thrum resonantly, like a deep note from a church organ. The lights in the cabin dimmed, and all but the essential controls in front of him powered down.

"Don't worry, it's the just my warp program redirecting all our available energy into the jump," Kendra explained.

Carter noticed that she had adopted a brace position, which didn't exactly fill him with confidence. He was about to question his happy-go-lucky engineer when the ship finally punched a hole in spacetime and tumbled through it, like a wedding ring falling down a plughole.

Carter hated soliton warp travel at the best of times, but the over-extended jump to TESS-961S was doubly unpleasant. After what seemed like minutes, but in reality, was merely the blink of an eye, the shuttle emerged at the other end of the wormhole, and straight away the cabin was filled with the screeching wail of alarms.

"We jumped in too close!" Carter announced, grabbing the controls and pulling up, despite not knowing for certain if up was even the right direction to climb.

A fork of silver lightning that looked like it had been thrown by Zeus himself flashed past the nose of the shuttle. A crack of thunder followed immediately, which was so loud and primal that Carter wondered how the cockpit glass hadn't shattered into a million pieces.

"The navigation system is fried," Carina called out. "I can't tell if we're rising out of the atmosphere or falling deeper into it."

Carter checked the scanners, but the electrical activity was rendering their systems useless. His own senses, however, were fully functional, and had been kicked into a higher gear by the stresses of the danger they were in. Forgoing all means of technological assessment, he instead relied on his most sensitive and vital instrument – his eyes.

"If we're falling then based on the altitude at which we exited the jump, we'll crash into the surface of the planet in less than fifty seconds," Kendra called out from the aux seat in the rear.

Carter heard his engineer but didn't answer. He was searching the violent skies outside for any crack in the soupy storm that would tell him which way to throw the controls.

"Carter?" Carina cut in. He could hear her heart beating almost out of control. In contrast, Kendra Castle was glacially cool. "Carter, did you hear Kendra?"

"I heard…" Carter replied. "Standby…"

Carina's mouth fell open and she glanced back at Kendra, presumably hoping to recruit her support. However, the engineer just closed her eyes and gave Carina the OK sign in return. In the meantime, Carter continued to stare ahead, allowing his superhuman vision and spatial awareness to do the job the shuttle's systems were no longer able to perform. Then he saw something. It was visible for only the briefest of moments, but it was enough to give him a bearing.

Throwing the controls into the correct position, he increased power to the main engines and engaged the ventral thrusters on full. The shuttle responded and changed trajectory like a pool ball bouncing off the side cushion of the table. The forces on their bodies were immense and Major Larsen blacked out, but Carter was able to withstand the pressure and hold his course. Then the forces eased as he pushed the shuttle above the cloud barrier of the barren, inhospitable world. The navigation systems re-initialized, and he locked in the autopilot for a low orbit, before blowing out a heavy sigh of relief.

"I think you should probably re-test for your pilot's license when we get back," Kendra said, smirking at him from the back row of seats.

Carter looked across to Carina, expecting her to deliver a caustic remark of her own, but the major was still out cold.

"Do me a favor and wake her up, will you?"

Kendra leaned forward and to Carter's horror, it looked like she was about to slap Carina across the face.

"Gently!" he cut in, just in time to save Carina from a very rude awakening. "Don't forget that she's your superior officer now."

Kendra grunted, slid back into her seat, and rooted around for a medical kit. He watched her out of the corner of his eye; Kendra was always an open book to him, and he could see there was something on her mind.

"What is it, Kendra? A century might have passed, but we're Longsword crew, and that means we don't keep secrets, at least not from one another."

Kendra frowned at him, torn between speaking her thoughts and keeping them to herself. A hundred years ago, there wouldn't have even been a need to ask her to speak up, but clearly a lot had changed, beyond the simple passage of time.

"Are you sure about her, boss?" Kendra said, tapping the stim injector against the side of Carina's neck. "I mean, I see why you like her. I like her too. But she's a home-grown 'normie', and not cut out for what's to come. Carina isn't like us, lucky for her."

"For the record, it wasn't my choice for her to be XO," Carter said.

The words tasted sour in his mouth; and he realized he was making excuses for himself, which was something he never did. Time had affected him too, he realized, perhaps more than he had appreciated.

"I guess I could have fought the admiral's decision, but I didn't," he admitted. This realization also troubled him.

"Just make sure you're doing this for the right reasons, Carter," the engineer said. "Because if she gets killed, you'll blame yourself, and don't say you won't, because we both know that's bullshit."

Carter considered his engineer's words. Events had happened quickly since Major Carina Larsen had landed on his forest moon, and almost got herself gouged by the boar-like alien Morsapri. She'd charmed and intrigued him enough to make him go along with her crazy ideas, without believing it would amount to anything. An amusing distraction, perhaps. But now they were faced with the very harsh reality of war with a post-human army that were faster, stronger and more ruthless than any human being. Kendra Castle was right that Carina should not be part of their crew, but the reality was that the deal was done.

"Let's get this mission in the bag, then I'll decide what to do about our fragile human executive officer," Carter said, turning back to his engineer. He glanced at Carina and saw that she was drooling onto the front of her uniform. "For now, though, how about you wake her up, before I have to find a mop amongst all the crap you lugged here with us."

FIFTEEN
SWORD OF TITANS

CARTER STUDIED the scan readings of the Aternien spy probe, pensively stroking his silver beard as he did so. Kendra had switched positions with Major Larsen in order to analyze the device, which they'd detected within a minute of arriving at TESS-961S; just soon enough to avoid being spotted by it.

"It turns out that exiting the jump inside the upper atmosphere of TESS-961S was a stroke of luck," Kendra said, as reams of data flooded across the shuttle's screens. "The electrical soup swimming around the planet masked our arrival, but if we'd dropped out of warp where we were supposed to, the probe would have picked us up in an instant."

"How the hell did we not know this was here?" Carina wondered, somewhat recovered after her blackout, thanks to Kendra's ministrations. "The terms of the armistice allowed both sides to monitor the Piazzi asteroid field, and Intelligence knew nothing about hidden probes."

"The more important question is how do we stop that thing from seeing us?" Carter said, focusing on the mission, rather than the Union's surveillance failures.

"I'm already on it, boss, just give me a few more seconds,"

Kendra replied. "This would be a hell of a lot easier if I had my gopher to help."

"By gopher do you mean a personal robot, like the one Carter had?" Carina asked. She was leaning over the back of the engineer's seat, watching with interest as Kendra worked her magic. "Kaleb wasn't it, or something like that?"

"His name was JACAB, not Kaleb," Carter cut in, a little huffily. "And I choose to believe he's still out there, like the Galatine."

"Sorry, Mr. Sensitive," Carina said, recoiling from him. She returned her attention to Kendra, who was working so fast it was impossible to follow what she was doing. "Does your robot have a cute name too?" she asked the engineer.

Kendra stopped mid-input and glared at Carina like she'd just insulted her mother. "I strongly suggest you don't call RAEB cute, or he'll zap you in the ass."

Carina recoiled again. "Jeez, you two are really defensive about your little robot buddies, aren't you?"

"They were more than just machines to us, Major," Carter said, continuing in a gruff manner. "You wouldn't understand."

"Okay, I'm sorry," Carina replied, holding up her hands in submission.

Carter grunted an acknowledgment of Carina's apology, glad that his XO had finally cottoned on to the fact that their gophers were a sore subject, and not one to be joked about. He could sense she wasn't done with her interrogation, but to her credit Carina changed tack, and began again with a more considerate line of questioning.

Does RAEB stand for something too, or was it just a name you gave it?"

"Him, not it…" Kendra corrected her, sternly. She had resumed her work at an even more frenetic pace. "The name is an acronym for R-class Autonomous Engineering Bot, not that we ever referred to our gophers by their technical designations. It's too impersonal."

"I hope I get to meet him one day," Carina said, and Carter could tell that she meant it. "JACAB too," his XO added, shooting him an apologetic smile.

"First things first; let's find the Galatine," Carter grunted.

Kendra completed her inputs with a flourish, like a pianist finishing a lively piece of music, then rocked back in her seat.

"There, I've hacked the Aternien probe and programmed it to ignore us," Kendra said, cracking her knuckles. "Any data it sends to whomever is receiving its transmission will contain no mention of this shuttle. The modification will only last for a few hours, though," she cautioned. "Aternien tech is sophisticated; before long, the probe will detect the modification to its base programming and correct it. When that happens, the Aterniens will see us, as clear as day."

"How long?" Carter asked.

"Maybe twenty-four hours," Kendra replied with a shrug. "If we're really lucky."

"I never bet on luck," Carter answered, staring at the probe with a wary eye. "But it looks like your criminal past as a hacker was all for a good cause in the end." He patted his engineer on the shoulder then grabbed the controls. "We'd best get moving."

Carter powered the shuttlecraft away from TESS-961S and toward the super-dense Piazzi asteroid field that orbited the system. His senses heightened as the shuttle passed into the field, knowing that one wrong move could leave the ship crippled and adrift. The risk of being detected by the probe was now a minor concern compared to the danger of being pulverized by one of countless rocks that were fizzing through space all around them. Piazzi was thought to contain literally billions of asteroids and rock fragments, some as small as tennis balls, and others as large as moons, all interacting in a chaotic melee driven by powerful gravitational forces.

"I've added the probable coordinates of the Galatine into the navigation system," Carina said, as the shuttle slipped deeper into the field.

"*Probable* coordinates?" Carter said. "I thought the Union knew where she was?"

"Well yes and no," Carina equivocated. "We don't have a spy probe inside Piazzi, like the Aterniens, so our information comes from probes stationed on the outskirts of the system. Based on their data, the Galatine crashed on a moon-sized asteroid in quadrant three."

Carter was less than impressed that this key piece of information had been left out of Krantz's briefing, but his Master Engineer remained upbeat and undeterred.

"Don't worry, boss, if she's out here, I'll find her," Kendra said, confidently. "I abandoned the Galatine once, and I'm never doing it again."

Carter grunted his agreement. Though he hadn't said it out loud to anyone, short of an act of God, or a fleet of Aternien warships warping in and atomizing them, he had zero intention of leaving Piazzi without his ship.

"Scanners are picking up the remains of other vessels," Kendra said, now focusing her considerable talents on the effort of finding the Longsword-class battlecruiser. "I'd say from the amount of debris and the composition of the metals, there's enough space junk out here to account for four of the five Longswords that were decommissioned."

"That's both distressing and encouraging," Carter said, speaking the words as one long sigh. "What about the Aternien Solar Barques? There were also five of those left at the end of the war, all of which were scuttled somewhere here."

Kendra was quiet for a moment, and her eyes narrowed and focused on the numerous screens of data that her augmented brain was manipulating and assessing in parallel, in a way that no regular human could match.

"I'd say that there's enough mass to account for at least three or four of the Solar Barques, but after a century of scatter and drift, large chunks of the vessels could be hundreds of thousands of miles from our position, and well beyond sensor range." Kendra then entered a sequence of commands to highlight and enhance an area of the asteroid field on the main screen. "There's one right there," she added, pointing to a bird-like object. "Its hull is largely intact too."

Carter steered the shuttle toward the remains of the old warship, while Major Larsen clung to the back of his seat, looking over his shoulder for the first tantalizing glimpse of an Aternien sun ship in over a hundred years. She was so close he could hear her breath rush past his ear.

"It's beautiful…" Carina said, speaking the words with deference. "I know the Aterniens named them after the ships from Egyptian mythology that transported the Sun god, Ra, but I never expected them to look so magical."

Carter nodded. The Aternien Solar Barques, and their Overseer commanders, had been responsible for millions of deaths, but a weapon was distinct from the one who wielded it. He could respect the tool while still despising the workman.

"They were comparable to our Union Longswords in almost every regard," Carter said, as his mind was filled with memories of battles fought long ago. "This was the Solar Barque Torkhon. Kendra and I fought it many times. It was a worthy adversary."

Carina let out a long, low whistle, which caused him to wince, since her mouth was still mere inches from his right ear. He adjusted the controls and flew past the remains of the Solar Barque, Torkhon, admiring its falcon-like swept wings, elegant neck, and diamond nose section, which resembled a quad-bladed broadhead arrow.

The ship itself gleamed under the starlight, displaying vivid ochres, golds, and azurites, while the hull was adorned with Aternien hieroglyphs, which told the story of its many battles and victories. It was, as Major Larsen had correctly observed, beautiful; but it was also deadly, and seeing it again after so many years chilled him to the bone.

Suddenly, the navigation system chimed an alert, and Carter reluctantly tore his eyes away from the remains of the Torkhon to check the update. Kendra, however, was way ahead of him.

"I've found her," Kendra said, the excitement of the discovery coloring her words. "It looks like the Galatine was caught by the gravity well of a massive asteroid and crashed into the surface."

Kendra worked the comp-slate and projected an enhanced image of the asteroid onto the main screen.

"That's an exo-planet, not an asteroid," Carina said. She was also running an analysis from the auxiliary station in the rear seat. "It's a mudball, but there's a breathable atmosphere, and I'm picking up massive heat and respiration indicators too."

Carter scowled and looked at his XO over his shoulder. "Are you saying there's something alive down there?"

Carina nodded, her eyes wide. "A whole crap load of somethings, if these readings are to be believed." She shrugged. "Who knows, they could be harmless and friendly, though."

Carter laughed. "Nature is cruel, Major, and alien nature is no different. You remember my wild boar friend from the forest moon of Terra Nine, right?"

Carina shuddered and scrunched up her nose, as if the memory of the enormous beast that had almost skewered her to death had attacked her inside her mind.

"I take it back," Carina said, before hooking a thumb toward the jam-packed cargo hold. "I assume we also brought weapons, in amongst that lot back there?"

"Enough to lay siege to a small town," Kendra commented. "Though I hope we don't need to use them. I've gotten far more used to cracking codes than skulls over the last hundred years."

"It's like riding a bike, Kendra," Carter said, smiling at his engineer. "You never forget."

Carter piloted the shuttlecraft low over the exo-planet that had the unadventurous designation, Satellite ZB-537. It was larger than Terra Prime's moon, but unlike that powder-coated rock, it had a syrupy atmosphere and steamy climate, both of which were perfect for harboring life.

"ZB-537 has a powerful magnetic core, so there's a good chance the Aternien spy probe wouldn't have spotted the Galatine," Kendra Castle said. "Frankly, it's a miracle the Union found it."

"We only did because we knew where to look," Carina cut in. "The location where each ship was scuttled was supposed to be kept secret, and the information destroyed, as per the terms of the armistice. But someone had the foresight to keep a copy."

Carter huffed a laugh. "It seems that Union Intelligence was more intelligent back then," he said, raising an eyebrow at his XO.

For once she didn't take the bait. Something else had stolen Carina Larsen's attention and kept hold of it, like the strangulating grip of a boa constrictor. It took him a moment to realize what, then he saw it for himself, and it ensnared him with the same authority.

"Is that the Galatine?" said Carina. She sounded even more wonderstruck than when she'd first caught sight of the Aternien Solar Barque.

"That's her, alright."

Carter felt his stomach flutter at the sight of his old ship. It was an adrenaline-fueled reaction that had been largely engineered out of his physiology by a Union that didn't want Longsword officers to experience fear, or at least the biological effects of it. But he was still human, and he could still be moved. In many ways, his emotions were even more powerful than those of a regular human, and the sight of the Galatine caused a tear to well in the corner of his eye.

"I've studied images and holos of the Longswords, but my god, seeing is believing..." Carina continued, utterly spellbound by the vessel.

Carter blinked the tear from his eye and allowed it to soak into his beard, hoping that neither Kendra nor Carina had noticed. He then adjusted the controls and programmed the shuttle to repeat a loop around the Galatine, which was part-buried in the mud of ZB-537. After a minute or two, he chanced a look at Carina, hoping she hadn't detected the crack in his gruff, surly exterior, and felt a swell of pride as he realized that his XO had fallen in love at first sight with the ship. The same had happened to him when he'd first seen the Galatine in the space docks above Terra Prime.

"Two-hundred and sixty meters long, it's sleek, fast and the deadliest weapon ever devised by human minds." Carter reached out in front of him, as if grasping the handle of an imaginary sword. "If I stood half a kilometer tall, I could reach down and draw the Galatine from this mudhole like unsheathing a blade. That's how they got the name, because in the grasp of a titan, it would look like a longsword."

His speech left Carina with a giddy expression on her face. It was like an archeologist gazing at the Tomb of Tutankhamen for the very first time. He smiled again; for some reason, her appreciation of the Galatine only made its rediscovery more satisfying.

"Unless your augments include the ability to turn into a five-hundred-meter-tall man, I suggest we land and try to remove the Galatine from this rock the old-fashioned way," Carina said, keen to move from observation to action.

Kendra punched in a sequence of commands, then landing co-ordinates flashed up on Carter's navigation screen. He disabled the autopilot and swooped toward the vessel, burning to get on board.

"There's a denser patch of ground near the auxiliary hatch in the engineering section at the rear of the ship," Carter said, descending as fast as the shuttle – and his nerves – would allow. "I'll set down there. That way, the shuttle hopefully won't sink into the mud and vanish, while we're inspecting the Galatine."

Despite their careful choice of landing site, the shuttle still touched down with a squelchy splat, and its struts sank unevenly into the mud, before finally reaching an equilibrium, tilted by almost ten degrees to starboard. Kendra opened the rear cargo bay door, and a sweltering heat permeated the shuttle from outside. It smelled like rotting meat and festering bog water.

"Wow, this a very special kind of stink we've discovered," Carina said, holding her nose. "I'll never complain about the locker rooms in Union gyms ever again."

"You have it easy," Carter hit back, sliding through the narrow gully between the crates stacked in the hold. "Just be thankful that you don't have an augmented sense of smell."

Carter got to work, making a priority of breaking out a trio of gauss rifles and sidearms, on the assumption that the exoplanet's natural inhabitants weren't friendly. Kendra wasted no time in deploying her tools, starting with a squadron of discus-sized flying drones, which hovered around the Galatine, constantly scanning, and analyzing their surroundings.

"What can I do? I feel like a fifth wheel around here," Carina said. She was at the bottom of the cargo ramp, hands on hips.

Carter tossed her a gauss rifle, and to Carina's credit she caught it, despite him not holding back on the throw.

"First, check our perimeter," Carter said, slinging his rifle then handing the third plus a sidearm to Kendra. "The last thing we need is for some alien monster to leap out and bite a chunk out of us, before we've even gotten inside the Galatine."

Carina loaded the rifle and held it at low ready. "To be honest, I wouldn't want that to happen *after* we've gotten inside, either. So don't worry; if an alien bug so much as looks at me the wrong way, I'll bury a slug into its slimy head."

"You can go with her, boss," Kendra said. "It'll take me maybe ten minutes to feed power to the auxiliary hatch and crack it open. Until then, there's nothing either of you can do to help."

"Roger that," Carter replied. He tapped the left lapel of his jacket twice to open a comm-channel between them all. "Stay on comms and stay alert."

Kendra saluted him with the wrench that was in her hand, and he returned the salute before loading his rifle and catching up with Carina, who had already begun her patrol.

"It looks like I'm your wingman, Major," Carter said, boots squelching in the mud in time with his XO. "I know that military intelligence types don't typically go into the field, so try not to shoot me, okay?"

Carina scowled at him. "I'll do my best, sir, but there's a pretty solid chance you're the ugliest and scariest-looking sonofabitch on this mudball, so I can't promise anything."

Carter laughed. "You have a smart-ass response for everything, don't you? Just how did you manage to climb the ranks and gain the admiral's favor with a mouth like that?" Carina's scowl deepened, and he was concerned that he'd genuinely offended her. "Not that it bothers me, Major. We Longswords were pretty up-front and frank with each other. Like I told you before, we were as much a dysfunctional family as we were a crew."

Carina seemed to accept his tactful climbdown, then considered how to answer his question. Carter noted that she appeared conflicted, perhaps wondering how much to reveal.

"I basically screwed my way up the chain of command," Carina finally answered, completely deadpan.

Carter stopped in his tracks and studied his XO's expression, but he genuinely couldn't tell whether she was serious or joking.

"Really?" Carina said, suddenly looking pissed off. "You actually believed that didn't you?"

Carter shrugged. "That's the problem with being such an effective bullshit artist; it's hard to determine the truth from the lies."

Carina continued to scowl at him. "If you must know, I was

a straight-A student and graduated top of my class at the academy. I got here on merit, Master Commander Rose, and without the benefit of biological and technological augmentation."

"You wouldn't think them a benefit, if you knew how being post-human has affected our lives," he countered. Any suggestion that his augments were somehow a gift always got his goat. "We weren't just ostracized after the war, but during it too. No-one wanted to be around us, Major. It wasn't much of a life."

Suddenly, his senses kicked into a higher gear, and the smell of blood shot to the foreground. He spun around, weapon ready, following the scent, until he spotted the carcass of an alien animal fifty meters away.

"Hold up, Major," Carter said. He raised his rifle to his shoulder and looked at the carcass though the scope.

"What do you see?" Carina asked, she was covering his back, but he could hear her heart racing.

"There's a dead animal, due North. It's about the size of a cow, and it looks and smells pretty fresh too."

A deep, rumble that was half-hiss, half-growl, surrounded them. It sounded like a pack of oversized Komodo dragons warning them to stay back.

"That noise came from all around us, but I don't see anything," Carina said, sweeping the barrel of her rifle across the mud-covered terrain.

"Fall back to the Galatine," Carter ordered.

Unlike his XO, he had spotted the source of the sound, or at least one of the beasts that had helped to produce it. And he had no intention of getting better acquainted with the animal.

"Kendra, how's it coming with that hatch?" Carter said, speaking though the open comm link to his engineer.

"I'm almost there, though I needn't have bothered. There's a tear in the hull big enough for us to climb through. It was likely caused by a collision with an asteroid before the ship crashed here."

"How big is the tear?"

"About two meters by half a meter," Kendra replied, though she didn't sound particularly distressed by this fact. "I have the right tools to patch it up, and once we get the Galatine back online, the nanomechanical armor will knit it together nicely. Though I still might have to hammer out a few dings."

Carter cursed under his breath. "Get the hatch open, Kendra, as fast as you can. And make sure you have a weapon in your hand, instead of a wrench."

"Why, boss, what have you seen?"

Carina was looking at him too; the same question that Kendra had asked was also on the tip of her tongue. However, he didn't need to answer either of them. At that moment, a reptilian beast the size of a polar bear rose out of the mud on hind legs as thick as tree trunks and roared at them through blood-stained rows of dagger-sharp teeth.

SIXTEEN
NATIVE DANGERS

CARTER RAISED his rifle and aimed it at the alien reptile, but kept his finger pressed along the frame. He didn't want to anger the beast in case its aggression was merely an act of dominance to ward them off, but he also didn't want to become its next meal.

"Back away, slowly," Carter said quietly, already taking a step back. "If we don't provoke it, then it might just leave us alone."

Carina stepped back alongside Carter; the rich squelch of their boots in the foul mud were still in perfect synchronization with one another.

"Did your hunting exploits on the forest moon extend to vicious alien reptiles?" Carina asked, speaking while barely moving her lips, like a bad ventriloquist.

"I'm afraid not, but I understand enough about creatures like this to know not to get clawed by them."

Carina laughed nervously. "Well, that much is obvious."

"I don't mean because of the physical damage those claws can do," Carter replied. The beast was now slowly tracking forward, tongue tasting the air as it stalked toward them. "Even a scratch could lead to an infection that would be deadlier than the wound itself."

Carina scrunched up her nose at this. "I thought you Longsword guys were largely immune to infection and disease?"

"We are." Carter met his XO's eyes to make sure she understood him plainly. "But you're not."

Another rasping growl stole their attention, and Carter spotted a second reptilian beast to their left. It had been lying completely still, camouflaged in the mud, but was now also stalking closer. He checked over his shoulder, his augmented eyes attuned to the subtle variations in color and texture that gave away the locations of other beasts. Cursing, he turned back to his XO.

"We got one on our left and at least another one to our rear," Carter said, as the hisses grew louder. "They're trying to surround us, and they're doing a good job of it too."

Carina squinted her eyes, but it was clear to Carter that she was struggling to spot the hidden reptiles. She then nodded toward the engine section of the Galatine, which was partly submerged in the mud.

"We can use the ship to cover our backs," Carina said. "But if it comes to a fight, we have to hope these things aren't as tough as they look."

Carter nodded, then together they retreated toward the Galatine, now stalked by three of the reptilian monsters.

"The hatch door is open, boss," Kendra called out over the comm channel. "What's your status?"

"Our status is that we're being hunted by a trio of six-hundred-pound carnivorous lizards, and our backs are against the wall."

The comm channel went quiet for a moment, then Kendra spoke up again. "I see them. They're closing in around me too. It goes without saying, but you might want to hurry things up."

"Copy that, Kendra, we're on our way. Keep your rifle handy."

Carter continued to cover two of the creatures, while Carina kept her rifle aimed at the beast that had first confronted them on hind legs. It was the largest of the group, and he estimated it was at least seven meters from its head to the tip of its spiked tail. However, for reasons he couldn't comprehend, the beast had stopped advancing. He checked on the other two, which also held their positions, though their tongues continued to taste the air, and their soulless, black eyes were locked onto them.

Suddenly, Carter felt his senses kick into a higher gear. There was another danger close-by, and he scanned the murky terrain looking for it, without success. Then he heard the scrape of claw against metal and looked up to see a reptilian beast perched on the hull of the Galatine, muscles coiled and teeth bared.

The beast launched itself at them and Carter shoved Carina out of danger at the last moment, propelling her clear of the alien carnivore. The mud cushioned her landing, but she was still dazed, and an easy target for the other reptiles.

The beast that had leapt at Carter lashed out with two-inch long claws, but he dodged back, avoiding the slashing strike by a hair's breadth. Turning the gauss rifle against the monster, he squeezed the trigger and fired three slugs at its head, but the beast's thick cranium repelled the shots like it was made of solid lead. More shots flew toward the beast and skipped off its thick hide and Carter saw that Carina was back on her feet, weapon also aimed at the beast in front of him.

"Fall back to the hatch, now!" Carter called out.

The beast attacked again, and he used the rifle to block the savage strike, avoiding being skewered by its flesh-tearing, four-inch claws. Even so, the force of the impact threw him back against the Galatine's hull, and he cracked his head on the metal, briefly stunning him. The beast pounced but was quickly beaten back by another barrage of gunfire. This time, a slug punctured the creature's eye and it roared in pain and drew back, snarling, hissing and flailing its powerful tail.

"I thought I told you to fall back?" Carter said, noting that Carina was still in the exact same spot she had been prior to the beast's assault.

"You're welcome," Carina replied, in her usual sarcastic manner. The hiss of another reptile cut across them, and she turned and opened fire, temporarily halting the beast's advance. "Now how about we get the hell out of here?"

Carter ran, but the cloying stickiness of the mud was making it difficult even for his augmented muscles to accelerate to more than a leisurely jogging pace. Understandably, Carina was struggling more, while the reptiles, with their wide, flat feet, were able to skate across the mud without impairment.

Carter reloaded then emptied an entire magazine at the reptile directly ahead of them, but even this was only just enough to kill the beast. Carina jumped onto the body of the felled creature and used its six-meter frame as a runway to gather more speed, and soon a gap had opened up between them.

"Come on, I can see the hatch!" Carina yelled, waving him over.

Carter stepped onto the dead lizard's head, which was pockmarked with holes from the solid projectiles their gauss rifles fired. Then he saw a flicker of movement in the mud close to where Major Larsen stood, and his senses honed in on the danger, like the needle of a magnet pointing North.

"Carina, get down!" he called out.

He raised his rifle to his shoulder, but Carina was standing between him and the beast, blocking his shot. The reptile sprang out of the mud and leapt at her, but before the animal could take down its prey, the beast itself was tackled from the side, and driven to the ground by Kendra Castle. It roared and thrashed its tail and claws, and Kendra was caught across the back. She didn't cry out – the engineer's sensation blockers did their job – but the strike had been clean, and the wound was deep enough that he knew Kendra wouldn't be able to immediately fight back.

His reaction times had accelerated to the point where life or death decisions were now made in the blink of an eye. Grasping the rifle in both hands, he sprinted across the long body of the dead animal at his feet, avoiding the pounce of another beast in the process, then powered into the air like a long jumper attempting a world record leap.

The reptile that had taken down Kendra was poised to strike again, its jaws gaping and curved teeth stark against the murky backdrop. Carter landed squarely on the beast's head, snapping its jaw shut before it was able to rip the flesh from his engineer's body. The lizard snarled and opened its jaw again, but Carter shoved the barrel of the gauss rifle down its throat and opened fire, splitting open its belly from the inside.

"Help Kendra up," Carter called out to Major Larsen, at the same time as ejecting the magazine from his rifle and slapping in a new one. "Once we're inside the ship, head to section G10, deck four."

"It's okay, I know the way," Kendra said, throwing her arm around the major and hauling herself out of the mud. Her hand was pressed against the wound, but blood was seeping through her fingers.

Four other reptilian beasts had climbed out of the mud, more than replacing the number they'd killed, but the creatures were holding back. Carter anxiously looked around him, worried that he might be the target of yet another ambush, but the real reason that the beasts had remained cautious soon became clear. The largest of the animals, perhaps the pack leader, had moved to the fore. It rose onto its hind legs, as it had done the first time Carter had seen the monster, and its growl shook the air.

Carter opened fire, but the slugs from his gauss rifle

rebounded off its dense hide, creating little more than scratches on the surface. The reptile dropped onto its front legs and the ground shook from the impact, but he wasn't about to wait around to see its next move. Spinning on his heels, he hurried toward the open hatch leading into the Galatine, and the reptiles immediately gave chase. Carina and Kendra were already through, but despite their lead, he knew it would be a tight race to the finish. He just hoped the area inside the ship that he'd selected as their haven was still accessible, and still held the item he desperately needed to find.

Throwing himself through the hatch, he tumbled across the deck and hammered into the wall. Hisses and roars filled the corridor and he saw the eyeshine of a reptilian beast glint from out of the darkness. He jumped up and ran at the monster, hammering shots into its head and finally cracking its skull and piercing its primitive brain.

The scrape and patter of more claw-tipped feet followed him as he jumped over the body and rolled through his landing. Ahead, he could see Major Larsen and Kendra Castle standing at the door to room ARM-01. One of the engineer's drones was humming by the side of her head, its probes embedded into the door's control panel, which was as dead as every other system on the once great vessel.

The roar of a reptile alerted him to another attack, and he dodged back, avoiding the slash of a muscular, claw-tipped leg. He hammered the stock of his rifle across the top of the beast's head, smashing its skull and the weapon in the process. Then the screech and groan of metal being bent and flexed echoed along the corridor, and the pack leader entered, dragging itself in through a fissure in the Galatine's hull. This time, however, Carter was unarmed and unable to stop its relentless advance.

"Boss, I've accessed the door controls, but the ship is on security lockdown; only you can open it!"

Carter turned toward the sound of his engineer's voice and

ran hard, accelerating so fast that an Olympic hundred-meter sprinter would have been left in his dust. Sliding to a stop in front of the door, he pressed his hand to the panel and waited for the security system to scan his face. A beam of light probed his features, but still the door remained closed.

"I hope to hell I don't look my age," Carter said, trying to smooth down his hair and wipe the mud and lizard blood from his silver beard. "It's been a hundred years since the ship last saw my face."

The scanning beam probed him again, but still the door remained locked. A resonant growl shook the deck plates, then the pack leader tore through the carcass of the last beast Carter had put down, splitting it open like it was a freshly-baked baguette.

"Come on, it's me, damn it!" Carter roared, hammering against the wall.

The beam reinitialized and scanned his face again, though Carter was aware that this would be their last chance. If the door remained shut, they would have to fight the colossal reptile hand-to-hand. Even with his unique abilities, it would be a fight he couldn't win, not without suffering critical injuries. The alien lizard roared, then finally the door unlocked and ground open.

"Inside, now!" Carter yelled, practically throwing Kendra and Carina through the opening.

The reptile charged, and Carter ducked inside the room, hammering the button to close the door with so much force that he almost pancaked it flat. The slabs of metal drew together, and at the same time the reptile hammered its head into the door. For a brief moment the mechanism faltered, leaving a gap wide enough for the beast's claws to wrap themselves around.

The monster drew back, ready to charge again, but Carter let out a roar of his own and forced the doors shut with the raw strength of his muscles and his indomitable will. More hisses and growls filled the air, and the beast continued to hammer and claw at the metal, but to no avail.

For now, at least, Commander Rose knew that his crew were safe; but for how long, he could not say.

SEVENTEEN
WEAPONS OF WAR

CARTER BACKED away from the door with the sound of the reptile pack leader trying to smash and claw its way in still ringing in his ears. The room they'd escaped to was without power and were it not for the lights emanating from Kendra's drone, it would have been pitch black.

"This is a dead end," Major Larsen said. While Carter had been barring the entrance, his XO had scouted their new space. "Why did you bring us here? Now we're trapped."

"Don't worry about that, I chose this room for a reason," Carter replied, calmly dusting down his hands. The scratches and cuts he'd sustained were already healing over.

"Why, what's special about this room?" Carina asked.

Carter was about to answer, when a moan of pain from Kendra Castle caused him to focus all his attention on his wounded engineer. Major Larsen also forgot about the question she'd asked, and dropped down next to Kendra, anxiously inspecting the gash to her side.

"This is bad, she's going to need a hospital, or at least the medical bay of a Union warship."

"There's a medical kit on the wall over there," Kendra said, nodding toward the door, which was still being assaulted from the outside. "If you wouldn't mind grabbing it, Major, then I can guide you in what to do."

"I don't wish to be alarmist, but I don't think a simple medical kit is going to cut it," Carina answered, sternly.

"She'll be fine," Carter cut in, unconcerned. He grabbed the med kit off the wall and slid it along the deck to Carina. "Just follow her lead."

His XO continued to frown but didn't argue and instead opened the medical kit that Carter had given her. At the same time, Kendra tore away what remained of the blood-soaked uniform surrounding her wound.

"Start by taking that white bottle with the blue stripe and use it to wash out the dirt," Kendra said. Her voice was strained, and sweat was beading on her face and neck. "And pass me that little silver canister too, if you would."

Carina removed the white bottle then hunted for the silver canister but couldn't seem to find it. Carter breezed past and knelt by her side.

"It's tucked under here," he said, lifting a flap in the med kit that had an 'n' symbol written on it. "It's called a nano-stim. It's an emergency supply of nanomachines," he added, as Carina removed the capsule and handed it to Kendra. "We have an implant close to our aortas which manufactures the nanomachines that inhabit our cells. They can replace any that are destroyed or lost through bleeding, but the process can take a up to an hour. In the case of a more serious injury like this one, it's best to give a little booster."

Kendra popped the cap off the bullet-shaped silver tube then twisted the dial to sixty percent. The engineer sucked in a deep breath then stabbed the sharp tip of the capsule directly into her wound. Straight away, Kendra was paralyzed with a wrenching agony that caused her body to contort and her face to screw up as if she was being tortured.

"Carter, something's wrong!" Carina called out; her voice strained with panic.

Carter dropped to Kendra's side, and held the engineer's hands in his own, allowing her to use his body to bear down against the pain.

"It's okay, this is normal," Carter said, speaking calmly, which helped to soothe his XO's fractious nerves. "Taking a high-dose nano-stim is not without risks, but this will soon pass. Just watch."

Carina didn't look at all reassured, but she turned back to Kendra and held her arms, hoping that the simple knowledge of her presence would lend enough moral support to allow Kendra to weather the storm. Then her face scrunched up as she watched the wound rapidly heal before her eyes, until no evidence of the savage gash in her side remained.

"That's… impossible…" Carina whispered.

"It's not impossible," Kendra replied. The pain was gone, but the engineer looked exhausted, like she'd just endured childbirth. "It does hurt like a fucking bitch though."

Carter rolled his eyes but allowed his engineer the use of the foul curse. On this occasion, he figured the circumstances merited it.

"Stay with her," Carter said, giving his XO what he hoped was an encouraging smile. "There's something in this room I need to find."

Carter resumed his search with renewed gusto, knowing that eventually the reptilian beast would break down the door. It didn't matter to him that the light from the drone was barely able to penetrate more than a few meters into the darkness. His augments allowed him to see in low light levels with the same fidelity as a domestic cat. A roar from outside then stole their attention, like a sudden crash of thunder. The hammering against the door intensified, and he could see that the metal was starting to buckle.

"Our weapons were barely any use against those reptiles, so I take it that you have a plan to fight them?" Carina asked, as Carter continued to search inside storage chests and lockers.

"I always have a plan, Major," Carter replied. He smiled again, though this was more sanctimonious than reassuring. "I told you that I chose this place for a reason. Room ARM-01 is the ship's armory."

Carina snorted a laugh. "Then I hope you're looking for a bazooka, or maybe even a light tank, because I don't see what else will have an effect against Godzilla and his buddies."

Carter laughed half-heartedly, but he was so engrossed in his search that he was only half paying attention to her.

"Nothing so extreme, or inelegant," he replied, while sifting through the contents of a long shelving rack. "But after a hundred years, I can't remember where I put the damned thing."

"That's because you never tidied up after yourself," Kendra called out. Though her wound had knitted together, it still looked red and raw. "You were always so damned messy that if it wasn't for me and Cai cleaning up after you, you'd have ended up fighting the Aterniens with your bare hands."

Carter stopped and scowled at his engineer. "That's a gross exaggeration. I wasn't that bad."

Kendra snorted. "I think age has addled your brain." To Major Larsen's clear astonishment, she then climbed to her feet, without any hint of discomfort, and pointed to the other side of the armory. "Try over there. Rack B12."

"Who was Cai?" Carina asked, following Carter with interest.

"Kendra is talking about Cai Cooper; the ship's Master Operator."

Carina tapped her fingers against her top lip, deep in thought. "Cai Cooper is still alive, if I remember rightly."

"That's what your intelligence reports say." Carter increased the urgency of his search, aware that the door was already on the brink of being bashed in. "I hope that's the case, because assuming we get out of this mess, we'll need to find him."

There was another hideous growl and snarl, then the top

quarter of the door folded inward, like a tin can being opened. The reptilian beast wrapped it claws around the edge and the armory was filled with the deafening screech and squeal of metal being warped and twisted out of shape.

"Right now, we need that bazooka," Carina said. Her attention was fully focused on the pack of alien monsters that were on the brink of breaking through the door.

Carter picked up a revolver and huffed. "I'd almost forgotten about this."

Carina's eyes flicked across to the weapon in his hand, then she glared at him wide-eyed, as if he'd lost his mind.

"A pistol? What the hell use is that going to be?"

"This isn't a pistol, it's a revolver," Carter hit back, with a touch of snobbery that he realized was perhaps unwarranted. "It's a Union Firearms 57-EX; a traditional five-shot revolver, with a twelve-inch barrel."

"That's nice, now about that bazooka?" Carina replied, clearly unimpressed.

Carter scowled at her in return. "This beauty shoots Osmium-tipped armor piercing .50 caliber rounds, with a seven-kilojoule muzzle energy. It was too powerful for regular humans to handle, so never went into production, but for an augment like me, it's like shooting a nine-millimeter."

"Unless it shoots anti-reptile bullets, I can't say that I really give a shit," Carina snapped. She glanced at the door; the beasts had almost torn it wide enough to break through. "Why the hell are you so calm? We're about to be cut to shreds!"

Carter smiled; he'd finally found the item he'd been searching for.

"Flesh will be cut today, Major, but it won't be ours," Carter said, lifting the weapon off the shelf and grasping it in his hand. It fit like glove, and it was like they'd never been apart.

"A sword?" Carina said, aghast. "Your answer to a horde of alien monsters is an old navy cutlass that's probably blunter than a dressing down from Admiral Krantz?"

Carter could see that his XO was on the verge of a mini nervous breakdown, and in many respects, he couldn't blame her; he'd hardly been transparent about the motives for his actions. However, he also knew that even if he had explained what he was looking for, she would have been none the wiser. The only way Major Larsen could be made to understand what it meant to be a Longsword officer, was to show her. And he intended to do just that.

"Take this," Carter said, loading five rounds into his 57-EX revolver and slapping it into Carina's hands. "But I'd recommend you don't shoot unless you have to. It's got quite a kick to it..."

"I know how to shoot," Carina said, huffily. "But why are you giving it to me; don't you need it?"

"No, I'll be fine with this." Carter unsheathed his sword and weighed it in his hand.

"Seriously, Carter, this is no time for jokes."

Carter adopted a grim expression. "I'm not joking, Major. This might look like an old nineteenth-century naval cutlass, but its blade was forged from a metal whose secrets are lost to time and ignorance. I used this during the first Aternien war, and I'm going to use it again now."

"I appreciate your sense of nostalgia, but even with your strength, a sword won't cut though a six-hundred-pound, bullet-proof reptile."

More deafening screeches and groans interrupted them, and Carina aimed the revolver at the door. The pack leader had finally torn the metal away from the opening and had pulled itself through. It let out a roar and locked its eyes onto Kendra Castle, who was closest to the beast. However, like himself, she was unafraid, because she knew what was coming, just as well as he did.

"I may be a little rusty after a century without practice, so don't judge too harshly..."

Carina simply stared at him, wide-eyed, and it seemed clear

that she still considered him mad, but the time for words was over. He flicked the switch on the handle of the cutlass and a burst of plasma ignited from the hilt and raced along the edge like flame following a trail of gunpowder. It lit up the room like a floodlight and exposed the true hideousness of the monstrous alien reptiles.

Commander Rose left a stupefied Major Larsen behind and advanced toward the pack leader, plasma cutlass in hand. The weapon hummed and vibrated with raw power, but the beast showed no fear. Roaring again, it charged at Carter, rising onto its hind legs, ready to pounce. He swung the sword with all his might and opened the beast's belly from one side of its meter-wide frame to the other. The creature's innards spilled out onto the deck, and the reptile roared, but this time it was a death cry, not a warning.

Marching past the mortally wounded beast, Carter advanced through the mangled remains of the door and into the hallway. Three more of the lizards were waiting for him, and the first wasted no time in making its move. A claw-tipped leg was slashed at his body, but he danced back and cut though muscle and bone, severing the limb cleanly from the creature's body. It screeched and lumbered back into the darkness.

Another of the reptiles darted forward, and he swung the sword over his head, cleaving the beast's skull in half, and killing it instantly. At the same time, the third reptile pounced and tried to sink its shark-like teeth into his leg. He dodged aside, drawing upon swordsman's instincts that he'd not used for more than a hundred years, and hammered the pommel of the sword against the monster's head. It roared and pulled back, allowing Carter to press his advantage.

Keeping his elbows close to his body because of the confined quarters of the ship's corridor, he cut the monster deeply across both of its broad shoulders, causing it to collapse under its own immense weight. It screeched and thrashed, unable to defend itself, but Carter was not a callous fighter, and did not revel in the creature's misery, despite its murderous intent. He thrust the sword through the reptile's dense armor and punctured its heart. The plasma-edged blade cooked and sizzled its flesh then Carter withdrew the weapon and disengaged the blade, as the beast let out a final, rasping breath of life, and expired.

Suddenly, there was a scrape and clash of claws on metal. Carter spun around to see the reptile he had dismembered charging toward him, moving at a frightening speed, despite the bloody stump that it was forced to use. He tried to reignite the blade but was too late. The momentum of the impact sent him staggering back and gave the reptile an opening. It rose onto its hind legs, jaws wide, then a blast shook the air and the beast's head popped like a ripe tomato.

Carter lowered the sword and scowled at the headless beast, at a loss to explain its sudden, gruesome death. Then he saw Major Larsen splayed out on her ass a few meters away. His 57-EX experimental revolver was clutched in her trembling hand, smoke issuing from the barrel.

"Major, are you okay?" Carter said, rushing to her side.

He expected to find her shaking with a combination of fear and muscle pain from the immense recoil of the revolver, but instead, she was laughing and had a broad smile on her face.

"Holy shit, that was intense! You can keep your sword; this is mine."

Carter scowled then grabbed the weapon out of her hand.

"Get your own damned gun," he said, gruffly.

Carina looked like a kid who's just had a lollipop snatched from her clutches. "Spoilsport... But you'd better have something else good in that armory for me."

"I'm sure I can accommodate you, Major." Carter stood up and offered Carina his hand. She took it and he hauled her off the deck. "Now, if you've had enough fun on this bug hunt, how about we gear up and head to the bridge?"

EIGHTEEN
THE ARMORY

CARTER CLIMBED over the dead body of the reptile pack leader, which was already beginning to stink thanks to the fact its guts were all over the deck, and approached Kendra. In the time it had taken him to dispatch the remaining alien beasts, with Major Larsen's assistance, she had changed into a new uniform. It was one of a style that he remembered well.

"Now, that's what I call a *real* uniform," Carter said, admiring his dapper-looking Master Engineer. He then tugged at his own jacket, which was torn and covered in blood. "Not like the crap the Union produces now. I never liked how this thing felt, and I like it even less now."

"What is that made of?" Carina said, circling around Kendra, who was making the final adjustments to her new fit. "I've never seen a material quite like it."

"That's because it doesn't exist anymore." Carter headed over to one of the storage racks and began sifting through the contents. "They're called battle uniforms, but the technology and method of fabrication were casualties of the Union's moratorium on advanced tech. Today's scientists and engineers would consider the material almost magical, like mithril, but Kendra knows how to work it and, more importantly, repair it."

Carter had continued to sift through the contents of the shelving racks while he was talking, then finally found what he was looking for. He pulled out another battle uniform and held it up against his body.

"Now, we're talking," he said, flashing his eyes at his XO.

She looked less than impressed. "I'm feeling a little left out here…"

Carter laughed and slung his uniform over his shoulder before pulling another off the rack.

"Don't worry, I've got you covered; literally…"

Carter tossed the garment at his XO, and she caught it awkwardly. The upper half of the uniform flopped over her face, like a bedsheet used to make a Halloween ghost costume. Carina clawed the uniform off her then held it up in front of her body, much as he had just done moments ago. It draped on the floor like badly cut curtains and looked several sizes too big around the waist and torso.

"Thanks, but I was hoping for a new uniform, not a tent," Carina said, evidently unimpressed with Carter's offerings.

"Just put it on and I'll show you how it works," Carter said, shaking his head.

He removed his jacket and was about to toss it, when he remembered the core block that he'd taken from his cabin on the forest moon. He found it and slid it into the pocket of his new uniform, before disposing of the mangled garment. Carina then watched with a mix of curiosity and horror as he pulled off his tank top and tossed it away with similar abandon. Carter spent a few moments checking the wounds to his hyper-dense shoulder and pectoral muscles, before he noticed his XO scowling at him, arms tightly folded.

"So, you're just going to strip off and get changed right there, huh?" she said, raising an eyebrow at him.

"This is an armory, Major, not a department store. Just put on the damned uniform, already."

"Not until you turn around," Carina hit back. "I don't know

you that well yet, sir. You could be a dirty old perv, for all I know."

Kendra Castle laughed freely, and Carter glared at his engineer, though this didn't appear to make any difference to her mirth. Meanwhile, Carina had continued her protest, giving him the evil eye, and he sighed and turned around.

"There, now I can't see you, not that I'm interested in looking, anyway…"

Carter removed his pants and added them to the pile then pulled on the two-piece uniform, which had pockets integrated in the chest section, shoulders and pants, plus magnetic fixing points for webbing pouches, holsters, and his sword's scabbard. He was pleased to discover that the high-tech uniform fit well, if a little snugger around the midriff than it had once been. Carter grabbed the left side of his collar and squeezed, triggering the auto-adjustment routine that made all the necessary modifications to account for how his body had changed over the last hundred years.

"You can turn around now, though if you laugh, then I won't be responsible for my actions…"

Carter turned and had to force back a snigger. His XO looked like she was wearing an oversized pillowcase.

"Grab the left side of your collar and squeeze," he said, pointing to the area in question on his own uniform to help guide her.

Carina did as she was instructed, and the battle uniform responded by analyzing her frame and shrinking itself to fit in a matter of seconds.

"You can make fine adjustments yourself, by applying shorter squeezes to the collar trigger," Carter added, whilst picking fluff off his sleeves. "Squeeze closer to your chin to tighten the fit, and toward your ear to loosen it."

"No, this actually feels great already," Carina said, flexing her arms and legs, like she was limbering up for a jog in the park. She then glanced at him and smirked. "Though you might try giving your collar a couple of squeezes on the ear-side, Commander tight-pants."

Kendra snorted another laugh, though she had the good grace to try to hide it this time.

"I'm fine just how I am, thank you very much, Major," Carter countered. "And that's Master Commander tight-pants to you."

Kendra Castle approached Major Larsen and began making some finer adjustments to the uniform, that were of a more technical nature, rather than related to its fit.

"This will supply the nanomachines that are dispersed throughout the fabric," Kendra said, attaching a domino-sized device to Carina's waist at the small of her back.

"What's the benefit of this uniform, besides making me look cool?" Carina asked, while allowing Kendra to work.

"It's a self-repairing nano-composite material that hardens like diamond when stressed, but it also dissipates heat energy in much the same way my engineered cells do, so it protects against directed energy weapons too." Kendra continued to fuss over the uniform for a couple more seconds before stepping back and nodding, like a tailor who was satisfied with her work. "It won't make you post-human, but it might just save your life."

"It used to belong to my Master Medic, Rosalie Moss," Carter said.

He could almost see Rosalie's face in place of Carina's, and the sudden recollection that his Master Medic had died hit him harder than he expected it to. He fought back the emotions, none of which were helpful to him now. If war was coming, he'd have to get used to forming a hard outer shell again, much like their advanced battle uniforms.

"But Rosalie doesn't need it anymore, whereas you do," Carter added, before returning his attention to the shelf rack and hunting for the last few items he needed.

"I'll be sure to honor her memory," Major Larsen said.

There was zero trace of her usual sarcasm, which stopped Carter in his tracks. While he'd gotten accustomed to Carina's straight-talking ways, her last statement was spoken earnestly, and with deep respect.

"Thank you, Major, she'd appreciate that," Carter replied, with matching sincerity. "And so do I."

He grabbed his 57-EX revolver and attached its custom holster to the mounting point on his new uniform, then connected the frog and scabbard for his cutlass to his left hip, before sliding the weapon in place. It all felt so natural, he couldn't believe it had been more than a century since he'd last worn the items. He was about to leave when he saw another weapon on the shelf and stopped. Sliding the pistol across the shelf, he checked it over first then turned to Carina.

"Here, this might suit you better than a seven-kilojoule hand cannon," he said, holding the weapon out toward the major.

Carina took the holstered pistol and inspected it eagerly.

"So, what's this thing's secret then? Does it shoot miniaturized black holes, or bolts of lightning?"

"Your second guess isn't all that far off," Carter said, taking back the weapon and removing its ammo cell. "This is a hydrogen fusion plasma pistol, or FPP for short. It's another piece of tech long forgotten to Union science. It's basically a miniature sun."

He gave Carina the ammo cell and she weighed it in her hand.

"The pistol uses a hydrogen fusion reaction to generate pulses of high-energy plasma, encased in magnetic capsules," Carter continued, showing Carina how to load the ammo cell. "Since Aterniens wear dense scale armor, directed energy weapons are more effective than slug throwers. "A good shot can melt holes in them, whereas gauss slugs tend to bounce off their armor, much as they did against our reptile friends outside."

Carina released the ammo cell then slapped it in again and

loaded the weapon. It hummed menacingly and he was pleased to see that she appeared to both appreciate and respect its power.

"I like it, thank you, Commander," Carina said, again with genuine gratitude rather than sarcasm. She then flashed her eyes at the revolver on his hip. "I still prefer your 57-EX though, so I feel duty-bound to inform you that should you die in combat, I'll be taking it from your still-warm corpse."

"That's very thoughtful of you, Major," Carter replied, deploying some sarcasm of his own.

Suddenly, the lights flickered on inside the armory and in the corridor outside, and Master Engineer Castle poked her head around the door.

"I've managed to engage the battery backups, and scanned ahead," the engineer said. It was impossible to tell that she'd been mortally wounded only an hour ago. "We're clear to proceed to the bridge."

Carter nodded. "Okay, then let's find out what condition the Galatine is really in and see if we can't haul her ass out of this disgusting quagmire."

NINETEEN
ELECTRONIC GRUDGES

CARTER LED the party out of the armory and toward the bridge of the Galatine. His internal early warning system had climbed down from its earlier high, and while he kept his hand close to his holstered weapon as they progressed along the central corridor of the vessel, he was relieved that there was no need to use it.

Before long, Carter found himself standing in front of the door to the bridge, and he took a deep breath, preparing for the worst, but hoping for the best. The ship had nosed-dived into the quagmire that was satellite ZB-537, so there was always a risk that the bridge had been wrecked by the impact. However, as he pressed the button to open the hatchway, he had a good feeling about what he'd find inside.

Stepping over the threshold, Carter marched inside the Galatine's command center, closely followed by Major Larsen and Master Engineer Castle. It was cold, damp and dead, like a cemetery. Lights flickered on in response to his arrival, then the computers and consoles at each station cycled on and began to boot up, and slowly the bridge of the warship returned to life.

"I don't recognize the layout of these bridge stations," Carina said, arriving at his side. Kendra had at once gone to a bank of consoles at the rear of the bridge. "Some are in the same place, like the navigation station, but even that looks wildly different to what I'm used to."

"That's because Master Navigators have a unique interface with the ship that the rest of us lack," Carter explained. "And there's also a place at the station for the navigation gopher, which can even pilot the Galatine if needed."

Carina nodded then looked around the bridge, once again wonderstruck by the long-lost technology that the vessel employed.

"What are the other stations?" Carina asked.

Carter first pointed to the left side of the bridge, which was occupied by a long console in a waning crescent-moon shape.

"That's the Master Operator's station, which would have been Cai on this ship," he said. "It's all the science and ops roles merged into one." He turned again and pointed to a slab-like console raised and to the rear of the captain's chair. "That's tactical, which was where Brodie Kaur would stand and wreak havoc on the Aterniens with our 120mm cannons and plasma weapon." He gestured aft of the tactical station, to where Kendra was working. "And at the rear is a bank of engineering stations. Kendra liked to be on the bridge when she could."

Carina nodded again then her eyes lit up, and she dropped into the captain's chair, before crossing her legs and making herself comfortable.

"And this is where I sit, right?" she said, knowing full-well that it wasn't.

Carter didn't take the bait, and instead tapped a button on the arm of the occupied captain's chair, prompting a second seat to rise from the deck to its right. He smiled at his XO and gestured to it.

"Longswords didn't have executive officers, but they came equipped to support the role if needed."

Carina pushed herself out of the command chair, eager to inspect her new station. She ran her hand along the frame and pressed the dense foam padding that was covered in a durable synthetic fabric. Her actions were performed with such care and reverence, it was like she was conducting a ritual. She then blew out a sigh and dropped into the chair with an even broader smile on her face.

"I've always wanted to sit on the bridge of a Longsword," Carina said, gripping the arms of the chair like she was on a roller-coaster.

"Well, now you're second-in-command of one," Carter replied. Again, the fact that Carina was clearly in love with his old ship made him swell with pride. "Assuming we can get her off the ground, of course."

"That might be more difficult than we first thought."

Carter had a sudden sinking feeling, and he turned to his engineer, observing that she had the look of a woman with problems on her mind.

"The damage is worse than I'd hoped, so I'll need a little time to run a deeper analysis," Kendra added.

The console she was working on suddenly sparked and spluttered, and the display flickered like a faulty TV. Kendra cursed and kicked the base of the console, making the machine warble and sputter again. Remarkably, however, her heavy-handed tactics seemed to have stabilized it.

"Don't take too long, Kendra. That dirty hack you did on the Aternien spy probe could unravel at any moment, and I don't want to be caught out here with our pants down."

"Yes, boss, you don't need to remind me," Kendra replied. She had removed a panel and was now part-buried inside the console. "This would be a lot easier if I had RAEB, though."

Carter stroked his silver beard and thought for a moment. "Have you tried looking in engineering? He must be here somewhere."

"I peeked inside while you were getting the XO acquainted with her new weapons. He's not there."

Carter grunted and headed back to his chair, still stroking

his beard. He dropped into the seat, and looked left to the cubby where his gopher, JACAB, would normally be situated. However, the location was empty. Then his augmented eyes spotted something on the deck, beneath the cubby, tucked underneath his chair. He dropped to his knees and discovered a volleyball-sized object, covered by a century's-worth of dust and grime.

"Wait a second…" Carter said, his heart rate climbing as he picked up the object and brushed away the accumulated detritus to reveal a familiar metal shell. "JACAB!"

Carter hurriedly cleared more dust off his old command robot, then cleaned the grime from its single ocular port, but the bot's normally glowing red eye was as dark as midnight.

"That's your gopher, right?" Carina said, moving to his side and looking at the spherical machine. "Your command robot?"

"Yes, but he appears to be offline," Carter replied, his excitement waning fast. He turned the device over in his hands and even tried shaking it, but JACAB was as lifeless as a stone statue.

"His power cell will be dead," Kendra called over. "Try this."

Carter looked up and his engineer tossed a domino-sized power block at him, which he caught with one hand. Popping out the discharged cell, he replaced it with the new one, and the bot immediately powered up.

"Once he's booted, see if he knows where RAEB is, will you?" Kendra added, before returning to her work.

JACAB's anti-grav repeller activated and the device hovered out of his hands under his own steam. Maneuvering flaps flexed and compartments popped open to reveal scanning devices and other tools that the robot was able to employ, like a hyper-advanced Swiss-army knife. Finally, the ocular sensor – a probing, expressive red eye in the center of the machine – turned on and slowly focused on his face.

"Hey buddy!" Carter said. He was so happy to see his old gopher, he almost kissed the machine. "Welcome back!"

JACAB's eye narrowed and he made a crude buzzing noise that was distinctly reminiscent of someone blowing a raspberry.

"Come on, buddy, don't be like that," Carter said, crestfallen. "You know I had no choice."

JACAB blurted another digital raspberry at him, then withdrew and turned his back to Carter.

"What's wrong?" asked Carina. "Is JACAB malfunctioning?"

"No, he's fine," Carter sighed. From his enormous high of a moment ago, he was now flatter than a slashed tire. "He's just pissed-off with me."

"Can you two speak to one another?"

Carter shook his head. "No, not exactly. His data outputs feed into my uniform's comp-slate through a brain-machine interface, which also allows him to pick up on my feelings and intentions. It's like he knows my thoughts, and I can sense his too."

"I think I know JACAB's thoughts pretty clearly, even without a brain-machine interface," Carina replied. "And I can see where he's coming from; you did leave him here, after all."

Carter bristled at the accusation, but JACAB's reaction was quite the opposite. The bot slowly turned toward Carina and his eye widened before JACAB made a sequence of brighter chirrups and bleeps, then hovered over to her and lurked by her shoulder.

"Oh, so it's like that is it?" Carter said, hands on hips.

JACAB blew another robotic raspberry at him then hovered even closer to Carina, so that the machine was practically nestling on her shoulder, like a pirate captain's parrot.

"He'll come around, boss, just give him time," Kendra called over. "Hey, JACAB, have you seen RAEB?"

The machine bleeped and warbled then hovered over to a compartment at the rear of the bridge, close to where Kendra was working. It cycled through a series of tools then used the implement it had selected to unlock and open the door. Kendra peered inside and squealed with excitement.

"RAEB!" she said, removing the engineering robot and cleaning it off.

A power block was swiftly inserted into the machine, and the device hummed into life. RAEB went through a similar boot-up sequence, which took longer on account of the significantly greater number of tools the bot had at its disposal, then a red eye lit up in the ocular sensor in the center.

"Good to see you RAEB!" Kendra said, rubbing the top of the machine's head as if it were a pet. "Damn, I've missed you!"

RAEB squealed and warbled then flew up to Kendra and nuzzled her like a cat.

"What the hell?" Carter complained. "How come you don't get the cold shoulder treatment like I did?"

"Because I wasn't the one who gave the order to scuttle the Galatine," Kendra hit back, bluntly and with more than a little repressed anger. "I'm still working on forgiving you for that, so you can't blame RAEB and JACAB for being pissed too."

JACAB blew another raspberry at him and RAEB quickly followed with one of his own. Carter cursed under his breath and shook his head. His happy reunion had turned sour quicker than a pint of milk left out in the summer sun.

"Just plug the damned thing into the computer and tell me if this crate will fly or not," Carter said, sulking.

Kendra and RAEB got to work, while JACAB observed. The two machines squawked and warbled to each other, speaking their own unique language. On occasions in the past, the noise had driven Carter to distraction, but he had to admit that hearing the electronic symphony again after so long felt wholesome.

"The good news is, I think she'll fly," Kendra said, after a few minutes of frenetic work. "But it looks like the Union butchers that decommissioned her also ripped out the primary core block. Without that, we're going nowhere fast."

"I expected as much, and so I've already given that problem some thought," Carter replied. "The main core block is basically just a beefed-up sub-core, which means we can run a few sub-cores in parallel to replace it."

Kendra considered this then looked at RAEB, who returned a shrugging motion with the maneuvering flaps on his shoulders.

"Okay, but if we pull sub-cores from other parts of the ship, it will just cripple our secondary systems," Kendra pointed out. "We'd be fixing one thing, only to break two or three more."

"That's why we're taking them from the other Longswords."

It was his XO who had answered, and Carter was impressed by her intuition.

"If we can find the remains of one or two other Longswords in the asteroid field, then we should be able to salvage enough sub-cores to network together a primary processor," Carina continued.

Kendra puffed out her cheeks and breathed a weary, rasping sigh.

"I guess it's possible," she said. RAEB appeared to nod in agreement. "But we'd need to install the core OS, and that code was purged from all Union archives more than century ago, as per the terms of the armistice. I might be a half-decent hacker, but I can't write an entire Longsword OS from scratch."

Carter smiled then removed the core block from his right shoulder pocket. JACAB and RAEB become suddenly very interested; their eyes glowed brighter and the machines chatted to each other at a rapidly increased speed.

"The Galatine's OS is all on here. Every last line of code."

It took a lot to shock Kendra Castle, but at that moment, her bio-engineered heart had stopped beating.

"You backed up the Longsword base code before you

decommissioned the Galatine?" his engineer asked, and Carter smiled and flashed his eyes.

"Do you realize how horrendously illegal that was?" Carina added. She was similarly aghast. "If the Union had caught you with that core block, you'd never have seen daylight again."

"Then it's a good job they never caught me," Carter hit back. "The fact is the order to decommission the Longswords was the stupidest decision the Union ever made. I knew it then, just as I know it now."

He tossed the core block across the full length of the bridge, and he heard Carina suck in a sharp intake of breath, but Kendra Castle caught it without even flinching. His engineer grasped the device in her fist and shook it, triumphantly.

"Find me some sub-cores and I'll get the Galatine back into action, like she was never gone," Kendra said. She was practically fizzing with nervous energy and excitement.

Suddenly, JACAB hummed back toward him and hovered about a meter away. His red eye narrowed and widened, then JACAB nodded and warbled cheerfully.

"So, am I forgiven?" Carter asked, beaming a smile at his gopher.

JACAB warbled again then blew out a loud, almost violent electronic raspberry, before hovering to Carina's side, and resting on her shoulder.

TWENTY
SHIP OF GHOSTS

MASTER ENGINEER KENDRA CASTLE slid into the rear seat of the Union shuttle, and was joined soon after by RAEB, her engineering bot. The automaton hummed and bleeped a message to JACAB, who was sitting on Major Larsen's lap like a cat, and Carter's personal gopher replied in kind.

"That's the last of the repair drones set to work," Kendra said, as the gull-wing door whirred shut. "There's nothing left in the hold of this shuttle now, but emergency equipment and our food rations."

Carter glanced over his shoulder from his position in the pilot's seat and could see the interior walls of the recon shuttle's hold for the first time. Without the mass of equipment that Kendra had packed into it before they'd departed from Station Foxtrot, the shuttle seemed surprisingly spacious.

"Will the repair drones be enough to fix up the Galatine?" Carter asked his engineer.

"I reckon so," Kendra replied, though she appeared more certain than her non-committal response implied. "Thanks to RAEB, we've taught the drones how to repair the Longsword's systems, and I found a supply of industrial nanomachines in engineering, which can restore hull integrity to the most severely damaged sections. Once we find the sub-cores from other wrecked Longswords and install the OS from your illicit core block, I think the Galatine will be able to limp home under her own power."

"Outstanding work, Kendra," Carter said with feeling, before returning to his instruments. "The Galatine doesn't deserve to be towed back to Union space like an old junker."

He engaged the take-off thrusters and lifted the shuttle out of the mud and into the muggy atmosphere of the exo-planet. From their newly elevated vantage point, he could see the small army of repair drones scuttling around the ship, fixing a century's worth of neglect and decay.

"How are we doing with locating another scuttled Longsword?" Carter asked, this time addressing his question to Major Larsen in the co-pilot's seat.

"I've loaded some waypoints into the navigation system already," Carina replied. Carter noticed that she was stroking JACAB like a pet, and he rolled his eyes. "It's lucky that JACAB was able to monitor the final trajectories of the other Longswords, at least for a time, because otherwise this would be a needle-in-a-haystack exercise," his XO added.

Carter checked the nav system and set a course for the closest waypoint marker. Before long, he was weaving the shuttle through the dense array of jagged rocks and planetoids that formed the Piazzi asteroid field. His senses were on permanent high, ready to conduct evasive maneuvers at a moment's notice to avoid the rocks that crisscrossed space all around them, any one of which could spoil their day in an instant. It was intense work that challenged even his augmented piloting skills and reaction times, though it would have been a cakewalk for his genius Master Navigator, Amaya Reid.

"I'm getting a strong signal, a few thousand kilometers ahead," Kendra said.

She was monitoring the sensor data closely, with the help of her gopher. RAEB bleeped and squawked, then interfaced with the shuttle's nav system and displayed an analysis of a nearby asteroid on the main screen.

"RAEB reckons there's something on that rock," Kendra said, leaning over the front bench to get a better look.

"It's about two kilometers across as its widest point, so it's certainly big enough," Carter commented. "It's unstable as hell though." He turned to JACAB, still relaxing with Carina's hand resting on his spherical metal shell. "What do you think, buddy? Is it worth a look?"

JACAB warbled then blew a raspberry at him before nuzzling deeper into his XO's lap. Carter sighed and shook his head.

"I know what you're trying to do, and if I'm honest, it's a little childish."

JACAB made another unpleasant sound then turned his glowing red eye away. Carina simply shrugged, so Carter returned to his controls and steered toward the target asteroid, muttering under his breath as he did so.

"There's definitely a Longsword down there, or least the remains of one," Kendra added, as the shuttle drew closer. Unlike Carter's bot, RAEB was hard at work, using his unique array of tools to analyze the scan readings. "It looks like it might be the Arondight."

Carter swooped in closer to the asteroid and swung around the reverse side. The wreckage of a crashed starship was apparent straight away, without the need for scanners.

"Damn it, there's barely anything left of the Arondight but scrap," Carter growled. "I'm heading to the next waypoint."

He felt a swell of anger building inside him. The Longswords were not just machines to their augmented crews. The relationship between Master Commander and Longsword was akin to that of a mythical dragon and their chosen rider. To see the ruins of the Arondight smote across the harsh and barren surface of the asteroid was like happening upon a comrade who had fallen on the battlefield and been left to rot.

An hour passed with little conversation between them, before a chevron denoting the second waypoint marker blinked up on the screen. It was followed soon afterward by a resonant chime, and excited warbles and squeaks from both RAEB and JACAB. The two gophers took to the air and hovered over the top of the console, chatting to each other, and waving their maneuvering flaps and sensor antennae in the same way people gesticulate with their hands when a conversation is in full flow.

"Swing around to the right," Kendra said, sounding just as excited as her bot. "I think it's the Caliburn, and if these readings are correct, it's reasonably intact."

Carter adjusted course, feeling a swell of excitement, despite his best efforts to remain realistic about their chances. Soon, the engine section of the Longsword came into view, but it had smashed clean off the rest of the ship and was mangled and broken. What hope had filled him quickly started to bleed away, then he saw the front section of the Caliburn and his grip on the controls tightened so hard that he bent the column.

"Bingo…" Carina said, smiling at him.

"It's the Caliburn alright," Kendra added. Unlike the others, she was focused on the scanner readout and hadn't even looked at the ship out of the cockpit window. "Whatever cracked her in half must have been a hell of an impact, but the forward section is intact, so there's a strong chance we can recover the sub-cores from the main bridge."

"I'm going in for a closer look," said Carter. He dove the shuttle toward the forward section of the warship, illuminating it with floodlights, like a submarine exploring the wreck of the Titanic.

"The emergency bulkheads between sections J and K are in place," he commented, while reading the fresh data that was being relayed via RAEB. "There are a dozen other minor hull breaches, but emergency seals are in place. It might even hold pressure."

JACAB hummed over to the bank of controls in front of him then interfaced with the navigation system. A second later, a docking hatch on the ventral hull was highlighted.

"You think we can get in there?" Carter asked his bot. The machine bleeped and nodded then returned to RAEB and continued its electronic conversation with him.

"Okay then, here goes nothing…" Carter said.

He adjusted his heading and skimmed the surface of the Caliburn to the docking hatch in question. On other occasions, he might have sanity-checked the decision with Kendra first. However, he was conscious that it had been his first interaction with JACAB since they were reunited that hadn't involved the bot giving him the cold shoulder, and he didn't want to risk upsetting him again by not heeding his advice.

A hard thump reverberated through the shuttle as it made contact with the Caliburn's docking hatch. The steady whirr of gears followed as the hatch mechanisms locked together, then a light on his console flashed green.

"That's a hard seal," Carter said, putting the shuttle into a mooring configuration and jumping out of his seat. "Last one on-board buys dinner back at base."

Carter and Kendra wasted no time in entering the cargo hold of the shuttle, but Carina appeared to be less enthusiastic.

"Hold up, the forward section of that wreck might hold pressure, but I'm not reading any oxygen, and the interior is colder than an Eskimo's nose."

Carter smiled at his XO. "You're in the A-team now, Major. We Longsword officers are equipped for every eventuality."

Carter tapped the top of his shoulder three times and the head covering built into his battle uniform engaged. In a matter of seconds, nanomachines in the unique material had fabricated a close-fitting helmet with a transparent visor.

"That's a neat trick," Carina said. She appeared suitably impressed.

"The nanomachines also produce oxygen from the carbon dioxide we breathe out, using a type of electrolysis." Carter shrugged. "Don't ask me how."

"You could ask me, if you wanted, but I'd advise against it," Kendra chipped in. She'd also activated her head covering. "It's boring as shit."

Carina laughed. "That's okay, I'm not interested in the how. I am, however, extremely interested in breathing, so it's good to know I'll still be able to do that, once this suit hems me in."

The major repeated the triggering action, and her uniform knitted the covering over her head. Carter laughed as the process took place; it looked like his XO was being mummified alive, and her petrified expression suggested she felt that way too. Carter then drew his experimental revolver and nodded to his engineer.

"Crank it, Kendra. Let's see what's in there."

Kendra grabbed the locking hatch on the door and turned it. There was a sharp hiss of escaping gas, as the air inside the shuttle equalized with the lower-pressure environment inside the stricken Longsword. Carter stepped through first, and his uniform began to luminesce. Combined with the light generated by his XO and Master Engineer, it was enough to see where he was going.

"It's freezing in this thing," Carina said, while rubbing her shoulders. "Is there a way to turn up the temperature?"

Carter frowned. "It feels fine to me. Maybe you're just used to the modern comforts of Union starships and bases."

"I don't have your superhuman biology, remember," Carina hit back. "You might not feel the cold, but I do."

"Just do some star jumps and you'll be fine," Carter replied, indifferently.

The look he got from his XO in return implied that she didn't particularly rate his suggestion, but he ploughed ahead regardless. If Carina was going to be a Longsword officer, then he couldn't make special allowances for her, as cruel as that sounded.

Suddenly, RAEB hummed toward them. Carter hadn't noticed that the engineering bot had already zoomed ahead and reconnoitered the ship. JACAB, meanwhile, was bringing up the rear. His bot was anxiously turning his red eye from one dark corner of the Longsword's interior to another, as the wrecked vessel creaked and moaned like a haunted ghost ship.

"It's okay, buddy, it's just the sound of the hull flexing," Carter said, in an effort to calm his bot's quivering circuits.

JACAB warbled anxiously then hovered closer, situating itself between Carter and Carina. Carina smiled at the automaton and rested a hand on his smooth surface.

"We've got you, JACAB," she said, warmly. "Just stick with us and you'll be fine."

The bot warbled again, this time more confidently, and hovered alongside the major with a touch more assuredness. Carter huffed a laugh and left them to it; he was eager to hear what RAEB had discovered on his scouting foray.

"According to RAEB, the bridge is safe and the sub-core processors we need are intact," Kendra reported. She was reading the information on a comp-slate that the nanomachines in her battle uniform had fabricated on her forearm. "But this asteroid is highly unstable, and the ship could be dislodged at any moment. It looks like we arrived just in time."

"Or at precisely the worst time, depending how you look at it," Carter replied. "Let's get the job done and get back to the Galatine." He turned to his gopher, who was sticking to Major Larsen like glue. "Hey, buddy, are you up for helping RAEB to recover to the sub-cores?"

JACAB's eye grew wider, and the machine appeared to shudder, as if someone was drumming on him like a high-hat cymbal.

"Don't worry, I'll be with you the whole time," Carina said, winking at the bot. "You can do it; I know you can."

JACAB looked at Carina, squeaked and warbled, then turned back to Carter and nodded.

"Good man," Carter said, smiling warmly at his gopher. "Now, let's get to work. I've already had enough of asteroids and ghost ships."

Major Larsen moved ahead to join Kendra and RAEB, and JACAB followed her like a puppy on a leash. Despite the fact his bot seemed to have formed an attachment to his XO rather than himself, he still felt glad that the machine was feeling better. In truth, he was guilt-ridden about the fact he'd left the automaton behind, despite being explicitly ordered to do so. In his heart, he felt like he didn't really deserve to have him back.

Carter spent a couple of minutes inspecting other rooms en route to the bridge, but quickly found the exercise to be depressing. His comparison of the Caliburn to a ghost ship was all too apt. Everywhere he went there were empty tables and sparse, abandoned rooms. Occasionally, he saw something that hinted at the life that once existed on-board, such as an old coffee cup or empty snack packet that someone had forgotten to put in the recycler. However, this only seemed to reinforce the tragedy and injustice that had befallen the once great ship.

Entering the bridge, Carter was pleased to see his skeleton crew hard at work recovering the computer sub-cores they needed to bring the Galatine back to life. He walked over to the commander's chair and rested a hand on it. The seat had once been occupied by Master Commander Erica Giambra, whose reputation as a fearsome warrior was well won. Yet, she was also a fierce friend to those who knew her well, himself included. Carter sighed and shook his head. Erica Giambra had died from a Trifentanil overdose only five years after the war had ended.

Like so many of his old friends, Erica Giambra had found the life of an ostracized loner to be too much to bear. She had been seventy-two years old at the time of her death, which Carter reasoned wasn't a terrible number. Yet, the fact he'd already lived for a century longer than his fellow Master Commander only reinforced how much more she could have given, had the Union only welcomed her home.

Suddenly, a shiver raced down his spine and he felt cold. At first, he simply attributed his reaction to the bleak memories that his visit to the bridge of the Caliburn had stirred up, but he soon realized it was something more. He glanced across to JACAB and saw that the bot was also looking at him. To anyone else, the machine's glowing red eye and fluttering panels and antennae would have simply looked random and synthetic in nature, but he knew his gopher as well as he knew his own face. JACAB had detected that something was wrong.

"Kendra, have RAEB interface with the shuttle's sensors," Carter said, returning to his crew-mates. "And see if you can get the main viewer online."

"Sure, boss, but what am I looking for?" Kendra asked.

His brow furrowed and he looked up, as if the dark shadow of his enemy was creeping above him. "I don't know, but something's not right," Carter replied. "How soon until you have the sub-cores in hand?"

"Not long; two or three minutes at most," Kendra replied, now also appearing apprehensive.

Carter nodded and grunted an acknowledgment, but still his uneasy feeling persisted. Then RAEB suddenly warbled and shook from side to side to get Kendra's attention. The engineer stopped working, checked her comp-slate, and her expression hardened.

"The shuttle's scanners are reading two new contacts in the TESS-961S system," Kendra said, her tone urgent. "Both are heading toward this quadrant of the asteroid field."

Carter cursed and turned to the viewscreen. He didn't need to ask if Kendra had managed to get it working, because a second later it flashed into life. The image was fuzzy at first, but quickly resolved, and before long a clear view of the new arrivals was displayed, front and center.

"One of those of is a Sesh-class Aternien scout," Kendra said, as Carter moved close to the screen. "And it looks like it carries Royal Court markings, including the Ankh of Aternus."

"The Grand Vizier…" Carter said, closing his hands into fists. "What the hell is that bastard doing out here?" He turned back to his engineer. "Has your hack of the Aternien spy probe failed?"

Kendra shrugged. "I have no-way to know from here, but it's possible."

Carina joined him, followed by JACAB, who hovered above their heads.

"What's that second ship?" Carina asked. She sounded more concerned about the mystery vessel than the possible arrival of the Vizier. "I've never seen anything like it."

RAEB warbled and JACAB spun around. The two bots conversed for a moment, then JACAB hovered in front of him, bleeping anxiously. Carter checked the comp-slate on his forearm and saw that his gopher had transmitted a technical analysis of the new vessel.

"It looks like a flying soliton warp engine, but there are no crew compartments or weapons. The whole thing is being piloted remotely. But why?"

Carina cursed and clicked her fingers. "They're here for the same reason we are. They're going to steal the Galatine."

Kendra plucked the final sub-core from the console then jumped up. RAEB squawked and her comp-slate chimed, urging her to check the new update.

"The XO is right," Kendra said. "The second vessel is a warp transporter. If they latch that onto the Galatine, we can kiss our old ship goodbye, this time forever."

Carter shook his head. "It's worse than that. If the Aterniens claim the Galatine then they'll wield her against the Union. And with a weapon like that, we don't stand a chance."

Kendra Castle marched toward him. The fire in her eyes was back; the same fire he remembered from their time at war.

"That's not going to happen, boss," Kendra said. "I'd rather blow her up myself than let those bastards turn her against us."

Carter felt his augments kick into gear, flooding his body with a burst of chemicals that ramped up his alertness, strength, and endurance to levels that a normal human body simply could not sustain. His hand instinctively went to his sword. The opportunity to use it again was coming far sooner than he imagined.

"No-one is taking the Galatine from us again," Carter announced, meeting the eyes off his engineer and XO in turn. "It's time we remind the Aterniens that they're not gods, and they're not immortal. If they want a war, I'll give them one."

TWENTY-ONE
MOVE AND COUNTERMOVE

CARTER SET the recon shuttle to autopilot then took his hands off the controls and studied the scan readout on the main screen, stroking his beard as he did so. The Aternien scout ship had already landed on exo-planet ZB-537 alongside the Galatine, while the warp frame that was intended to steal his ship remained in orbit above it.

"The Aternien spy probe is back online, and scattering outbound signals," Kendra reported. While he was focused on the scout, his engineer had been trying to reach the Union to warn them what was happening. "I've tried to get a message to Admiral Krantz, but no joy."

"Can we take out the probe then call for backup?" Carina asked.

"That won't work either, I'm afraid," Carter cut in. "The Aternien scout is also scattering outbound comms. Even if we destroy the probe, we'd need to effectively exit the asteroid field to get a clear transmission to the Union. By the time we contact them, and they get here, the Galatine will be long gone."

Carina cursed under her breath then began drumming her fingers on the arm of her chair. Carter didn't need his post-human senses to know that she was deeply frustrated.

"Maybe the Union spotted the Aterniens jumping into the TESS-961S system and are already preparing to send a force to help us?" Carina suggested.

From the halfhearted way she offered the thought, his XO knew she was grasping at straws. For his own part, he'd already given the matter due consideration and come to the simple conclusion that they'd been soundly outmaneuvered.

"That ship warped in right on top of the Galatine," Carter said, still stroking his silver beard. "They knew exactly where to look, and what sort of ships to bring in order to remain undetected. My guess is that the Grand Vizier was watching us this whole time, and we basically led him right to where X marks the spot."

Carina stopped tapping her fingers and closed her hand into a fist. Clearly, she didn't like to be made a fool of, and neither did he. However, they weren't beaten yet.

"Kendra, what sort of opposition are we looking at?" Carter asked.

Kendra worked her consoles for a second, ably assisted by RAEB, then a tactical analysis was overlaid on the shuttle's main screen.

"The scout ship delivered a platoon-strength troop of Immortals onto the exo-planet, which have deployed to secure the entry point into the Galatine," Kendra began. "And as we suspected because of Royal Court markings, I spotted a familiar face down there too."

The screen updated and Carter found himself staring at the Aternien Grand Vizier. The imperious Aternien leader and second-in-command to Markus Aternus himself was personally overseeing the operation to steal the Galatine.

"There's someone else with him," Carina said, pointing to a figure that stood to the Vizier's left. "But I don't think I've seen her before."

Kendra frowned then worked her consoles for a moment, before shaking her head.

"I can't get a clean image of whoever that is." She gently tapped her gopher with the knuckle of her index finger, and the machine bleeped and warbled, eagerly awaiting her instructions. "Hey, RAEB, do you think you can get us a better look at the goldie standing next to the Vizier?"

RAEB warbled again, nodded then interfaced with the shuttle's systems. The vessel veered off at speed, and even with his super-human reactions, Carter was caught off guard and almost head-butted the side window.

"Damn it, RAEB, a little warning next time, please?" Carter said.

The machine bleeped, apologetically, then the shuttle resumed its original vector. Shortly after, the screen updated to show the mystery Aternien soldier in vivid detail. To Carter, at least, the figure's purpose was no longer a mystery.

"That's an Overseer," he observed, recalling the few times he'd faced one of the fierce Aternien warriors. None of the memories were pleasant. "They're effectively middle-ranking officers, who command ships and larger troops of Immortals."

Carter studied the elegant warrior, who was dressed in Aternien scale armor like the Immortals, but with the addition of a Tyrian purple sash, a color often reserved for elites and royalty in ancient Egyptian culture. The Overseer also wore a golden helm and cloth face mask that covered the nose and mouth, made from the same Tyrian purple material as the sash. Even so, from what little he could see of the Aternien's face and gleaming blue eyes, it was clear that this Overseer was a woman.

"What is that she's carrying?" Carina commented.

"They call it a war spear, but the name doesn't really do it justice," Carter replied. The unpleasant memory of being struck by similar weapons was vivid in his mind. "The pointy end is bad enough, but those spears can also shoot blasts of particle energy that are far deadlier than the rifles the rank-and-file Immortals are armed with."

Carter turned away from the screen and frowned at his XO. "I'm surprised you don't already know everything about the Overseers, considering your studies. Any additional insights would be valuable, especially if we have to face her in battle."

Carina shook her head. "The Union archive has barely any information on the Overseers," she admitted. "But I can offer some insight." She worked the controls and focused the image on the Overseer's golden, dragon-scale armor, then added an image of the Vizier's armor for comparison.

"Spot the difference," his XO said, rocking back in her chair again.

"I don't like games, Major," Carter grunted. "What am I looking at?"

Carina tapped a control, and a section of each suit of armor was highlighted.

"The Overseer's armor doesn't bear Royal Court markings, which means she's yet to ascend to the inner circle," Carina explained. "To gain a position at Markus Aternus' court is the highest honor an Aternien can aspire to."

Carter grunted, understanding his XO's logic. "That means this Overseer has a point to prove, which means she'll fight tooth and nail to stop us."

"So, what's the plan, boss?" Kendra cut in.

Carter had already turned his bio-engineered mind to the problem of what to do about the Aterniens, and while tactics and cunning were traits he often employed in battle, on this occasion, the Aterniens held all the cards.

"The plan is simple," Carter said, turning to his officers. "They know we're coming, so we have no tactical advantage. To retake the Galatine we have to win her back in a straight fight."

"That suits me just fine," Carina said, returning to tapping her fingers impatiently on the arm of the chair.

While he appreciated his XO's eagerness to fight, they were outnumbered and outgunned, and facing an enemy that didn't tire and didn't feel pain. He had personally endured a brutal regime of genetic modifications and technological augments designed specifically to make him more than a match for the Aterniens. The simple truth was that Carina Larsen was only human.

"Look, Major, I know I agreed to take you on as my XO, but this is where it gets real," Carter said. He'd put off confronting her for as long as possible, but he'd run out time. "I value you as an officer, and you've proven that you can handle yourself, but the hard fact of the matter is that against these Aterniens, you're vulnerable."

Carina frowned. "What are you saying?"

Carter knew he was making a pig's ear of his explanation. He sighed and was about to try a more direct approach, when his engineer beat him to it.

"He means that in this fight, you're more of a liability than a help," Kendra said. She shrugged. "And I mean that in the nicest possible way."

Carina snorted. "Calling me a liability is you being nice?"

Carter shot his engineer a dirty look, and tried to dig himself out of the hole she'd hurled him into.

"What Kendra means is that you're at far greater risk than we are, even wearing that battle uniform," Carter said, trying to make his point as succinctly as possible. "This fight will be hard and fast, and while Kendra and I are built for this sort of action, you're not. Having you out there with us is a dangerous distraction. We can't be responsible for your safety, and still focus on the mission."

Carter had fully expected his XO to fight her corner with the same sort of tenacity she'd shown on other occasions, but to his surprise, she nodded and appeared to accept his points.

"I get it, so I'll make this easy for you," Carina replied. "On the field, you treat me no differently than you would Master Engineer Castle or any other Longsword officer. That means if I go down, you continue on mission. I don't want or deserve any special considerations."

Carter frowned; it wasn't the answer he had expected, and he was stuck for how to respond. However, Major Larsen wasn't done talking.

"I'm your XO, so I'll obey your orders, whatever you decide," Carina continued. "But the admiral gave me this position, and I intend to fulfill my duty. Unless you wish to relieve me, of course."

Carter drew in a deep breath and looked at Kendra Castle in an effort to gauge her reaction. However, his engineer just shrugged, which was her unhelpful way of saying the decision was all on him. As if to highlight that time was limited, the navigation computer chimed an update, and the tactical system followed soon after.

"The Aternien scout has taken off from the exo-planet and is heading our way," Carina said, calmly communicating the update. She turned to him. "What are your orders, Master Commander Rose?"

Carter shook his head and growled through gritted teeth. "Don't get killed, those are my orders, Major," he snarled, jabbing a finger at his XO. "Oh, and give me a tactical analysis of that ship too."

"Aye, sir," Carina replied, immediately getting to work. "And while I intend to fully comply with both of your orders, you should know that I will pay especially close attention to the first one…"

"Good," Carter grunted. He was already regretting his decision.

"The Aternien scout is twice our size, and coming in fast," Carina continued, as a sensor scan of the enemy vessel appeared on the screen. "Even if we wanted to run, we'd never outpace it. I'm also detecting what appears to be a variant of the Aternien energy weapon we saw on the larger Khopesh destroyers. It's difficult to know how powerful it is, but it's a good bet they pack enough of a punch to reduce this shuttle to atoms."

"Kendra, this is where you get to work your magic," Carter said, glancing back at his engineer, while resuming full manual control of the shuttle. "Use RAEB and JACAB and see what you can do to boost our engines and thruster capacity. We might not be able to outgun or outrun the scout, but we can surprise it."

RAEB and JACAB both hovered into the rear section of the shuttle and before long, an access panel and maintenance hatch had been levered open. Both bots swiftly disappeared inside to work on the shuttle's systems directly, much in the same way that the nanomachines in his blood boosted his own capabilities.

"Engine power is up by thirty percent," Kendra reported, while making her own adjustments. "And I've got you up to fifty percent more thruster capacity, but don't go mad, because at that level, they won't last long before burning out."

"If this works, it'll be enough," Carter replied. He had already adjusted course and had placed a large asteroid between them and the Aternien scout. He turned to his XO. "This shuttle is armed with missiles, right?"

Carina nodded. "Yes, but we only have two."

"That's fine, I only need one. Let me know as soon as you get a lock on the scout."

He tightened his hands around the controls, aimed the shuttle at the apex of the asteroid and maxed-out their boosted engines. Every deck plate and metal panel on the ship began to shake and rattle like they were at the epicenter of a major earthquake.

"Not that I don't have absolute confidence in you, but what the hell are you doing?" his XO asked.

Carina's hands were wrapped around the arms of her chair, holding on so tightly that her knuckles had drained of blood, while her eyes were locked onto the asteroid that was directly ahead, and looming larger by the second.

"Since the Aterniens seem to always be a step ahead of us, I'm guessing they know the capabilities of this shuttle just as well as we do," Carter replied. He'd tightened his hold on the control column such that it was the only thing on the ship that wasn't shaking. "They'll expect to intercept us before we clear the asteroid. I intend to give them a little surprise."

Warning alarms lit up the consoles all across the dashboard, but he ignored them. All ships had built in tolerances, and he was going to test them to their very limit.

"Structural integrity is falling fast," Kendra called out. She'd been forced to raise her voice to be heard over the pulsating thrum of their engines. "This isn't a Longsword, boss; there's only so much RAEB can do to hold her together."

"Just a few more seconds," Carter said. "Standby on missiles…"

His eyes were fixed on the point in space where the surface of the asteroid met the void. He slipped his hand onto the thruster controls and felt his senses kick into overdrive. Despite their hazardous velocity, their rapid progress appeared to him like nothing more than a leisurely drive down a country lane. Then another alarm blared out inside the cabin, but Carter knew the reason even before his XO had managed to call out the danger.

"Collision alert!" Carina cried. "Contact, dead ahead!"

The Aternien scout ship rocketed past them, so close that Carter could make out the vexed expression on the face of the Aternien pilot. At the same time, the shuttle blasted over the surface of the asteroid, vaporizing the top layer of rock into a smokey plume, like a jet aircraft taking off from a dusty runway. He pulsed the thrusters and spun them around in the blink of an eye so that the nose of the shuttle was pointed directly at their enemy.

"Target lock!" Carina called out, her eyes wide and voice shaking even harder than the shuttlecraft.

"Fire!"

Major Larsen reached out with trembling hands and flicked the switch to launch the shuttle's only two missiles. The weapons launched and tracked the Aternien scout ship, as it desperately attempted to alter course and reacquire them. Countermeasures were launched and one of the missiles took the bait, veering off course, but the second was not fooled. An explosion lit up the darkness, but his augmented eyes could already see that the weapon had struck true.

"Direct hit, heavy damage to the scout," Carina reported. Her heart was beating so hard that Carter could hear it even above the tumult of the shaking deck plates and strained engines. "It's no longer pursuing."

Carter nodded and grunted an acknowledgement. "I'm resuming course to the exo-planet…"

He swung the shuttle back on course and reduced the power to the already strained systems. Suddenly, another alarm rang out, but this time there was no opportunity for Carina to give her report. An Aternien energy blast hammered into the aft section of the shuttle and punched a hole through the cargo bay door, causing an explosive decompression of the main cabin. All their remaining tools and provisions were blown into space in an instant, and were it not for their harnesses, he and his crew would have been swallowed by the void too.

The head coverings in their battle uniforms automatically engaged to protect them from the cold ravages of empty space, and soon the alarms were silenced. RAEB and JACAB hummed out of their respective access hatches and directed angry warbles and squawks in his direction. Both machines were pinballing off the inner walls like they were drunk.

"Sorry about that, guys," Carter called out, holding up his hand. "Are you both okay?"

The automatons whirred and blew raspberries at him, before setting themselves down on the rear passenger bench beside Kendra. Both were quivering like plates of jello on a washing machine.

"I'll take that as a yes," Carter said, managing a weak smile.

Despite everything, he still found their childlike impudence to be endearing.

"It may not look like it, but we actually got lucky," Kendra said. She was assessing the damage, while stroking JACAB and RAEB with her free hand. "That blast missed our engines, though we still took heavy damage."

"Will we make it to the exo-planet?" Carter asked. He didn't care if the shuttle collapsed into a pile of scrap, so long as it did so after they'd successfully made it to the surface.

"We'll make it, but only just," Kendra confirmed. "As long as we don't get blown out of the sky first, of course."

Carter nodded, while continuing to fight the controls to keep them on course. The Aternien particle blast had knocked out several thrusters and part of their navigation system, making the shuttle handle like a yacht with a damaged rudder.

"What's the status of the Aternien scout?"

His question was not met with an immediate response, and he turned to his XO to see her in a catatonic state, staring blankly out of the cockpit glass.

"Hey, Carina," Carter said, snapping his fingers in front of her face. "Stay with us, okay?"

Carina met his eyes and nodded, before letting out a shaky sigh and placing her trembling fingers back onto the consoles.

"The scout came off much worse out of that exchange than us. It won't be able to catch us before we land, but it is still flying."

Out of nowhere, an energy blast flashed through the open bay door and punched a hole through the cockpit glass, like cigarette ash burning through the arm of a couch.

"It looks like it's still firing too," Carter said, staring wide-eyed at the gaping hole in his cockpit. "The sooner we touch down, the better."

He increased power to the engines, despite the risk of overloading them, and soon the exo-planet had filled the view ahead. Blasts continued to chase them as the Aternien scout tried desperately to shoot them down, but the volleys became increasingly wayward as the distance between the warring vessels grew larger.

"I'm going to set us down in that swampy forest, about five hundred meters from the Galatine," Carter said, locking his proposed landing coordinates into the barely-functional navigation computer. "It's on an elevated plane, and will provide natural cover, while we figure out how to assault their position."

Carter maneuvered them into the sticky atmosphere of the exoplanet and friction began to blister away the damaged sections of the shuttle's beleaguered hull. Flames licked at the insides, threatening to turn the craft into a pizza oven, but fire suppression systems, combined with their heat-resistant battle uniforms, proved sufficient to ensure they survived entry uncooked.

"Thirty seconds till we're down," Carter said. For the first time in what seemed like hours, his augmented senses had wound down to the point where his engineered heart wasn't beating at a million cycles per second. "Salvage whatever weapons and ammunition you can, and be ready to move out as soon as we land."

"Got it boss," Kendra said. She was already loading cells into her twin energy pistols.

Carter glanced at his XO and was pleased to see that she looked calmer and less drawn. "Are you still with us, Major?"

Carina tapped her new energy pistol and smiled weakly. "Just let me at them, sir."

Carter nodded, then his senses spiked into overdrive, like he'd been injected with pure adrenaline. He checked the shuttle's scanners, but there were no obvious threats, and the Aternien scout had long since stopped firing at them. Then he saw something glinting under the sunlight at the edge of the tree line; a golden figure, holding a golden staff. He cursed and tried to alter course, but it was too late, and a blast from the

Overseer's war spear destroyed their engines in a single shot. The shuttle lost all power and dropped like a dead weight. He fought the controls, but they were unresponsive, and there was nothing he could do to slow their descent.

"Hold on!" Carter called out.

The shuttle fell through the sky, screaming like a Stuka dive bomber on an attack run, and crashed into the forest in full force. The cockpit glass exploded inward and tree branches and splintered wood burst inside, threatening to skewer him like a knight's lance. Then the ship hit the rocks and cartwheeled out of control, tumbling end over end for what seemed like an eternity, until it thudded into the base of a hill and came to a sharp and agonizingly painful stop.

TWENTY-TWO

THE OVERSEER

CARTER BRUSHED fragments of glass off his face and body then tore his harness clear of its mounts to free himself from the confines of his broken pilot's chair. The hull of the shuttle was split open, and the exo-planet's muggy atmosphere now filled what remained of the cabin.

"Report!" Carter called out through the internal comm system built into their battle uniforms, but there was no answer.

Pushing himself up, he saw fires crackling in the rear compartment, which had spread to the trees outside. Then he saw his XO slumped in the corner, and he shuffled across to her. Through her visor, he could see blood on her face and neck from where she'd hit her head in the crash, but her head covering was still intact and had likely saved her life.

"Kendra?" Carter called out again, trying to see his officer through the smoke. "Kendra, where are you?"

Suddenly, a smoldering mass of wood and shuttle wreckage was hurled into the cargo compartment, and Kendra Castle pushed herself out of the footwell of the rear seat, like a zombie rising from a grave.

"I'm here, boss," she said, brushing burning splinters off her uniform. "Just about, anyway."

"Check on Carina; she's hurt," Carter ordered.

Kendra nodded and leapt over the front row of seats to begin her assessment, while Carter climbed onto the instrument panel to get a look outside the ship and survey their crash site. The path that the shuttle had carved through the forest extended for several hundred meters, and though he couldn't see the Aternien Overseer who had shot them down, he could sense she was nearby.

A flurry of distorted warbles and bleeps caught his attention, and Carter ducked back inside the shuttle to see RAEB and JACAB shaking debris from their outer shells. Both bots then hovered unsteadily into the air and began using their tools to clean the wreckage off each other's coverings. Suddenly, JACAB saw Carina and his glowing red eye widened. The bot squawked desperately and flew over to her.

"She'll be okay, buddy, don't worry," Carter said. He could feel the machine's anxiety as keenly as if it were his own.

"Her pulse is weak and fading, boss," Kendra said, snapping shut the box of a med kit. "I can't treat her here. The fires are getting out of control and in just a few minutes this shuttle will be an inferno."

"Carry her out onto the forest floor and do what you can," Carter said. He turned to his gopher. "JACAB, you're with me. I need you to scout for Aterniens."

Carter vaulted the bent and twisted frame of the shuttle cockpit and traversed the three-meter drop with the dexterity of a cat. Due to the dense canopy of leaves above them, the forest floor was dryer and harder than the mud that covered most of the exo-planet. If it came to a fight – and Carter fully expected that it would – the solid ground would make it easier to defend their position. Then the sky rumbled, and he saw the Aternien scout ship ploughing through the atmosphere to the west. It was heavily damaged, and no longer an immediate threat, but he made a mental note of its projected landing site in case he needed to find it again.

He looked for his gopher and saw the bot still hovering beside Major Larsen, as Kendra carried his XO out of the shuttle and into a patch of the forest that wasn't on fire. JACAB had remained at Carina's side, like a faithful dog.

"JACAB, come on, I need you," he called out to the machine. "The Aterniens could attack at any moment."

JACAB looked at him then turned back to Carina. Kendra had now placed her on the ground. She looked drawn and weak, and Carter could barely hear the beat of her heart.

"Kendra will take care of her, but none of us will survive if the Aterniens ambush us while we're distracted."

JACAB let out a distressed warble then nodded and hovered above his head. The machine's scanners activated, and the device began probing their perimeter.

"It's not good, boss," Kendra said. She was on her knees beside Carina. "The battle uniform helped to protect her body, but her head took a hard knock in the crash. The bottom line is that she's dying."

Carter clenched his fists and his stomach knotted just as tightly. He had known his XO was badly hurt, but Kendra's bleak evaluation had completely blindsided him.

"Can't you do something?" Carter said. He was afraid for her life, but his dominant emotion was anger. "I just started getting my crew back together, and I'm not losing anyone today."

"She's not like us, Carter, these injuries won't heal on their own," Kendra explained. "I wish I could save her, but I can't."

Carter growled in frustration and felt like tearing down every tree in the forest, but he needed to save his strength and fury for the real enemy. Even so, despite his apparent helplessness, he refused to give up on her.

"We're not going anywhere," Carter said with determination. "Give her a nano-stim at a fifty-per cent dose."

Kendra got to her feet. "Boss, an infusion of that quantity of nanomachines will kill her. She's only human."

"If we do nothing, she's dead anyway," Carter grunted. "If it doesn't kill her, it'll make her stronger, at least for a time. Give her the stim, that's an order."

"Yes, boss," Kendra replied, without delay.

He could sense that his Master Engineer disagreed with his decision, and she was right to do so. Quite apart from the fact that infusing nanomachines into a body that lacked the bio-engineering and technological augments to sustain them was easily fatal, it was also highly illegal. It was in direct contravention of the Aternien Act, which forbade any post-human practices or experiments. It was also true that he didn't give a damn about the law. If there was even the slightest chance he could save Carina Larsen, he was going to try.

Carter watched as Kendra dialed the nano-stim to fifty percent then deactivated Carina's head covering and injected the capsule into the side of her neck.

"Assuming this works, it'll only make her stronger for a few hours at most, before the nanomachines stop functioning," Kendra said, anxiously waiting by Carina's side for the excruciating side-effects of the stim to kick in.

"It'll be enough…" Carter said, willing it to be so with every fiber of his being.

Suddenly, Carina's eyes sprang open, and she screamed as if someone had pressed a searing hot poker into her flesh. Kendra grabbed her body and held her down as she thrashed and convulsed, continuing to howl cries of anguished pain. Blotchy patches formed on her face and neck, and her body swelled and bulged, like there were a hundred scarab beetles burrowing beneath her skin.

"It's okay, Major, we gave you some meds," Kendra said, as Carina's terrified, bloodshot eyes looked up at her. "Just fight through it. You'll be okay."

Carina screamed again, and Carter noticed that JACAB was quivering. Even so, the machine continued to carry out his orders and scan the perimeter. Carter rested a hand on the bot's trembling frame, which helped to calm his anxious gopher, but it didn't change the fact there was nothing further he could do to help his XO. If she was strong, she'd survive.

"She'll be alright, buddy, you'll see," Carter said to his bot, though he was painfully aware that he was trying to convince himself, as much as his loyal gopher.

Anxious seconds passed and finally the screams and convulsions died down, and Carina appeared more at ease. Carter listened carefully and was relieved that he could still hear the beat of her heart.

"She's alive, but barely..." Kendra reported, releasing her hold on the major. "All we can do now is wait."

Suddenly, JACAB sounded a warning and the machine's red eye sharpened and turned South, in the direction of the Galatine. Carter felt his forearm vibrate, and he tapped his comp-slate to read the report his bot had just transmitted.

"A force of Aterniens is headed this way," Carter said, relaying the news to his Master Engineer.

"They're not just headed this way, boss," Kendra replied. She had tensed up and her eyes were fixed into the distance. "They're already here."

Carter had sensed it too, and he turned to see the Aternien Overseer standing at the end of the three-hundred-meter-long furrow that the shuttle had carved through the mud. Two full squads of Immortals stood ready to her rear.

"We should fall back and regroup," Kendra said, while drawing her plasma pistols, one in each hand.

Carter shook his head. "I'm not leaving Major Larsen behind."

"Boss, we can't fight that many Immortals and an Overseer, and also carry the XO."

Carter met his Master Engineer's eyes then drew his cutlass and ignited the plasma-edged blade.

"We're not going anywhere without the XO," he repeated,

the light from his sword casting one side of his face into deep shadow. "We stand and fight; that's an order."

In that moment, all of Kendra Castle's doubts and fears were pushed aside, and his Master Engineer stood with him, ready to engage the enemy. Despite the grueling process of augmentation that all Longsword officers endured, they weren't immune to emotions, and each of them had their unique quirks and personal failings, just as he did. However, there was one thing that all Longswords had in common; when a command was given, it was obeyed without hesitation.

Carter turned back to the Overseer and pumped his left hand into a fist three times in rapid succession. His battle uniform reacted to the input and fabricated a buckler shield on his left forearm. He could have simply drawn his 57-EX revolver and attacked the advancing forces from range, but that was not his way. It was also too easy. His anger was raw, and to channel it properly required that he get into close action with his enemy.

The Immortals advanced ahead of the Overseer, and particle blasts flew toward him, but Carter dodged with the swiftness of a shadow, avoiding the shots like they were moving in slow-motion. Yet despite his augmented speed, his actions were nothing compared to the fluidity displayed by his Master Engineer. While Kendra Castle's greatest talents lay in engines and computers, she was also a formidable fighter, and the fastest gunslinger Carter had ever seen.

Kendra opened fire with both pistols, while darting from tree to tree, moving so fast it was like she was in multiple places at once. Six Immortals were immobilized within the first few seconds, forcing the rest to regroup and take cover. However, Kendra wasn't merely taking out targets at random; she was funneling the enemy directly toward Carter, which was exactly where he wanted them. Drawing up his augmented senses, Carter deflected a succession of Aternien blasts with his buckler then took cover behind a cluster of trees. Kendra was doing a good job of harassing the Immortals, but he needed a little more help.

"JACAB, RAEB, go high and give the Aterniens something else to think about," Carter said to the two gophers through the comm system built into his uniform.

The bots complied, springing weapons from inside their shells and zipping into the sky, one heading to the left of the Aterniens and the other to their right. Before long, needles of plasma energy began to rain down on the Immortals, like dozens of tiny bolts of lightning. The low-energy blasts were not enough to harm the Aternien warriors, but it was enough to distract and harry them, like being caught unawares in a severe hailstorm.

Carter took full advantage of the diversion and charged headlong at the enemy, cutting down three Immortals before they'd even seen him coming. Now alert to his attack, a team of warriors advanced, but he blocked their shots and ran them through with savage efficiency, his plasma-cutlass crackling like hot fat as it split their golden armor and severed their synthetic limbs.

The Overseer was close now, but she chose not to engage, instead content to observe Carter like a true student of war. He pushed on, as the Immortals energized the bayonets attached to their rifles and moved to take him on at close-range. He blocked the first thrust with his buckler and parried another, before he was struck to the chest by the butt of a third rifle and stopped in his tracks. His counterattack was brutal, slicing the synthetic body of one Immortal in half before crushing a second warrior's face flat with a punch from his buckler. The remaining Immortal fired at close range, and the blast scorched his side, but Carter had driven his cutlass through the warrior's neck before the Aternien could fire again. A quick flick of his wrist was all it then took to remove the Immortal's head. It landed at his feet, and he kicked it like a soccer ball, sending it flying within inches of the Overseer's face. The Aternien officer didn't flinch.

Even with the carnage that was left in his wake, there were still more Immortals behind the Overseer, but the Aternien officer raised a hand, and they obediently stood down. Carter nodded to Kendra, who was still progressing stealthily through the trees in an attempt to flank the warriors, and she also stood down, understanding Carter's intention without him needing to spell it out. The Overseer had challenged him to single combat, and he was not about to turn her down.

"Your efforts are in vain, Master Commander," the Overseer said, advancing toward him, war spear in hand. Carter detected the hint of an accent, but like the woman's human origins, it was distant, like an old memory. "Once I have dealt with you, I will collect the souls of these Immortals, and they will be reborn, wiser and stronger."

"And they'll remember who killed them too," Carter grunted in reply. "Just as you will, after I've removed your head from your neck."

The bottom part of the Overseer's face was covered by the purple mask, but from her eyes, Carter could see that she was smiling. She was confident, he realized – perhaps overconfident – and that would work to his advantage.

"I survived the first war, and I will survive this one," the Overseer said. The two were now circling each other, sizing each other up before crossing blades. "I even killed the Master Operator of the Longsword Evalach, which is how I attained the rank of Overseer."

Unlike the Overseer, Carter was not about to underestimate his enemy. To kill a Longsword officer was no small feat, and the fact she had fought in the first war meant she was a veteran, most likely as old as he was, or close to it. Yet, this Overseer had not ascended to the Royal Court, which meant that Master Commander Rose was much more than just her opponent – he was her ticket to a place at Markus Aternus' side.

"If you fought in the first war, you'll know I've put down hundreds of goldies like you," Carter replied, emphasizing the disdain he held for all Aterniens. "Immortal, Warden, Overseer, Vizier… it makes no difference to me. All of you are my enemies, but right now, you're the one standing in my way."

The Overseer flourished her war spear then adopted a fighting stance.

"Aternus is immortal," the woman said. "Aternus is forever…"

The Overseer attacked, spinning her war spear then lunging at his leading leg. Carter parried the blow then dodged another swift thrust aimed at his heart, but a follow up glanced his shoulder and cut through his battle uniform. Carter struck the spear away and slashed his cutlass at the Aternien's neck, but the Overseer had already danced out of range, using her reach advantage to full effect.

"Not bad," Carter said, touching a hand to the wound. The cut had already sealed, and his uniform was in the process of knitting itself back together.

"You will find that I am more than your equal," the Overseer replied, displaying perfect fighting form. "And when I kill you, the Grand Vizier will ascend me to the Royal Court as a reward."

The Overseer leaped forward and tried to lunge over the top of his guard, forcing Carter onto the back foot. He blocked the attack with his buckler, but the Aternien's speed and agility allowed her to thrust the spear at his throat before he had chance to counter. He parried, though barely, and the Overseer continued her elegant assault, smashing the staff against his shoulder, before slashing low and cutting his thigh with the energized spear head of the powerful weapon.

"I expected more from you, Master Commander," the Overseer said, mocking him from behind her mask. "Perhaps the years have dulled your abilities and made you weak?"

The Overseer's goading tone was designed to provoke his anger and force him to make a mistake, but Carter was not so easily baited. The same, however, was not true of his opponent.

"I'm just a little out of practice," Carter countered. "It's been a while since I killed an Overseer, especially a low-born nobody like you, who isn't even a member of the Royal Court."

The Overseer's azurite blue eyes flashed with rage, and she charged, spear tip angled toward his heart, but this time Carter was ready. He held his ground and deflected the attack, before driving his shoulder into the Aternien's chest. The blow staggered her, and he hammered his buckler into the Overseer's face, smashing her golden helm and causing the purple mask to slip from her nose and mouth. Dazed, the Overseer backed away, but not before he sliced through her golden armor, opening a deep gash in her synthetic gut.

Without her mask, Carter could see the shock and embarrassment at having been bested writ plain on the woman's face. She was young, or at least she had been at the time she ascended, and the soft lines of her cheeks and jaw didn't suit her dark intentions.

"It looks like you won't be ascending today, Overseer," Carter said, pouring salt on the wound.

The Overseer cradled her split synthetic flesh, then her young face twisted with rage and resentment, and her blue eyes drew daggers on him. Howling a war cry, she charged and thrust the spear at his head, but her attack was wrathful and clumsy, and Carter caught the weapon and tore it from her grasp. A split-second later, his energized cutlass was at the woman's neck, slowly melting her synthetic skin like candle wax exposed to a flame.

"It doesn't matter if you kill me," the Overseer said. Despite her synthetic body and undying soul, her voice still trembled with fear. "I'll return, stronger than before," she hissed, defiant in defeat. "Nothing and no-one will stop me from taking a place at Markus Aternus' side."

"That's where you're wrong," Carter said, pressing the spear tip of the Overseer's own weapon to her throat. "You can come for me again and again, and I will put you down every time, until the shame of your failure consumes you." He kicked the Aternien's legs and forced her to her knees, sword and spear still pressed to her neck. "It's time to meet your god-king, Overseer. Tell Markus I said hi…"

Carter pulled back his cutlass and was about to strike the killing blow when a blast of energy struck him in the chest and bowled him over. For a moment, he was disorientated, then he saw an Aternien Immortal charging at him, rifle barrel and bayonet angled at his chest. He raised his buckler and deflected the first shot, but the impact left him open. He braced himself, ready to take a blast to the chest, but it didn't come. Instead, the enemy warrior was shot twice in the head, and the energy of the plasma blasts melted the Aternien's synthetic face and neuromorphic brain.

Carter scrambled into cover and looked for who had saved him, but his guardian angel hadn't been Kendra Castle, or even his loyal gopher, but Major Carina Larsen. She was lying on her stomach, propped up on one elbow and with her energy pistol clutched tightly in her hand. Suddenly, Kendra darted out of the trees and forced the remaining Immortals to retreat with a furious barrage of plasma fire. Carter took the opportunity to look for the Overseer, but she was gone, as was her war spear. Then the shooting stopped, and an eerie calm fell over their dank and sweltering woodland hideaway.

"Sorry if I spoiled your duel," Carina said, climbing to her feet. The fact she could stand at all was a miracle.

"Don't worry, I somehow doubt that's the last we'll see of her," Carter replied. The woman's bitterness had left a sour taste in the air, and he could still feel her presence. "Revenge is a powerful drug, even for an Aternien."

"Speaking of drugs, what the hell did you give me?" Carina said, brushing dead leaves and dirt from her uniform. "I remember crashing, then I must have been knocked out, because I had the weirdest dreams. It was like there were things crawling around inside me."

Carter wasn't quite sure how to explain it to his XO, though her nightmarish imaginings weren't all that far from the truth. Kendra Castle then arrived and solved the problem for him, by tackling the subject in her usual blunt fashion.

"How are you feeling, Major?" Kendra asked, staring at Carina like she was flesh risen from the grave. "I've never seen a human survive a high dose of nanomachines before, so you must be tough as old boots."

"A high dose of what now?!" Carina cried.

"You were dying, Major, so we gave you a fifty-percent dose from a nano-stim capsule," Kendra explained. "I said it would kill you, but the boss made the right call, which is why he's the boss."

Carina's mouth fell open, but whatever questions his XO had would have to wait. They were still in a bad position, and while they'd fended off the Aternien attack, there were still many more Immortals on the exo-planet.

"The nanomachines will make you stronger, for a time, so make use of them while you can," Carter said, focusing on the benefits of her unintended temporary augmentation. "But remember that you're still human. You died once already today, and I'll be damned if I let you die again. Is that clear, Major?"

Carina still looked stupefied, but she managed to nod her understanding and compliance. Satisfied, Carter ushered his XO and Master Engineer further away from the crash site, and in the direction of the Galatine. JACAB and RAEB were both hovering above his head, generating a sensor scattering field, while visually scouting the way ahead. Under the watchful eyes of their gophers, Carter checked their surroundings and saw a jagged outcropping of rocks a few hundred meters away that stretched above the tree canopy.

"There, we can climb those rocks to get a better look at the Galatine," Carter said, pointing the way. "We need to find out how many Immortals we still have to contend with, before they manage to lift our ship out of the mud and steal her from us."

Carter set the pace and to his surprise Major Larsen was able to keep up. The infusion of nanomachines had not only saved her life, but temporarily imbued her with some of the traits of a Longsword officer. He had no idea how long it would last, but intended to take full advantage of his rejuvenated XO until the effects wore off, and she was subjected to the mother of all hangovers.

"Shit, we haven't got long," Kendra realized. She had reached the top of the outcropping before the others. "They've already fixed grav lifters all around the Galatine's hull. From the size and number of the devices, it's more than enough to raise her into orbit."

Carter scrambled to his engineer's side and focused his augmented eyes onto the Longsword. The bulk of the remaining Immortals were positioned around the side entrance hatch, standing guard. Then he saw why; the Aternien Grand Vizier was waiting on the steps leading up to the Galatine, and the Overseer was with him.

Suddenly, the ground shook and a rumble like thunder rolled across the horizon. The grav lifters illuminated and the vibrations began to shake the years of clotted mud and detritus from its hull.

"They've activated the grav lifters," Kendra confirmed, eyes focused on her comp-slate. "If they manage to dock her with the soliton warp frame, we'll have lost her forever."

"That's not happening," Carter grunted. "I told you that we're not losing anyone today, and that includes my ship." Carter got to his feet and fixed his eyes onto the Grand Vizier. "Now stay close behind me, and let's give these bastards hell."

TWENTY-THREE

ROSE AND THORNS

PARTICLE BLASTS SMASHED into the trees and flashed above Carter's head, forcing him and the others to take cover at the edge of the forest. A squad of Immortals had been diverted to intercept them, and though the Galatine was now in sight, the powerful Longsword-class battleship had already been raised part-way out of the mud.

"We're not going to make it," Kendra said, returning fire and taking down one of the advancing Immortals. "We need a plan B."

"We haven't lost her yet," Carter answered. In his head, he knew his engineer was right, but in his heart, he refused to believe the Galatine was lost. "Cover me!"

He ran at the line of Aterniens blocking his path, and plasma blasts quickly overtook him as Kendra and Carina rained down fire on their enemy. Carter's assault was no frenzied charge because his senses were now acutely attuned to every move the Immortals made. The aim of their weapons, the position of their feet and bodies, and even every pull of a trigger was captured by his augmented eyes and processed by his bio-engineered mind. Carter had anticipated the track of their particle blasts even before the shots left the barrels.

Shots zipped past his face and body, while others he swatted away with his buckler. He took a hit to the chest, but his sensation blockers nullified the pain, and soon he was within cutting range of the front rank of warriors. He swung his cutlass, dismembering any Aternien that was foolish enough to stand in his path. His super-human strength combined with the searing-hot plasma edge his blade sliced through their bodies with frightening ease. The Aterniens fought back, slashing, and stabbing at him with their energized bayonets, but he blocked and parried with inhuman speed, then cut the warriors down with ever more savage swings of his sword. Combined with the accuracy and power of the covering fire from his officers and gophers, the Aternien squad was obliterated within seconds. Yet it still hadn't been enough.

"No!" Carter roared, as the Galatine cleared the ground and began to climb higher.

The Grand Vizier stood in the open hatchway, peering down at him with imperious, glowing blue eyes. The Aternien leader and second only to Markus Aternus then vanished inside the Galatine, and the Overseer appeared in his place. Carter's senses heightened, but there was no time to shout a warning before the Overseer took aim with her war spear and opened fire.

The blasts hammered into the ground around them, exploding with the force of plasma grenades. He turned and ran, intending to grab his XO and pull her into cover with him, but Major Larsen was caught in a blast and sent flying back into the forest, like a tumbleweed blowing across the desert. Another blast exploded ahead of him, and he was sent crashing into the mud, the skin on his face and neck burned and his silver hair scorched black. Sensation blockers numbed the pain, and his augments kept his fear in check. Looking around him, he saw Kendra Castle on her knees, her mass of chestnut hair alive with flickering yellow and orange flames.

The barrage of fire from the Overseer's war spear had

ceased, and Carter looked up to see the Galatine climbing into the clouds under the influence of Aternien grav lifters. JACAB hummed to his side and the bot warbled at him, anxiously. He disengaged his buckler and deactivated his sword before checking his comp-slate to read the message from his gopher, but it only confirmed what he already knew. The Galatine had been stolen.

"Don't worry, buddy, this isn't over yet," Carter said, climbing to his feet.

JACAB's eye widened, and his bot stared at the ground, unconvinced, but Carter had not made a hollow promise. He was under no illusion that the situation was bleak, but he had no intention of letting the Galatine fall into enemy hands, not while there was still a way to stop it.

"I thought these nanomachines were supposed to stop you from feeling pain?" Carina said, loping toward him. Her uniform was scorched, and she was cradling her ribs, but by another minor miracle, she had survived again.

"I'm afraid the sensation blocker is a different system," Carter replied. He turned to JACAB and waved the bot over. "Give her something for the pain, buddy, but nothing that will dull her senses."

He quickly checked over his XO while JACAB got to work, but other than a few broken ribs and a dozen more cuts and bruises, she was okay. The pain of his own injuries were also starting to assert themselves, but he wasn't interested in treating them yet. Pain could focus the mind just as keenly as his augments could.

"Is everyone okay?" Kendra asked, ironically at the same time as dousing the flames that were licking at her scalp.

"We're still in the fight, if that's what you mean," Carter answered, gruffly.

Kendra looked into the sky and Carter recognized the fury in her eyes as his Master Engineer watched the Galatine slip away.

"What's the plan, boss?" she asked, turning back to Carter. "Our shuttle is totaled, and last time I checked, our augments didn't include the ability to fly, or breathe in the vacuum of space."

"Our shuttle isn't the only spacecraft still left on this mudball," Carter replied, turning his attention West, to where the Aternien scout ship had set down. "They stole my ship, but two can play at that game."

"But won't the Galatine be thousands of light years away by the time we reach the scout?" asked Carina.

"Not if we act quickly," Kendra explained. "To jump her, the Aterniens will have to dock the warp frame and calibrate it to the mass and profile of the Galatine. That buys us some time, but not much."

"How much?" grunted Carter.

"An hour, maybe a little more, if we're lucky." Kendra had tried not to make her estimate sound gravely unworkable, but there was no hiding the truth.

"It will have to be enough," Carter said, returning his focus to where the Aternien scout had landed. "Follow me, if you can..."

Carter set a pace that would ordinarily have been impossible for Major Larsen, or any human being, to match, but the nanomachines still flowing through her veins allowed her to keep in lockstep with him and Kendra. As he ran, his mind worked through dozens of hypothetical solutions to their problem, but it always came down to one possible option. They had to hope that the Aternien scout could still fly, and he had to commandeer it before it left the planet.

Carter reached the edge of the woodland and suddenly the sound of engines firing up shook the branches of the trees, sending Carter's senses into high alert. The Aternien scout ship was visible in a clearing a few hundred meters ahead, but the vessel was preparing to leave. Three Aternien warriors were waiting to board, and one of them was a Warden, the equivalent of a high-ranking NCO in the Aternien soldiery, and one step below an Overseer.

"Damn it, we're too late," Carina said, hunched over with her hands on her knees, breathless from the sprint. "And we can't take out its engines, because that just strands them here with us!"

Carter had checked their surroundings and formulated an idea in the time it had taken Carina to make her observations. A steep hill climbed sharply to his right, sweeping around the clearing where the scout ship had landed. He admitted it wasn't the best plan he'd ever come up with, even at such short notice, but it was all he had, and there was no time to explain it to the others.

"Stay here, I'll take care of this," Carter ordered.

"Take care of it how?"

It was Carina who'd called out the question, but Carter was already accelerating like a dragster, eyes fixed on his target, and his XO's words simply tailed off like police sirens speeding into the distance. His augmented mind had calculated the various angles and speeds he needed to make the jump, without requiring any conscious effort on his part, so while it seemed that he was acting on pure instinct, the reality was more complex.

By the time he began his steep ascent of the hill, the three Aterniens had boarded the scout, and the ship's thrusters had fired to lift it off the ground. The vessel teetered a few meters off the surface, as its pilot compensated for the damage the vessel had sustained. The scout then began to climb higher, and Carter exploded off the hillside with the full force of his augmented muscles, drawing and energizing his cutlass in mid-air.

He soared toward the Aternien scout like a missile, and drove his energized cutlass through the side hatch, latching him onto the vessel like a harpoon. The scout rocked from side to side in a desperate attempt to throw him clear, but his grip on the vessel could not be broken. Using the plasma-edged blade of his cutlass, he sliced through the door hinges like a can-opener through soft aluminum, before tearing open the hatch and sending it spiraling to the mud below.

Particle blasts smashed into his body as Carter pulled himself inside the Aternien scout and charged headlong at the Immortals inside, cutting two down with ferocious strikes of his sword. His armor saved him from critical injuries, but the close-range shots still burned his flesh and blackened his bones. The Warden remained, but Carter was already alert to the danger, and managed to hack the Aternien's rifle in half before the warrior could kill him. A powerful front kick from the Warden sent him barreling into the rear of the compartment, but without his rifle, the Aternien would be forced to fight him, hand-to-hand.

"If you know what's good for you, then you'll throw yourself out of that hatch," Carter grunted, before pulling the cap off a nano-stim with his teeth and injecting the vital treatment into his burned gut.

"Aterniens do not run," the Warden answered, defiantly.

The warrior crouched down and removed the energized bayonet from the severed off barrel of his rifle. He displayed the flickering blade to Carter, like a fencer saluting his opponent, before adopting a fighting stance.

"Aternus is immortal..." the Warden whispered reverently. "Aternus is forever."

"So you people keep telling me," Carter replied.

He was hissing the words through gritted teeth as the effects of the nano-stim ravaged his body with excruciating pain. Then his ordeal was over, and his eyes sharpened onto his target. Carter pumped his left fist three times to engage his buckler, then raised his sword and met the Warden's advance.

In the confines of the scout's hold, his longer blade was no advantage, and the Warden moved swiftly to close the distance between them. As Overseers-in-waiting, the Warden-class were skillful, cunning fighters, but Carter was in no mood for a protracted battle. His body was in pain, and his ship was minutes from being stolen by his enemy, all of which meant that the Warden had picked the wrong time to face Master Commander Carter Rose in single combat.

The Aternien thrust the bayonet at his injured gut, but Carter deflected the strike with his buckler then trapped the Warden's arm against the wall of the scout. His augmented and boosted strength was unconquerable, and the Aternien could do nothing but watch as Carter brought his cutlass down so hard that he split the warrior in half from shoulder to groin. For a moment, the warrior's blue eyes registered the terrible shock, before they fizzled to nothing, and the Warden collapsed at his feet.

Suddenly, the pilot of the craft – now the only Aternien left on board – scrambled out of his seat and tried to reach for a particle rifle. Carter met the warrior half-way and swatted the Immortal out of the open hatch with the flat of his cutlass, like hitting a home run. He watched for a moment as the warrior's arms and legs flailed helplessly in mid-flight. He idly wondered if the Aternien was experiencing fear, or whether the assurance of its rebirth would make it immune to such primal emotions, but he'd already turned away and climbed into the pilot's seat, before the Immortal had smashed into ground,

The Aternien scout ship was his, and it was now his last chance to save the Galatine. It was a chance he was not about to squander.

TWENTY-FOUR
EXTREME BOARDING ACTIONS

CARTER TOUCHED down the scout ship far harder than he had intended, on account of the fact he hadn't quite gotten to grips with the Aternien control system. The vessel bounced twice then ground to a stop a hundred meters from his intended landing site. However, this had the unintentional benefit of bringing him closer to where Kendra Castle and Major Larsen were standing in the mud, waiting for him.

"All aboard," Carter called out, waving at the others to get inside.

Carina arrived first, still hobbling on account of her injuries, then Kendra pulled herself through the open hatch a moment later and helped the major into the co-pilot's seat of the craft. He noticed that his XO was scowling at him, as if he'd made a terrible faux pas.

"What's that look for? I thought you'd be impressed with my heist of this ship?"

"I am, but that Aternien you lobbed out of the door landed less than ten meters from where I was standing," Carina replied. "It scared the shit out of me!"

Carter shook his head at her. "I'll make sure to aim the next guy a little further away."

RAEB and JACAB hummed through the opening, and both bots were warbling and chirruping excitedly, as if they were having a heated conversation.

"What's gotten into them?" Carter asked.

The two gophers stopped chatting and looked at him. JACAB nudged RAEB and the bot burbled indignantly, before transmitting a message to Master Engineer Castle.

"RAEB says they've detected a power surge in orbit. They both agree that it's the soliton warp frame spinning up but disagree on how long it will be before the Aterniens can jump the Galatine out of the system."

"What are the two options?" Carter said.

RAEB warbled again, and the information appeared on Kendra's comp-slate. "JACAB reckons we have less than five minutes, but RAEB says ten."

"Engineers always overestimate how long things take, so I'll go with JACAB's figure," Carter said, returning to the ship's controls.

RAEB blew an indignant digital raspberry, while JACAB intoned a whine that sounded very much like, "I told you so!" to Carter's highly attuned augmented ears.

Carter engaged the maneuvering thrusters and lifted the Aternien scout ship out of the mud splat he'd buried it in. The craft rocked unsteadily, though he didn't know whether this was due to the extensive damage it had sustained, or his piloting skills.

"Kendra, see if you can smooth out the ride, a little," Carter said, aiming the nose of the craft skyward and increasing power to the engines. "This thing handles like a damned bucking bronco."

"A lousy pilot always blames his ship," Carina said in a sing-song voice.

She was smiling at him, but her eyes were glassy and distant. His XO then laughed and threw her head back, and

Carter scowled at her. If he hadn't known better, he'd have said she was drunk.

"The regular meds weren't helping, so JACAB gave her a shot of Trifentanil while you were off doing hero stuff," Kendra explained, perhaps aware of Carter's concerned expression. "She'll be okay in a couple of hours."

"Trifentanil!" Carter blurted out. He looked at his gopher, but the bot simply turned its eye away and tried to look innocent. "I said give her something that won't cloud her mind. That stuff will turn a human brain to mush."

JACAB was still pretending not to hear him, though Kendra appeared unconcerned. "He only gave her a tiny amount, boss, don't worry."

"Yeah, chill out, *boss*..." Carina added, at the same time as slapping her hand on his thigh. "You're so uptight. Loosen up. Live a little!"

Carter muttered a curse under his breath and focused ahead. The last thing he needed was a drugged-up XO and co-pilot, especially considering they still had to re-take the Galatine.

"Everyone, activate your head coverings," Carter said, tapping the initiator on his collar. "Aternien ships aren't pressurized with oxygen-nitrogen atmospheres. And besides, this ship has a massive hole in it."

Kendra activated her head covering, and Carter was pleased to note that Carina still had presence of mind enough to activate hers too. Before long, the scout ship had left the muggy atmosphere of the exo-planet, and the Galatine came into view ahead of them. The hull sparkled with light reflected from the sun like a sword that was still wet with the blood of its victims.

"How are we supposed to get on board?" Carina asked. She was staring at her hand and flexing her fingers, as if they were alien appendages that had been grafted to her body. "It's not like we can just dock and open the door."

"That's exactly how we get on-board," Carter replied. "The

Galatine is still my ship, and it will respond to my unique biometric signature and command codes. All we have to do is latch on to the port-side hatch near the command level, then storm the bridge."

Carina leaned over, rested her elbow on his shoulder and looked him dead in the eyes from no more than a few inches distance.

"Come on boss, we'd be outgunned at least twenty-to-one," Carina said, wiggling her fingers at him, as if to illustrate the number disadvantage. "I know you're good at this ass-kicking malarky, but those odds are pretty steep, don't you think?"

"Fighting against the odds is what we do, Major." Carter removed his XO's arm from his shoulder and maneuvered her back to her seat. "Do you still want to be one of us?"

Carina blew out a sound that resembled the digital raspberry that RAEB and JACAB were fond of using, then wafted a hand at him, dismissively.

"Bah, you know I do, but you don't think I'm up to it." Carina wagged her finger at him and Kendra in turn. "I see you two talking. Don't think I don't see…"

Carter sighed and turned to JACAB. "This is your doing, so fix her. That's an order…"

JACAB squawked indignantly, but obeyed his command and began cycling through a selection of medical capsules, one of which Carter hoped would counteract the euphoric effects of the Trifentanil. The bot then hovered behind Carina's head and injected her neck. Moments later, she was unconscious.

"Damn it, JACAB, I said revive her not sedate her!"

The bot shrugged with its maneuvering flaps, but before Carter could give the machine a piece of his mind, RAEB suddenly bleated an alert.

"Boss, according to RAEB the warp frame is almost charged," Kendra reported, jumping into action. "They'll be able to jump in ninety seconds."

"Damn it, we're still two minutes out," Carter said, trying to urge the scout ship on harder, but the damage it had sustained was too severe. "How do you activate the weapons on this thing? We know it has them."

"I'm working on it…" Kendra called back.

The Master Engineer had pulled open panels to allow her gopher to interface directly with the ship's systems, but the bot and Aternien computer still didn't speak exactly the same language. Meanwhile, Carter aimed the nose of the shuttle directly at the warp frame, fingers on the triggers and ready to fire at a moment's notice.

"Thirty seconds, people, I need those guns!" Carter shouted.

"Almost there!"

RAEB was now completely consumed inside the scout ship, and sparks and smoke were erupting from consoles all around the cockpit.

"Ten seconds. It's now or never!"

Suddenly, energy hummed through Carter's console and a shining blue targeting reticule appeared in front of him.

"Weapons are hot, but targeting is manual only!" his engineer finally called out.

"Manual targeting is all I need…"

Carter aimed at the largest section of the warp frame and focused his gaze into the reticule, like looking down an iron sight, before squeezing the triggers. Pulses of golden energy erupted from the scout's cannon and struck the warp frame cleanly, causing a cascade of explosions to ripple across the mid-section of the device.

"Great shot boss!" Kendra called out, thumping her fist on the wall of the ship. RAEB re-emerged from inside the ship and updated the information on his engineer's comp-slate. "The warp frame is heavily damaged; they're not going anywhere."

Suddenly, energy blasts flashed back at them, and the scout ship was hit. Carter took evasive action, but not before another volley of blasts smashed the cockpit glass, missing Carina's head by the narrowest of margins. Changing course again, Carter ducked below the level of the console, and was forced to maneuver blindly to avoid being hit by blasts that continued to flash above his head.

"What the hell is shooting at us?" Carter said, as the scout ship raced past the Galatine. "I thought the warp frame didn't have any weapons?"

"It doesn't," Kendra replied.

His Master Engineer leaned into the cockpit and showed Carter a magnified image of the Galatine on the screen of her comp-slate. Six Aternien Immortals were stood on her hull, guarding the hatch that Carter had selected as his entry point into the ship.

"That last volley took out the energy cannon," Kendra continued, while her gopher worked frantically to keep the scout flying. "There are still a couple of functional Aternien particle rifles back here. Maybe we can use those?"

"I don't need any Aternien weapons," Carter replied. He had another plan in mind, and it was no less audacious than his scheme to capture the scout ship. "Take the wheel, Kendra, and point us back toward my ship. When the coast is clear, dock to the hatch and wait for further instructions."

"You got it, boss," Kendra said, taking over control of the scout. "Call me nosy, but where will you be?"

Carter gave her a look that suggested it was better if she didn't ask, and his engineer took the hint. It was far from the first time he'd gone ahead with a plan that to any sensible, un-augmented human being would have seemed plain crazy, but he had a habit of making things work.

Kendra steered the scout back toward the Galatine, and at the same time, Carter hauled the unconscious body of Major Larson into the rear compartment and made sure she was shielded from incoming fire.

"Hey, buddy, take care of her, okay?" Carter said, turning to his gopher. "And no more drugs. At least not ones that will make her trip out or fall asleep. I need her awake and sensible, okay?"

JACAB warbled and nodded his agreement, then hovered beside Major Larson. He gently patted his bot's spherical shell then moved across to the open side hatch and drew his 57-EX revolver. Energy blasts from the Aterniens on the Galatine's hull were already hammering into the scout, but Kendra held her course and her nerve.

"We're taking a pounding boss, how close do you want me to get?"

"Close to fifty meters, then bug out," Carter replied. "You'll know when it's safe to return."

Kendra tossed up a salute using two fingers of her right hand then ducked as a blast raced through the cockpit and punched a hole through the rear door.

"Two hundred meters..." his engineer called out.

Carter pulled himself outside and got ready to jump.

"One hundred... Seventy... Fifty!"

The scout ship veered away sharply and at the same time Carter hurled himself out of the vessel and sped toward the Galatine like a human cannonball. His augmented senses processed his environment at a rapidly accelerated rate, allowing him to time his move to perfection. Five meters from the ship, he spun his body around, magnetized his boots and landed on the hull like a gymnast dismounting from the parallel bars.

The entire daredevil maneuver had taken only a few seconds to complete; the exact same amount of time that it took the Aterniens to realize what had happened. The Immortals spun around and aimed their rifles in his direction, but Carter had the element of surprise, and a more powerful weapon. Opening fire with the five-shot revolver, he blew a hole in the chest of the closest warrior, before engaging his buckler and advancing.

Soon, blasts were flying at him, but he deflected the shots and returned fire. The Aternien golden scale armor was no match for his high-power rounds, and one shot, no matter where he hit, was enough to incapacitate his enemies. Making each shot count, Carter dispatched another three Immortals before he took a hit square to the chest that dropped him to his knees. Cursing, he checked the integrity of his battle uniform; it was hanging on by a thread. Another shot grazed his thigh, and he returned fire, blowing the head off a fifth Aternien, but there was one remaining, and he was out of bullets.

Holstering his revolver, he drew and energized his plasma cutlass and charged at the Immortal. The mag-lock system in his boots made progress slow and clumsy, and he took another two hits, first to his right shoulder, then to his ribs. Even his sensation blockers couldn't spare him from the searing agony of his injuries, but his resolve to recapture the Galatine drove him on.

Disengaging the mag lock system, Carter launched himself at the final warrior. The Aternien fired and missed, and a second later, he had sunk the blade of his cutlass through the Immortal's chest. The momentum carried them both toward the edge of the ship, and he engaged his boots again, but couldn't reach the hull.

Suddenly, the Aternien grabbed him around the throat. Carter fought back then realized to his horror that the Immortal wasn't trying to strangle him, but remove his head covering, so that he'd suffocate in the vacuum of space. Their struggle sent them spinning end over end, out of control, and he lost sight of the Galatine completely.

Then out of nowhere, the scout ship surged in front of him, and he slammed into it like a wrecking ball. The impact drove his cutlass deeper into the Aternien's body, and the two halves of the warrior were split apart and began floating into the ether. Carter pressed his boots to the hull of the scout and finally regained his balance and his bearings, though his head was still spinning like a roulette wheel.

"I'd forgotten how much I enjoy watching you work," said Kendra, speaking through the internal comm system inside their head coverings.

"And I'd forgotten how good it is to know you have my back," Carter replied, sincerely. "Thanks for the pick-up."

Carter climbed back inside the scout ship and saw that Major Larsen was sitting up, holding her head like she'd just woken up from a heavy night on the beers.

"How are you doing, Major?" Carter asked, while dropping into the co-pilot's seat. "Are you ready to fight? I wouldn't blame you for sitting this one out."

Carina climbed to her feet, ably assisted by JACAB, and dusted down her uniform.

"I'm ready, Commander," she said, before sucking in a deep breath. "Let's take back your ship."

"*Our* ship, Major," Carter grunted. "The Galatine is ours, and we're going to make the Aterniens wish they'd never set eyes on her."

TWENTY-FIVE

UNTO THE BREACH

CARTER RESTED his hand onto the Galatine's docking hatch, as if trying to soothe an anxious stallion that had been stolen by horse rustlers. Major Larsen and Master Engineer Castle were by his side, and they were flanked by RAEB and JACAB. To gain entry, all Carter had to do was input his command override codes, then the fight to retake his ship would begin, and wouldn't end until either the Aterniens were dead, or they were.

"Get ready, I'm unlocking the hatch now…"

Carter punched the codes into his comp-slate then drew his 57-EX revolver. The obscenely powerful handgun was in his left hand, while his ignited plasma cutlass was held ready in his right. It made little difference which hand wielded which weapon – he was adept with either. However, when it came to close quarters fighting, and especially hand-to-hand, he favored his right.

His comp-slate bleeped three times and the hatch unlocked. There was no need to wait for the pressure to equalize, since the Aterniens hadn't pressurized the Galatine, nor was there any air in the scout ship, which had more holes in it than a sieve. The lack of atmosphere would make the fighting more difficult, but

Carter didn't care. Nothing and no-one could stop him from taking back his ship.

"Kendra, your objective is to install the core OS and get the systems back online," Carter said, poised to open the hatch. "The Major and I will make sure no-one gets in your way."

Both officers acknowledged the order, then Carter threw open the hatch and charged inside the Galatine, buckler held outstretched, and head tucked low behind it. Aternien Immortals were lying in wait, but Carter flattened their ranks like a hurricane tearing across a coastline, leaving chaos and destruction in its wake. Major Larsen and Kendra shot the Aterniens that had fallen, while he focused on the enemies that still lay ahead.

With his elbows tucked in tight to his body because of the restricted space, Carter continued his charge, and hacked through the second rank of Immortals like a scythe cutting hay. The enemy regrouped and fought back, but Carter unloaded his 57-EX into the mass of synthetic bodies that stood in his way, dropping them with the power of a gatling gun.

More warriors advanced, but Carter and his company had already pushed beyond the choke point at the docking hatch. Pulling into cover, he reloaded his revolver then knelt and fired, clearing a path along the central corridor leading to the bridge. Carina and Kendra added their plasma blasts to the assault, and Carter advanced again.

"Keep pushing…" Carter called out, emptying the spent cartridges in his 57-EX and reloading them so quickly the whole process looked like a magician's sleight of hand. "And if you see the Grand Vizier, and have a clear shot, make sure you take it. We're not here to negotiate."

Immortals piled out from the bridge, but this time Carter had the upper hand. His officers and bots lit up the corridor with burning spears of light, and the warriors were engulfed in the onslaught and mowed down before they could even get a shot off. He stepped over the incapacitated Aterniens, shooting any that still posed a threat, then fixed his eyes on the door to the bridge, willing himself toward it, like the finishing line of a grueling endurance race.

The door was almost in reach when two Wardens charged out of connecting corridors and hammered him against the wall. To a normal human, the Aternien's strength would have been impossible to resist, but Carter had been engineered with the might of Hercules. He grabbed the closest Warden by the neck and smashed him first through one wall, then the wall opposite. The stock of a rifle was clubbed across his back, but it was the Aternien weapon that broke, rather than his augmented bone.

Releasing the mangled body of the first warrior, Carter crushed an elbow strike into the face of the second Warden, collapsing the Aternien's perfect synthetic bone structure, before driving his plasma cutlass through the warrior's gut and pinning him to the wall. He released the handle of the sword then grabbed the upper and lower halves of the Warden and ripped the Aternien in half, like breaking bread.

Carina and Kendra arrived and assumed positions next to the bridge door. He accessed his comp-slate, but the lock jammed, and even with his augmented strength, he knew he wouldn't be able to force it.

"RAEB, see if you can get this open," Carter said, glancing back to the engineering bot, before meeting his own automaton's glowing red eye. "And see if you can scan the bridge, buddy. I'd like to know who's waiting for us on the other side."

The two bots hummed into action without delay and Carter used the opportunity to reload his revolver. He could feel the effects of injuries starting to assert themselves, but he ignored the pain; treating himself would have to wait until the fighting was done.

JACAB chirruped and Carter's comp-slate updated with the bot's scan data. He read the analysis with a confused frown.

"JACAB is only picking up one life form on the bridge," Carter said, after re-reading the data to double-check. "There are sporadic indications of other Aterniens elsewhere, but it doesn't make any sense."

"Why only one Aternien to guard the bridge?" Carina asked. "Something about this seems off."

His XO was resting against the wall and Carter noted that her skin was clammy. The heady combination of drugs, combined with the withdrawal effects of a high dose nano-stim was starting to take its toll on his human second-in-command.

RAEB was next to chirrup an update, and the bot had a short electronic exchange with JACAB, before sending its report to their comp-slates.

"RAEB says he's unlocked the door," Kendra said. She had both pistols raised and ready. "So, I guess we go in and see who's waiting for us?"

Carter's senses were also telling him something was wrong, but he had little choice other than to continue. He faced the door then raised his buckler and cutlass, which was still humming with deadly plasma energy. He considered going in shooting, but he needed the bridge intact, and his 57-EX would likely do more harm than good.

"Open it…" Carter said, glancing back to RAEB.

The bot nodded then the door slid aside. He expected to be met with a barrage of enemy particle fire, but the only sound was that of his own breathing. He stepped onto the bridge of his ship, but it appeared deserted. Then he noticed that someone was sitting in his command chair. He approached closer, and the Aternien Overseer rose to greet him, war spear in hand. Carter saw that she had regenerated the cut he'd sliced through her belly, and that her golden dragon-scale armor was fully intact again too.

"Kendra, get the core OS installed, and get the Galatine online," Carter said, speaking the command over their comm channel, without taking his eyes of the Aternien.

"You got it boss…" Kendra replied.

The engineer and her bot hurried to the console that housed the primary core block and set to work. Meanwhile, Major Larsen stalked to the port side of the bridge and was covering the Overseer with her energy pistol. Suddenly, relays thumped, and the lights switched on. Soon after, gravity was restored to the bridge, and the space was flooded with breathable air. Carter watched the indicators on his comp-slate until the pressure and oxygen readings were nominal, then deactivated his head covering.

"Where's the Grand Vizier?" he asked, careful to remain out of stabbing range of the Overseer's war spear.

"The Grand Vizier regrets that he cannot grant you an audience," the Overseer replied, in a high-handed manner, though her smug tone suggested she was hiding something. "He has already departed."

"What do you mean, departed? Departed for where?" Carter growled.

A short, sharp thump reverberated through the deck, and Carter heard JACAB quietly warble and squawk somewhere to his rear. His comp-slate updated, and he carefully raised his arm to read the update. Sighing, he shook his head and turned back to the Overseer.

"What is it?" asked Carina. Like Carter she had also removed her head covering.

"The scout ship just detached from the docking hatch," Carter said, speaking loud enough that Kendra could also hear him. "The Vizier was on-board."

The consoles on the bridge powered up, and the main viewer illuminated. It was like the front quarter of the bridge had suddenly dematerialized and opened a window directly into space itself. However, it wasn't the millions of asteroids surrounding the exo-planet that had grabbed his attention, but the single Aternien scout ship. It was battle-scarred and weary, like himself, but it was still operational and still a threat.

"I've restored power to the bridge stations, but the core OS is still building," Kendra called out. "It'll be a few minutes before it has fully compiled, and I can get the reactor, engines and weapons powered up. We're operating on battery backups right now, which are already highly degraded."

"Understood, Kendra, but focus on main power, nano-mechanical armor and weapons as a priority," Carter replied.

Kendra acknowledged the order then redoubled her efforts, with RAEB assisting.

"Major, get on tactical and scan the scout," Carter said to his XO. "I want to know if its cannon comes back online." Carina hesitated; her weapon still trained on the Aternien. "Don't worry about her," he added, sensing her unease at leaving him alone with the Overseer. "I can handle our guest."

The Overseer snorted and looked down her nose at him, but Carina reluctantly complied, holstered her pistol, and jogged to the tactical station. Carter took a step closer to the Overseer, dropping his sword lower at the same time. The Aternien tightened her hold on her spear and her glowing blue eyes sharpened.

"Scanner resolution is still poor, but the scout doesn't seem like a threat," Carina reported. "From what I can tell, its particle cannon is too badly damaged to fire."

The Overseer laughed then jabbed the point of her spear in Carina's direction.

"This is what you fight so hard to protect?" the Overseer said, making her contempt for Major Larsen clear. "Their primitive organic minds cannot even grasp what is happening." She lowered her spear and her innocent-looking, youthful face smiled at him. "Yet you understand, don't you?"

The tactical station chimed an alert, and Carina cursed bitterly. She was about to report the update, but Carter already knew what she was going to say.

"The scout has torpedoes," Carter said, taking another casual step toward the Overseer. She was now inches from being within striking range of his sword. "Without our nanomechanical armor, this ship won't withstand a direct hit at this range, not in her current condition. That's why the Grand Vizier left. If he can't steal the Galatine, he'll destroy her."

The Overseer gave him a mocking smile and tapped her hand against the shaft of her spear. The weapon generated a resonant chime, like a silver fork striking a crystal champagne glass to announce a toast.

"Well done, Master Commander," the Overseer said, her comment thick with condescension. "At least you're smarter than the worthless sacks of meat and bone you serve, like the loyal dog you are."

The tactical station chimed another alert, and he could hear his XO's heart-rate climbing sharply.

"The scout is arming torpedoes," Carina reported. "The vessel's targeting systems are still down, but it won't be long before it's ready to fire. One or two minutes at most…"

"I'm on it…" Kendra called out. She didn't need to be told that time was of the essence, more so than ever.

"Why are you even here?" Carina said, fixing her gaze on the Overseer. "If the Grand Vizier destroys this ship, you'll die too."

"Control your animal," the Overseer snapped, growling like an angry bear. "Every word this human speaks to me is an insult."

Carina pulled her pistol and aimed it at the Overseer's head. "Keep talking shit about me, lady, and I'll display your neuromorphic brains all over the damned bridge."

Carter could tell that his XO was sincere in her threat, but the Overseer brushed it off like it was inconsequential.

"My soul is already safe," the Aternien said, continuing her tone of abject disrespect. "As an Overseer, my mind is permanently linked to the Soul Crypt through the conduit of spacetime. Immortals are reborn from their soul blocks, but kill me, and I will simply live on in a new body, with all my memories intact, right up until the moment I cease to function." She mocked Carter with another cruel smile. "It is not me who dies today, commander, but you and your crew."

Carter could sense that the Overseer had made peace with her situation. She had been left behind to make a point, not to fight, since the woman knew that she couldn't face Carter and the others alone. However, the fact that she would be reborn with all her memories, up until the inevitable point at which Carter killed her, presented an opportunity too.

"Why are you doing this?" Carter asked, eager to gather what intelligence he could from the condemned woman. "The war ended over a century ago, and in that time, humanity hasn't bothered you. We were no threat."

"Humanity will always be a threat to us," the Overseer countered. "Better than anyone, you know how their fears and prejudices drive their actions. Whether now, or in another hundred years, or even ten thousand, humans and Aterniens will cross-paths again, and the Union, or whatever it becomes in the future, will still see us as the enemy." She paused to read Carter's expression, and he realized that the Overseer was no simple warrior; she was intelligent, and insightful, and believed every word she was saying. "We are not all that different, commander. We both fight for a cause we believe in. The difference is that you fight for a people who despise you, while I fight for my god-king, who loves me, as he loves all Aterniens."

Carter considered her answers, which were reasoned and, in many ways, rational and understandable. However, regardless of what the woman's real age might have been, she still had the naivety of youth.

"You place too much faith into your god-king, Overseer," Carter replied, respecting her honesty by keeping a civil tone. "The real reason for this war is far simpler than you realize. Revenge."

There was a flash of anger behind the woman's glowing blue eyes, and her synthetic muscles tensed.

"You see, I do understand," Carter continued. "I know how it feels to be cast out and rejected. It made me angry and bitter too, just as it did to Markus Aternus. And now he's going to make humanity pay for their actions."

"And why shouldn't they?" the Overseer hissed. Carter could see that she was on the verge of snapping and launching an attack. "Why shouldn't we take revenge upon those who wronged us?" She paused and shook her head at him. "And why, of all people, are you defending them?"

"Because I took an oath to protect the Union," Carter answered. His senses had peaked – he was ready. "Because, unlike your god-king, I'm an honorable man."

The Overseer exploded with rage, and leapt at Carter, spear pulled back, ready to strike. He watched the angle of the thrust and waited until the last possible moment, before deflecting the attack with his buckler, and using the Overseer's momentum to drive his cutlass through her chest all the way to the hilt.

The war spear fell from the Overseer's grasp and clattered against the metal deck plates, like the sound of glass smashing. He left the sword buried deep in the woman's body, and held her in his arms, so that she didn't fall. Despite the certainty of her rebirth, she still looked terrified. Deep down, the human fear of dying was still ingrained into her psyche; a base human instinct that even Markus Aternus' programming could not eliminate.

"We are the future, Commander…" the Overseer said, her voice barely more than a whisper. "You and I should not be enemies."

"I agree," Carter replied. He could feel the Overseer's strength fading fast. "Tell me your name. At least give me that."

The Overseer rested her hands onto Carter's shoulder, and for a second, he thought she was trying to strangle him, but her hold was warm, not threatening, and she pulled her mouth closer to his ear.

"Though I fall, I also endure…" Her voice was weak, and her words ebbed and flowed like a meadow stream, drying up in the sun. "Aternus is immortal. Aternus is forever…"

The Overseer's blue eyes went cold and dark, and she fell limp in his arms. Carter grunted a sigh and threw the woman's synthetic body to the deck, treating it as the empty husk it now was.

"The Aternien scout has a target lock," Carina said, snapping Carter back to the sobering reality of their situation. "They'll be ready to fire in moments."

Carter stepped away from the Overseer and turned to Kendra and her robotic helpers.

"Kendra, RAEB, if ever you wanted to impress me, now is the time…"

RAEB bleeped cheerfully then energy hummed through the ship, and the whole vessel seemed to snap together like two powerful magnets coming into contact.

"Main power restored and nano-reactive armor is online," Kendra said. Her face was covered in grease. "I'd say it was a team effort, but RAEB was the real star player."

JACAB warbled indignantly, and Kendra bowed her head to the bot. "Ably assisted, by another star performer, of course."

This appeared to appease JACAB, who chirruped and hummed closer to the engineer.

"Torpedoes incoming!" Carina called out.

"Relax Major," Carter said, turning to the view screen. "They can't hurt us now."

The Aternien torpedoes thudded into the Galatine's hull, but the energy was dissipated throughout the vessel, which acted like a giant heatsink. Carter dropped into his command chair and used its comp-slate to check for damage, but their armor had held fast.

"Lock on to that ship and prepare to fire," Carter ordered,

enjoying the snug and perfectly-contoured fit of his chair. "Let's deliver the Vizier back to his god-king with a message of failure."

Carina acknowledged the order, then another alert chimed from the tactical console.

"The scout is hailing us," Carina reported. She huffed a laugh and rested her elbows on the console. "He's seen the writing on the wall, so of course now he wants to talk…"

Carter snorted a laugh then shrugged. "Put him through."

Carina connected the two ships and the face of the Grand Vizier appeared on the screen, larger than life, and still impossibly perfect in every detail.

"If you're calling to offer your surrender, Vizier, you can shove it up your shiny ass," Carter said, making his position clear, before the Aternien had managed to speak. "You're outgunned, and that scout is going nowhere fast."

To his surprise, however, the Grand Vizier was smiling.

"I think not, my old friend," the Aternien noble replied. "This war is only just getting started."

Another alert rang out from the tactical console, but this time it was more urgent, and from the rapid beating of his XO's heart, he knew it was bad news.

"Warp signature detected…" Carina said, breathlessly. "Another ship just arrived, right on top of us, but I don't recognize the configuration."

"Put it on the screen," Carter said, his senses spiking.

Carina worked the controls and the vessel appeared. Carter was not one to succumb to feelings of fear or despair, but on this occasion, his human side won out.

"That's the Solar Barque, Mesek-tet." Carter turned to his XO, stony faced. "That's Markus Aternus' ship…"

TWENTY-SIX
GLORY OR DEATH

MASTER COMMANDER ROSE silently cursed the Grand Vizier as he watched the Mesek-tet swoop in and collect the damaged scout ship into its hold. The Aternien Solar Barque then maneuvered itself in front of the Galatine, and held position, nose-to-nose with them.

"Kendra, tell me that we have weapons," Carter said.

His aching muscles were tense, but his augments, along with his years of combat experience, kept his nerves in check.

"We're working on it, boss, but so far nothing that will put a scratch on that old bird," the engineer replied. "I'm hoping you can buy us some more time."

Carter checked his comp-slate, but so far, the Mesek-tet had not attempted to signal them, nor was it preparing to fire.

"Maybe he's waiting for me to make the first move," Carter considered. "I guess that picking up the horn and calling me would be beneath the mighty Markus Aternus."

Carter turned to his XO, who was transfixed, as if the arrival of the Mesek-tet had turned her to stone, like a troll suddenly exposed to sunlight.

"Major, if you're done gawping, I need a tactical analysis on that ship," Carter said. His question succeeded in jolting Carina out of her stupor, and her eyes snapped to his. "It seems the Aterniens had the same idea we had about recovering ancient weapons of war, but I need to know the condition of the Mesek-tet, because if that thing is fully-operational then we're toast."

Carina nodded then returned her gaze to the Solar Barque on the view screen and swallowed hard. Her hands were still frozen in place on the deck of the console.

"Focus, Major, I need you sharper than ever," Carter snapped. For the first time since they'd met, he'd spoken to her sternly, in the manner of her superior officer. Their relationship had begun in an unusual and abnormally casual manner, but right now he needed to assert his authority. With an Aternien Solar Barque bearing down on them, there was no room for complacency.

"Sorry, Commander, I'm on it," Carina said, reacting in a professional manner, just as he'd hoped she would.

Carter nodded then glanced at his gopher. "JACAB, give her a hand, buddy. Our sensors are still shot to hell."

JACAB bleeped then hovered beside Major Larsen and interfaced with the tactical console, lending his own processing power and unique computer intuition to the task. Carter returned his gaze to the ship on the screen. He could hardly blame his XO for being mesmerized by it; the Mesek-tet was achingly beautiful in a way that inorganic objects rarely were.

The aft section of the ship was like a symmetrical battle axe, forged from a mythical, golden metal known only to the gods. This curved elegantly toward the middle-section of the vessel, where blade-like superstructures rose from the hull like the fins of a jet fighter plane. The forward section of the Solar Barque was no less elegant and dangerous-looking, narrowing to a diamond nose that resembled a four-bladed broadhead arrow.

The entire ship gleamed in the sunlight of the nearby star, reflecting intense golds, ochres, and azurites, like it was a jewel embedded into the very fabric of the cosmos. Etched across the hull were the hieroglyphs of the Aternien Royal Court, and the symbol of Markus Aternus – a golden ankh imprinted with the face of the god-king himself.

"I've got some good news and some bad news," Major Larsen reported. Ironically, it was now his XO that had shaken him from an entranced state. "There's little doubt they've had the Mesek-tet for longer than we've had the Galatine, but it's still far from one hundred percent."

"Go on…" Carter said, joining his XO at the tactical station.

"We got lucky with the Galatine having crash-landed on the mud-soaked exo-planet, because it meant she remained intact, structurally, anyway."

Carina nodded to JACAB and the bot projected a schematic of the Solar Barque in front of them as a hologram.

"The Piazzi asteroid field really went to town on the Mesek-tet during the century it was out here." She pointed to specific sections of the vessel's hull. "These areas show evidence of recent repairs, and in many cases, they've yet to graft their scale armor on top."

"What about its offensive capabilities?" Carter asked.

He welcomed the news that the Solar Barque wasn't yet fully repaired, and noted its weak points with interest, but what he really needed to know was whether it could blow them out of the water.

"That's where things are less rosy, I'm afraid," Carina answered. "The Aterniens have clearly focused on refurbishing weaponry above all else, and we know it already has soliton warp capabilities. Based on these scans, it has four active banks of particle cannons, which is all it needs to spoil our day."

Carter assessed the scans and concurred with his XO. "If that's the case then what the hell are they waiting for?"

Carina shrugged. "I suppose you'd better ask."

Carter grunted an acknowledgment then returned to face the viewscreen and pressed his hands to the small of his back.

"JACAB, open a channel to the Mesek-tet."

The bot chirruped a reply and a few anxious seconds later the image of the Grand Vizier appeared on the screen.

"You're on the wrong ship," Carter said, though he noted that the Aternien was not seated on the command throne of the vessel but was someplace else on its regal bridge. "The Senuset was your Solar Barque, remember?"

"I remember all too well," the Grand Vizier replied, unimpressed with Carter's flippant opening line of attack. "And the god-king does not speak to merely anyone. I wanted to be sure that it was you who was requesting an audience with the great Markus Aternus, and not your human pet."

To his rear, he heard Carina snort with derision, but continued to focus on the Vizier.

"I don't want an audience," Carter answered. "I just want to tell your boss, face-to-face, to stay the hell out of Union space, and never come back."

"That would be unwise, especially as it seems that our actions were justified." The Vizier extended a hand toward the screen, as if gesturing to the bridge that surrounded Carter. "The Aternien Act forbade you from maintaining Longsword-class battleships, did it not?"

"It did, but then you've hardly room to talk, do you?" Carter said, pointing right back at the Aternien. "Don't try to pretend that you only just recovered the Mesek-tet in response to us finding the Galatine. We scanned your ship and know that you've been working to restore it for some time, so how about you cut the shit?"

The Grand Vizier considered his next words carefully, then appeared to relax his posture.

"Very well, Master Commander, we shall speak plainly to one another; one post-human to another." A scan of the Galatine appeared on the screen, and Carter had to bite his tongue to stop himself from cursing. "We too have scanned your vessel, and it is clear that you are in no condition to resist us."

"Get this over with and shoot already," Carter hit back. He was done talking.

"The god-king has an offer for you," the Grand Vizier replied, shocking Carter with the unexpected response. "That is, assuming you are humble enough to listen?"

Carter glanced at Kendra and his engineer held up two fingers. The comp-slate on his forearm then updated and he saw that JACAB had transmitted the progress report to him, relayed via RAEB. A normal human being would have experienced a sudden rush of adrenalin, sparked by the excitement of the news he'd just received, but his primal instincts were different. There was no flight – only fight – and what he'd seen told him that a fight was still on the cards, so long as he could stall the Aterniens for another couple of minutes.

"Very well, Grand Vizier, I will hear what your leader has to say," Carter replied, doing his best to sound cooperative and respectful, as the Aternien had asked.

"First, you must ensure that your human officer does not address the god-king, or speak in his presence," the Vizier added, with a darker tone.

Carina laughed out loud. "You can tell Aternus he can kiss my homosapien ass."

Carter winced and turned to his XO, shooting her a look that he hoped conveyed his sincere desire for her to bite her tongue and take it on the chin. Carina growled under her breath and folded her arms across her chest but exercised her better judgement and stayed silent.

"The Major will respect your request," Carter said to the Vizier, though he could feel his XO's eyes burrowing into the back of his head.

The Grand Vizier nodded then bowed his head low, and the scene switched to display the command throne. This was the equivalent of Carter's captain's chair, except it was impossibly grander. Golden in color, like the Solar Barque itself, and set on a plinth above the main deck that was accessed by a bejeweled flight of steps, the command throne was every bit the seat of a king. The Ankh of Aternus seemed to hover above and behind the throne, gleaming like polished diamond, while a pair of ornate braziers sat to either side, burning with ethereal azure flames.

The god-king was seated on the throne, and though Carter had seen Markus Aternus before, it had been on only a few, fleeting occasions. The man who was famously the first human to ever transition into a synthetic mind and body was taller and more physically imposing than the lither Aterniens that served him and called him a god. His sculpted features were unrealistically beautiful, such that he was barely recognizable from the flesh-and-bone human being that had been born at the turn of the twenty-third century.

The god-king's clothing was equally magnificent. A bejeweled, golden band ran around his head like a crown, while a long and narrow metal beard protruded from his strong chin. This was complimented by an ornate golden neck-covering, like the Usekh collars worn by the Egyptian pharaohs on whom he had based his visage. Like the Grand Vizier, Markus Aternus also wore elaborate scale armor adorned with Royal Court hieroglyphs and his personal Ankh. All things considered, the leader of the Aternien Empire looked more alien than human, and had Carter not known the man's origins, he would have assumed Aternus to be from another universe entirely.

"You have grown old, Master Commander Carter Rose," Markus Aternus observed. The faux-deity's voice possessed an unearthly resonance, as if the words had been spoken from the summit of mount Olympus.

"I quite like the silver, actually," Carter replied, stroking his beard. "You don't look any different, though, Your Majesty. I guess being synthetic helps."

"I am ageless, Commander," Aternus replied, continuing to speak with an otherworldly whimsy that was both absurdly theatrical and eerily disturbing. "Nor do I forget. While the Union has grown complacent, fat, and lazy, my empire has been rebuilt and made strong."

"Good for you," Carter said, offering the god-king a congratulatory nod. "Though, it's the first I've heard of it, since you folk didn't bother to show up at the Diplomatic Outpost even once." He paused to correct himself. "Apart from when the Vizier attacked us, and all but declared war on the Union."

"Negotiation is irrelevant," Aternus countered, with a brief flash of irritation. "The word of a human cannot be trusted. In the end, it would always come down to war."

Carter shook his head. "I can honestly tell you that the Union has no interest in a war, and even less interest in your empire. You've been gone for a century; so long that no-one even remembers who you are, anymore. So, my advice is to take your ship and head on back to whatever gold-encrusted planet you live on these days, and never return."

Aternus' sparkling eyes sharpened and glowed brighter, and his thin cheeks were sucked in, making his angular face appear chisel-sharp.

"Humanity may have forgotten, but I remember everything," Aternus replied, betraying his anger more clearly this time.

The god-king rose from his throne, revealing the full scale of the Aternien's physical grandeur. Not only was the synthetic man built like a mystical warrior-king, but he also stood at least eight feet tall.

"It is in your nature to fear that which is different from you," Aternus continued, speaking as if giving a lecture. "It is why you demonized us, and cast us out, and it is why you stole our lands. I will not wait for humanity to take up arms against the Aterniens once again. I will crush your Union and reclaim that which was taken from me."

Carter glanced across to Kendra and she casually gave him a thumbs-up signal. His engineer had attempted to disguise the gesture, but in so doing had managed to make it more obvious. Had it not been for the imposing aura of the god-king staring down at him, he might have smiled.

"The Vizier said you have an offer to make?" Carter said, hurrying the conversation to a conclusion, so that their inevitable battle could finally begin.

Markus Aternus began to pace down the steps from his command throne, so that his long, inhuman-looking face filled the screen and appeared even more intimidating.

"I am offering you a position by my side, at the Royal Court," Aternus said.

Carter was struck dumb. Out of the possible scenarios he could have imagined, this particular offer had not even factored amongst them.

"I offer you the chance to fulfill your potential, amongst those who appreciate your uniqueness," Aternus continued, mistaking Carter's stunned silence as a sign of interest. "Human beings despise you. To them, you are merely a disposable tool. You know this in your heart. But amongst the Aterniens, your post-human qualities are revered. You would live a life of purpose and respect. You would be valued."

Markus Aternus held out his hand, as if inviting Carter to take it, even though they were separated by the void of space.

"Join me, Master Commander Rose," Aternus said, compelling Carter with his powerful voice. "Become a member of my court, and together we will usher in a new era of peace and prosperity; one where the cruel whims and desires of human beings are no more."

Carter stroked his beard then cast his eyes across to his engineer. Kendra Castle looked as stupefied as he had felt only moments earlier. He could usually read her like a book, but this time he drew a blank. Next, he turned to his XO. At the best of times, Carina Larsen wore her heart openly on her sleeve, but the look of sheer terror in her eyes spoke volumes. She was afraid that he was going to accept the god-king's offer, and for this he blamed himself. If Carina had doubts it was because he had given her reason to.

"Join me, Carter," Aternus said again, his voice somehow even more resplendent and convincing. "You know it is the right choice."

Carter sighed and looked around the bridge of his old ship; a ship that had carried him into battle on more occasions than he cared to count. She had always brought him home, and whether he liked it or not – whether they wanted him or not – home was the Planetary Union of Nine.

"Go back to your world, Your Majesty," Carter said, returning his gaze to the mesmerizing, glowing eyes of the god-king. "Go home and stay there, because if you invade Union space, I will personally put your so-called immortality to the test."

Markus Aternus lowered his hand and stepped back. The drawn look on the king's face became almost skeletal, like that of an ancient pharaoh of Egypt, risen from his tomb by an act of arcane magic.

"Very well, Master Commander Rose, of the Planetary Union of Nine," Aternus said. The king climbed the stairs to his throne and lowered himself onto it. "Instead of an eternal life of peace and respect, you shall have death."

TWENTY-SEVEN
SWORD VS. STAR

"THE MESEK-TET IS COMING ABOUT!" Carina announced, as Carter raced to the vacant navigation station. "Weapons lock detected… they're firing!"

The Galatine was rocked by a volley of energy blasts, then the Solar Barque slipped out of view as it soared above their stricken and immobile warship.

"Kendra, time's up, I need engines and weapons *now*!" Carter called out, hammering inputs into the navigation controls, but the ship remained unresponsive.

"I've got our one-twenties online, but the plasma cannons will take a little longer," his engineer reported.

"The one-twenties will do for now," Carter replied, trying again to engage their engines without success. "But right now, we're a sitting duck."

A reverberant thrum shook the deck, and he recognized it at once as the sound of the Galatine's massive engines sparking into life.

"Engines are online," Kendra reported, as another volley of particle blasts lashed the ship. "I can give you propulsion, but at no more than fifty percent."

Carter tried the controls again, and this time the Galatine

lurched forward under its own power for the first time in a century.

"It's like maneuvering through treacle, but at least we're moving," Carter muttered, turning away from another volley of energy blasts, which whipped past their aft quarter. "I'm going to try to get an angle on the Mesek-tet. Major, be ready to fire, and don't wait for my order."

"Aye, sir," Carina replied, her response snappy and alert. "The one-twenty millimeter cannons are loaded and ready, but targeting is manual only."

"Then here's where you impress me, Major," Carter called back.

The smooth-bore cannons fired mass-projectiles, but they were far from dumb instruments of destruction. The shells used nano-adaptive armor piercing explosive warheads, which could take out Aternien destroyers in a single volley. The Mesek-tet, however, was another matter.

Carter drew a bead on the god-king's ship and the twelve guns opened fire, but despite its weathered state, the Aternien Solar Barque was still nimbler than the Galatine, and the shots flew wide.

"Shit!" Carina cursed, hammering the palms of her hands against the console.

"You get one miss, Major, and that was it," Carter said, veering off in pursuit of the Mesek-tet. "Make sure you nail the next shot."

"Aye, sir," Carina replied, furious with herself.

In truth, Carter didn't blame her. The Galatine's targeting system was shot, and the guns were misaligned and hadn't been fired in a century. If she had scored a hit on the first attempt, it would have been a one in a million shot. Even so, he needed to focus his XO's mind, because they wouldn't get many more chances to take the Mesek-tet down.

"Kendra, do we have warp drive?" Carter asked, throwing

the Galatine to starboard, but not before a particle blast ripped into their port wing.

"With the core OS installed, I can squeeze one jump out of her, boss, but it won't be pretty," Kendra called back. She was still half-buried inside consoles. "I've already got the soliton warp drive spinning up, but it'll be a few minutes before we can jump."

Another enemy volley hammered into the ship and the auxiliary stations along the starboard wall exploded, showering Carina with blistering sparks and razor-sharp shards of shrapnel, but the ship's XO bit down against the pain and fought on.

"We don't have a few minutes," Carina reported, brushing burning debris from her hair. "Structural integrity is down to sixty-eight percent, and our armor is buckling. This old bird can't take much more."

"She'll hold together," Carter answered, willing it to be so. He knew the Galatine better than anyone, Kendra Castle aside, and she was a fighter, just like himself. "Get ready on the cannons and target their structural weak points. We can't outgun the Mesek-tet in our current condition, but with Markus Aternus on-board, they'll be cautious. We only need to bloody their nose and they'll turn back."

Carter threw the ship to port and powered the Galatine in pursuit of the Mesek-tet. At their best, the two vessels were evenly matched in terms of firepower, but while the vainglorious Aterniens had invested time and energy into creating a battleship that looked as elegant as it was deadly, the Union had forged the Longswords as pure weapons of war. This meant that the Galatine could cut through space more sharply than its rival.

"Look alive, Major," Carter called out, baring down on his enemy. "I can give you a clear shot in seven seconds; make sure you take it."

Despite a century wallowing in a muddy grave, the Galatine had taken to its role like a duck to water. He could feel the beat of the reactor and the thrum of the engines, like a driver being in tune with the road through a steering wheel. Before long, the Mesek-tet appeared directly ahead. Carter had out-turned the Aternien flagship, which was now trying to evade their guns like a Messerschmitt Bf 109 trying to shake off an attacking Spitfire.

"Major, take the shot!" Carter called out, struggling to maintain his turn and keep the Mesek-tet in their sights.

"Cannons away!" his XO responded, and the deck rumbled as the Galatine's array of twelve 120mm smooth bore guns unloaded at the Aternien ship.

Carter's super-human eyes were able to trace the path of the warheads, in a way that normal human vision could not, and he already knew that Carina had struck true before the shots had even landed.

"Direct hit!" Carina called out, hammering the console with her fist, this time jubilantly. "Moderate damage to their portside, aft. We cracked their shell, but they're still coming!"

Suddenly, the Galatine was hit out of nowhere and Carter felt the engines falter. He turned sharply to starboard, abandoning pursuit of the Mesek-tet in the process, but his senses told him it was the right move.

"Report!" Carter ordered.

"We just ran into a torpedo," Carina replied. The blast had thrown her clear of her console and she was clawing herself back to it. "It was from the Mesek-tet. They dropped it into our path like a mine."

Carter cursed and tried to reacquire the powerful solar barque, but the Aternien warship was almost on top of them. More than ever, he wished that his Master Navigator, Amaya Reid, was at the helm, because without her piloting genius, they were sorely disadvantaged.

A savage blast then rocked the bridge, and if it wasn't for his augmented strength, Carter would have been thrown clear of his station. Fires erupted and smoke clouded his vision, but he clung on. So long as power still coursed through the Galatine like blood through his veins, he would fight to the very end.

"Damage report!" Carter ordered, while coaxing more thrust from their tired engines.

"Engine two has all but given out," Carina replied, waving smoke away from her screens. "And our nanomechanical armor has failed in sections C4 to C7. If we take another hit there, we're done for."

Carter gritted his teeth and swung the longsword around, rolling its blade-like frame to keep the damaged sections away from the Mesek-tet's guns.

"Kendra, how are we doing on that plasma cannon?" Carter said. Their one-twenties weren't going to be enough; they needed a bigger gun.

"I can give you one shot, but that's it," the engineer called back. Her uniform was scorched black, and blood was trickling down her face and neck from exploded debris that had peppered her like a blunderbuss. "Make it count…"

Carter turned to his XO, but she was way ahead of him.

"Just get that ship in our sights and I'll blast the Aterniens back to whatever rock they crawled out from," Carina said. Her trembling hands were gripping the sides of the console for support, and she looked ragged and worn out, but her determined stare told him she meant business.

More shots flashed past, but this time Carter was in-tune enough with his old ship that he managed to evade them. Even so, the Galatine was bleeding out and couldn't last much longer.

"RAEB, get to engineering and see if you can boost the power," Carter said. "JACAB, you assist Kendra while he's gone."

RAEB chirruped then sped off the bridge like a cannonball, and at the same time, JACAB hummed to Kendra's side, and dutifully awaited her instructions.

"Where's my target, Commander?" Carina called out.

She sounded like a stern schoolteacher, demanding to see a student's homework. However, he liked the fact that she was pushing him as hard as he was pushing her. Everyone needed to be at their sharpest, the captain included.

Another particle blast raced past, but this time the Aternien ship had overcooked its attack and missed. Carter seized the opportunity and threw the Galatine hard to port. The Mesek-tet tried to shake him, but while the Aterniens had advanced their technology in the last hundred years, their tactics had remained the same. The two vessels remained locked in a deadly ballet powered by fusion engines and thrusters, until Carter finally zeroed-in on his prey.

"Got them!" Carter called out, as the Solar Barque appeared dead center in the viewscreen.

"Plasma cannon locked on… Firing!" Major Larsen hit the initiator to fire so hard that she almost smashed the console, and the resulting energy blast was equally as violent. A bolt of searing plasma raced from the sword-like tip of the Galatine and struck the Mesek-tet cleanly across its elegant belly. There was an explosion and debris flew off the ship, which began to list out of control.

"Great shot Major, now hit them again with the one-twenties," Carter ordered, shaking his fist at the screen. "Let's blow them back to hell!"

"Yes, sir, locking on," Carina replied.

There was now a broad smile on his XO's scorched face, and though her hands were still trembling, they moved across the console screens with more assuredness. Then the smile fell off her face, and her heartbeat doubled.

"Weapons malfunction," Carina reported. "Our one-twenties are offline."

Carter gritted his teeth and turned back to the viewscreen. The Mesek-tet had regained control, and its arrow-like nose was now pointed straight at them. All it would take was one more shot to put the Solar Barque down, but the same was true of the Galatine, and the Aterniens had them dead to rights.

"Kendra, can you scrounge enough power to deploy the plasma shield?" Carter called out. It was now their only chance.

Carina scowled. "Plasma shield? What shield?"

The plasma shield was an energy barrier held in place by an intense magnetic field, which vaporized conventional weapons on impact, and absorbed energy blasts like a sponge. The problem was that it ate power, and worked both ways, which meant that while they couldn't be shot, they also couldn't shoot back. Ordinarily, he would have been more than happy to explain this to his XO, but there was simply no time.

"I can do it, but I'd have to steal power from the warp drive," Kendra replied, after rapidly working through the calculations on her comp-slate. "It'll save us, but it'll also strand us here for another ten minutes, at least."

Carter understood the stakes. If he stole power from the warp drive, it would force them to fight the Mesek-tet to the death, but if he didn't, they were dead anyway.

"Do it, Kendra; a slim chance is better than none," Carter replied, before meeting his XO's confused gaze. "Stand by to deploy the shield."

"You'll have to show me how," Carina answered, looking increasingly frazzled, both from the flames licking at her console, and the stress of battle.

Carter leapt from his station, and hurdled his command chair, landing at Carina's side in the blink of an eye.

"It's okay, Major, take the helm," Carter said, assuming control of tactical. "Instead of shooting things, I now need you to make sure we don't get shot."

"Aye, sir, make us squirrelly," Carina answered, rushing to the navigation station, which was barely functional, like the rest of the ship.

"The Mesek-tet is about to fire," Carter said, again turning to his beleaguered engineer. "It's now or never, Kendra."

"Then it's now," Kendra replied. "Hit it!"

Carter engaged the plasma shield just as the Mesek-tet fired a full volley of particle blasts from its forward cannons. The shield was hit, and a cocoon of pure energy lit up the space surrounding the Galatine. Another volley came at them, and explosions rippled across the bridge, like they'd been strafed with particle blasts from a squad of Immortals.

"Navigation is down," Carina reported.

"Plasma shield is critical!" Kendra added, having to shout to be heard above the roar of the ship falling apart around them.

Fire and smoke filled the bridge, and JACAB hummed away to help fight it, since the suppression system was also damaged. Carter tried their weapons again, but their one-twenties and plasma cannon were inoperative. They were dead in the water, and toothless.

"Plasma shield is down," Kendra shouted. "That's it, boss. I can't give you anything more."

Carter roared with anger and frustration and hammered the tactical console so hard he split it down the dead center.

"Come on!" Carter yelled into the air, pleading with the Galatine directly. "Fight, damn you! I need you to fight!"

The tactical console flashed then chirruped and Carter looked at the screen in disbelief. Their plasma cannon had come back online, but at a quarter of its maximum power.

It'll be enough... Carter told himself. *It'll have to be...*

He fired blind, knowing that Carina could do nothing to affect their aim, then peered at the viewscreen, as the ball of plasma raced toward the Mesek-tet and struck it cleanly across its stern quarter. Explosions rippled across the body of the golden vessel and its engines flickered on and off, like a faulty light bulb. He was about to call out in celebration, when a conduit next to the navigation console exploded, and Major Larsen was blown across the bridge like a kite in a storm.

TWENTY-EIGHT

HARD CHOICES

CARTER VAULTED the tactical station and ran to where Major Larsen had landed in a crumpled heap on the deck. She was still conscious, though her eyelids were fluttering, and a shard of broken metal had penetrated her battle uniform and impaled itself through her shoulder.

"JACAB, get over here, she's hurt!" Carter called out, before turning to his engineer. "Kendra, what's the condition of the Mesek-tet?"

"She's stricken, to put it mildly," Kendra replied. "The Mesek-tet's weapons are offline, but she's still got power."

"So long as she can't fire, she can't destroy us," Carter replied. "For now, that will do."

JACAB hummed over to Carina and began to scan her. At the same time, Carter pulled the shard of metal from her shoulder, like it was an arrow. Carina cried out in pain, but her battle uniform quickly repaired the hole to seal the wound and stem any bleeding.

"Your job now is to keep her breathing, understood?" Carter said, looking his bot directly in its glowing red eye.

JACAB nodded and warbled meekly, before setting to work. He left his gopher to it and returned to the command chair. The dense seat padding suddenly felt less comfortable, as if it were filled with needles.

"Kendra, check our weapons," Carter called out, massaging his smoke-blackened silver beard.

Kendra dashed to the tactical station and worked the console, but she was soon shaking her head. "The plasma cannon and one-twenties are both offline, and our missile system is shot to hell too," she reported. "I suppose we could try standing on the hull and firing at them with pistols?"

Carter managed a gruff laugh, but it was because of the absurdity of their predicament, rather than Kendra's joke. He had the god-king, Markus Aternus, dead to rights, and couldn't do a damned thing about it. One shot could end the war before it had even begun, but he didn't have so much as a cork-gun to shoot at them. Then he had an idea and massaged his beard even more deeply.

"I know what you're thinking," Kendra said, quietly.

Carter scowled at her. "How do you know that? *I* don't even know what I'm thinking."

Kendra just raised her eyebrows at him and gave him a look that said, "don't bullshit me." Carter nodded and sighed. He agreed that he owed her that, at the very least.

"We could end it right now, Kendra," Carter said, choosing to come clean. "We could ram that sun ship and split it wide open, spilling the god-king and his minions into space." He shrugged and met his engineer's eyes. "Hell, we might even survive."

His engineer's eyebrows remained almost at her hairline.

"Fine, we probably won't survive it," Carter admitted, grumpily. "But who's to say we won't get blown up tomorrow, or next week? At least this way, our deaths are for something. At least this way our lives *meant* something."

Kendra was silent for a time, but Carter could sense she still had questions and doubts.

"Would Aternus even die if we blew up his ship?" the

engineer eventually asked. "He'll just get reborn like his foot soldiers."

Carter shrugged, but admitted that Kendra had a point. "He probably will regenerate, but even if we can't kill Aternus the man, we can kill the legend. Just think about it, Kendra… the god-king beaten by a couple of humans and his sun ship reduced to atoms."

"Post-humans," Kendra corrected him.

"My point stands." Carter was adamant that he was right. "And this may be the only shot we get at Aternus."

He knew what he was asking, but like himself, Kendra Castle had lived a long life. Neither of them knew how many more years they had ahead. Conceivably, their engineered physiology could extend their lifespan by another century or even two, but he'd already spent much of his life alone. At least in war, he had a purpose, and that purpose was to defeat his enemy. After that, he was back to being an outcast and a leper, and he'd had enough of that life already to know he didn't want more.

"What about her?" Kendra eventually said. She was looking at Major Larsen, who was still being attended to by JACAB.

Carter looked at his human XO then sucked in a deep breath and let it out slowly. Carina Larsen was a grown woman and a senior officer of the Union Navy, but compared to himself and Kendra, she was a baby with her life still ahead of her.

"We could rig up an escape pod and punch her into space," Carter suggested. "The pod will put out a beacon and the Union will pick her up." He laughed. "She'll probably spend the rest of her life cursing my name to the heavens, but whatever. At least she'll be alive."

Kendra slid over the top of the tactical station and landed in the XO's seat beside Carter. She tutted and shook her head. "Don't take this the wrong way, but I wish you hadn't found me on Terra Three," his engineer said.

Carter managed another half-hearted laugh. "I'm sorry, old

friend. This isn't exactly what I had in mind for us." Then he frowned as another thought struck him. In retrospect, it was obvious, and he cursed himself for not thinking of it sooner. "You don't have to stay, Kendra," Carter said, careful to ensure his expression and tone of voice conveyed the absolute sincerity of his words. "You can escape in the pod with Carina and go home. This ship is largely automated. I can fly it by myself."

"Trying to get rid of me so soon?" Kendra hit back, smiling, and jostling his shoulder. Her expression then became more serious, and she shook her head. "No, I think I prefer it this way. It seems right, somehow."

Carter nodded then walked over to where Major Larsen was still flat out on the deck and scooped her into his arms. JACAB hummed away, looking sullen and sorrowful; the bot had obviously heard him and Kendra talking.

"Don't worry buddy, you're going with her," Carter said, walking to one of the escape pod hatches at the rear of the bridge. "And let RAEB know to haul his ass up here too."

JACAB let out a solemn bleep while Kendra opened the hatch to the escape pod. The pods were small and not exactly luxurious, but they would keep his XO alive, and that was all that he cared about. Working in silence, they strapped Carina into one of the seats, and by the time they'd finished, RAEB had hummed onto the bridge from engineering.

"Okay, you guys, in you get," Carter said, pointing to the escape hatch. RAEB hovered next to JACAB then neither bot moved. "Are your auditory sensors malfunctioning? I said get inside."

RAEB rocked its spherical body from side to side like a head shaking, while JACAB merely blew out a loud and particularly unpleasant sounding electronic raspberry.

"Come on you guys, this isn't the time to be horsing around." Carter had his hands on his hips and was trying to look and sound as strict as possible. "Just get in."

JACAB hummed over to the escape hatch and interfaced

with the control panel. The door slammed shut a second later and the pod ejected into space. Carter simply stood there with his mouth wide open.

"Damn it, JACAB, that's insubordination!" Carter roared. "I could have your circuits lobotomized for this."

JACAB blew another raspberry then returned to RAEB's side. To his surprise, Kendra was laughing.

"Looks like it's all of us then," the Master Engineer said. She pointed to the navigation station. "Mind if I take the helm? I always fancied myself as a Master Navigator."

Carter resigned himself to the situation. "She's all yours, Kendra. Try not to crash her, on your way to crashing her."

"Very funny," the engineer replied, drolly.

Carter returned to his command chair and JACAB hovered next to him, while RAEB stuck to Kendra's side like glue. The Mesek-tet was still listing, but it was clear that the vessel was rapidly repairing itself. Like the Galatine, it had regenerative capabilities, and it was aggressively employing them to get itself back into the fight. Carter, however, didn't need to repair the Galatine in order to win the battle. His Longsword-class battleship was a weapon in itself.

"Set a collision course and engage at maximum thrust," Carter ordered.

Kendra worked the console, and at the same time an alert blared out. He checked the comp-slate built into his chair and cursed.

"The Aternien scout ship just launched from the Mesek-tet," Carter said, trying to piece the puzzle together as he spoke.

"But the scout's cannon was destroyed, and they already used its plasma torpedoes," Kendra remembered. "What can they hope to achieve by launching it now?"

Then it hit him, and Carter rested his head in his hands.

"The scout is on a collision course, Kendra," he realized. "They're going to do to us what we intended to do to them. Except in their version, they walk away, and we don't."

Kendra cursed and hammered the navigation console with her fist, denting the metal. She then frantically worked the controls, operating at a level far beyond normal human functioning. Carter knew what she was trying to do, but he also knew it was pointless.

"We can't outrun it, we can't evade it, and we can't shoot it down," Carter said, as his engineer finally came to the same realization.

Kendra looked more pissed off than he'd ever seen her in his life, but her anger quickly melted, and a resigned expression materialized on her ageless face. She stepped away from the navigation station, before perching herself on the arm of his command chair, with her hand on his shoulder.

"I guess you win some, you lose some, right?" Kendra said, with dignity.

"Personally, I prefer winning," Carter replied, shooting her a sympathetic smile. He then took her hand in his and squeezed it gently. "I'm glad you're here, Kendra," he added, as the scout ship accelerated toward them like a flying bomb. "I would have hated to die alone."

Kendra nodded, and the two post-human officers waited in silence for the end to come. Then with the scout ship still a minute away, the comp-slate in the command chair chirruped an alert, though since Kendra was sitting on the screen, Carter couldn't read the message. A moment later, the tactical station and operations stations chimed too, and JACAB came suddenly whizzing over to them, bleeping, and warbling like it had a transistor loose.

"What's up, buddy?" Carter asked.

Kendra blurted out a laugh and slid her arm off his shoulder. She was grinning like she'd just won the lottery.

"Can someone tell me what's so funny?" Carter added. It didn't matter that he was about to die; he still hated being out of the loop.

Suddenly, a bright flash lit up the viewscreen, and the scout ship exploded in a ball of orange flame. Carter jumped out of his seat, propelling Kendra forward with him.

"What the hell is going on?" Carter growled, arms thrown out wide.

"It looks like the cavalry just arrived," Kendra explained, still grinning from ear to ear.

The viewscreen updated and Carter almost fell back into his seat. The Dauntless – Admiral Krantz's battlecruiser – had just warped in, at the head of the entire Union First Fleet. The comm system bleeped, and Carter answered it without delay. The face of Admiral Clara Krantz appeared inset on the viewscreen.

"I take it you could use a hand, Master Commander Rose?" Krantz said, looking and sounding impressively composed.

"Your timing is impeccable, Admiral," Carter replied, jubilantly. At that moment there was so much electricity racing through his body that it was threatening to arc out of him like lighting. "Markus Aternus is on the Mesek-tet. Take that ship down, and this ends today."

The admiral's features hardened like obsidian. "You're sure?"

"I'm sure, Admiral, but that ship is regenerating fast, and our weapons are down," Carter answered. "You have to strike now; we won't get another chance like this."

Krantz nodded then turned to an officer off screen. "Order the fleet to advance on the Mesek-tet and engage," she said. "I want that ship destroyed."

A chorus of "yes sir" rang out and the fleet began to mobilize against their enemy. From the very bowels of despair, Carter felt elated. They were about to snatch victory from the golden jaws of defeat.

"Shit, I'm detecting more warp signatures," Kendra called out. Carter felt like his blood had suddenly flash frozen. "They're Aternien... A least two hundred ships inbound!"

Carter cursed and turned to the viewscreen. A fleet of Khopesh-class Destroyers, along with many more supporting craft, arrived through folds in space and surrounded the Mesek-tet like the shell of an armadillo.

"We can still take them," Carter said, addressing the admiral. "All that matters is defeating the god-king. Without Aternus, this war dies."

Krantz looked unsure. "Commander, we could lose our entire fleet. And what's to say Aternus won't just return, like the Immortals?"

"It doesn't matter, Admiral," Carter said, feeling like a stuck record, since Kendra had made the exact same counter-argument. "If we take down Aternus now then we shatter the myth of the god-king and prove that he's fallible, even weak. We could bring down the whole house of cards right now."

Krantz clamped her jaw shut. He could see the vein in the side of her head pulsing. She then straightened her tunic and fixed her laser-blue eyes onto his.

"Very well…" Krantz said, each word striking him like a bullet to the chest. "Continue the attack. The priority target is the Mesek-tet."

Carter shook his fist and turned back to the viewscreen. He wished that the Galatine was in a condition to fight, because he wanted nothing more than to strike the killing blow. However, he'd settle for watching the Union fleet atomize the god-king instead.

"The Aternien fleet is maneuvering," Kendra reported; she was back at the tactical station. "But they're not moving to attack."

"What?" Carter spun around. "Then what are they doing?"

Kendra was about to answer when a message arrived. It had been transmitted directly to Carter's comp-slate in his battle uniform. His read it then growled a bitter sigh and lowered his wrist.

"What did it say?" his engineer asked. She was astute enough to realize who had sent the communication.

"It said that this is just the beginning, and that we will meet again," Carter answered, while watching the Aternien fleet regroup. "Then it ends, 'Aternus is immortal. Aternus is forever'."

The Aternien motto stuck to his teeth like treacle, and he couldn't get the taste of failure out of his mouth. Then the Aternien ships began to blink out of the system, one by one, but he kept his eyes fixed onto the Mesek-tet. He had broken the sun ship's back to the point where the mighty Solar Barque was a mere plasma cannon blast away from being defeated. Yet today was not its time, nor was it the end for the Galatine.

The Mesek-tet flashed out of view, tumbling through a hole in space time, back to the secret star system of the Aternien Empire. The god-king was gone, but Carter knew in his bones that he would meet the leader of the Aternien Empire again before the war was done.

TWENTY-NINE
MASTER COMMANDER

CARTER GRABBED the railings in the viewing gallery of Union Station Alpha and peered out at the Galatine, docked in the orbital repair bay nearby. With the assistance of Admiral Krantz, they had recovered his Longsword and returned it to Terra Prime – the planet once known as Earth – to be repaired and refitted. From the outside, the Galatine looked like barely more than a wreck. It had been in a sorry state even prior to the pounding it had taken from the guns of the Mesek-tet, but he was still surprised at how much damage the vessel had sustained. That it was still in once piece at all seemed like a miracle.

JACAB bleeped, hummed closer and peered up at him. Through the brightness and aperture size of its glowing, red eye, to every adjustment of its maneuvering fins and twirl of its antennae, he knew what the bot was thinking. The machine's movements told a story that he could understand as plainly as the expression on a person's face.

"I'm okay, buddy," Carter said, resting a hand on the bot's spherical shell. "Hell of a few days, though, huh?"

JACAB warbled and nodded, and even appeared to chuckle

in an oddly electronic manner. The machine then looked out at the Galatine, and its antennae drooped.

"Kendra will fix her up, you just wait and see," Carter said. "There's nothing that ever broke that she couldn't put back together."

He knew that it was wishful thinking to believe the battered Longsword could be repaired, especially considering Union engineers didn't have the first clue how its systems worked, but he chose to remain positive. JACAB bleeped then looked at him, eye brighter and wider than before.

"Don't worry about me, buddy," Carter replied, patting his gopher affectionately. "I've had worse injuries, and I'll probably suffer worse still before this is over. I'm already mostly healed."

JACAB let out a mournful warble then hummed so close that he butted up to his side. Carter huffed a laugh and put his arm around the machine.

"I can't fool you, can I?" he said, as they both returned their attention to the repair dock. "I can't deny that what Aternus said hit a nerve, but I'm not about to turn my coat. I'm a Union Master Commander, and that's what I'll always be. Even if the people I serve continue to see me as a freak and a demon, that's my cross to bear."

JACAB blurted out a disgusted squawk that sounded like a mix between white noise and a car horn. Carter laughed quietly to himself and hugged the machine more tightly.

"At least you still like me, so that's something," he said, smiling at the bot.

JACAB blew out a raspberry then its chassis vibrated like an alarm call, as if the machine was trying desperately to stifle an electronic chuckle but failing miserably to do so.

Carter shook his head at his gopher, then his thoughts were suddenly consumed by the exchange between himself and god-king of the Aternien Empire. In particular, he wondered whether Kendra had been drawn by the Aternien's offer, even if only for a fleeting moment. When he'd looked her in the eye, he genuinely couldn't tell, and he desperately wanted to know. If he was being brutally honest with himself, Markus Aternus had touched something within him, and it made him sick to his stomach to admit that part of him had been tempted.

However, what worried him the most was that Aternus had not tried to manipulate him with lies; the god-king had spoken words of truth. Humanity despised him and those like him. If Markus Aternus was to contact other surviving Longsword officers – all of whom were deeply embittered at the end of the war – he worried that some might be swayed to join him.

The door to the observation lounge opened and JACAB perked up, hovering above Carter's head to check who had entered. However, the bot's excited sequence of bleeps and warbles told him who it was before he'd even turned around to look.

"I wondered where you two reprobates had gotten to," said Major Larsen.

Her left arm was in a sling, and Carter could tell from the stilted way she was walking that other parts of her body were strapped, pinned, and bandaged too. JACAB zoomed over to greet her, and the major returned the gesture by giving the bot a hug with her only available arm.

"How is she?" Carina asked resting up against the railings and looking out toward the Galatine.

"In all honesty, not great," Carter admitted, though it pained him to do so. "We got her back though, which is what matters. It gives us a chance, at least."

"You got me back too, by the way," Carina said, turning her back to the viewing window and shooting him a surly look. "Or the admiral did, anyway. You can't believe how spooked I was waking up in that metal coffin, floating through space like a rogue comet."

JACAB looked at Carina then at Carter and hovered out of the way. The bot was smart enough to know when he was about to get caught in a crossfire.

"Are you seriously mad at me for putting you in an escape pod, rather than letting you die with Kendra and me?" Carter asked.

"Of course, I'm mad!" Carina snapped, throwing her one good arm out wide in dismay. "I mean, I'm not especially mad that you thought to save my life, but... it's the principle of it!"

Carter raised an eyebrow and folded his arms across his chest. "What principle are you talking about? The principle of me not wanting you to burn up in the fiery wreckage of two ancient warships?"

"No, not that," Carina replied, sharply. She pushed herself off the railing and stood toe-to-toe with him. "I'm supposed to be one of you, and you said you'd treat me no differently to Kendra, or any other Longsword officer. Yet that's exactly what you did."

"If I recall, it was you who asked me to treat you no differently, and I never agreed to that," Carter hit back, standing his ground.

Carina looked genuinely hurt by his rebuttal. "So, you don't consider me to be one of your officers, even after everything we've been through?"

Carter sighed and rubbed his beard. He didn't want an argument, but he had to face facts, and so did his XO.

"Carina, the truth is you're not like us; me and Kendra, I mean. You can wear the battle uniform and crew a Longsword, but it doesn't change the fact you're human, and I'm not. Not entirely, anyway."

"I don't care that you're different, or that I am," Carina said. She was sticking to her guns just as much as he was. "If other people want to fear you and vilify you for being post-human then screw them. If I could be like you, I would."

"That's easy to say, but the reality is different, Carina. You can't know what it's like, and I wouldn't wish it on you for a second."

Carina shook her head and looked out of the window,

though she was staring blankly into space, rather than at the Galatine. "I don't understand what's not to like," she continued, with less anger. "You're stronger, smarter, and more resilient than a regular human, not just physically, but mentally too. You've lived with persecution for more than a century and a half, and it hasn't made you bitter."

Carter laughed. "If you think that, you haven't been paying attention."

Carina didn't see the funny side. "I'm not saying that you're immune to feelings, or that you don't suffer, but most people wouldn't have lasted as long as you have, given how the Union treated you."

"You're forgetting that most of us *didn't* last," Carter countered, remembering the report of all the deceased Longsword officers that Carina had showed him in the bar, back on his forest moon home. "And, in case you've forgotten, I was about to sacrifice myself on the altar of duty not twelve hours ago."

Carina was silent for a moment, during which time he again became aware of JACAB. His gopher was hovering above their heads out of sight, but the bot hadn't missed a word that was spoken. Carter noted that JACAB appeared to be slightly closer to Carina than he was to him, and he wondered whether this was an indicator of who the machine thought was winning the argument.

"Why were you about to commit hara-kiri out there, anyway?" Carina asked, unexpectedly. "You could have set the Galatine on a collision course and escaped in the pod with me, but you chose to die. Why?"

Carter could tell that she was angry, and he knew that he had to be careful with his reply. Merely shrugging her off or telling her to mind her own business – as much as he felt like saying so – would only inflame tensions between them. Yet, he also didn't know how to convey his feelings in a way that she could appreciate.

"You'd need to have spent a lifetime walking in my shoes to understand that, Carina," Carter said, choosing the deflect the question as subtly as he could. "There's no simple answer that will satisfy you."

His XO, predictably, looked unhappy with his response, but she didn't push him to say more. He sighed again and shuffled up closer to her.

"I'm not trying to block you out, Carina," Carter added. Opening up to people was hard for him, but he felt like he could genuinely trust his assertive XO. "I wish I could explain, but there are some things that I just can't put into words."

To his surprise, Carina then placed her hand on top of his and squeezed it gently. It was a simple act of friendship and solidarity that he'd never received from anyone who wasn't post-human like him.

"If you ask me, and I know you didn't, you're a goddamn hero, Carter Rose," Carina said, offering him a warm smile. "I wish more people were like you." She laughed. "And no matter what you say, I wish I was too."

"Be careful what you wish for," Carter said, remaining stern. "I'll never have a family, or a real home. I'll never have grandkids, or someone to grow old with. I'll never experience love, not like you can." He took her hand and squeezed it gently between his own. "Don't envy me, Carina. You can have everything I've ever wanted, but never will."

Carina's face fell, and she suddenly appeared faint. It was as if his words had drained the blood from her body like a vampire bite. The door to the observation lounge opened again, and Carter quickly released Carina's hand and placed his own at the small of his back, before sharply turning to greet whoever had entered. Admiral Krantz and Kendra Castle were approaching, joined by another officer whom he didn't recognize.

"Master Commander Rose, Major Larsen," said Admiral Krantz, nodding to each of them in turn. She extended her hand to the unknown officer. "This is Captain-Engineer William Schultz. He heads up Union Fleet Engineering here at Station Alpha."

Carter had seen the look on the engineering captain's face a million times before; it was the look of someone who regarded him with suspicion and fear, and even a little disgust, like he might be a plague carrier.

"Good to meet you, Captain Schultz," Carter said, offering the engineer his hand, as well as an olive branch, but predictably the man didn't take it.

"I just wanted to let you know that the Galatine is in the finest repair dock in the fleet," Schultz said, keeping his hands firmly at the small of his back. "We'll fix her up and get her into the fight, don't you worry."

Carter withdrew his offer to shake hands and matched the engineer's standoffish posture.

"Do you know a lot about Union Longsword-class battleships, Captain Schultz?"

He'd asked the question with a deliberately barbed tone, knowing full-well that the man wouldn't have had the first clue how to fix up the Galatine.

"I can assure you, Commander, that I have read everything there is to know about the Longsword-class," the engineer replied, puffing out his chest and looking down his nose at him. "My team is the finest in the fleet. I do not envisage any problems."

"That's good to hear, Captain," Carter replied, shooting the man an insincere smile. "In that case, I'm sure you won't mind if Master Engineer Castle asks you a few questions?"

He looked to his engineer, who had been unusually quiet since entering the room. However, it hadn't taken him long to notice the raw anger and indignation that had been festering beneath her flawless, bio-engineered skin. It seemed clear to him that she had been itching for an opportunity to call bullshit on the Captain-Engineer's claims, and Carter fully intended to expose Shultz in front of the admiral, so there was no doubt who should head up the repair efforts.

"Of course, she can ask me whatever she wants," Shultz replied, still with an air of haughtiness.

Carter felt like taking the man to task himself for the clear disrespect he had shown to him and Kendra. The fact that Shultz had simply referred to his Master Engineer as "she", rather than by name or rank, pissed him off more than anything else. It was belittling and had been done on purpose. However, he was pleased to see that Kendra seized the opportunity Schultz had provided with both hands, while managing to remain polite and dignified as she assassinated the captain's competence in front of everyone.

"I wanted to get your input on the magnetic containment system for the plasma shield," Kendra said, thrusting a comp-slate in front of the engineer. "Does this field design for the rebuilt generator look correct to you?"

"Um, well…" Shultz hesitated as he looked at the screen with scowling eyes. "Well, I'm not exactly familiar…"

"Don't worry, I can take care of that then," Kendra cut in, quickly swiping to the next screen. "Maybe you can help by suggesting alternative materials to manufacture a replacement for the liquid armor that was lost in the battle with the Mesek-tet?"

"I am not yet familiar with the precise nature of…"

"Oh, I see, never mind…" Kendra cut in, causing Schultz to look even more cross and embarrassed. "I imagine that fabricating new sub-processor cores to replace the ones that were damaged is something you can help with, though?" Schultz was silent. "I assume you can at least help with overhauling the soliton warp drive?"

"The blueprint for the warp technology used in the Longsword-class was hard-deleted more than a century ago, as you well know!" Shultz blurted out. The man's hands were now clenched into fists.

"Really? So, what you're telling me, Captain-Engineer Shultz, is that you're completely clueless when it comes to repairing the Galatine?"

Kendra had skewered the man like a kebab, and Carter was enjoying every excruciating second of Shultz's trauma. The Captain-Engineer looked ready to explode, but Kendra held up a hand to cut him off and appeared suddenly apologetic.

"Actually, what I said isn't quite fair," she continued. "I could give you a hammer and a wrench, and you could probably manage to bolt some new deck plates in place."

"Admiral, this is intolerable!" Schultz erupted, turning his back on Kendra, and addressing the admiral, as if there was no-one else in the room. "This is *my* repair station, and I will *not* have this deviant freak of nature question my abilities, or my authority!"

Carter raised an eyebrow at the use of the phrase, "deviant freak of nature". It was just one of many slurs that had been leveled at him and Kendra over the years, but it was also one of the most offensive. That was because it went further than merely implying there was something physically wrong with them; it suggested they were mentally deranged too. It put them in the same bracket as child molesters or psychopaths, and it revealed exactly what Captain Schultz thought about them. However, the verbal assault presented an opportunity, because how Admiral Krantz responded to Schultz's overt bigotry would reveal tomes about her character too.

"I agree, Captain, this is intolerable," Krantz agreed, and Carter raised his eyebrow higher.

Schultz at once calmed down, presumably happy that the admiral was taking his side. However, Krantz then did something that Carter never expected.

"Master Engineer Castle, you are hereby given full authority to manage the repairs to the Galatine as you see fit," the admiral said, addressing Kendra with her back to Captain Schultz. "You may select a team and request whatever materials and tools you require."

Kendra's eyes widened then flicked across to look at Carter, but he was just as surprised as his engineer was. Captain Shultz, on the other hand, looked like he was ready to blow a gasket.

"Admiral, I must protest!" Shultz roared. "I will not have this post-human abomination made responsible for my people and my dock."

The admiral's eyes snapped toward Shultz and the man clamped his jaw shut harder and faster than a bear trap.

"Another word from you, Captain Shultz, and you are done!" Krantz barked, delivering the line with a powerful bite that almost knocked Shultz off his feet. "In all matters relating to the Longsword Galatine, you will take your orders from Master Engineer Castle. Is that clear?"

The initial shock subsided quickly, and the Captain-Engineer looked ready to explode again, but Krantz was quick to interject.

"I advise you to choose your next words wisely, Captain, or they will be your last as an officer of the Union Fleet."

To his credit, Shultz shut his mouth and kept it shut, at least for long enough to regain control of his emotions.

"I understand, Admiral," the engineer finally replied, before snapping to attention. "Am I dismissed?"

"Get out of my sight," Krantz replied nodding toward the door. "I will deal with you later."

Captain-Engineer Shultz saluted, then marched away, but not before shooting dagger eyes at both him and Kendra. The admiral waited until Shultz had left, before addressing Kendra.

"Master Engineer Castle, if you run into any similar problems when recruiting your team, I order you to bring the matter to me directly, is that understood?"

"I prefer to deal with malcontents myself," Kendra began. However, the look that Krantz shot her in reply encouraged his engineer to quickly change her tune. "But I understand, ma'am, thank you."

"Thank me by getting that Longsword back on the line," Krantz responded. "Without it, and you, we stand little chance against the Aterniens, especially in light of the fact they have an operational Solar Barque at their disposal."

"Don't worry, Admiral, the Galatine is my baby," Kendra said, confidently. "No-one knows her like me, and no one can." Kendra then smiled and flashed her eyes at Krantz. "I don't suppose this new gig comes with a promotion, does it? Captain-Engineer has a nice ring to it."

Carter winced. As an attempt at humor, it was sorely misjudged and mistimed.

"Don't push your luck." The admiral replied, her tone as unyielding as the grave.

"Kendra will fix her up in no time, won't you Kendra?" Carter cut in, eager to end their meeting on a positive note.

"I'll make her right," Kendra said, wisely adopting a more serious manner. "I just hope that when you're done with her this time, you don't cast her out again." She paused then added, pointedly, "or us."

Not for the first time, Carter raised an eyebrow. Kendra's comment was borderline insubordinate, but on this occasion, he allowed it, because he was just as keen to hear the admiral's answer as his engineer was.

"What you ask is not in my power to grant," Krantz replied.

Carter could sense that the admission had angered and shamed her, but he appreciated the admiral's frankness, and was about to thank her for being honest with them, when Clara Krantz surprised him for a second time.

"What I *can* promise is that I will do everything in my power to ensure that you, and the Galatine, are treated with the dignity and respect you deserve."

"I appreciate it, Admiral," Carter said, bowing his head

slightly. He then looked to his engineer. "We both do, don't we, Kendra?"

Kendra still looked aggravated, but she appeared to accept that the admiral was at least trying. It was more than anyone else had ever done.

"Thank you, Admiral," Kendra replied. "And thanks for the job too. I won't let you down."

Krantz nodded then half turned, intending to leave. However, something stopped her, and she spun on her heels again. This time, however, it was Major Larsen she spoke to.

"I trust that you are healing well, Major?" Krantz asked.

Carter frowned; there was an odd familiarity between the two women that was more than just professional interest in her wellbeing.

"Don't worry, I'll be right as rain in no time, Admiral, but thanks for asking," Carina replied.

Krantz nodded again and Carter was sure he detected the hint of a smile, but in a flash the admiral was marching away before anyone else could get a word in.

"Well, I guess I'd better put my team together," Kendra said, once the admiral had left the room. "Any special requests for the refit? A coffee machine in your quarters perhaps? Or maybe a hot tub?"

"Just get her fighting fit, Kendra, and I'll be happy," Carter answered, smiling at his engineer.

Kendra gave him a jaunty salute then smiled and nodded at Major Larsen, before also departing. There was a definite spring in her step, he noted, and for good reason. The admiral had just given her a blank cheque and put her in charge of the largest and most sophisticated repair dock in the Union. It was like all her Christmases had come at once. It was then he noticed that his XO was staring at him. He stared back, but she didn't flinch, and the standoff quickly became unsettling.

"What? What the hell is it?" Carter said, finally blinking first.

"Am I still your XO or not?" Carina blurted out.

"Well, I didn't hear the admiral reassign you, so what do you think?"

Her aggressive question had gotten his back up and made him antsy and bad-tempered.

"I'm not asking what the official records say, I'm asking you," Carina snapped. "I want to know whether you're going to stuff me inside an escape pod and jettison me into space every time things get hairy."

Carter scowled; he felt like stuffing her into an escape pod and jettisoning her right there and then. However, he didn't get the chance, because a young officer raced through the door, comp-slate in hand, and practically collided with him.

"Slow down, Lieutenant," Carter said, stretching out his hand, like a police officer stopping traffic. "What's all this about?"

"Urgent message from Admiral Krantz, sir," the lieutenant said, breathless from running. He then held out the comp-slate.

"Krantz was just here, Lieutenant, if there was anything urgent, she would have told me."

"I don't know about that, sir, but I think you'll want to see this."

The officer thrust the device toward him again, and Carter snatched it angrily from the man's grasp. He hated unnecessary hustle and bustle; it smacked of being ill-prepared.

"What does it say?" Carina asked, trying to look at the comp-slate over his shoulder.

Carter read the message then lowered the device to his side. "Thank you, Lieutenant. Inform the admiral that we'll be there presently."

The lieutenant saluted then raced out of the room, looking even more flustered than when he'd entered.

"Carter, I'm dying here; what did it say?"

Carter handed the comp slate to his XO then looked out at the Galatine.

"It says that the Aterniens have invaded Terra Six," Carter said. Already he felt frustrated that he couldn't just warp out there and fight his enemy. "It says they have blockaded the planet and launched a ground assault."

"Shit..." Carina hissed, while reading the report. "Our ship is still in pieces, so what do we do?"

"Kendra is putting the Galatine back together, but she still needs a crew," Carter replied, watching as hundreds of repair drones began swarming around his ship. "Others from my old team are still alive, and I need to find them."

"I think you mean *we* need to find them," Carina corrected him. "And *we* don't have a moment to lose." She turned to him and stood to attention. "Assuming, I'm still a part of your crew, that is?"

Carter grunted and faced the major. Everything he'd said to her previously still held true. Carina Larsen was only human, and it was true that this made her vulnerable. However, the unpleasant experience with Captain-Engineer Shultz, and the man's subsequent dressing down by Admiral Krantz, had reminded him that prejudice was the real enemy. His XO had served him well, and despite his own fears and biases, he believed that she would continue to do so.

"You're still part of my crew, Major," he said, standing tall. "In fact, I'm damned lucky to have you."

Carina smiled. "Steady-on, tiger, I'm not that easy."

Carter rolled his eyes and shook his head. Then the rhythmic patter of bootsteps in the corridor outside reminded him that all hell was about to break loose. Officers and crew were racing to their posts, and soon after that, to war. It all felt so familiar, like he'd stepped back in time and the first conflict had never ended.

"This time it will be different, Carina," Carter said, meeting his XO's gaze. "This time, there will be no armistice. No negotiations. This time, we'll crush our enemy and make sure they never return."

Major Larsen nodded. "I'm with you, Carter. Every step of the way."

Carina tossed the comp-slate onto a table and together he and his XO marched out of the observation lounge on Station Alpha. They didn't yet have a ship, and they barely had a crew, but they had a mission. More than that, for the first time in a century, Master Commander Carter Rose had a purpose again. Maybe it wasn't everything he'd wanted or dreamed of having, but it was something. It was enough.

His old enemy had returned, and so had he. The Galatine would rise again and this time, it would cleave a path of destruction throughout the galaxy until every trace of the Aternien Empire was eradicated for good.

The end (to be continued).

CONTINUE THE STORY

Continue the story with book #2 - Enemy Within.

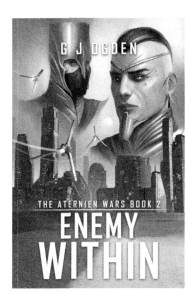

ALSO BY G J OGDEN

Sa'Nerra Universe

Omega Taskforce

Descendants of War

Scavenger Universe

Star Scavengers

Star Guardians

Standalone series

The Contingency War series

Darkspace Renegade series

The Planetsider

Audible Audiobooks

Star Scavengers - click here

The Contingency War - click here

Omega Taskforce - click here

Descendants of War - click here

The Planetsider Trilogy - click here

G J Ogden's newsletter: Click here to sign-up

ABOUT THE AUTHOR

At school, I was asked to write down the jobs I wanted to do as a "grown up". Number one was astronaut and number two was a PC games journalist. I only managed to achieve one of those goals (I'll let you guess which), but these two very different career options still neatly sum up my lifelong interests in science, space, and the unknown.

School also steered me in the direction of a science-focused education over literature and writing, which influenced my decision to study physics at Manchester University. What this degree taught me is that I didn't like studying physics and instead enjoyed writing, which is why you're reading this book! The lesson? School can't tell you who you are.

When not writing, I enjoy spending time with my family, walking in the British countryside, and indulging in as much Sci-Fi as possible.

Printed in Great Britain
by Amazon